HIS FROZEN HEART

BREWER BROTHERS SERIES, BOOK ONE

NANCY STRAIGHT

Text set in Cochin LT.
Book design by Inkstain Interior Book Designing

ACKNOWLEDGEMENTS:

As I finished this story, there were many people I needed to thank. First, Lisa Henderson, although I have never met you in person, I look forward to the day that I do. Lisa was a fan who read my Touched Series and told me it was the first Paranormal Romance she had ever read. She told me she would love for me to write a Contemporary Romance; it was her prodding that made *His Frozen Heart* a reality.

To Charles Young, Melissa Balentine and Rebecca Ufkes: Do you know why football teams have cheerleaders? Me either, but my goodness, you all make me feel like the starting line-up for the Green Bay Packers. Your support means the world to me. No author could ever be more fortunate than I – to have three of the best beta readers and friends on the planet.

Jaime Radalyac, there are no words to tell you how much I appreciate everything you do. I like that when I say something crazy like, "Hey, let's do a cover reveal this week," your only response is, "You bet!" I'm convinced there is nothing you cannot do, and it is my privilege to know you and call you my friend.

To all the book bloggers who have supported me since I started this career a few years ago, "Thank you," is inadequate. I have never met a group of people who are more giving of their time. Your willingness to take a chance on my work has humbled me from the beginning, and I grow more grateful every time I discover a new one of you in the blogosphere. Your passion inspires me every day. Thank you for doing what you do for me and for all the other independent authors out there.

To the citizens of Charles City, Iowa – you have my deepest apologies. I'm certain you have had to ask for resupplies of red ink pens from neighboring cities since my editor, Linda Brant, has bled the town dry! Linda, this has been quite an adventure. I wouldn't have wanted to go on this journey with anyone but you!

To my sons, Alex and Zack, your imaginations, humor, and enthusiasm inspire me every day. I feel blessed to have two of the coolest kids in the world. Thank you for finding a way to make me laugh even when I am buried in my fictional worlds.

Finally, Toby, thanks for all the nights you played Plants vs. Zombies® with Zack so I could write and for never rolling your eyes when I said, "How about take-out tonight?" Few wives are lucky enough to have a husband who not only believes in them, but encourages them to chase their dreams. I am the luckiest wife/mom/author I know.

All my love,
Nancy

HIS FROZEN HEART

CHAPTER I

I ran to the shadow of an enormous maple tree and crouched low to the ground. I couldn't believe I had let Libby talk me into this. We had set our alarm clock for 2 AM, then sneaked out of my house while my parents were sound asleep. Libby was ticked off about some stupid science assignment over spring break. She believed she had been purposely singled out by Mr. Brinks. I pointed out that her entire class had a project to work on over the break, but she insisted her assigned project was more difficult than everyone else's.

Still confident that this was the dumbest idea she had come up with in months, I asked, "You're sure this is his house?"

"Of course, I'm sure. I wrote down the house number today, 811 Stone Avenue."

I eyed the small scrap of paper in her hand – only the number was scrawled down. "You're sure this is the right street?"

"C'mon already. Yes, his address is 811 Stone Avenue. Do you need me to break in and steal a piece of his mail?"

I was struggling to find a way to talk her out of her plan. Delaying, I pointed at the driveway, "I thought he drove a blue four-door car?"

Her gaze drifted to the driveway where a red SUV was parked. She shrugged my question off, "Maybe he keeps it in the garage."

"Or maybe this isn't the right address." I eyed the upscale neighborhood where the two-story brick home stood. It had a three car garage, and there looked to be a detached guest house in the back. This didn't look like the sort of home a high school science teacher could afford.

Libby scowled at me, "It's the right address. Are you going to help me or not?"

I took another look at the SUV. The license plate caught my eye: it was a vanity plate that read: SUPRINT. "What do you think the license plate stands for?"

Libby barked, "Surprise instantly, super instantly, super instructor. . . who knows, he's a dork. If you aren't going to help me, go wait in the car."

As much as I hated this idea, I couldn't let Libby do it on her own. I grabbed a roll of toilet paper, "Okay. I'm helping. I'll take the trees, you do the house."

"You're the best." Those were the last words spoken before the two of us set off an external alarm and the house lit up like Caesar's Palace. A computerized voice began to broadcast, "Intruder alert," every five seconds. Flood lights poured down onto the grass from several points on the roof. Lights in the house turned on, then the computerized voice coming through the loud speaker shut off. We had obviously awakened Mr. Brinks, and he was about to catch us red-handed teepeeing his house. I froze. I willed my legs to move, but they ignored me.

The front door opened and Mr. Brink's voice shouted from the front porch, "Who's out there?"

I was sort of hidden in the shadows when I heard Libby's voice whisper to me. "Candy, I'll distract him. You get home. You were never here."

Before I could stop her or try to tell her I wasn't leaving her, Libby skipped from out of the shadows – not walked, not ran, but skipped. She overexaggerated her movements, nearly dancing in circles in the glow of all the lights. The man on the porch adjusted his glasses, cinched his bathrobe up tight, then reality hit me that this was definitely not Mr. Brinks. Whoever this man was, he was not happy about a girl skipping through his yard with a roll of toilet paper in the middle of the night.

The man shouted, "Who are you? What are you doing?"

In a shrill voice, Libby shouted, "I'm the gingerbread girl, and you can't catch me." She sprinted around the side of his house and into the side yard. As soon as his attention was diverted, I ran across the street and tucked behind his neighbor's garbage can. My heart raced, I wiped my palms on my jeans, and it sounded like I was breathing heavy enough to be a prank telephone caller.

I couldn't leave Libby. I needed to delay the man who was now rounding the side of his house chasing her. It was my turn to create a distraction for her. I looked at the SUV, which had a small red flashing light above the rearview mirror indicating the alarm had been set. I knew what I needed to do. I darted back across the street, ran up to the side of the SUV and kicked it as hard as I could.

The vehicle's alarm blared to life as I ran back to the safety of the garbage cans where I had taken cover minutes before. The SUV flashed its lights, a loud siren awoke every neighbor who had managed to sleep through the previous alarm and the man's shouting. The man ran from around the side of the house where he had chased Libby, onto the porch, and through his front door. A minute later he reemerged from his front door holding a remote to turn off the vehicle's loud plea for help.

This had been enough time for Libby to run over to my side of the street and squat down beside me behind the garbage cans. I whisper shouted at her, "Couldn't stay up and watch old movies. Couldn't surf YouTube. No, you have to teepee your teacher's house. Oh, wait, scratch that, teepee a stranger's house."

She answered me with an enormous smile and mischievous eyes, "Admit it. This is soooooo better than braiding each other's hair and painting our nails."

A voice shouted from directly behind us. "They're over here. There's two of 'em. I already called the police."

The two of us popped up from behind the garbage cans and ran full-speed down the street away from the ruckus we had caused. We ran the four city blocks straight to where we had left my car. Libby made my life interesting. She was never one to see the flaws of a plan before initiating it – life with Libby was an adventure. We both watched for police cars as I drove home, but didn't pass a single squad car. I turned off the car and coasted it into place so as not to wake up my parents. We both sat there in front of my house for several minutes before our breathing slowed and Libby asked, "What do you want to do now?"

"Now? We almost got thrown in jail. I want to go to bed."

Libby snarked, "We did not almost get thrown in jail. We didn't even see one police car."

"And that's a bad thing?"

"Well, no. But since we already sneaked out, maybe we should make the most of it. It might be risky trying to sneak back into your house."

"So, what's your plan? Sleep in my car?"

"We could go out to the lake and see if anyone were there tonight."

"The lake? If anyone was there, the police have already sent them packing and confiscated the beer. C'mon, let's get in before anyone notices we've gone."

She reluctantly followed me inside; we had been gone less than an hour. The next morning, Libby was on the computer when I woke up to, "Oh, crap, it was 118."

Rubbing the sleep from my eyes, I asked, "What was 118?"

"Mr. Brink's address. I just wrote the house number down because I knew I could remember the street. His address is 118 Stone Avenue; we went to 811 Stone Avenue last night." She paused for a minute, "Want to try again tonight?"

She handed me the slip of paper from last night which read 811; when I turned it upside down it read 118. That was Libby. Once she got something in her head, the only way to get it out was to follow her blindly on whatever objective she had set her sights on.

The memory of that adventure played through my head as I tuned out the commencement ceremony. Returning to reality, I listened to our class valedictorian's speech drone on. A smile formed when it hit me that every happy high school memory I had was with Libby. When the valedictorian's speech ended with the cliché, "This is the first day of the rest of our lives," I was sure I would puke.

Luckily the rest of the ceremony moved faster. The superintendent stood in front of the lectern handing diplomas to each student. Beads of sweat formed on my brow as I accepted mine, and decided he looked even more intimidating in a suit than he did in his bathrobe at two in the morning. SUPRINT on the red SUV did not stand for "super instructor," as Libby had surmised. I was already back in my seat holding my diploma when Libby's name was called, and I was anxious to see her reaction to the superintendent up close. A slurred voice shouted from the risers, "That's my girl."

I saw her stop to look where the shout had come from. Her dad was here. She placed one hand on her square hat, holding it in place, while her other hand waved like crazy to the voice above. Libby had ridden with me to the ceremony. When I'd asked her if her dad was coming to graduation, her answer sounded defeated, "He doesn't like crowds."

Libby had grown up with only her dad. He had a tough time holding a job, and for the same reason had a tough time keeping a decent place to live. She moved a lot. Growing up, Libby had spent almost every weekend at my house. When I was younger, I never understood why I couldn't go to her house to spend the night. Mom always manufactured a good reason for why I couldn't go over, but welcomed Libby to stay with us. It wasn't until I was a teenager and could drive that I saw where she lived first hand and was grateful Mom had never given in to my pleading.

After the ceremony was over, we found each other. I asked, "Is your dad giving you a ride home?"

"No. I'm going back to your house with you." Libby had stayed with me the last two weeks. She said it was because she didn't want me to have to drive across town and pick her up, but I was guessing her dad had drunk their rent money again, so they were locked out of the apartment. There was a month when we were in eighth grade where both of them lived in his truck. A few of the nights were so cold that they had to stay in a homeless shelter.

Not wanting to pry about her dad's abrupt departure, I said, "Great. I got you a present."

A huge smile formed on her lips, "Oh, me, too!" She reached into her pocket and took out a handmade red and white friendship bracelet. I'd seen her make these before. It was made of knotted embroidery floss, but she had made it with my name in it: Candy. I'd watched her make simple ones that took all weekend: one with my name in it must have taken her several weeks.

I looked at the wrapped box in the back seat of my car. After seeing the bracelet she had made for me, I felt like I had cheated her. She tore through the wrapping paper and stared at the two little eyes peering out through the box's lid. Libby had collected turtles for as long as I could remember – she had hundreds in all shapes and sizes.

I watched in horror as tears welled up in her eyes. I stammered, "What's wrong? If you don't like it, I can take it back. I thought you liked turtles."

She shook her head. She reached across the bench seat of my car and grabbed my neck in a tight embrace. I froze. Libby let me go, then wiped her eyes trying to keep her eyeliner from running. "Until I met you, I was a turtle. That's how I saw myself. Anytime someone got too close to me, I would hide in my shell. You were the first person I could be out of my shell around."

So the valedictorian's speech hadn't been that monumental. I was sort of excited for Libby that her dad had sobered up long enough to watch her get her diploma. But it was Libby's response to the little stuffed turtle that yanked on my heart.

She smiled, "Let's go see if Mom needs help getting ready for the party." Libby never knew her mom: they had met a few times, but it was Libby's dad who raised her. One day she just started calling my mom, "Mom."

When we pulled up to my house, a huge banner hung down from the roof of the front porch. "Congratulations Candy and Libby." We may not have been sisters by blood, but in every other sense of the word we were. It was a typical graduation party: relatives I hadn't seen since my older sister's high school graduation, neighbors, my parent's friends – snore. After the last of the guests departed, Libby and I went upstairs to my room to change so we could go to a couple fun parties. Mom knocked on my door, peeked through the opening and asked, "Got a minute?"

"Sure. C'mon in."

Mom was beaming when she said, "We're so proud of both of you girls." She sat on the edge of my bed, "Libby, have you picked a college?"

"No. I'm going to work for a year or so to figure out what I want to do."

"Good. Maybe you can help Candy with rent."

I couldn't believe my ears. "Rent? You're going to charge me to live here?"

Mom smiled. "That's up to you. Dad got a job in New Mexico. He needs to start there in two weeks."

Did I hear her right? "You're moving to New Mexico? But why?"

"Dad's company has wanted to transfer him for years, but he wouldn't move while you and your sisters were still at home. His boss offered him a promotion if he transferred – Dad accepted."

I had heard my parents talk about a transfer a few times, but each time I started to get seriously nervous about it, Dad told me he wouldn't uproot me or my sisters. Now I was officially an adult: I had turned eighteen last month, and, as of four hours ago, I was a high school graduate. It was supposed to be the kids who grew up and moved away, not the parents.

Awkwardly, I asked, "So how much rent are we talking?"

Mom smiled warmly. "We think $500 is fair."

Five hundred dollars was a bargain. Libby and I could easily swing $250 each. "So how soon are you going? You said a couple weeks?"

"Dad starts his new job in two weeks. We're planning to drive down this weekend. We have to find a house and get situated. No more Midwest winters! I can't wait."

"Why didn't you say something before now? You're just leaving?"

Mom answered apologetically, "Dad wasn't sure the promotion was going to happen. He wouldn't have accepted the transfer without it. He found out last night. The timing was right, and it was too good of an offer to turn down."

Libby piped in as if to convince me that this wasn't the strangest event ever. "I'll be working full-time. I could pay half, maybe even more than half since you're going to school. It'll be great. Just you and me."

It was sort of great, at least in the beginning it was great. My parents moved away the Saturday after I graduated. What few possessions Libby had were moved in Saturday night. So began my adventures with Libby.

CHAPTER 2

21 months later

I had been standing in front of the massive metal cabinet that doubled as a pantry in our back hallway. I shoved the empty orange and yellow Ramen Noodle packaging aside, only to find an empty macaroni and cheese packaging wadded up behind it. My angry stomach growled in frustration.

My eyes roved to the next shelf, hoping to find another delicacy. The only semi-meal I could see was rice and soy sauce . . . maybe. My stomach complained as my hands slid the rice aside. Something, there had to be something in here to eat. A lonely can of stewed tomatoes invited me to pick it up. What were we thinking to have bought that?

Onto the third shelf: two cans of generic Dr. Pepper – I'd rather drink water. Backing away from the pantry to get a better look, my hunger tried to take control of my legs, imploring me to find something. Where was all the food? The Ramen and mac and cheese should have lasted us another couple days.

It hit me – Doritos! I'd given Melinda a ride to school. She was notorious for leaving half-eaten bags of chips in the back seat of my car. Her bag still had to be there.

Not even bothering to grab a coat, I launched myself off of our front porch, bounded down the steps in front of our house, and sprinted thirty feet up the street to where my car was parked. I had just parked it a couple hours before when I got home from work at the restaurant, and it was already like a deep freeze inside. The door complained as I swung it all the way open. Tipping the seat forward, I found McDonald's bags, Burger King bags, empty pop cans, a couple empty cigarette packs – then I saw it, the bright red corner of the Doritos bag peeked at me from beneath all the crap on top of it.

I freed the bag from the pile of garbage. My fingers greedily dug into the bottom of the bag to find nothing but crumbs. Telling myself there was no shame when hunger was involved, I tipped the bag upside down, so I could free the few slivers of chips. It was just enough to make my stomach complain for more. The watchful eyes of Mrs. Bavcock stared at me through the front window of her house.

It was seriously cold; I hoped she wouldn't take the time to get her coat on to come outside. I tossed the now completely empty bag back onto the floor of my car, plastered an over-sized smile on my face, and waved at her.

Her congenial expression didn't change as her hand excitedly waved back at me through the frosty glass of her front window. When the weather was decent and she saw me anywhere near the street, she nearly tripped over herself to talk to me. Conversations were always the same: she would tell me about her cats. . . her grandchildren, her cats. . . her ailments, her cats. Growing up, I'd always believed Mrs. Bavcock to be wealthy, but as she grew older, she didn't migrate south for the winter with all the other old people. Maybe she was as broke as the rest of us.

I liked my street. It was an old neighborhood. All the other houses were occupied by empty nesters whose grown kids would occasionally show up on the weekends. When my sisters and I were little, I remember watching all the visiting cars, hoping for grandkids of my neighbors to stop by to visit so I could play with someone other than Kim and Carly.

That was the way it was supposed to work – the natural order of things. Kids grew up, moved away, came back and visited their parents on the weekends, maybe for Sunday dinner, birthdays, or anniversaries. Too bad my family didn't fit the mold: it had been almost a year since I had seen my parents.

Growing up here, my sisters and I had been the only kids on the whole street. Kim was twenty-four and Carly was twenty-two: both moved away after high school. Now Kim was all business. She was a receptionist for some law firm and was too wrapped up in her own life ever to be bothered with mine. It had been months since she had even returned a text.

Carly was different. She was the middle child. Carly was the social butterfly of the three of us. She was on a full-ride academic scholarship and had been since she graduated. Carly was always too busy studying to see me other than winter and summer break when she was thrown out of the dorms. That left me, here, surviving.

Libby's voice called from the house, "Damn, Candy, too hot for you in here or what?!"

When I had sprinted down to the car on a quest for stale Doritos, I hadn't bothered to pull the front door shut behind me. I called up, "Naw, just scavenging for food. Did you throw a party last night or what?"

Ignoring my question she yelled, "You're going to go into hypothermia. Get in here!"

Standing in seven inches of snow in a pair of sweat pants, flops and a t-shirt in the dead of winter was not the brightest thing I'd done today. Sadly, it wasn't the dumbest thing, either. I wasn't supposed to work at the restaurant during the week, but I had been so hungry I went in hoping to pick up a shift. The manager said he didn't need me as a waitress, but the janitor had called in sick. I ended up having to scrub the bathrooms; I had gotten three hours of work on the clock, but no tips and no food. I chalked my poor wardrobe choice up to being close to passing out from starvation. When she pointed out that hypothermia was a possibility, I shoved my car's heavy metal door and sprinted back up to the house.

Our entryway was warm and welcoming after the arctic temperatures. My eyes darted around looking for her when I zeroed in on Libby standing in the kitchen. "Where's all the food?" I accused. "I don't get paid for another three days."

Her dismissive answer frustrated me, "Oh, stop it. You get paid every day."

"Yeah, tips today were a big fat goose egg. I couldn't even score six bucks to cover lunch. I don't have hours at the restaurant again until Saturday."

Libby stalked over to the cabinet and started shoving boxes around the same way I had right before I decided to scavenge for food in my car. She didn't find anything either. Still concentrating on the metal cabinet, she asked, "Where'd the peanut butter go?"

Further frustration ebbed into my voice, "Gone last weekend. You were supposed to pick more up."

"What about the tuna fish?"

My nose crinkled, "Ewww . . . gone and no need to get any more."

"We had some Ramen noodles in here last night."

I walked up behind her, reached around her into the cabinet, and held up the cellophane that had held the case of noodles, "Yeah, they're gone, too."

"All right. Let's go to the store." She walked up to the stove and grabbed the coffee can where she hid her money. "I've got twelve bucks." Twelve dollars. Was she kidding? That wouldn't even cover a gallon of milk, a case of macaroni and cheese, and bottle of vitamins. We'd both proven that those three staples were enough to survive on. I was sick of just surviving: I was hungry for real food.

I could usually count on a meal at the restaurant during my shift: something a customer had sent back or a special that got cold, something – not today. The new manager backed my hours off at the restaurant, too, so that meant even fewer meals with real meat. I'd been late twice this month, both because of school, so all of the sudden I was no longer reliable enough to be scheduled for the weekday lunch crowd. I'd been tempted to slash his tires, but I couldn't afford to lose my job, at least not the one that I could count on to get tips to keep gas in my car and a hot meal when the cupboards were bare.

"Twelve bucks isn't going to cut it. Didn't you just get paid?"

Her cheeks flushed, and I didn't need to hear her say it. Dammit. This happened every time I was working and she had money. She'd invite some friends over, order pizza, get some beers, then wings: the next thing our cupboards were empty, she was broke, and rent was due. If it wasn't rent it was the electric bill, the gas bill, the water bill, or the trash bill – this had to stop.

Unapologetically she said, "Go throw on a skirt."

"Shit, no frickin' way! Your check's gone, isn't it?" I accused.

"Don't worry about my check. Get a skirt on, and we can go to the grocery store afterwards."

"No. Find someone else. I've got a test tomorrow I haven't studied for, and I have to be at the gas station at midnight."

She looked at the clock on the stove. "It's only six. That's plenty of time."

"Are you deaf? I have to work tonight, all night. I have to study, and I haven't slept yet today."

"Do you want to eat or not? You know I hate taking anyone else. Get a skirt and wear the black sweater you wore last time."

Unbelievable. I didn't try to mask any of my contempt at her suggestion of the short black sweater, "It's like twenty below out!"

"Okay, fine. Wear what you want, but the less skin showing, the less food in the pantry."

My stomach let out a furious rumble. Mrs. Bavcock across the street probably heard it. "It's a Tuesday night. Where are you going to find a chump on a Tuesday night?" I asked incredulously.

Libby was as sympathetic as a paperclip. "Dammit, Candy, stop bitching and get dressed!"

She stalked out of the room and up the stairs. I hated this. I hated that my wellbeing was tied to someone who wasn't responsible enough to adopt a puppy from the pound. I went back to the cabinet, begrudgingly pulling the rice and soy sauce from it. The shower turned on upstairs as my water started to boil on the stove. I shook my head to no one in particular. She couldn't be serious. No one would be at the bars on a Tuesday night in the bitter cold beyond the alcoholics and the regulars. She couldn't get money from either of those two groups – they all knew her.

Five minutes later my instant rice was ready. I took a seat in front of the television, grabbed my notes for my test tomorrow, and eyed my pathetic meal as enthusiastically as I could. The bowl nearly emptied itself. It wasn't great, but the sharp pains in my stomach eased. Libby's hair dryer blared to life upstairs – if she thought I was going with her, she was insane.

Trying to decipher the scribbles in my notebook, I tuned out everything else. School sucked, but no way was I going to live like this the rest of my life: three jobs, full-time school, and no boyfriend.

As irresponsible and carefree as Libby could be, there was no one I was closer to in the world. It drove me crazy, because for every time I was ready to kick her out in favor of a roommate who I could count on, she would do something amazingly selfless and remind me why she had been my best friend since grade school. She had an enormous heart. Blowing her paycheck the night she got it and having friends over who cleaned out what little food we had in our cabinets sucked, but it wouldn't have been in her nature to tell someone "no."

As I zoned out over my notes, I noticed her standing at the entryway to the living room.

My eyes about popped out of my head. She wore two scraps of fabric: an emerald green halter top and a short black skirt. Black leather boots with sky-high heels went up over her knees, letting little of her muscular legs peek through. Her blonde hair stretched half-way down her back and was smoothed straight. She must have been hungrier than she was letting on; in an outfit like that, no one would stand a chance against her. In a voice normally reserved for drill instructors, she barked, "Get dressed."

Absently I answered, "I told you, I have a test tomorrow, and I have to be at work in a few hours."

She looked at the clock. "You said midnight. That's almost six hours from now. Get dressed."

"Barely five hours, and I haven't slept yet today," I growled.

"You can nap at the gas station tonight. C'mon, I can't do this tomorrow night, and we don't have enough food to make it until then anyway."

My eyes took in her scant clothes. Instead of agreeing to wear a short skirt and half a top, I simply said, "Julia Roberts called. She wants her *Pretty Woman* outfit back."

"Shut up and get dressed."

Decisively I looked her square in the eye and told her one last time, "I'm not going. Call someone else. But rent's due next week, so if it doesn't work out at the bar, you may want to stop by lower Third Street. You'll fit right in."

My insult, "lower Third Street" where all the prostitutes hung out, was ignored. Instead she hurled a low-blow in my direction, "If you go with me, I'll make manicotti tonight."

My stomach lurched at the offer. Libby's manicotti was my favorite, and she knew it. I shook my head, trying to keep from taking the bait. "You say that now, but five hours from now you'll be sleeping, and I'll be going to work."

She held her pinky up in the air, "I swear. Two hours tops at the bar. I'll go to the grocery store after, you take a nap, and it'll be ready before you have to go to work."

Arguing was a waste of time. She had me. I would do all the chores around here she didn't want to do at the mere hint that she would make a pan of it. Throwing on a skirt and helping her find a chump in a bar was a lot less work than what I would have been willing to do for her manicotti. Dammit. I tossed my illegible notes on the floor, put my empty rice bowl in the sink, and was in my room changing before I could convince myself that I was an idiot.

We rolled into Bank Shot at the end of happy hour. The aroma of the happy hour food, the stale alcohol smell which permeated the air, and the loud music blaring through the sound system was a familiar welcome. The sad remains of free chicken wings were lined up on the bar. I started for them like a toddler to chocolate.

Libby's hand grabbed my arm when she reminded me, "We're not here to eat." If my stomach could have controlled my hands, they would have slapped her for that comment. Was she for real? We were here to get money for food, and there were dried up, cold chicken wings just a few feet away.

Libby's eyes roved over the room: there were ten pool tables, all with players – a surprising crowd for a Tuesday night. She studied each table, cautiously sizing up each player. Libby could have been a professional – she and I hadn't played pool for fun in years. Her eyes stopped on table four, where a tall slender guy with a bad case of acne was racking. He was probably about our age. The one getting ready to break was shorter, muscular, and was at least early thirties. Both had raven-colored hair.

The two she picked were average Joes, nothing special about either one. Neither was overly attractive, nor were they painful on the eyes. They didn't wear designer clothes, but both had brought their own pool cues with them. Sizing them up, I shook my head, "No, not needy enough."

Libby shook her head, and said, "I've never seen them here before. It'd be easy."

Chris shouted from behind the bar, "Candy, you two better not be doing what I think you're doing!"

Libby flinched. She shot him one of her perfect smiles then spoke to me through clenched teeth, telling me, "Go talk to him. Give him a sob story so he doesn't give us any trouble. I'll find a spot for our coats."

I was a little surprised at Chris' outburst. We'd been coming to Bank Shot since we were still in high school; he'd never given us an ounce of grief. I shook my head, "You do it. This was your idea."

Libby's bright smile diminished as she confessed, "I took him for three hundred bucks the last time I was here. You think he'll listen to me?"

I hadn't been with her that night. Libby was the best pool hustler around. A few of the bars around town had banned her, which was a pretty decent accomplishment for a girl who was still shy of the legal drinking age. It wasn't like her to take money from a bar employee. That was the quickest way to be shown the door, as we had both learned during our senior year of high school when we were trying to get money to go on the senior class trip. I was the decoy. In my own right, I wasn't half-bad, but I couldn't shark on my own.

Begrudgingly, I strode up to the bar. "Hey, Chris. I haven't seen you around. Been working much?"

He ignored my attempt at small talk and pointed an accusing finger in Libby's direction. "She better not be sharking tonight."

"Oh, come on. She's just blowing off steam. It's not her fault she's better than most of these guys."

Chris looked me dead in the eye. "You know she took me for more than a hundred dollars."

She had just told me she had taken him for significantly more than that, but letting on that I knew would only bruise his ego further. I played it off, "Yeah, she was really excited when she came home that night. Thanks, by the way. We were able to pay the electric bill. I hate seeing my breath in my bedroom."

Chris had been glaring at her, but my confession softened his stare. His voice changed when he prodded, "For real?"

I rarely let anyone in on how dire our circumstances were, but if I didn't share the truth, there was a good chance he'd toss us. If that happened, we were completely screwed. "Yeah. You should see our pantry right now. The mice have moved out and have applied for food stamps."

His eyebrows rose. There was a kindness showing through when he asked, "Why don't you two get regular jobs like everyone else?"

"We have regular jobs. It's not enough to cover the bills. She only does this when we're really in a pinch." I forced a smile and added, "I'm not exaggerating about the mice."

He shook his head. Without another word he grabbed what was left of the chicken wings from happy hour and put them all on a paper plate. He filled a big plastic glass with ice water and placed both in front of me.

The smell of the wings did something to me. I picked up the first one as my hand began shaking – I was hungry in a big way. I didn't care if Chris thought I was some kind of animal. I devoured the whole thing, not setting it back down until it was a naked bone.

I didn't hear the music or conversations around me, and I couldn't feel Chris's eyes – even though I was sure he was staring. I had inhaled the first five wings before Libby's hand on my shoulder brought me out of my eating ecstasy.

She reached around me and picked up a wing off the plate. I felt like a feral dog ready to bite her hand, but resisted the urge. Libby winked at Chris, no doubt trying to make nice, "I love that shirt."

I hadn't paid attention before, but she was right, he was wearing a nice shirt. Chris was okay to look at – not an Adonis by any stretch of the imagination. He was average height, average build, and usually wore an easy smile: the kind of guy you wanted to leave a big tip for if moths weren't flying out of your wallet.

Chris forced a smile back at her. He shouldn't have bothered, because it looked like it was painful for him. The shirt he wore was a black button down: the material had a sheen to it with designs woven into the fabric. Something about the shirt made him look more attractive than normal. Or maybe it was that he had just fed me and somewhere deep within my primal being that bumped him up on the attractiveness scale.

Chris warned Libby, "I already told Candy, no bets tonight. If you're playing, it better be for fun."

Libby actually batted her eyes. She shouldn't have because it made her look disingenuous. Her voice was sweet as she answered, "It's always for fun. Some times are just more enjoyable than others."

Chris wasn't budging as he pointed toward the exit. "There's the door. Feel free to use it if you have anything beyond a friendly game of pool in mind."

She leaned up on the bar, so far up that her toes were barely on the floor as she balanced her body weight with her forearms. She leaned all the way across the bar and put her mouth right up against Chris's ear. Although she whispered, I could still hear her words, "Twenty bucks if you look the other way."

He pushed her face away from his ear and shot her a glare. "Twenty?" He looked around the bar, then quietly answered, "If any of these chumps complain, it's my job. I have to eat, too."

She rolled her eyes. "I'm not taking the title to anyone's car. We just need groceries."

She held his glare. I wondered if something more had happened between them? It wasn't like him to hold a grudge. His eyes darted to the floor while he considered her words. When he finally looked back at Libby, he nodded his head. "Fine. Twenty bucks. You've got fifteen minutes, that's it."

Her victory smile emerged, "I need forty-five."

Chris scowled and looked at me. I answered his scowl with a smile, quietly adding, "She needs to play at least three games, maybe four."

Yes, there was a psychology to taking someone's money in a bar. "Taking" was the wrong word: convincing them to wager with us. Libby was great at it. She let them know she had moves, but never ran the table in the beginning. It was a series of, "I can't believe I just made that shot!" or "I wish I had a video of that one," or one of my all-time favorites, "Have you ever lost to two girls?"

She always dressed for the part, too, choosing attire that would make her opponents pay more attention to her than to the game. This was the only part that bothered me: some of her outfits covered less than a bikini. I wouldn't so much care if it were just her, but she insisted I wear the same sort of uniform regardless of the temperatures outside.

Within one game she could size up who would be willing to part with some money. She always threw the second game, then would offer to bet on the third. Usually, whoever she was talking to was so enamored with her, they weren't even concentrating on the game.

Chris reached over and put his hand on my forearm, "Forty-five minutes, not a second more."

Libby had the green light she needed and didn't waste one second of it. She went to table four where the two guys were still playing. I didn't have to hear her to know she was successful. The shorter of the two stood up from his shot and slid all the balls into the center of the table, put coins in to retrieve the balls which had already gone in and began re-racking. She motioned for me to come over.

I set the last chicken bone down on the plate, smiled at Chris, and said, "Wish me luck."

CHAPTER 3

The tall guy with the bad case of acne kept his eyes averted, preferring instead to look at the pool table rather than watch my approach. I wasn't dressed as skimpily as Libby, but I knew the skirt and boots I had on normally drew men's eyes to me. I smiled at him as I approached to introduce myself, "Hi, I'm Candy."

His eyes roved from the pool table, down to my boots and shyly made their way up to mine. He looked nervous, as if two women didn't normally invite themselves over to play a game of pool with him. His answer was stiff, "Tony."

Libby beamed from across the table, "That should be easy to remember, Teddy and Tony," as she gestured to the shorter man closer to her, letting me know his name, then she introduced me to Teddy, "This is my friend, Candy."

The first game went quickly. Teddy racked, Libby broke, and she put four balls into the pocket. Teddy took their first turn and dropped five. I put in two and Tony sunk one. There were only three balls left on the table, and Libby won without even having to do any fancy bank shots.

Teddy leaned toward Libby, his eyes glued to her outfit as if he were an inspector in a sweat shop. “Damn, that was fast. You two want to play again?”

Libby smiled, “Sure, we don’t have to be anywhere for a half hour.”

Teddy’s curiosity was piqued, “Where are you two off to? A date?”

Libby dismissed the idea brazenly, “On a Tuesday night? No. Candy has a test she has to study for. I promised if she came out with me to play a couple games, I’d make dinner so she could study.”

Close enough to the truth not to raise suspicion. Teddy eyed me, “A test? You’re in college?”

It was a fair question. Libby and I were both twenty, so we didn’t drink, at least not in bars. We looked young enough that we could easily be jail bait, so good for him for checking to make sure I wasn’t in high school.

I nodded, “Yeah, my sophomore year.”

His attention turned back to Libby, “So, you two stay in the dorms?”

Libby flirt-punched him, “No, we have a house on the east side of town. High school was enough for me. I work.”

Tony had quietly racked the balls without asking if we wanted to play again. Teddy gestured to the table, his eyes fixed on Libby, “It’s your table. You’re going to play us again so we can get it back, right?”

I felt eyes on me from across the room. I turned expecting to see Chris staring our way, but was surprised to see a different set of eyes watching me. It took me a second to place who they belonged to: Dave Brewer leaned up against a wall. I hadn’t seen him since the summer after we graduated. Dave was stalky, tall, but built solid. He was wearing dark blue jeans, a black t-shirt stretched taut across his chest, and black boots. I held up my hand in a half wave, but he didn't return my wave or nod in my direction or anything. That was odd. The two of us hadn't kept in touch after high school, but we were good friends our senior year. I wanted to go over and say hi, but Libby would blow a gasket if I did.

I couldn't help but steal glances in his direction: each time I looked his way, he was staring at me. Dave had changed a lot since high school. He had been stringy and awkward looking, but he had filled out the last couple years. Libby shot me a warning glance reminding me I needed to stick to the routine. She broke again, but this time she only got three balls in. Teddy sunk six. I put in one, Tony dropped one, and it was her turn again. We still had three balls on the table, Teddy and Tony were on the eight ball, Libby made it look good but missed her shot. Before I had a chance to shoot again, the men had won.

So far we were seriously keeping to Chris's original timeframe. We'd been playing with them for less than ten minutes. Libby went into shark-mode, "You two got lucky. If I hadn't missed that last one, you'd be racking again," she challenged.

Teddy answered in a self-deprecating way, "I know. You're pretty good."

Damn, I hated it when she took money from nice guys. I actually kind of liked it when she took money from the cocky ones. After all the chicken wings from Chris, I wasn't nearly as desperate for manicotti. She answered slyly, "I think your luck's about to change. We've got time for one more before we have to leave."

Stroking his pool cue slowly, Teddy argued, "One more? Come on, you two just got here."

Libby shook her head, "Nope, I promised."

Attempting to barter for our company, Teddy suggested, "If you're so sure my luck's about to change, how about if we win this next one, the two of you have to stay and play."

Libby raised an eyebrow. "Really? What makes you so sure you can beat us?"

He tipped an invisible hat and put on a slow-southern drawl, "Darlin', this ain't my first rodeo."

Libby smirked, "Pretty confident. So, if you win, we stay and play, if we win we leave? That's the worst bet I've ever heard."

Teddy's cocky nature reared its head when he countered, "Name your price, Sweetheart."

Watching Libby shark was a thing of beauty. She was reeling them in, "If you win, we'll stay and play another game, but if we win, you make it worth our while. Fifty dollars."

Teddy's surprise registered. "That's pretty steep."

"Only if you're going to lose."

Teddy shook his head. "You're serious?"

"Yes."

Teddy eyed Libby more cautiously. "If I didn't know better, I'd think you were trying to take advantage of me and my little brother here."

Libby set her cue on the table, "Never mind, Candy and I can go."

He held up both of his hands with his palms facing Libby, "Now, I didn't say the two of you had to go. But I'm not willing to lay down fifty bucks for the pleasure of anyone's company – well, at least not for their company in a bar. You want to bet money, the wager is equal on both sides."

Libby gave her innocent smile, "Okay, fifty bucks on both sides."

Tony shook his head at Teddy, but Teddy wasn't budging. Teddy pulled out his wallet and took a crisp fifty dollar bill and laid it on the table. Libby's eyes got big when she scolded, "Put that away! Gambling is a quick way to get tossed out." Her voice softened as she added, "I know you're good for it. Put it back in your wallet."

Teddy did as instructed, but grabbed his cue. "I'll break."

Libby didn't even get a turn. Teddy ran the table, sinking all of his balls and the eight. Shit, we barely had enough gas to get to the bar. We didn't have the fifty we now owed Teddy.

Before Teddy had an opportunity to gloat, Libby offered, "Double or nothing."

Teddy shook his head in a condescending way, "Sweetheart, you aren't going to win."

Tony walked over to where I stood, his voice low, "Hey, don't let your friend get suckered in. Teddy's really good. He sharks all the time. Tell her to cut her losses and walk away."

I looked at him incredulously. Was he serious? If these two were pulling the same stunt Libby and I were, then his warning would get him in all kinds of trouble with Teddy. Tony was Teddy's decoy, but unlike me, he had a conscience about who they took money from. How many times had I seen Libby take some hard-working stiff for every penny he had? I'd never once given one a warning. Damn.

I had to play naïve – that was my job, "Really?" I countered, "Libby's pretty good."

"Not good enough. Tell her to walk away." Tony looked me square in the eye as if embarrassed at how badly his partner would beat us on the pool table.

I couldn't believe what I had heard. There was no way I was letting on that we were trying to play them either, so I asked, "Why are you telling me this?"

"Teddy's my brother. He's a jerk and has a real gambling problem. When he sees dollar signs, he turns into a different guy. Just have her pay up and get out of here."

I didn't share Tony's warning with Libby, and I didn't share with Tony that we didn't have the money to cover the loss. Libby racked again, and Teddy did it a second time. Two shut out games in a row. I started to get worried, because in all our games, since we were juniors in high school, we'd never run across another team like ourselves. Libby and I now owed him a hundred dollars. Shit, this was so not how tonight was supposed to go down.

Libby walked over to Teddy and flirtatiously put her hand on his chest, "Double or nothing again. You at least have to let me shoot."

"I can do this all night, Sweetheart. You sure you want to go for two hundred? You got that much on you?"

"I've got it." No she didn't, but I kept my mouth shut, as she racked for a fifth game.

After the third shutout I began sweating. Not like little beads of sweat, but the "Oh, my God, she was gambling with our rent money – that she didn't have" kind of sweat. I tapped her on the shoulder, drawing her attention away from the table. I whispered low to keep Teddy and Tony from hearing. "That's it, Libby. You can't do it again. You don't have four hundred dollars."

Confidently she smirked, "I don't need it. Watch this."

She racked for the sixth game, Teddy had sunk four of the balls and looked like he was focusing as if his life depended on the fifth.

Libby innocently stood behind the pocket he was aiming at and dropped her pool cue on the floor. The sound of the cue hitting the floor distracted him for a fraction of a second. In that fraction of time he saw her bend down to retrieve it, and I heard music to my ears. A good shot had a solid sound to it: Teddy had been distracted enough to miscue.

Libby didn't play with him. When she bent over the table, she ran it. She had won the game before Tony or I even had a chance to shoot.

Teddy looked pissed. He threw his cue on the table and went to rack. Libby's sing-songy voice echoed, "Oh my God, that's four hundred dollars! Wow. I'm sorry about your shot, well, not really." She looked at the clock, and we had just crossed Chris's time limit.

She squatted down next to Teddy who was slamming balls onto the table in the rack hard. Her voice was sweet, too sweet. "Sorry, maybe another night. We've got to go."

His cocky voice had turned to anger when he growled, "Double or nothing again."

Libby shook her head, "No can do. I only had four hundred. I couldn't afford to pay you if we lost again, and you are *really* good."

That was a lie. If she had scraped all the change in the bottom of her purse together, she might have had fifty-two cents to go with the twelve dollars from her coffee can. Four hundred dollars would have been catastrophic if she'd lost.

Teddy stood to his whole height glaring at Libby, "I don't carry that kind of cash."

She pointed to a dark corner of the bar, "No problem. There's an ATM right over there."

Teddy was fuming, his words angry and measured. "I'm not paying."

Tony walked up to Teddy casually and softly offered, "They won. Just pay and let's go."

Teddy snarled, "No. I'm not paying this bitch."

Others around us were suddenly very interested in what was going on at our table. I wanted to blend into the wall. I'd seen scenes like this before, and normally they didn't turn ugly because we had friends around, but tonight the only ones we knew in the whole place were Chris, who didn't want us here to begin with, and Dave Brewer, who I hadn't seen in almost two years, neither of whom would go to bat for us if we needed them.

Tony stepped up to his brother, towering over him with his lanky frame. "You've told me a hundred times, a bet's a bet. A man's only as good as his word. Pay up or I will."

Was he for real? Teddy's little brother was sticking up for us? He stood quite a bit taller than his older brother, but Tony was willow thin. If looks were any indication, Teddy, who surprisingly enough had seemed about as aggressive as a teddy bear earlier, could beat the crapola out of his brother without any effort at all. Tony didn't back down, instead demanding, "Now."

Teddy shoved Tony hard into the pool table behind him. Tony righted himself after he had smashed into the pool table and narrowly missed the light hanging above it with his head. Teddy glared at Tony for a couple seconds as if silently challenging his brother to come at him. Tony didn't. He stood against the pool table staring at his brother. Teddy shook his head as if he were going to say something to his brother, but reconsidered and walked toward the ATM in the far corner, mumbling an explicative under his breath.

I flew over to Tony, "Are you okay?"

"Fine. When he pays you, the two of you better get out of here. I've never seen him come after a lady, but he's a bad loser."

"Will do." He didn't have to tell me twice. Chris was watching in earnest from behind the bar. I'm sure a small part of him was hoping Libby would lose, after her doing essentially the same thing to him. The larger portion of him was no doubt thrilled that she was going to make good on her offer to him for letting her shark.

I felt like I owed Tony for sticking up for us, but I didn't know how to say it without sounding disingenuous. "Hey, thanks."

"No problem." He watched his brother returning from the ATM, "Here he comes. You two better go."

When Teddy returned with a pile of twenties, he tossed them at Libby: they all floated to the floor. She squatted down to gather them. Teddy crossed over into Slimeville when he spat, "Go ahead, Honey, you can stay down there if you are looking for some more cash."

Out of nowhere came a booming voice neither I nor anyone in a twenty foot radius expected. "Teddy, you sneaky son-of-a-bitch, I thought that was you. Just got beat by a girl? Careful, your rep may never recover."

I turned to see Dave towering over Teddy. Up close, Dave looked even more different than when I had last seen him. When he was across the room from us, I'd noticed his shirt was tight, but up close I could see his chest stretched every stitch of fabric on it, rivaling any body builder I'd seen.

Dave moved in closer to Teddy, and Teddy took a step back giving Dave some room. He shot a dazzling smile my way, and said, "Ladies, if you're done with Teddy, I need to talk to him for a minute."

Libby had gathered up all the twenties off of the floor and shoved them in her purse. "Sure. We were just leaving."

In a commanding voice, meant to knock Teddy down a couple inches, Dave asked, "I saw you toss her winnings at her. You weren't disrespecting the ladies, were you?" Libby was a few steps ahead of me, but I was frozen in place by Dave's question to Teddy.

Teddy's voice answered in a friendly tone, "No. Of course not, Boss. Just wrapping up a friendly game."

"That's what I thought." Dave turned toward me, held out his hand and said, "I'm Mark. I'm sorry we couldn't meet under better circumstances. Can you stick around for a drink?"

Mark? What the hell? His name was Dave. I took his hand in an odd way, not understanding the game he was playing. I'd known him since the day he turned my piece-of-shit car I'd rescued from the scrap heap into a muscle car. He had to have recognized me. Regardless of what was going on between the two men, he had definitely come to our rescue with Teddy, so I decided to play along. "It's nice to meet you, too, Mark. I'm Candy."

Dave's eyes locked on mine as he asked a second time, "A drink?"

"Um, no thanks. Libby and I were just leaving."

In a smooth voice he answered, "My loss. I'll be here next Tuesday night. Maybe I'll see you then."

There was something weird about Dave's voice. It sounded deeper than the last time I had heard it – older for sure. Not a surprise, he was two years older than the last time I had seen him. As big as his chest was, maybe he had taken steroids or something, but I think those make a man's voice rise not get deeper.

"Maybe. I don't usually go out on Tuesdays, but I'll try." I turned my attention to Libby who stood several feet away. "Ready?"

With my back to Dave, I heard him say, "I've got some business with Teddy. I hope you two lovely ladies have a good evening."

With that, we had been dismissed. None too soon, either. Libby's eyes had taken in all of Dave, as well. From her expression, she was just as impressed with the changes as I had been. I watched her sizing him up, but I grabbed her shoulder to move her away from all the testosterone. Libby made a straight line to the bar; she had agreed to give Chris twenty, but it looked like she slid him closer to sixty.

He nodded his thanks then jammed the cash in his pocket. We were outside in the frigid air a few seconds later. The temperature did nothing to quiet her when she asked loudly, "That was Dave Brewer? Holy shit, did he move into a gym?"

I shook my head, "I don't know, maybe. You want me to go back in and ask?"

She pushed me toward my car, "Funny. Drive."

CHAPTER 4

We got home after 8:00 PM. Libby was right: I had just enough time for a quick nap before I had to go to work at midnight. She promised to go to the grocery store in order to have manicotti waiting for me when I woke up. The free chicken wings I had eaten at the bar had taken the edge off of my hunger, so getting to sleep would be easy enough.

I wondered how long she would be able to keep this pool sharking up. Libby was good, really good. She'd make more money in a bigger city like Omaha or Chicago, but there was a much better chance that she'd get knifed there, too. There were nights she lost, but few, if any, where she lost big. Tonight was the first time in a really long time that I worried she might have to come up with money she didn't have.

I lay down and snuggled into my pillow. The cool caress of my sheets was short-lived. I awoke briefly when I heard Libby's high-pitched call from downstairs, "Candy! Candy!!" Startling awake, I propped myself up on my elbows, picked up my phone from my nightstand and saw that I still had five minutes before I needed to wake up.

I wondered if I had heard my name in a dream or if Libby had called to me. I sat up for a few seconds to listen for her – nothing. Libby was always screwing with the settings on the clocks in the house, so none of them were the same time. The one on the stove was five minutes fast, the one in the living room was ten minutes ahead. I eased my head back onto my pillow – the few hours of sleep wasn't enough, and I desperately wanted my other five minutes. It felt like my eyes had just barely closed when my phone began ringing.

The ring was easy to ignore – I was too tired to talk to anyone. I used the alarm on my phone instead of my alarm clock, which sounded different than my ring tone. I tuned out the annoying caller in favor of my final minutes of much needed sleep. Whoever was calling me could wait. I dozed off again.

My phone rang again. I reached over to push "ignore" when I saw the time. 12:20 – shit, I was twenty minutes late for work! Leaping out of bed, I grabbed a pair of jeans and a sweater and flung them both on, not even bothering to look at myself in the mirror. My fingers weaved through my hair, tying it in a messy pony tail, then began lacing my leather boots. They stopped just below my knee, so I skipped half the eyelets and tucked the laces in the top. I shoved my books, which had been scattered around my room, into my backpack as the smell of Libby's manicotti wafted upstairs.

I bounded down the steps, two at a time. Libby was lying still on the couch in the dark living room with the television on. A small casserole dish with stuffed manicotti was waiting for me on the kitchen table. Something was on the wall behind the couch, but before I could get a closer look, my phone screeched to life again – how many calls was that? I saw the caller

ID: it was Maria at the gas station, the lady who I should have relieved over twenty minutes ago. I accepted the call and blurted into the phone, "Maria, I'm so sorry. I overslept. I'm on my way right now."

She was wholly pissed off, "My babysitter charges me by the minute after twelve-thirty."

"I'm sorry. I swear I'll be there in ten minutes. No pass down, you can jet as soon as I hit the parking lot. I'll relieve you an hour early tomorrow night." I grabbed my coat, bolted into the cold night air, rushed down the front steps to my car, not even bothering to shut off the television or to tell Libby thanks for the dinner.

"I'm telling Mr. Sanders you're late again."

I was already in my car. The roar of the engine momentarily drowned out the swear words she was firing at me. I pleaded, "Please don't. I swear I just overslept. I'm in my car now."

I gunned the engine, and my car responded immediately. I loved my car.

Maria hung up on me. I hoped she didn't make a big deal about it to our boss. Of my three jobs, this was the one I liked the best. Midnight to seven, five nights a week. I could bring my books with me and study most of the night. Customers weren't allowed in the store after ten, so other than the occasional request for a pack of cigarettes, there were very few disruptions.

Maria was already in her car as I flew into the tiny parking lot. She rolled her window down and threw the keys toward me before I had even shut my car off – they landed in the snow a few feet away. Damn, she *was* going to tell Mr. Sanders. I couldn't afford to get fired from this job. I needed it.

I slung my book bag over my shoulder before I reached down to the ground, digging through the pile of snow for the keys. Hopefully Mr.

Sanders would come in early tomorrow *before* Maria could call him. That would give me a chance to explain. I thought of all the little crappy jobs around the store that I could do tonight to make up for being late.

An old Chevy Nova pulled up to the pump as I was unlocking the door to the store. It was tricked out with wide wheels, chrome everywhere, and a black matte finish. I couldn't help but check it out as I secured the deadbolt behind me after I was inside the store. I took my perch behind the window, finished lacing up my boots, brushed my hair into a more presentable pony tail, and put some lip balm on.

I sat in the booth, and if anyone needed something besides gas, I could sell them pop, snacks, cigarettes and beer, but I did it through the nifty little drawer. No one came inside. Most customers just needed fuel and paid at the pump, so I could go hours without talking to anyone on my shift.

As all-night convenience store jobs go, this one was better than most. Mr. Sanders didn't like to talk about it, but one of his clerks had been shot and killed a few years ago. After it happened, he changed the policy: the doors stayed locked from 10 PM to 6 AM, and bullet-proof glass was installed on every window. Occasionally, someone would come in who was too dense to figure out how to work the pumps, so I'd go outside to help, but that almost never happened.

The driver of the Nova made his way to my window after he had pumped and paid for his gas. I didn't recognize the car, and the driver reminded me of a little Banty rooster. It was minus ten degrees, yet he was only wearing a sweatshirt, strutting up to the window. "Hi. I need a Coke and a pack of Salems."

I reached over and grabbed the cigarettes, then leaned into the pop cabinet to retrieve his drink. "Six, forty-nine."

He slid a ten into the drawer then cocked his head toward my car. "Nice wheels. Is that a '68?"

I placed his items and change into the drawer and slid it to him. I was used to compliments on my car. It was a classic and by far one of the sexiest cars on the road. "'66."

"Nice. If I had a car like that, I wouldn't be driving it. That'd be in the garage."

Trying to be polite, "Your Nova's not bad. Why isn't it in your garage?"

"Yeah, it's a '76 and it's nice, but it's not a Chevelle."

"Driving it is my only alternative to walking, and I'm not hoofing it in this weather."

"I hear that. Rebuilt the Nova myself. Hey, it's freezing out here. Can I come inside?"

"Sorry, against store policy. If you need anything else, I can get it." Every now and again, someone would ask for something that wouldn't fit through the little drawer. When that happened, I would open the door and hand their item to them, but that wasn't anything I offered up unless someone needed a frozen pizza or a bottle of windshield wash.

He jerked his head toward my car, "Any girl who drives a '66 Chevelle is worth getting to know. Let me in for a minute. It's freezing out here." I sized him up. I liked his car, but I would tower over him, and he couldn't be all that bright if he was out in this weather with just a sweatshirt.

I pasted on my sweetest smile, "Sorry, I'd get fired if I let you in."

Oblivious to my disinterest, he asked, "How about your number? I'll give you a call." Something was off about this guy. He was coming on a little too strong. I'd seen plenty of guys come through at all hours of the night: none had given me a second look. My car was awesome, but I'd never had anyone who wanted my number because of it.

"Sorry, again. I have a boyfriend." I didn't, but something bothered me about this guy. I was anxious for him to get into his car and leave.

He pursed his lips together in a grimace, "That's my luck. Hey, can I get the key to the men's room?"

I slid the key through the drawer. As he walked around the side of the building, I watched him on the security camera. He walked around back, but didn't try to use the men's room. He lit up a cigarette outside the restroom and stood there huddled against the wall. That was odd.

Keeping an eye on the surveillance monitor, I reached into my book bag and pulled out my business law book. I hated that class and had been neglecting the reading assignments because of it. I'd spend the first hour tonight doing the last couple days' reading assignments, then a few hours prepping for my test. I needed to fit in some "crap job" time, like restocking the cooler or refilling the pop display by the window, to make up for my tardy arrival.

I saw the guy throw his cigarette butt on the ground. He still didn't use the restroom. Strange. The guy walked back to my little convenience window. When he stood in front of me, he didn't put the key back in the drawer. Instead he said, "Hey, the door is jammed or something. It won't unlock."

Warning bells started going off in my head. I'd watched him the whole time. He never even tried to open the door. Unsure what type of game he was playing, I accused, "I was watching the camera. It didn't look like you tried the key."

His forehead wrinkled as his eyes narrowed. "You calling me a liar?"

Attempting to keep any alarm out of my voice, I offered, "Um, do you want to try the key to the ladies' room?"

"Yeah, sure." The man made no move to return the key he already had.

I slid the drawer forward, "I'll need the key to the men's room first, then I can give you the other key."

"Oh, right. I must have left it in the door. Just a minute."

Now I was thoroughly nervous. He went toward the back of the place a second time. A big Ford pickup truck pulled up to one of the pumps. I was trying to watch the guy around back on the monitor but had lost him when the truck pulled up. Damn it, where had he gone? I watched the grainy security images from the cameras around the perimeter of the building, but it was like he had just vanished. The man's Nova was still waiting patiently near pump one.

By the time the woman from the Ford had finished pumping her gas, I began to get tense because there was still no sign of the guy. She got back in her truck and was pulling out when I saw a flicker of him on the back side of the building. The camera had captured his movement, but not him. That was it – I'd had enough. We had a panic button under the counter; if I pushed it, the police would be here in five minutes. I re-angled the camera near the pump to get a good visual of the guy's license plate then wrote it down on a slip of paper.

The camera on the back of the building went from a grainy black and white image to nothing but black. I tapped the monitor. Had it been an equipment malfunction or had the man done something to the camera? I turned the camera which had been zoomed in on his license plate and reangled it toward the back of the building. It wouldn't turn far enough to provide a clear view of the back of the building. Shit. Where was he?

The tiny hairs on the nape of my neck stood up. The lady who had my job before I was hired had pressed the silent alarm three times in a month, each time over nothing. Mr. Sanders let her go after the third false alarm, so I didn't want to press the button unless I really needed the police.

I took another look at the black monitor in front of me. A suspicious man was here while I was alone. He said the bathroom door was jammed, yet I knew he hadn't even tried to open it. He had tried to get me to let him inside even though there were signs everywhere saying no entry after 10 PM. I pushed the panic button under the counter before I could talk myself out of it. The device sent a silent signal to the police station – if it turned out to be a glitch in the surveillance system, I would apologize profusely to Mr. Sanders tomorrow. My eyes went to the clock: 12: 43. The police should be here by 12:48.

My eyes continued looking at the three working monitors, attempting to find him somewhere in the shadows. A second monitor went out. There were four cameras on the premises: one on the pumps, one on the front door that showed the front of the store, one on the back near the restrooms, and the fourth around back aimed in on the dumpster.

The cameras by the restroom and dumpster were now both out. The one by the pumps worked, but it could not see the back of the store, and the one aimed in on front was taking footage of me through the glass getting more freaked out by the second.

I picked up my cell. Who could I call? What would I say? I'm in a safe place but a customer who refuses to use the restroom is scaring me. Yeah, the few friends I had would think I'm a head case. I watched headlights on the street whiz past the gas station, praying one of the vehicles might pull in. I didn't want to be alone.

An object flew through the air in front of the window where I sat. The camera in front of the store now only registered black like the other two. This wasn't a glitch: he was breaking the security cameras. My heart had been gaining speed and was now beating so loudly that it drowned out all other sounds. Heat welled up in my body as I felt my face flush with fear.

I looked at the clock: 12:45. For God's sake, where were the cops? The man was slithering toward me along the side of the building. What did the guy look like? I tried to get a good look at him in case he left before the police arrived. He was shorter than me, maybe five feet, six inches on a good day. He wore a black sweatshirt that zipped in the front, well-worn black jeans which were too long, rumpled at his feet. Tan work boots stuck out under his over-sized jeans. He looked to be in his early to mid-twenties. It was freezing outside, but he wore no gloves or hat. His brown hair was short, sort of wavy, and his ears and cheeks were beet red from the cold.

I tried to mask the fear I was feeling. I tucked my shaking hands under the counter so he couldn't see them.

He positioned himself directly in front of me, leering at me through the glass, "The men's room still won't open. Here's the key." He held the key up that was attached to a ridiculously large sign that said "men's." I slid the drawer open for him to drop the key into it.

He held the key high above the drawer with his index finger and thumb, dangling it in the air. My voice shook like a dog in a thunderstorm. "Put the key in the drawer."

The man gave me a thin smile and offered, "Maybe you could come out and give the door a try?"

I shook my head that I couldn't, but said nothing.

"Oh, come on. A big tough pool hustler like yourself? You're not scared of a guy like me, are you? Come on out and give me a hand."

Pool hustler? Who was this guy and what was he talking about? My mind whizzed through all the recent games Libby and I had played – I'd never even seen him before.

He held his smile, but his eyes narrowed. "Swimming with the sharks can be hazardous to your health." He dropped the washroom key into the outstretched drawer with a loud thud, then reached his hand inside the pocket of his sweatshirt. I grinned to myself, knowing he had to have left a fingerprint on it and pulled the drawer closed. My grin must have ticked him off, because he asked, "You like swimming with the sharks, Princess? Teddy wants his four hundred dollars back. Give me the money, or you'll never swim again."

My heart lurched in my chest. Teddy? That was the guy from Bank Shot earlier tonight. Libby had hustled him out of four hundred dollars. Teddy sent a thug to get his money back from me? Teddy hadn't even paid *me*. Why wouldn't he have tried to get it from Libby? My phone lay on the counter to my left. I dropped his gaze and looked at it on the counter.

"That's right, Princess. Call the police. They won't get here in time." This moron had obviously never heard of an alarm system. I wasn't about to correct him and let on that I wanted to call my roommate to warn her that Teddy might show up at our door. She had won the four hundred dollars from him fair and square; he must have believed otherwise if he sent this jerk to try to get his money back from me.

My eyes darted to the clock: 12:46. I listened hard, hoping to hear sirens in the distance – nothing. I swallowed a lump in my throat, doing my best to steady my voice. "I was there; she didn't cheat. Teddy lost. Why would he send you to get his money back?"

"That's the thing, the money he gave you girls tonight – it wasn't his. It was mine. You've got to the count of three to push four hundred fifty dollars through that drawer."

"Four hundred fifty?"

His eyes widened as he shrieked, "You think my time is free? Give me my money back and add another fifty for me having to chase you down in this ice box, and I'll let you live."

Let me live? My stomach knotted as the hairs on my arms joined the fine ones at the base of my neck now also standing at attention.

I shook my head. Whatever volume I had been able to produce before evaporated: a small whisper was all I could get out, "I don't. . . I don't have it."

Condescendingly he said, "That does create a bit of a problem. You're a resourceful girl. I bet you could get it."

My mouth opened but nothing more came out. I couldn't tell him we had spent it already, or that Libby had whatever was left of it. I looked at the clock: 12:47. The police should be here any minute. If I could just keep him calm until they arrived, I'd be fine.

The fear I felt sharpened my thoughts when it hit me: how did this guy know where I worked? Did someone from Bank Shot know I worked here? No – none of our friends were with us tonight. Had he already stopped by my house? Would Libby have told him I was here? "Um, I could call my friend. She could bring it here."

His answer accompanied a toothy smile: a shiny gold tooth beamed at me where one of his canines had been, "You think I'm dumb? I was already at your house. There's no money there."

"You were at my house? How do you know where I live?"

"I'm a resourceful guy." If he knew my last name, he wouldn't have had any problems finding me. Libby Googled me a couple weeks ago; she had told me all my information was posted in their directory.

Libby kept all of her money in a coffee can above the stove. Whatever had been left over after she went to the grocery store would have been in the can. If this guy would have tried to get money from Libby, it wouldn't have been in her purse. She could have told him I had the money. "Libby can tell you I don't have it."

"Libby's not going to be talking to anyone again, Princess. Now, give me my money."

CHAPTER 5

The hand he had inside his sweatshirt emerged holding a gun. My hands shot into the air as if he were a typical robber. Mr. Sander's voice echoed in my head, *"It's just money. If it's your life on the line, give them whatever they ask for. We're insured."* He told me that my first night on the job. Anything in the store could be replaced, but there was nothing worth an employee's life.

The man's voice was low and calculating when he slowly counted, "One. Two. . . "

"Wait! Hold On!" I pushed the "cash sale" button on the register and pulled a handful of twenties, dropping them into the drawer without even counting them. I did bank deposits every morning after my shift, and I knew the pile I had just given him was well over $500. I was safely behind bullet-proof glass, but, until this second, it had never occurred to me to ask how well it would stop a bullet. Libby and I had watched a show on the Discovery Channel where it said armor-piercing rounds could get through bullet-proof everything. There was no way to know what kind of rounds he had until he pulled the trigger.

His left hand reached into the drawer, groping for the cash and shoving it in the pocket of his jeans. He smiled and nodded appreciatively to me. I let out the breath I had been holding when he menacingly said, "Three."

His finger pulled the trigger, and I saw the muzzle flash. Inside my robber-proof cage, the bullets ricocheted off the glass as one giant mark puckered the glass. At least three hit the glass before I was able to react. I threw my hands over my head and sprawled onto the floor. Images of my life began assaulting me. I saw myself playing with my sisters on a merry-go-round. . . baking a cherry pie with Mom. . .riding the school bus holding my pink Hello Kitty backpack . . . a slow dance with Dad at my cousin's wedding . . . hundreds of images flashed before my eyes. My hands were jammed hard over my ears, trying their best to keep the sound out. He kept firing. The sound of the bullets ricocheting off of the thick glass were deafening. I lost count on the number of shots. It seemed as if they would never stop, and time had slowed down for them to echo on forever.

The shots finally stopped. I didn't dare look at the shooter's face. For all I knew he was reloading while I was paralyzed with fear on the floor. There was a ringing in my ears as I heard the man's muffled words shout at me through the window. "The next time you see me, you better hope I'm in a good mood, Princess."

The lottery machine, which I hadn't heard at all before the assault, was the only sound in the room. Some hypnotic computerized voice announced the upcoming jackpot as I lay there on the cool tile floor, my body shaking like a teenager after a six-pack of Red Bull. What had just happened? He wasn't trying to hold up the store: he had come here looking for me.

I scrambled to my feet, crouched down below the counter so I could steal a glimpse of the pumps. His Nova was gone. My hands trembled as I fumbled for my phone. I called Libby's phone number – no answer. When her voicemail came on, I nearly shouted into it, "It's me! Are you okay? Some guy just came to the gas station! Oh, my God, are you okay? Call me as soon as you get this!"

A police cruiser eased into the parking lot: lights on, no siren. I stood upright, my whole body quaking, trying to make sense of what had just happened. The cop shined his spotlight throughout the parking lot, as if looking for a criminal to pop out of a shadow and say, "It's me! Arrest me!"

Why was he still in his car? I started to feel sick. I looked through the glass directly in front of where I had sat. One giant mark puckered the glass: my finger touched the dented glass from the inside. Each shot he had fired had been exactly where the previous one was – he was trying to create a hole so he could shoot me. The enormous puckered hole was where my chest would have been, had I not been cowering on the floor.

A second police cruiser arrived. His spotlight was also fully lit and scanning the dark parking lot. Both policemen seemed to be in no hurry whatsoever. After what felt like a union-break, both exited their cruisers and talked briefly together between the two cars. What in the hell were they discussing? Couldn't they see the enormous bullet mark in the glass? Shouldn't they be asking if I were okay?

Slowly, the first officer to arrive walked toward my window. He calmly asked, "You triggered an alarm?"

My finger pointed to the puckered glass, "Uh, yeah, there was a robbery."

In a none-too concerned tone he asked, "Have you phoned the owner?"

Mr. Sanders? Shit, I hadn't thought to call him. "Not yet."

"We're going to need him down here or at least talk to him on the phone." He pulled a notepad from his pocket, "What's your name, miss?"

"Candy Kane."

He wrote down my name, then looked up from his notepad with a raised brow. He wore the same look I got from everyone when I introduced myself. Sheepishly I responded, "I know. My mom had a strange sense of humor." My sisters both got normal names – I was the one who got screwed. Dad told me he left the hospital to go home to take care of Kim and Carly, and when he came back the next morning, she had already filled out my birth certificate.

The police officer smiled empathetically at me, "Don't feel bad, mine named me Charlie."

I looked at the name tag on his uniform, displaying the last name "Brown." His humor gave me some relief from the fear camping inside me. I confessed, "I'd rather be a cartoon character over a Christmas decoration."

He smirked, "Maybe, but to make it worse, she gave me a beagle when I was six – guess what his name was."

Despite my fear, that made me laugh. "No way! Snoopy? She didn't dress you in a yellow shirt with black zig zags, did she?"

"No comment. Just remember, as bad as it gets, it could always be worse." I liked this guy. I hated all the stupid jokes I had heard growing up, but my childhood had to have been a cakewalk compared to his. Officer Brown turned his business voice on and asked, "You want to tell me what happened tonight?"

"You want to come in out of the cold?" He nodded and I let him in. I relayed everything from the time the guy had first pulled up until I was on the floor; I omitted the part about owing him money and what he had said about Libby. He took notes and asked a few questions. When I mentioned the part about him knocking out the security cameras, I added, "It shouldn't matter, though. I zoomed in on the guy's license plate, and I know I got a few pictures of his face. All the camera footage is backed up on the internet. He bought gas with a credit card, too; it was the last purchase on pump one."

Officer Brown stopped taking notes and asked, "Can you show me the surveillance footage from here?"

"You got a computer in your car?" I knew he did – I could see it on his dashboard. I reached for the rumpled up piece of paper Scotchtaped to the wall behind the tray of cigarettes, scrawled down the information on a clean sheet of notebook paper, and handed it to him. Go to the website and use those credentials. The guy pulled up after 12:30; you'll be able to see all four camera feeds."

Officer Brown took the piece of paper with all the info on it. "I'll go take a look. Pull up the credit card information for me and notify the owner." I locked the door behind him as he returned to his car.

I picked up the phone, wanting desperately to try calling Libby again. His words echoed in my head, *"Libby's not going to be talking to anyone again, Princess."* He knew where we lived. He'd already been there. If I told the cops, they'd know this wasn't a regular robbery. Instead of calling Mr. Sanders, I tried Libby's cell it went to voice mail again. She'd been sleeping when I left, and she always turned her ringer off at night. Maybe the man was just trying to scare me.

Before I'd gotten up for work, she had called for me. Was she trying to wake me up or had she been calling out for me to help her? My stomach lurched at the thought that Libby may have screamed for my help and I ignored her. No, I had seen her before I left the house: she was sleeping. . . or was she?

I racked my brain trying to think of someone I could call to go check on her. It was after 1 AM. Who would answer their phone this time of night, then be willing to go to the house? I'd locked the house up before I left, or had I? I'd been in such a hurry, did I leave the door unlocked?

Officer Brown was in his squad car – I wanted to get his attention, but my feet were planted. They didn't want to leave the security of my booth. I eased myself around the counter and made it as far as the thick glass double-doors. My hands were shaking so hard I looked like a Parkinson's patient.

"*Get it together, Candy,*" I told myself. Reaching for the heavy metal deadbolt, I turned it a quarter-turn and cracked the front door open. Officer Brown hadn't noticed that I'd budged, so I stood in the cracked doorway and shouted, "Excuse me!! Hello???"

The officer looked up from his computer, but made no effort to get out of his squad car. I motioned for him to come to the door. It was freezing outside, so I didn't blame him for wanting to do as much investigating as possible in his car, but I kept waving until he slowly exited his sedan. I held the door open for him to join me inside. "Hey, that guy, um, he said something that bothered me."

"What's that?"

"I don't remember exactly what he said, but it was something about seeing my roommate and me at a bar." That was close to the truth. "I tried calling her, but she's not answering. I think she's probably sleeping, but do you think someone could check on her?"

For the first time since his arrival, a look of concern flashed in his eyes. "Did you recognize him?"

"No. I mean, I don't remember seeing him, but he was... I don't know. Could someone see if she's okay?"

Less concerned than he had been a second ago, he asked, "If you didn't recognize him, what makes you think he knows your address?"

I shook my head, "I don't remember exactly what he said, but he knew my roommate's name. We live alone, and she isn't answering my calls."

"What's your address?"

I gave it to him. He didn't waste any time asking for a car to be dispatched – he radioed my address in from the radio's microphone that he wore on his shoulder. When he turned his attention back to me, he asked, "You're sure she's at home?"

"Yes. I mean, she was asleep on the sofa when I left for work less than an hour ago." Libby slept like a rock. It wouldn't be like her to wake up in the middle of the night and go anywhere. She was probably still on the couch where I left her. I hoped she was.

The guy was here within five minutes of me showing up. He couldn't have done something to her, then sped over here, could he? He didn't have enough time. The guy had to have been trying to scare me.

Then it hit me – I hadn't seen Libby before I left, not really. I saw her on the couch – but could she have been hurt and I hadn't noticed? I had left the house in such a rush, I really hadn't seen her. Could he have been in the house when I was there, and he followed me here? I was in such a hurry that I wouldn't have noticed a jumbo jet following me to work.

The second policeman joined us inside. He had been checking the perimeter of the building while Officer Brown was watching surveillance video from his car. The second officer began briefing Officer Brown, "Three of the four cameras were disabled, damage to the front window, and a shot through the windshield over there." He was pointing at my car. "I didn't find any other damage. You think gang initiation?"

I couldn't help myself, "The jackass shot my car?"

Officer number two answered in a clinical tone, "Looks that way. Unless you drove here tonight with a bullet hole through the driver's side of the windshield. The forensics team is going to need to recover the slug."

I careened my neck to try to see my windshield over the rack of candy bars. There was a hole in the driver's side with cracks spread out encircling it in an ugly spider web. Great, more money I didn't have.

Officer Brown's radio shrieked to life, "Ambulance requested at. . ." I heard my address as my ears strained to hear each word. "Female, early twenties, head trauma, lacerations to her face and hands – unresponsive. No sign of forced entry. Victim was seen through a window." The words had crackled out through the radio on his shoulder, and my knees went out from under me. Libby, he had hurt Libby.

No sign of forced entry. Had she let him in while I was sleeping? Was he still in the house when I left? Libby had called out to me a few minutes before I was supposed to get up to leave for work. I thought she was giving me a wake-up call. Had she been calling for my help?

I ran around to the other side of the counter, grabbed my phone and called Mr. Sanders. His voice was groggy when he answered. I don't know what all I said to him as words spewed out of me, but I heard him say, "I'm on my way."

The second officer guided me toward my chair as I numbly took a seat.

My body went into robot mode. The two officers asked questions as I answered one after another – but I felt disconnected. Someone asked me for the keys to my car to dig the bullet out of wherever it was lodged. I could only think of Libby. They had called an ambulance for her. What had he done and when had he done it? He had to have been right there in the house, but I didn't see him as I rushed out the door. Would he have attacked me, too? My mind came to one conclusion: yes, he would have.

I had left the house so quickly, I wouldn't have noticed a polar bear in the house unless it was holding my car keys.

Playing pool and watching Libby take money from strangers never seemed dangerous – never. Sure, guys got pissed off lots of times, but it was more of an assault on their egos. None had ever threatened either of us before. The manicotti Libby had made me was still in the casserole dish on the counter where I had set it when I arrived – I hadn't even had a chance to lift the lid. Raw emotion grabbed hold of me as my eyes focused on the casserole dish. She had to be okay. Trying to reason with myself, I remembered the voice over the radio had said "unresponsive," not dead.

I described the robber, then proceeded to tell them about our encounter with Teddy and Tony earlier tonight. "They were on table four at Bank Shot tonight. Tony was a tall slender guy. He had a lot of acne. He looked my age – early twenties. His older brother was Teddy; he was shorter than Tony, muscular, and seemed to be in his early thirties. Both had dark hair."

Officer Brown was scrawling down my words in his notebook. "My roommate and Teddy were betting on games. She took Teddy for four hundred dollars. He was seriously mad, but he paid her. The bartender working tonight was Chris. If they paid with a credit card, he might know their last name. I know Teddy used the ATM while he was there."

The place closed at midnight during the week, so Chris would already be long gone. Had Teddy seen Libby give Chris money before we left? Was he in danger, too? At this point I didn't know what to think, so I blurted out, "Hey, the bartender, Chris – Libby owed him some money and paid him before we left tonight. Do you think they would have done anything to him?"

Both sets of eyes widened. Officer Brown squeezed the microphone on the radio at his shoulder, "Dispatch, we're going to need a squad car to Bank Shot on Tipton Drive."

A static filled response came back and Officer Brown responded, "Right, Dispatch, check the perimeter. Verify that no incident happened with an employee there tonight."

The next fifteen minutes were a blur. I told them everything I could think of about Tony and Teddy. The robber had said Teddy gambled with *his* money. Teddy had pulled money out of the ATM, so it wasn't like he was holding the money for anyone else. Each of the officers continued asking questions, and I answered each as earnestly as I could. I didn't care if we got prosecuted for illegal gambling later, I didn't care if Mr. Sanders made me pay back every penny I had handed the guy through the drawer – I only wanted this guy caught.

Libby had to be in the hospital by now. I wanted to stop the interrogation to call the hospital, but they needed my answers to find the animal who had attacked her. I hadn't seen Mr. Sanders drive up, or him walk into the store, but I felt his arms wrap around me as he lifted me off my stool. "Candy, I'm so sorry." As I clung to his chest, he asked, "Are you okay?"

I shook my head that I wasn't okay, and, in his embrace, tears began streaming down my cheeks. The sobs, which hadn't even threatened to surface through the hundreds of questions and answers with the police, rocked my body when he held me tight and told me everything was going to be okay. Why did this always happen? I could go through any ugly situation and never even threaten to tear up, but when someone showed me even the smallest kindness, my body would revolt and start bawling like a little baby.

Mr. Sanders was tall and slender. He always wore dress slacks, a button down shirt and a tie – there was never a hair out of place on his head or a hint of five o'clock shadow on his face. He looked like someone who should be running a Fortune Five Hundred company rather than owning a couple of convenience stores. One time when we had problems with one of the pumps, he was down on the ground pushing the reset button on the pump in his slacks and tie. Tonight was the first time I had seen him in blue jeans and a sweatshirt – I wouldn't have guessed he even owned casual clothes.

The police told him that they believed I had been targeted and this wasn't a run-of-the-mill robbery. Mr. Sanders didn't mince words, "Whatever it takes to find this guy – do it. You have our full cooperation."

Mr. Sanders had always been great to me. He moved all the other schedules around so I could have the shift I did – he knew I was putting myself through college and needed the study time. He had even asked me why I didn't take out bigger student loans so I wouldn't have to work so many hours just to survive. I only took out enough to cover my tuition so I wouldn't be in as bad a shape as all the unemployed college graduates my professors kept talking about.

He kept one arm wrapped around me as he fished his cell out of his pocket. He dialed a number as he shot me a reassuring smile. "Marjorie, I'm sorry to call you at this hour. It's Glen Sanders. There has been an incident at the store. Can you come in and cover the rest of Candy's shift?" There was a short pause while she gave him his answer, "Thank you. No. Overtime won't be a problem. Candy is going to need a few days off. We'll work that out when you get here."

Shit. He was firing me. I locked onto his eyes, pleading with him while my mouth started spewing rapidly, "I'm sorry. I didn't mean for this to happen. I'll pay for everything. Please don't fire me."

His arm tightened, still holding me against his chest. Mr. Sander's voice was gentle as he answered, "It's okay. I'm not firing you. I'm just glad you're okay. You've been through a lot."

My words came out in a rush, "I can finish my shift. I swear I'm okay."

Mr. Sanders did something I never expected: he put his phone away and wrapped both his arms around me, then gently kissed the top of my head. His voice was sweet, with not a hint of anger toward me, "I never liked you working this shift. It's too dangerous."

I didn't know what to say. Dangerous? It was the least dangerous shift here because no customer could even get into the place. If I hadn't have been working this shift, I might be dead right now. It was only because I was in a bullet-proof cage, in a locked store that had cameras on every angle, with a panic alarm hooked directly to the police station, that I was able to stand here and cry. Didn't he understand that this shift at this place was safer than taking Santa photos at the mall at Christmastime?

Ignoring the two police officers still in the store, I pleaded, "I'm okay. For real. It's not dangerous."

Mr. Sander's eyes roved toward the glass with the enormous indent from the bullets – he didn't agree, but he didn't argue with me either.

Officer Brown piped in, "Miss Kane, nothing out of the ordinary at Bank Shot. Do you know Chris's address?"

I didn't. I didn't even know his last name. I described him to Officer Brown, and he left to try to figure out who one of my favorite bartenders really was. My stomach tightened. I should have known his last name. I'd talked to him hundreds of times. He had given Libby and me free food nearly every night we came in. Why didn't I know his last name?

Mr. Sanders poured me back into my chair, squeezed my shoulders, and then walked to the far side of the room in front of the forty ounce singles. I watched him make one phone call after another. A third squad car pulled into the parking lot at the same time Marjorie pulled in.

Marjorie was supposed to be my relief in the morning. She wasn't supposed to be here until 7 AM. I had always liked her; she was older than me by a decade but, by far, my favorite employee here. She didn't look like she had just been woken up in the middle of the night and called into work five hours early. Marjorie eased herself behind the counter as her eyes looked at the glass that had been shot to hell, "Damn, girl. You all right?"

My eyes were dry. My adrenaline was waning and my thoughts were consumed with my best friend. I looked in her direction, but not at her eyes; I couldn't afford to break down again. "Yeah, I'm okay. Thanks for coming in."

Mr. Sanders spoke to the three officers; I hadn't seen the third one come into the store. "If you need me," he pulled a business card from his wallet, "you can reach me here. I'm going to get her to the hospital to make sure she is okay."

Hospital? I didn't need to go to the hospital. Nothing had happened to me. I'd followed all the rules that he had drilled into us: Stay in the cage. Don't let anyone in the door. Push the panic button if you need help.

Mr. Sanders' voice prodded me, "C'mon, Candy. Let's get you checked out."

Like a robot I stood up from the chair. Libby's casserole dish still set on the counter. Looking at the dish, memories of Libby assailed me. I was fine, but I needed to see Libby. I slung my backpack over my back and reached for the dish. Somehow my hand didn't work right, and the dish crashed to the floor, spewing bits of marinara sauce all over everything. When I kneeled down to pick it up, one of the sharp pieces of glass sliced the palm of my hand.

It was surreal – the red from the marinara sauce clinging to surfaces as it had splattered the floor, while the fresh blood dripped down my wrist. Mr. Sanders grabbed a t-shirt off of a rack and wrapped it around my hand, took my elbow in his hand, and guided me to my feet. "Marjorie will clean it up. Let's get you to a doctor."

I didn't argue. He held my coat for me as I slid my good hand through the armhole and let it hang loosely over the shoulder of my bleeding hand. Mr. Sanders carried my book bag for me and guided me toward his car.

CHAPTER 6

The cut from the casserole dish hadn't been deep. We had only driven two blocks when I pulled the t-shirt off of my hand and saw the bleeding had slowed. Mr. Sanders had insisted on driving, and as much as I hated leaving my car at the gas station, I couldn't drive it. The bullet hole had been placed directly where my face would be while I was driving, and the glare from headlights in all the cracks would have blinded me if I had tried to operate it. The shots in my safety cage had been well-placed, and I wouldn't ignore the message of the one in my windshield. The shooter was sending me a message, and I received it.

We pulled up in front of the hospital's emergency entrance where the ambulances parked. I didn't feel like this was any kind of an emergency, so I pointed to the garage across the street. "Let's leave this spot for someone who's missing a limb, okay?"

Mr. Sanders furrowed his brow at me, as if to disagree, but must have decided he would be wasting his time. Instead, he did as I asked, and parked in the adjacent garage. As we got out of the car, the below zero temperature took my breath away as I pulled my coat tight around my chest. Mr. Sanders shoved his hands into his thick downy coat, tucked his head down and ushered me toward the entrance to the skywalk for the hospital. Once we were sheltered from the wind and cold in the skywalk between the two structures, he awkwardly said, "You may not feel too bad now, but I think that's just because it hasn't sunk in yet. I want you to take a week off."

I couldn't afford to take a week off. If he knew how broke I was, he wouldn't have even suggested it. My monetary situation was what got me into this mess to begin with: we would have never gone to Bank Shot tonight if we hadn't needed money for food. If he knew how strapped I was, he'd probably let me cover some of the other workers' shifts. "I'm fine, Mr. Sanders. My hand's okay. I just want to check on my roommate. I'll be back to work tomorrow night."

Compassionately he offered, "Sometimes the stress of something like this isn't immediate. I'm taking you off the schedule until next Tuesday. If you need more time, call me and let me know."

We were midway through the glass enclosed skywalk between the parking garage and the hospital when I stopped him. I didn't want to sound like I was ungrateful, but with Libby banged up, I was somehow going to have to come up with her share of the rent. My hand was still wrapped in the t-shirt he had given me, and I allowed myself to concentrate on it when my small voice confessed, "I can't afford to be off work that long."

He stepped into me and hugged me hard to his chest, much the same as he had done at the gas station when I broke down – the same way Dad used to hold me whenever I needed it. Mom and Dad moved to New Mexico a couple years ago, so neither were going to hold me and tell me everything would be fine. Mr. Sanders was old enough to be my father, and I worried I might fall apart all over again in his embrace. He lifted my chin so I was forced to see the kindness waiting for me in his eyes. "It'll be a week with pay. This is on me. You don't have to use any of your accrued vacation time. I just want you to be a hundred percent before you come back."

He released my chin, and I burrowed back into his embrace. I stood there clinging to him, unable to let go or to say anything. I was grateful, but more than that, I wondered what kind of Karma I had to get this guy for a boss. He knew this hadn't been a normal robbery: this was someone Libby and I had pissed off. His store was shot up, three of his security cameras were toast, yet he wanted to give me a paid week off. It didn't add up.

Not wanting to take advantage of his generosity, I told him, "I don't need a week off. I'm sure I'll be okay by tomorrow."

He stepped back from me, distancing himself by several feet. His pained smile focused on my still wrapped-up hand. "Then treat it like a well-deserved vacation."

I didn't know how "well-deserved" he would believe it to be if Maria called him in a few hours to tell him, on top of everything else, I had been thirty minutes late to work. He guided me forward through a second set of double-doors. A hospital information desk greeted us as we stepped out of the skywalk. An older gentleman in a security guard uniform was posted behind the desk. He didn't seem at all surprised to see us. Maybe there were security cameras discreetly placed in the skywalk. Instead of telling him we were looking for my roommate, I held up my hand with the bloodied t-shirt wrapped around it. He gave me an understanding smile and pointed to the left, "Emergency is down the steps on the first floor."

Mr. Sanders waited with me for over an hour. He filled out the mountain of forms saying it would be a workman's comp. claim, so thankfully I wouldn't have to put the hospital on the payment plan. When the nurse finally called me back to meet with the doctor, I told him, "You don't have to wait for me. I can catch a cab back to pick up my car when they're done."

He looked at his watch. It was now well after 3 AM. He started to answer when a lion-sized yawn escaped him. I cut him off. "Mr. Sanders, honestly, thank you. There's no reason for you to stay. Once I see the doctor, I want to go upstairs to check on Libby. You should get some sleep."

He looked like he was going to protest, but instead he stood up and kissed my forehead. "If you need anything, anything at all, call me."

The doctor examined my hand and came to the same conclusion I had – it wasn't much more than a gnarly scratch. He glued it shut and had a nurse wrap it. After reviewing the information Mr. Sanders had written on my admission paperwork, the doctor wrote a prescription for anxiety. I insisted I didn't need it, but he told me at least I would have it if I began to feel overwhelmed. I shoved the slip of paper in my back pocket.

As I was signing out of the emergency room, I asked the nurse behind the desk, "My roommate, Libby Merrick, was brought in a couple hours ago. Do you know if she's still here?"

Her fingers whizzed on the keyboard, then she turned to me, her eyes grave. "She's in the intensive care unit on eight." I turned toward the elevators as her voice warned me, "You won't be able to see her. Visitors are restricted to family only."

I wanted to glare at the nurse and tell her I was family, but instead thanked her for her help and stood by the elevator anyway. When the elevator deposited me on the eighth floor, there was a large waiting area, with several lounge chairs and sofas. As I made my way to the nurse at the ICU desk, a voice behind me stopped me short. "Candy?"

I turned to see Libby's ex-boyfriend, Loser Larry, sitting alone by an enormous window. What she ever saw in him was beyond me. The guy made my skin crawl. He worked as a salesman at the Ford dealership, so he always drove nice cars, but Libby had never been one to embrace material things. He had the personality of a well-trained terrier: lots of energy, always happy, not that bright. "Hi, Larry. How's she doing?"

His eyes were bloodshot and glossy. "The doctor just came out. He won't tell me anything, but I overheard him telling a detective that she was awake when she arrived. They gave her a blood transfusion. Her brain was swollen, so he gave her some drugs to keep her sleeping until the swelling goes down."

"They induced a coma?"

"Yeah, he said it would be a day or two. Any idea what happened?"

Larry had never been a friend. Truth be told, I had never kept it a secret how little I admired him. For some strange reason, Libby liked him. He was twenty-five and could be pompous, but most men I knew had a touch of arrogance every now and again. At first I thought she felt sorry for him because he had the intellect of a stop sign, but after a while I figured out she gravitated toward him because he was always upbeat. She hadn't had an ideal life, and I think she enjoyed being around someone who was happy for no good reason.

I hardly knew where to begin. I motioned for Larry to take a seat while I took the one next to him. I remembered every detail of our trip to the bar as they all came crashing in on me. "We were out of food." The rest of the words poured out of me, and I didn't stop until I told him what had happened at the gas station and about the police finding Libby at the house.

He didn't interrupt once. It was much different than answering the barrage of questions from the police at the gas station. I didn't understand why, but telling him what had happened somehow calmed me. When I was done, Larry asked, "This Dave guy you went to high school with, do you think he's involved?"

I shrugged my shoulders. I didn't think so, but after the last several hours, I wasn't prepared to rule anything out. Larry's knuckles were balled into white fists. His angry accusation took me by surprise, "Why would you let her shark like that? I thought you two only did that when you had back-up with you. She swore to me she would never go alone."

This was the first time I had ever seen Larry angry. I didn't have an answer; this had been a last minute decision. He was right; normally if Libby knew she would be playing at a bar, she would call and ask a few friends to come along. We had never had any real trouble, but there was strength in numbers, and we had gone in alone last night. He interrupted my internal argument when he said, "You could have called me."

No. Libby could have called him, but she wouldn't have. She told me he took their break-up really hard, and I think if she had been going to play in the ghettos of Los Angeles tonight, she still wouldn't have called him. Which led me to the question, "How did you know she was hurt?"

"I programmed my phone number into her cell as ICE when we were together. She must have never changed it."

"ICE?"

"First responders are trained to look for an 'In Case of Emergency' contact in cell phones."

"What about her dad?"

"I tried calling him. The only number I had has been disconnected." Libby's dad never stayed in one spot for long. From a very young age, she had essentially been taking care of herself. Libby used to pick on me when we were young about how I never knew how to do anything. I could load the dishwasher, but had never washed dishes by hand. I put my clothes in the laundry basket, but didn't have a clue how to sort them into colors or work the washing machine. When we were girls, she always seemed so much older than I was.

When she moved in with me, after my parents moved to New Mexico, I needed her. I had been able to boil water, but Libby could make a meal out of almost nothing. She once made some casserole thing out of just rice, tuna fish, and Italian dressing. Reality punched me hard in the stomach: for all of her flaws – I still needed her.

Larry interrupted my thoughts, "Do you know where he's staying?"

I shook my head, biting back the tears that wanted to form. He looked intently, "Where's he working now?"

I shook my head again. Libby rarely talked about her father. From time to time we would see his truck in the parking lot of a bar, but if Libby caught a glimpse of it, she'd always tell me to go somewhere else. I had never met her mom. She told me once that her mom had Libby when she was sixteen and wanted to give Libby up for adoption. Her dad wouldn't sign the papers, so her mom signed over full custody to him. She told me she had seen her mom a few times, but never elaborated on anything about her.

The ache inside me grew. I was her family. I was all she had in the world, plus I had a hand in why she was here tonight. She had just gotten paid, but she had blown her paycheck and there wasn't even a package of Ramen Noodles in the house – I guilted her into the bar. If I hadn't been such a baby about there being no food at the house, she never would have gone to the bar tonight. We could have had a quiet Tuesday in front of the television. If something happened to her, and the last few hours I spent with her were really our last few hours together, I would never forgive myself.

Larry must have seen I was about to implode because he reached over and pulled my head to his chest. It was awkward, because despite me unloading everything that had happened tonight on him, we weren't close. My body was stiff up against his. Rather than acknowledging the awkward feeling, I asked, "Have you seen her?"

He shook his head, "No. Family only."

I stood up on instinct. I was her family. I went to the nurse positioned in front of the doors that led into the ICU, "I'm Libby Merrick's sister. May I see her?"

In a sorrowful tone she answered, "Visiting hours aren't until 8 AM."

"I just want to see her. Just for a minute. Please."

The nurse wore scrubs with Scooby Doo all over them. She was older with graying hair, and eyes that understood I wasn't going to take "no" for an answer. Compassion came through in her words when she replied, "Let me get the doctor, so he can give you an update on her condition." She spoke quietly into a phone; the only thing she said that registered was the word "sister."

Within minutes a handsome doctor came through the doors guarded by the nurse in the Scooby Doo scrubs. He motioned for me to take a seat as he took one in between Larry and me. "Your sister underwent significant trauma to her head and lost a great deal of blood. She had some defensive wounds on her hands and arms as well, but those are less troubling. We gave her a blood transfusion. The injury which is most concerning is that her brain had swelled, so we needed to put a hole in her skull to allow for the fluid to drain. She is responding well to the treatment, but we need to give her time to heal safely."

Still holding it together, my voice barely audible, I asked, "Can I see her?"

The doctor's hand took mine, lying loose on my lap. His answer was tender, "She doesn't look like your sister right now because of the swelling and bruises. I can assure you, she is getting the best care we can offer."

My voice broke as a single tear escaped down my cheek, "Just for a second. Please."

He nodded sympathetically. "For right now, I don't want you in her room. I'll take you to where her room is, so you can see her through the glass."

I turned around to see Larry looking hopefully. As little as I liked him, I knew he loved her, too. "Would it be okay if her boyfriend came, too?" There was no need to qualify him as her ex-boyfriend, just like there was no reason to tell the doctor that I wasn't her sister by blood. He agreed and led us both to an enormous glass wall looking in on Libby.

The doctor bowed his head, "I'll give you two a second." He went two windows away from us, scribbling notes with his finger on an electronic tablet outside another patient's door.

The doctor had been right – Libby was unrecognizable. Her face was bruised and swollen, hair above her left ear had been shaved, and a tube ran directly into her skull as her body lay still just feet away from the window. Machines set on the far side of her with their displays recording her pulse, temperature, breathing, and I didn't know what else.

Neither of us spoke. Larry and I stood in the dimly lit hallway, transfixed on the dark room and the girl who meant so much to each of us. She had to be okay. Too much of my heart was wrapped up with her. If she died, Libby would take that piece of my heart with her, and it would be lost forever. The doctor hadn't mentioned brain damage, but if she lived, would she be the same Libby?

Guilt washed over me: I had to have been in the house when this happened. How could I have slept through such brutality? How had I heard nothing? My house was old; I was upstairs and she downstairs. The assailant may not have known I was even there – or maybe he hadn't taken his turn with me yet. The man had to have been in the house when I left for work. An ache welled up from deep inside when it hit me that I had slept through the beating and didn't even notice the perpetrator hiding in the shadows of my own home. If I had just checked on her before I ran out the door, maybe I could have done something. Maybe she wouldn't be lying in front of me with an oxygen mask on her face.

Larry's arm, wrapped around my side, squeezed me gently, "We should go."

I couldn't take my eyes off of her. Her beauty was still visible through her delicate hands draped gracefully beside her covered-up body. Libby's clear polish on her fingernails shined up against the white blanket covering her. Her toes were covered up by the blanket, but I knew she wore an emerald green polish with white daises appliqued on them, because mine looked the same. We had done them together three nights ago. I tried not to look at her face, but to concentrate on the rest of her. Larry squeezed my side a second time, silently prodding me to walk away.

I turned to him and saw tears pouring down his face. He didn't share in my guilt, nor was he looking for the parts of her that this monster hadn't touched. Larry only saw the woman he had given his heart to, dancing with the reaper before his eyes. I wrapped both my arms around him and whispered, "She's going to be okay. It's Libby. She's too tough to let something like this take her away from us."

The doctor saw us walking toward the door. He handed me his card. Answering my unspoken question in his clinical tone, "We will keep her sedated for at least another two days. Call me anytime if you want an update on her condition."

"Thank you. I'll be back later to check on her."

I could sense he wanted to tell me that looking through the window at her wouldn't do either of us any good, but gratefully he said nothing. As Larry and I emerged into the waiting room, I could see the first rays of dawn showing through the large windows. My mind was slowly breaking free of the guilt that had been weighing it down. That guilt was quickly being replaced by the need for vengeance. Whoever this monster was, I wanted him caught. I wanted him to pay. I wanted him stuck in a room with machines keeping him alive.

The police were doing their investigation, but the key to everything might not be video tapes and finger prints. The key might be the one person who could not only tell me who the dirt bag was, but also tell me where I could find him.

I gave Larry a quick hug. He saw I didn't intend to stay in the waiting room and asked, "Where are you going?"

"I'll be back. I need to see what I can find out about who did this."

"The police are already doing that. If she wakes up, one of us should be here."

The doctor had already told us both that Libby wouldn't be waking up any time soon. I forced a smile at him as I brushed a stray tear from his cheek, "I'll be back later. I'm going to see what I can do to help the cops."

Almost absently he answered, "Someone should know something."

I was that someone. I did know something, or at least I knew someone who might know something – I had to find Dave. I gave Larry a soft kiss on the cheek. "I'll be back later. You look like hell. You should get some rest. You don't want Libby to see you like this when she wakes up."

Larry's eyes clouded again, but he nodded and told me, "Be careful."

CHAPTER 7

Dave Brewer had been at the bar last night. He knew that creepy Teddy guy. If anyone would know where to tell the police to look for Teddy or the guy who tried to turn my safety cage into Swiss Cheese, he would.

I hadn't seen or talked to Dave in almost two years. The two of us had been thrown together by circumstance. We had been sort of friends but hadn't kept in touch after graduation. He acted strange at the bar last night. He really wanted me to call him Mark, but given what had transpired the last few hours, I could see why he wouldn't want those guys to know his real name. I googled Dave's name on my phone, and a half-dozen David Brewers popped up – none of them seeming to be the right one.

He had been a talented mechanic, so maybe he worked for one of the dealerships in town. I could try calling the local service departments. My heart sank as I thought about randomly calling every repair shop in the city looking for him. Even if I stumbled across someone who knew him, I would sound like a stalker. There had to be another way. It hit me – Kendra Brennan.

Kendra had always been the busybody in our class who seemed to know everyone, all their business and then some. I hated talking to her because she was a gossip, but if anyone might know where to find him, she would. I looked at my watch: it was after 7 AM. I opened the Facebook app on my phone and searched for her – she had already posted something 10 minutes ago. I typed a personal message, "Hi Kendra. I need your help. Can you call me as soon as you get this?" I inserted my phone number, hating the fact that she would now be able to call me whenever the mood struck her, and pushed "send." Less than 30 seconds passed before my phone rang.

Her syrupy sweet voice blared through my phone, "Caaaaaandy! I haven't seen you since high school! How are you?"

She hadn't seen me since high school for a reason – I didn't like her. I hated that I needed her help, but I did, so I made my voice sound happy to hear from her. "Hi Kendra, thanks for calling me. I need to get in touch with Dave Brewer, and I thought you might know where I could find him."

"Dave Brewer? That greasy loner guy who was in our class?"

"Yeah, he did some work on my car, and I need to talk to him. Any idea where he might be?"

"I think he works in a body shop on the west side. Not someplace to go after dark, if you know what I mean."

The west side? That narrowed it to fifty or so possibilities. "Any idea what the name might be?"

"Brewer's Body, or Body by Brewer or something. I drove by there once – very ghetto. Hey, I have a great mechanic if you're looking for one!

It's my boyfriend's brother – he's amazing. Al can fix anything from a mower to a semi-truck." She added in a sing-songy voice, "He's single, too."

That was just like Kendra. Not only was she in everyone's business, she was forever trying to be a little matchmaker. "Thanks, I just need to get a hold of Dave, but I'll give you a call if I ever need a mechanic."

Gushing, she asked, "So did you hear my big news? I'm sure you did. I posted like fifty times on Facebook, and I changed my profile on Twitter."

Oh brother, did I even want to know? "Um, no, I haven't really been paying attention. What's new with you?"

"I got accepted to do a year at Oxford in a study abroad program! Eeep, I'm so excited!"

Trying to match her enthusiasm, "Wow, that's great, Kendra." What I really wanted to say was, "Wow, I'm thrilled I have another spoiled rich friend with parents who have more money than sense" – but I kept my thoughts to myself.

"I'm going next fall and I can't wait . . ." She went into full-blown excited-school-girl mode. I promptly engaged my tune-out mode. Maybe it was jealousy, maybe I just didn't want to hear a blow-by-blow account of how she was going to experience college at a prestigious international university while I was still trying to figure out how I would ever pay back my own student loans to go to college in my hometown. I tried several times to interrupt, but she just kept talking. She wouldn't even let me wedge in a word to let her know I needed to hang up.

After enough details that I wanted to find a blindfold and a firing squad, she finally took a breath and I politely let her know I had to go. I wished her luck in her semester abroad and hung up. I opened the browser on my phone and quickly found "Bodies by Brewer Repair and Restoration" on Google. It didn't have a website, but the yellow pages on my phone said it opened at 8 AM. That gave me just enough time to catch a cab back to the gas station to pick up my car and be there when the place opened.

The cab I had phoned from the hospital dropped me right next to my car, which was patiently waiting for me on the frozen parking lot. Mr. Sanders was inside the convenience store working the register. Part of me wanted to go inside to say hello, but looking at him through the puckered glass stopped me short. Fear I had carefully tucked away until now rushed in on me like a tsunami. I stood paralyzed, too scared to take a step toward the store. I took a deep breath and tried to force my feet forward, but they had grown roots.

A black sedan pulled up next to pump one as a flashback of the Nova crashed on me. I ducked down below my fender, my lungs sucking in air faster than a Kirby while my hands began to shake uncontrollably. I closed my eyes, forced an exhale before I could hyperventilate, and told myself it wasn't the Nova. He wasn't here. No one was going to shoot me.

Peering around my bumper at the offending car, relief washed over me when I saw it was a Nissan Maxima. It looked nothing like the Nova with the matte finish and mag wheels that had been parked in the same place last night. Gritting my teeth and forcing my muscles to work, I stood up slowly, looking around to see if anyone had witnessed my little freak out.

Satisfied that Mr. Sanders hadn't seen, nor any of the patrons, my eyes settled on my Chevelle. The hole in the windshield was even more pronounced in the daylight than it had been last night. The bullet had gone through the windshield, the driver's seat, and the back seat.

I took a step toward it to get a better view, my fear evaporating as anger began to emerge. My hand felt the jagged edge of the hole. Parts for old cars were next to impossible to find, and when I could find them, they cost an arm and a leg. I took a more thorough look to see if he had shot anywhere other than the windshield. A sigh of relief escaped me when I learned the damage was isolated to the windshield and the seats. My car had been perfectly restored. I was pretty sure the seats could be repaired, but if nothing else, I could get by with some black duct tape for the time being.

I loved my car. It didn't look like anyone else's. It didn't sound like anyone else's, either. I'd never seen another one like it. It was a 1966 Chevelle Super Sport. I'd bought it off an old guy when I was fifteen for six hundred dollars. The car had been a bucket of rust that wouldn't start, but I saw the potential. I bought it my sophomore year, a full year before I could even drive.

Shaking my head at the irony, my car was how I met Dave Brewer to begin with. I sat down in the driver's seat, cranked the engine, turned the heat on full-blast, and waited for it to warm up. My mind wandered back to my first meeting with Dave. It was hard to believe that it had been five years ago.

My high school offered classes on vehicle repair; one of the requirements to sign up for the class was every student had to have a broken car. This one definitely qualified. Still all aglow from my six hundred dollar bargain car, I went to the guidance office to sign up for the automotive repair class as an elective in the fall semester.

The guidance counselor refused to let me sign up. She said the class was only offered during the same periods as AP English and Chemistry. She refused to let me slide out of either class, which was bogus. Her reasoning for not letting me register was that I was listed as "college-bound," and auto repair was reserved for "non-college-bound" students. I left the guidance office frustrated beyond belief. Never one to take "no" for an answer, I decided to work a different angle.

Mr. Kravitz was the teacher who taught the auto repair classes. My freshman year I had gotten busted skipping school. I wasn't smoking dope, I wasn't running amuck around the city; I just took the day off to hang out with friends – all of whose parents excused the absence. My parents refused to lie: mine were pissed and wanted to make sure I learned my lesson. In addition to them grounding me and taking my phone away, the school sentenced me to three days detention. My parents thought the school's policy was too light, so they called the school and demanded I serve two weeks instead of the typical three days. The only good that came from it was I got to know the teacher who seemed to be the permanent detention teacher, Mr. Kravitz.

After my two weeks of detention, an unheard of long sentence for such a minor rule infraction, he was always really nice when he saw me in the hallways. I thought he might be able to help me get registered for his class. Making a beeline from the guidance office, I bounded into his empty shop and saw him elbow deep in an engine. "Um, Mr. Kravitz, hi. Do you have a second?"

He stood up, grabbed a rag from the fender of the car he was working on, and wiped some grease off of his hand. "What can I do for you, Miss Kane?"

I plastered on my most winning smile and said, "I just came from Guidance. I tried to sign up for your Auto Repair class this fall, but they told me I couldn't register. I was hoping you might be able to help."

He looked at me from my toes to my head. It hit me that my wardrobe choice wasn't helping me make my case. I was wearing sandals, a short white skirt and an Hawaiian print top in pastels. My pink fingernails and toenails had appliques of flowers on them which matched my Hawaiian shirt perfectly. He wore blue coveralls, brown leather work boots, and seemed to have permanent grease stains etched under his fingernails. Mr. Kravitz shook his head. "I've got limited class space, and it's already full."

I blurted out, "I have a car. It doesn't run, but I have one."

Kravitz raised an eyebrow, "It's full. Sorry, Candy."

Not wanting to be shut down a second time, I began pleading, "You don't understand, it's a '66 Chevelle. I really want this car, but the only way I can afford to get it running is if I'm in your class."

"A 66 Chevelle?" His interest was piqued, "Convertible or hardtop?"

I had set the line; I just needed to reel him in. "Convertible."

"Super Sport?"

I could feel my face glowing, "Yes!"

He shook his head, taking a second to look at me. "My class is full, but I wouldn't mind the class seeing how the older engines function compared to the new ones with computers on board. Could you leave it here for the whole semester?"

What was he saying? Was he going to let me in the class or not? "Uh, yes, the class description says once I'm signed up, I bring the car in, and you teach me how to fix it."

"I don't have room for another student, but I may have an idea." Kravitz called into the other room that I had believed to be empty, "Mr. Brewer, can you come out here for a minute?"

Feet shuffled from the other room as a student came through the doorway. He glanced in my direction, but his eyes settled on Mr. Kravitz's boots, "Yeah?"

The student wasn't anyone I would have ever given a second look. His jeans begged for detergent. The stench of stale cigarettes permeated his clothes. Those were just surface issues. The most disturbing thing about him was that he kept his eyes focused on the floor instead of looking at either Mr. Kravitz or me. Mr. Kravitz introduced us – Dave looked like he was thousands of miles away. "I may have a solution for you, Candy." Kravitz was nearly beaming.

My heart skipped a beat when I thought he was going to tell me he'd find a way to make room for me in his class. Maybe we could double-team my stupid counselor with the idea that knowing how to fix a car was a skill I could use while I was going to college to help cover expenses. His big arms gestured to Dave, "I have a student without a car." He looked at me and gestured with his other arm, "Dave, Candy's got a diamond in the rough, but there's no room for her in my class. I thought you two might be able to strike a deal."

A monotone answer, laced with irritation responded, "No, thanks." Still focused on the floor, his thick leather boots, scuffed raw, shuffled against a free standing toolbox.

Kravitz answered optimistically, "You found a car?"

Dave shrugged his shoulders, his eyes still refusing to leave the floor. "Found one at the salvage yard."

Mr. Kravitz eyed Dave suspiciously; he must have known a great deal about this student because he asked, "So you've got the money to buy it and all the parts you'll need?"

Dave shrugged his shoulders again.

I saw my dreams getting ready to disappear into a puff of smoke. "Pleeeaaase," I dragged it out like a seven year old begging for a later bedtime.

Dave shook his head, shoved his hands in his pockets, and walked out of the room.

Mr. Kravitz huffed as we both watched him take a quick turn down the hallway and disappear into the sea of other students. Kravitz gave me a sheepish look, "The class is offered in fall. If he doesn't have a vehicle to repair in the next couple of weeks, he'll be reassigned to another elective.

I know he wants in my class. Get your car here this week. You know you will be responsible for all the parts?"

Confused, I said, "But he just said, 'no.'"

His voice lowered, not that there were any others around to hear, "Mr. Brewer is in the foster care system. He's got great instincts for cars, and he hangs out here after school helping me with odd projects. I've never seen someone with his attention to detail. Unfortunately, the state only covers his basic necessities. A car for my class isn't a necessity, so he can't enroll in my class."

My heart went out to Dave. I didn't know him, but I had heard awful things about foster care. His clothing choices and absence of detergent seemed significantly less revolting with that tidbit of information. I was ashamed of my initial assessment of him when he walked in – who was I to judge? My parents weren't the greatest people on the planet, but at least they made sure I had everything I needed. I'd bought the car with babysitting money – money that I had earned from watching their friends' kids.

As if to drive his position home, he added, "Dave's been jerked around his whole life. He's one of those kids who has to warm up to an idea. You get your car here, and I'll see that he stays in my class."

I'm sure the disappointment showed on my face at his unwillingness to help me out with Guidance. I really wanted this car, so I asked one more time, "If he's not in your class, does that mean you would have room for me? Could I be put on a standby list?"

Mr. Kravitz must have wanted to persuade me this was the best solution because he answered, "Candy, you have options. That boy who just walked out of here? He doesn't. He needs this class more than you do. Get your car here this week, and I'll convince him to do the repairs."

Mr. Kravitz walked back over to the car he had been working on and leaned back down into the engine where I had found him.

I wasn't convinced, but Mr. Kravitz had made it clear he wouldn't be advocating with the guidance office for me to get into his class. If Dave Brewer wouldn't agree to repair it, I'd be stuck with a six hundred dollar car that didn't run. Defeated, I made my way to the door when Kravitz added, "Get the registration up to date. Every car we keep has to be legal."

A friend helped me tow the car to the high school the next morning. We put it inside the automotive repair fenced-in area just like Mr. Kravitz had told me to. Two weeks later I got a note to come to the auto shop around the back of the school. When I peeked around the corner of the building – I was elated. Kravitz was standing there with a clipboard; Dave was leaning up against the brick wall with a frustrated look on his face. Mr. Kravitz tapped Dave on his shoulder with the clipboard, "C'mon, Mr. Brewer. You agreed to it. You're going to have to go over the list of parts her car's going to need."

Dave shoved himself off of the brick wall. If he'd been a cartoon character, a huge "Bwong" would have shot up from behind his back. He nearly ripped the clipboard out of Kravitz's hand and shoved it at me. "Need those parts by this fall." His hair looked greasy and hung in stringy waves just above his shoulder, his face was all scraggly, and stale cigarette smell clung to him. His jaw was set in an angry way as if he were challenging me to argue with him about the parts I needed to purchase. Dave wore the same faded black jeans and scuffed up boots he was wearing the first time I had met him. His clothes didn't matter; if he was going to fix the car – he could do it naked for all I cared.

Mr. Kravitz watched Dave walk back into the classroom and removed the paper from the clipboard, "Take this sheet to Advanced Auto on South

Tenth Street. They've got a deal with the school district. If you give them this sheet, they'll order and sell you the parts at cost."

I put on my bright, cheerful, and grateful face, pretending to be surprised – I wasn't. This was the reason I'd tried to sign up for the class to begin with. I wouldn't have to pay any labor and the parts were dirt cheap. Every repair made by a student, no matter how big or small, got a sign off by Kravitz that it was done right. Six hundred for the car and another few hundred dollars in parts, and I'd have solid transportation by the time I had my license.

Once the fall semester rolled around, I saw Dave in the hallways lots of times. It didn't matter how many times I said, "hi," or smiled at him – he never gave me a second glance. It almost seemed as if he preferred to sneer at me. I'd sneak down every few days and see Mr. Kravitz after school. My car was progressing faster than most of the other cars that had a lot less work to be done. For what Dave lacked in personal skills and hygiene, he made up for in mechanical ability.

When it was all done, the engine had been rebuilt, the brakes were replaced, as well as the radiator, the battery, and most of the electrical wires behind the dash. Mr. Kravitz told me before Thanksgiving break that my car was ready. The right thing to do was to thank Dave, but since he preferred to believe I was invisible every time I saw him – I wasn't sure how to accomplish it.

The first day of Christmas break, I decided to thank Dave the only way I knew how. I'd always seen him wear the same black jeans and boots. He seemed to be as tall as my sister Kim's boyfriend and about the same body build, so I asked him what size clothes he wore. I bought Dave a pair of dark blue jeans and a rugby shirt. Libby had her license. My sister Kim let us borrow her car. Libby knew which house was his from the bus route she had ridden on. I went up to his front door, a little nervous, and rang the doorbell.

Instead of someone answering the door, a hateful female voice yelled, "What?"

The television was blaring in the background, so I couldn't be sure if the voice was a person's inside the house or if it had shouted from the television. I rang the doorbell a second time.

I heard loud footsteps stomping toward the door, and a woman flung the door open wide with a menacing look on her face, "You better not be sellin' anything." She was a very large lady with long greasy hair and a permanent scowl etched on her face. Her looks alone made me shrink an inch or two on the spot. This was his mom? Then I remembered Kravitz told me he was a foster care kid. What idiot state worker would place anyone with this woman?

I stood there relieved that there was a storm door separating the two of us. My voice came out meekly, "I was looking for Dave Brewer. Does he live here?"

She stomped away from the door without acknowledging my question and bellowed like he might have been on Jupiter, "Dave, door!!"

I stood there, losing my nerve by the second. The stale smell of the house began seeping through the cracks around the front door. Dave appeared in front of me, and I figured in this circumstance he might actually look at me – wrong again. He stepped out into the frigid December temperatures with just a t-shirt and jeans, onto the little cement steps where I stood. Dave didn't sound the least bit happy to see me, "What're you doin' here?"

Damn, nice to see you, too. I shook off my snottiness, and responded cheerfully, "You never let me thank you for my car. I wanted to give you something." My shaky hands held out two white boxes tied together with a thick shiny red ribbon.

He eyed the boxes, but made no move to take them from me. "I did it because Kravitz made me do it."

Wow, that was a whole sentence. Dave hadn't talked to me all semester. Still holding the two boxes out, I began to think this was an awful idea. "I know, but without you doing the repairs, I wouldn't have a functioning car. Here," I pushed the boxes in his direction, "it's no big deal."

His hands reluctantly took the boxes out of my hands. An awkward silence hung for a few seconds. I wasn't sure what to say, and he didn't have any conversational skills. I tried feebly, "So, do you have any big plans for Christmas break?"

He shook his head, peering over his shoulder into the house. "Look, I gotta go." He stammered, as if trying to find the words, "I . . . hope. . . you like your car." Dave did a one-eighty and disappeared inside the house, shutting the door hard behind him. I stood there for a second, realizing I had just been dismissed.

I could hear the vile woman inside shout at him, "Well, don't just stand there. Dinner won't make itself!"

I understood in that moment why Mr. Kravitz took such an interest in Dave. He didn't have another person in the world who looked out for him. I never saw him walking with or talking to anyone at school – ever. I'd waved and smiled a few times to him in the hallway, but I'd never gone out of my way to try to have a conversation with him. Standing on his cement steps, knowing where he lived and the woman the state had assigned to care for him, my heart ached for him. I decided when break was over, I would look for him in the halls. I would do more than just a shallow greeting – I owed him. If the only way for me to pay that debt was to befriend him, to let him know someone in the world besides the shop teacher gave a crap about him, that's what I'd do.

I didn't have to wait for school to start up. Two days after Christmas, we got an outrageous snow storm that dumped eight inches of snow. I was clearing the sidewalk in front of our house, ticked off that both my sisters had miraculously had things to do and were gone, leaving me with the snow removal job all by myself.

I still didn't have my driver's license and wouldn't be able to get it for another couple months, but every few days I'd go out and start my car just to hear the engine rumble. It sounded bad-ass. After the shoveling was done, if I could still feel my toes, I'd go out back and start it – that would cheer me up.

I had just finished the sidewalk and started on the steps when I felt someone's eyes boring into me. I turned around quickly to find Dave staring at me. He wore a light leather jacket, his signature scuffed up motorcycle boots, and the blue jeans I had given him a week ago. When I realized it was Dave and not some deranged freak leering at me, I asked, "Hey. How was Christmas?"

He shrugged his shoulders but didn't answer. Grappling for something to say, I commented, "The jeans look great." I was wearing a winter coat, faux fur lined gloves, a hat and a scarf, while he stood there in a jacket with his hands shoved in his pockets. Did he not own gloves or a hat?

He prodded some snow with the tip of his boot, and quietly offered, "Thanks." It didn't roll off of his lips, and it occurred to me that he didn't have much cause to use the word. It didn't seem like he had poor manners, but the more I knew about him, the less I thought he had much to be thankful for.

The temperature was dropping fast, and I'd already been out for at least thirty minutes. I was beginning to feel the cold tingles in my fingers and toes, right before the numbness set in. Now was a perfect time for a break. "Hey, you wanna come inside? I could use some hot chocolate and toast."

Dave shook his head. Remembering the woman at his house, I couldn't imagine why he'd be in a hurry to go back there. "I'm not taking no for an answer. C'mon, I'm freezing."

I turned my back on him and marched up the steps that were still covered in snow. I would go back out and finish the steps after he left. When I got into our entryway, I held the door open for him to follow. He hadn't budged an inch from his spot on the sidewalk.

Almost daring him I said, "You got something against hot chocolate?" A slight smirk showed on his face when Dave reluctantly followed me into the house. I walked into the kitchen and dumped a packet of instant cocoa into a mug, and put the cup under the Keurig machine, dispensing the hot water. Stirring quickly, I handed the cup to him. I made mine and then threw some toast in the toaster. He didn't say anything, but I saw his bright red fingers wrap themselves around the steaming mug.

"I like my toast with just butter on it, but we have jelly and peanut butter if you want."

He shook his head. I wasn't sure what he had just said "no" to, so I pulled out all the toast toppings and put them on the table.

His house was over two miles from mine. I was sure he didn't have a car, so he must have been freezing. Dave devoured four pieces of buttered toast, the mug of chocolate bliss, and seemed to be stealing glances around the kitchen. He was content with the silence, but it sort of creeped me out.

About the time I could feel my toes again, Dave surprised me with a question. "What color?"

What color? I stared at him clueless as to what he wanted. I'd heard him speak less than ten words up until now, and I was beginning to question if he were capable of regular conversation. I was grateful for his help with my car, and no matter how bad his personal skills were – I owed him. "What do you mean, what color?"

"Kravitz wants to know what color for your Chevelle."

I was stunned, "You're painting my car?" Dave gave me his signature shoulder shrug, but didn't answer. "Wait, you're taking Auto-Body Repair next semester?"

He nodded.

"Um, I'm just glad it's running. The rust doesn't really bother me."

His eyes fixed on mine briefly, as if I'd stolen a prized toy. "I can't use your car?" Dave had made eye contact with me for the first time ever. His eyes were a deep brown, not a pretty brown like a chestnut, but a dark walnut, almost swallowing his pupil. I couldn't place his expression – it looked like a cross between frustration and, I don't know, – anger?

"I never said that. I mean, I would really appreciate it if you could paint it. How much will it cost?" I had tanked every bit of my babysitting money for the car, the parts it needed last semester, and Christmas gifts. However, I'd found an awesome website that the rich people in town used to find short-notice babysitters – I could maybe find some more jobs before Christmas break was over.

"Body-repair isn't much unless we have to replace a bumper or something. Yours are fine. Maybe a hundred dollars for chrome from the salvage yard and the primer and paint."

This was too good to be true. I didn't know whether the shock on my face was from the second incredible bargain, or the fact that he'd said more to me in the last thirty seconds than he had in the previous four months. "Uh, okay. What color do you think would be good?"

"Original was maroon. I'd keep it the same."

In my mind I had envisioned a canary yellow with black interior – I knew I'd seen one like that in a hot rod magazine, but making those kinds of changes to the interior would be way more than a hundred dollars.

"Okay. When do I bring in the money?"

"First day. Kravitz is expecting it." Without another word, he stood up from our kitchen table, pulled his jacket off the back of his chair and began walking to the entryway.

"Wait!" I couldn't let him go back out dressed like that. It was too cold. He gave me a weird look, but I held up a finger, "Just give me a minute. Don't go anywhere."

I ran to the mud room by the back door where there were more boots, mittens, gloves, hats, and scarves than Wal-Mart. I grabbed a black ski cap, a black sweatshirt, and a pair of black leather gloves, then sprinted back to where he waited by the front door.

Handing them over, "Here, it's freezing out there."

His eyes narrowed on me, "I'm not a charity case." To think just a few hours ago I'd never seen his eyes, now I had the privilege of them glaring at me.

"I didn't think you were. Friends help each other out. Just say thank-you."

Dave cocked his head to the side as if studying me. I added, "It's dropped twenty degrees in the last hour. It's not as warm now as when you left your house. Take them, you can give them back if you don't want to keep them."

He shook his head as if he intended to turn me down, but I grabbed his shoulder and said, "Look, if you're going to do the body work on my car, I'm pretty sure you're going to need all your fingers. Just take them." I forced the pile of winter attire at him and walked back to the kitchen.

Half an hour later when I bundled up to go outside to finish removing the snow from the steps, they had already been shoveled, and someone had put salt down to stave off any ice that might try to appear overnight. I started to find Dad to thank him when it hit me that Dad hadn't left his home office all afternoon.

A warm glow sparked inside me. Dave must have done it before he left. We still weren't friends, but this was what put us on the path to being more than acquaintances.

CHAPTER 8

The air from my car's vent was blazing as I stopped reminiscing about Dave in high school. Mr. Sanders was watching me from inside the store. I gave him a friendly wave as I eased my car out of the parking lot. I rested my wounded hand on the top of the steering wheel, using my good hand to shift and to drive. As soon as I turned onto the main street, the frigid outside air took my breath away, blowing straight at me through the hole in my windshield. The car's heater was doing the best that it could, but my feet were in hell while I worried an icicle was forming on my nose. I had to scrunch down to try to see through the glass under the hole. To top it off, the sun was glaring through the cracks around the hole, making it almost impossible to see.

Ten minutes later I pulled up outside Bodies by Brewer to see several sweet classic muscle cars parked in front, peeking out from the piles of snow around them. The two-story building was made of cinder block. I couldn't guess how many times the blocks had been painted over, but the top coat was gray and was desperately trying to separate itself from the building. Two large roll-up doors staring at the street were closed. The sidewalk in front of the shop had been shoveled after the last snow storm, revealing cracks running its length. Large naked maple trees stood on either side of the building. A retaining wall was crumbling behind the building. The place reminded me of a scene from a Tim Burton movie.

I had a clear view from my car of the door on the front of the building. The door had been painted the same Navy Warship Gray as the rest of the building with a single small window in its center. A closed blind blocked my view into the shop through the glass, but a sign hung in front of the blind indicating the place was open. Other than the glass in the door, the building didn't have any windows on the first floor. It was just after 8 AM, but the place looked locked-up tight. Someone may have forgotten to turn the sign around before closing last night.

I started to have second thoughts about being here alone. No one knew I was here, and Kendra hadn't been embellishing anything. It felt like I should be wearing a bullet-proof vest if I were going to leave the safety of my car. Trash cans lined the curbs, several of them knocked over and in the street. A vacant building stood directly across from the garage; from the weathered paint on the door, it used to be a drycleaner. A large window to the right of its door was boarded up with a "keep out" sign in the corner. Bushes and trees sprinkled throughout the neighborhood were overgrown, and several of the sidewalks hadn't been shoveled all season. Junker cars seemed to be collecting in one driveway several addresses down from the garage, and I couldn't help but notice many of the nearby homes sported bars on their windows. Our neighborhood wasn't the high-rent district by a long shot, but compared to this place, we were living on Boardwalk.

I thought of Libby's still body in a hospital room right now. She had been attacked in our home. The weight of what I was about to do crashed in on me – I needed to ask Dave how I could find the predator who had attacked Libby, left her for dead, and then came after me last night. Dave and I had never been that close, and despite my attempts to befriend him in high school – he remained a near stranger. A lot could happen in two years – he could have gone from an angry lonely teenager to a killer. He might even have been the one responsible for what happened to Libby.

Dave had seemed happy to see me at Bank Shot yesterday evening. It was strange that he had wanted me to call him *Mark*, and he had seemed so charming and charismatic compared to the boy I had known. He had told Teddy to respect Libby, and it was obvious the two of them knew each other. It hit me in that moment – after Libby and I left, he could have been the one to tell Teddy where we lived – or at least where I lived. I'd seen it on television lots of times: without making a scene in public, the criminals find their mark, follow them home and attack.

Had Dave had a hand in what happened last night?

I sat in the warmth of my car, trying to decide what to do. I could just give the police Dave's name and address. They were investigating. A flash of Libby in her hospital bed shot through my mind. Investigating may be the police's job, but the Dave I knew would never have been mixed up in anything like what happened last night. Remembering how shy he was, if the police did come to ask him questions, he might shut down and tell them nothing.

"Don't be a baby, Candy." I told myself aloud as I eased out of my car, as if the sound of my voice could calm all the crazy thoughts shooting through my head. A few feet from the gray door, I stopped and noticed there had been no traffic on the street and no passersby since I arrived. If anything happened to me inside, there would be no one to hear my cries for help. This was a bad idea.

I should just call the police and tell them I remembered seeing Dave at the bar, and *he* knew Teddy. They could ask him what he knew. Doing this on my own, I might end up sharing a room with Libby at the hospital, which wouldn't do either one of us any good.

Sprinting back to my car, I reached for my car's door handle when I heard a voice call from inside the shop through the open front door, "Candy? Candy, is that you?"

I stood frozen behind my car. Crap. "Um, yeah. I was in the neighborhood and thought I'd say hi. It looked like you weren't open."

"Naw, I'm open, come on in. I just unlocked the door."

Great, now if I didn't go inside, what would he think? My hand rested on the cold door handle as thoughts assaulted my mind. Did he tell Teddy where I lived? Did he know the guy who tried to shoot me last night? Were they friends? Self-preservation took control of me, "Maybe some other time. I just remembered I have to be somewhere."

A disappointed look shown on his face, "Are you sure? I haven't seen you in forever."

Forever? He saw me last night. Maybe he didn't count seeing me when he was pretending to be some other guy. My body went on high alert when I remembered how he wanted me to call him Mark. "Sorry, I'll come back another time. I need to. . . go visit a friend – she's expecting me."

I swung my heavy door open and crawled inside the still warm car. I turned the key in the ignition and the car instantly responded with its throaty rumble. Just as I was ready to pull away from the curb, I saw a finger poking through the bullet hole in my windshield, and I screamed like a little girl. What was he – an Olympic sprinter? How the heck did he get to my car so fast?

Dave motioned for me to roll my window down. This was preferable to getting out of the car. I rolled it down a couple turns as I heard his disappointed voice say, "I thought this was a social call. Sorry. I can replace your windshield if you want."

My windshield? That was the least of my worries right now. Fear gripped me as I considered he might be partly responsible for putting the hole in it to begin with. I stammered, "It's okay, I'll take it to a glass place later."

Dave looked confused. He stood beside my car in the freezing cold wearing a thin black hoody over a gray t-shirt and jeans. I bet if I could see his feet through my car's door, he would be wearing scuffed up black motorcycle boots, too. Dave squatted down next to my car, peering in through my partially rolled down window, and asked, "So, was this a social call or business?" With his face just inches from mine, my breath hitched. Dave's looks had changed dramatically since high school. His hair was styled, trimmed neatly, his face was freshly shaven, and his deep brown eyes held mine. His cologne invited me to roll my window down further.

Before my hormones could let me do something really stupid, I reminded myself that there was a good chance he was somehow involved with what had happened last night. I put my hormones in check and stopped surveying him.

Dave's voice sounded different, not the scared kid I'd forced to talk to me in high school, but a man. When I looked at his face, his eyes were staring back into mine. I couldn't remember him ever holding my gaze for any length of time, and it was a full ten seconds before I realized I was the stalker watching him. I stammered, "Social, sort of. It's not important. I need to go." I pressed the clutch and put the car into gear, ready to pull away.

In a pleading voice, Dave said, "Come on, five minutes. I'll make hot chocolate." He opened my car door in a gentlemanly way, trying to coax me out of the car.

I forced a smile, not wanting to give away just how frightened I was to be here. There was no one else that I could see inside. Going in there with him would be a mistake. Anything could happen. For all I knew, he had a wood chipper out back to dispose of bodies on the premises.

I tried to tug the door closed from his hand, when he asked, "What, you got something against hot chocolate?" I was prepared to snarl in his direction when I saw he had the brightest, widest smile I'd ever seen him wear. Dave Brewer knew how to smile? Even when I'd forced him to talk to me in high school, no matter how funny the story was I was telling him, he barely ever smirked. Here, now, it looked like he was practicing for a Crest commercial.

It disarmed me. Not just his smile, but his choice of words – the same thing I had said to him the day he told me he was going to restore the outside of my car. I couldn't help but smile back at him. "Nothing against hot chocolate; I just forgot I had to be somewhere. I'm late."

Still holding my door open, peering down at me he offered, "If you're already late, what's another five minutes?"

I didn't know what to do. My mind was telling me to get out of here, but something about *this* Dave in front of me – was a draw. All those times I'd only ever seen his guarded shell, I was sure, somewhere deep down, this Dave existed. He looked and acted like a different person, as if he finally decided he wanted to be a part of the human race.

I caved, cutting the ignition. "Five minutes, then I have to go." I grabbed my phone and put it in my pocket, so it would be at the ready if I needed it.

I followed Dave inside a tiny reception area which smelled like lemons. The inside was a stark contrast to the dilapidated exterior. Shiny white floors glared up at me from below, without a speck of dust on them. The smell of lemon permeated the air, not the light lemony scent from an air freshener, but powerful lemon from an industrial cleaner. On the desk was a fine leather appointment book, opened to today's date with very neat handwriting annotating appointments sporadically throughout the day. A two burner coffee pot set in the corner, one with hot water and one patiently waiting for the morning coffee to be brewed.

Dave took two white mugs from a cup tree and set them on a white marble countertop by the brewer. He ripped open a couple packages of instant hot chocolate, added the water and stirred them, then handed a cup to me. "I don't have any toast to offer you, but there are some fresh bagels and cream cheese in the refrigerator."

My stomach lurched at his offer, my last meal having been the dried up chicken wings at Bank Shot. I shook my head to decline, but he took one out, ripped it in half and handed a piece to me. The toast reference meant he must have been having the same flashback I'd had on my drive over. I tore a piece of the bagel off and let it melt in my mouth.

As I looked around, I wasn't sure what to make of the immaculately clean showroom. Any garage I had ever been to had been – grungy. "Um, what kind of garage is this?"

"Restorations mainly. Sometimes I do a little repair, but most of the cars that come through here are on their last leg. It's my job to get them off life support and back to their glory days."

"This place is yours?"

"Yeah, well, mostly. I have a silent partner who helped me get it off the ground."

I tensed when I remembered Teddy had called Dave "Boss" last night. I could guess who his silent partner might be as my fingers began shaking in earnest. I wrapped them more tightly around the mug to try to calm them, and ended up spilling some hot chocolate onto the pristine floor. "I'm sorry." Without a moment's hesitation, Dave grabbed a napkin near the brewer and wiped up my dribbles on the floor.

I set the mug down. My fingers absently traced the smooth surface of the marble countertop, as I plied for more information. I wondered if he would own up to who his silent partner was. "Anyone I know?"

Dave's smile stretched across his face, "The only person other than you who ever gave me more than a dirty look in high school."

His answer caught me off guard. Confused, I asked, "Kravitz?"

"Yeah, he helps me out on the weekends and when there are breaks during the school year, sometimes even on snow days."

My fingers seemed to like his answer and picked the mug back up. I brought the hot chocolate to my lips. I couldn't remember the last time I had had a cup. It was sort of a luxury item; when it came to groceries, Libby and I could rarely afford to buy anything like this. He interrupted my silent pity party by setting his mug on the counter. Dave motioned for me to take a seat in the leather chair behind the desk and perched himself on the desk next to me. "So, what are you doing these days? College?"

"Yes. Here in town." Until he mentioned it, I'd completely blown off the fact that I had school today. It hadn't even been twelve hours since the attack last night at the station. If necessary I could bring in a copy of the newspaper tomorrow. No way would my professors give me a hard time for skipping today.

He leaned back against the wall and confessed, "I had always pictured you as a sorority girl. I bet you live on campus and are the life of all the parties."

Was that a slam? Trying not to take offense, "What's that supposed to mean?"

Dave wrapped his fingers around his mug innocently, "Oh, come on. With your looks and personality, you're bound to be pretty popular on campus."

"Okay, I'm not sure if I should be offended or thanking you for a compliment."

Another bright smile formed when he said, "Say thank-you." For the first time since I walked in, Dave's eyes left mine. He stood up from the counter, walked to the sink, washed then dried his cup, and hung it back on the cup tree. As I watched him, I wondered if he had grown since high school, then it hit me: he looked taller because he was standing up straight. How had I never noticed how tall he was? He was well over six feet. While I was ogling him, he caught me off guard as he confessed sheepishly, "I always had the biggest crush on you."

Who was this guy? What happened to the introverted loner who couldn't even make eye contact with me? I laughed, "A crush? You're not serious."

He turned and looked at me, his voice sincere, "I am serious. You were out of my league back then." His smile wavered when he added, "You still are."

The warmth of a blush spread on my cheeks – not the reaction I would have expected. "I don't know. I don't own my own business or anything. You look like you're doing okay for yourself. What else have you been doing since graduation?"

His cheeks darkened as his eyes hit the floor. "Not much. Working mainly. I've gone to the high school a few times to help one of Kravitz's students. He's got one kid who reminds me a lot of me. He's laser focused on cars, but doesn't have the most supportive home life. He was in the same spot as I was: plenty of talent, no money. I found an old Charger that he's restoring now."

"That's pretty cool of you. Is it for one of your customers?"

"No. I rescued it from a farmer's barn and hadn't gotten around to the restoration. When I found it, it had been buried under a pile of rusty equipment, bird droppings, and two decades worth of dust. The kid loves it. He doesn't know it, but I'm signing the title over to him as a graduation present."

"Wow, that's pretty awesome of you."

"I remember how hard it was to give you your Chevelle back when I was done. I'd hate to take the Charger away from him. He's poured his heart into it."

Suddenly I felt bad. He'd never told me he was attached to my car. He had treated it like a means to an end. He needed it to enroll in Kravitz's classes. "You never said anything."

Dave grinned. "Well, the car was a big reason for me following you around in high school. It wasn't the only reason, but it was a big one. I kept secretly hoping it'd break down so I'd have a reason to see you after we graduated. I guess I did too good of a job restoring it." His mischievous grin grew, "Enough about me. Do you want me to order you a new windshield, or what?"

Was he flirting with me? I'd been on two dates in the last six months – both sucked. Remembering why I had come, I stammered, "Um, no. This was a social call." His smile grew in front of me. Neither of us spoke for a minute, so I answered one of his earlier questions. "I'm not in a sorority. I never pledged."

"Why not? I thought that was part of the whole college experience."

"Only for the girls who have more money and time on their hands than I do. My college experience consists of a full class load and three jobs."

Dave cocked his head to the side, "You aren't still living with your parents?"

I laughed, "No, they moved away."

He had the same reaction everyone did when he asked skeptically, "To where?"

"Dad got a job in New Mexico a few days after I graduated. My older sisters were already out of the house, so they didn't waste time downsizing once they figured I could fend for myself."

"So, you live in the dorms?"

"No, it was actually cheaper to stay in the house and get a roommate. My parents are my landlords. If rent is late, not only do I get the threat to be evicted, I get the added, 'We're so disappointed in you' speech. You remember Libby?"

Dave scowled, "How could I forget? She coined the name 'loner guy' for me. That probably got printed in our yearbook instead of my name. She was never much of a fan."

My stomach cinched. Could he have been harboring bad feelings toward Libby all this time? Is that why she was in a hospital right now? I was having a tough time wrestling with the two Daves: the quiet one who preferred to be left alone in high school and the successful charismatic one standing before me now.

The fear I had felt outside began ebbing back. He was asking a lot of questions. Too many questions. It was my turn. Glancing at the door, I had a clear shot at it if I needed to bolt. I needed answers. "Look, this has been fun catching up, but I need to ask you about Teddy."

Confused, Dave answered, "I don't know a Teddy."

"The one from last night at Bank Shot?"

His shoulders arched as his perplexed look deepened, "I was here last night."

"Working?"

"No. The shop closes at five, but I have an apartment upstairs."

"I talked to you last night at Bank Shot. You stuck up for Libby when Teddy threw his money at her."

He shot me a wary look, "Candy, I told you, I was here all night."

Dave was trying to hide it. Did he think I was some bubble-headed girl? Or maybe he was trying to do some mind-control thing on me to try to convince me he hadn't been there. "Uh, so, you didn't tear into Teddy for throwing the four hundred dollars on the floor for Libby to pick up instead of handing it to her?"

"Holy shit, Libby won four hundred dollars? Doing what?"

He seemed genuinely surprised. Dave should be living in Hollywood. "Uh, playing pool."

"I didn't know she played. If you two want, there's a great bar a couple blocks from here. It's a pay by the hour table instead of seventy-five cents per game."

Dismissing his suggestion, I answered, "Yeah, Deuces Wild. She and I play there every now and again."

I couldn't wrap my mind around things. Did he have multiple personalities or something? He had always been so quiet, and this was like a completely different person. Last night he had wanted me to call him Mark. Was it possible he didn't know he was there?

I never knew much about him other than he was in foster care. It never occurred to me that there might actually be something wrong with him. He reached out a warm hand to my shoulder as concern deepened his tone, "Candy, are you okay? You're white as a ghost."

"Um, yeah, I'm fine. Hey, I gotta go. I must have seen someone who looked like you."

I stood up quickly, his hand remained on my shoulder, "Sit down for a minute. You don't look so hot. Eat some more of the bagel."

He's got multiple personalities and he wants me to eat a bagel? "I'm fine. I'm just late. It was great seeing you again." I turned away from him quickly, knocking the mug to the floor where it smashed into slivers. "I'm sorry." My memory of last night flashed before my eyes of a smashed casserole dish with bits of marinara sauce everywhere. I stumbled away from him.

"Candy, relax. What's wrong?"

"I'm fine. I'm sorry about the mess." I continued backing away from him toward the door.

"It's okay, I'll get it. You sure you're all right?"

"Yeah." I grabbed the door, flung it open and practically flew to my car. I was inside with the ignition turned over pulling away from the curb before he could follow me out. I kept looking in my rearview mirror to see if he was following me, but he wasn't.

I couldn't make sense of what he'd said. I knew he was at the bar last night. He made fun of Teddy for being beaten by a girl, and now he pretends he wasn't there. If he didn't have multiple personalities, he was the best actor I'd ever seen. He had to have been involved in the attack on Libby and was trying to cover his tracks. Maybe that's why he had said the stuff about having a crush on me and hoping my car would break down. What did he take me for?

CHAPTER 9

I couldn't go back to the hospital – not yet. I didn't have the strength to see Libby's lifeless body again so soon. Was it the guilt that I was responsible for what had happened to her, or the knowledge that the same thing could just as easily have happened to me? Or worse, if I hadn't been working behind bullet-proof glass, I could be lying in the morgue right now.

I didn't want to go to school. My mind was all over the place, and there was no way I was going to pass a test or sit through a bunch of lectures today. Mr. Sanders had given me the week off, so picking up hours there was a non-starter. I wasn't scheduled to work at the restaurant again until Saturday. I worked as a housekeeper for a couple bachelors, but I had just cleaned their house last week, so they wouldn't want me back again until next week. Bank Shot didn't open for a couple hours, so trying to find Chris wouldn't be possible, either.

Home. I needed to go home, to take a shower, to attempt to wash some of the fear off of me. Pointing the car in that direction, my mind continued scrolling through several possible scenarios.

The guy who tried to shoot me last night had gotten his money back, courtesy of Mr. Sander's cash register. He had broken the security cameras, probably betting that they weren't hooked up to a recorder. Idiot. Even if the picture wasn't clear enough for facial recognition, I had zoomed in on his license plate, and I was sure he had left his fingerprints on the restroom key. The cops shouldn't have any problem finding him. What he had done to Libby was grisly – no one inflicts that kind of pain unless they enjoy it. Even if he did have his money back, I needed to be careful until he was apprehended.

The hole in my windshield made driving a nightmare. I leaned as far to the left as I could to keep my face out of the path of the arctic air blowing directly on it. I wished I had a piece of gum to try to stuff into the hole.

After the longest trip across town that I could remember, I parked the car in front of my house. Expecting to see police tape on my front door and neighbors speculating over what had happened, I was surprised to see a typical quiet morning on the street. Based on the number of cars along the curb, most of my neighbors had gone to work. I climbed out of my car and locked my door just in time to look up and see Mrs. Bavcock standing inches away from me. Her proximity startled me – that was twice today I'd been sneaked up on. She urgently pleaded, "Have you seen Henrietta?"

I had learned long ago not to ask which cat was which. She had a slew of them, and one always seemed to escape for a few days. She would comb the neighborhood looking for the escapee with little luck, but eventually it would come back. Dismissively, I answered, "No, sorry, I'll keep a lookout for her."

She lowered her voice conspiratorially, "I saw the ambulance last night."

My heart lurched. I wasn't ready for questions from nosey neighbors. What could I tell her? How much did she already know? I wanted a few minutes of solitude in a hot shower followed by bundling myself in my comforter and shutting the world out for a little while. I did not want to face the reality of what Libby or I had gone through last night. I couldn't walk away from Mrs. Bavcock. She wanted an explanation – I didn't understand the details any better than the police and struggled with what to tell her. "Yeah, Libby's at Saint Elizabeth's. I just left a little bit ago."

Mrs. Bavcock took my hand in hers, her voice an urgent whisper, "I didn't want to get involved. Those types of men prey on women alone."

My eyes widened as I pulled her hand toward me, "Did you see something? Did you see the guy?"

She looked to her right, then her left. She answered in a sweet grandmotherly voice, "Why don't you come over for some tea?"

Tea? What the hell? Did she see something or not? "Mrs. Bavcock, if you saw something, you need to tell the cops. Libby's still unconscious."

Her voice was louder as she pried her hand away from my grip. "No, of course not, dear. I go to bed too early. The lights from the emergency vehicles woke me up last night."

Frustrated, I turned my back on her, and stomped off toward my front steps. I didn't need a grandmother or a prying neighbor right now – what I did need was my loofah sponge and enough hot water to cloud the bathroom in a blanket of steam.

"Oh, say, Candy," her voice echoed toward me, "I need you to help me move a box."

I stopped before my foot could climb the first step toward my front door. Blowing out an exasperated breath, I couldn't tell her "no" outright, but I was far too wound up to be polite. "I'll stop by later, Mrs. Bavcock. I need a shower."

She nearly shrieked, "Candy, please! It's very important. The box is leaking on my carpet."

A box is leaking on her carpet? Why wouldn't she just empty out the contents of the box or slide a rug under it? I turned around not even attempting to hide my incredulous look, but saw pure fear staring back at me through her aged eyes. Before I could turn her down a second time, a voice inside me told me I needed to help her. She was old; for all I knew, she was recycling motor oil or something dumb, and I'd never hear the end of it if I didn't save her carpet today.

Reluctantly I answered, "Okay, lead the way."

She smiled warmly and wrapped both her hands around my elbow, I assumed to use me for support crossing the packed ice on our street. She let me in the side door of her home, closed the door behind us and secured the deadbolt. I wandered into her living room to find the offending box, but nothing seemed out of place. One thing I could say for her, she knew how to clean. Her house always smelled like warm cookies with a hint of vanilla, despite the number of cats that shared her home.

As I turned back toward her to ask where the box was she needed help with, her feeble hands were gripping an ornate wooden chair from her dining room set. Confused, I asked, "Mrs. Bavcock, are you all right?"

"Help me with this, Candy, quickly," she demanded.

I took the beautifully handcrafted chair from her as she pointed to the door we had just come in. Unable to make sense of her request, I asked, "I don't understand. I thought you needed help with a box?"

"For God's sake, Candy, there is a man in your house! He's been there for hours. Secure the door and call the police."

A shot of adrenaline ripped through my body as my hand dropped the chair. "What? Who?"

I stood paralyzed with fear as she rushed in front of me, scooped the fallen chair up off of the floor and rushed to the door to wedge it under the door knob. She answered me urgently, "I don't know. I couldn't see his face. He's been looking through the curtains most of the morning. I don't think he saw me watching him. What are you waiting for? Call the police!"

Still in shock I challenged, "Why didn't you already call them?"

"I'm an old woman, Candy. Until you came home I wasn't sure what to do, but I couldn't let you go in there with him waiting." She shoved an old-time rotary phone at me.

Instead of using hers, I fished my cell out of my pocket. Just as I was dialing 911, a throaty rumble reverberated down our street. My thumb hovered over the send button as I looked through her front window at the unfamiliar car crawling down the narrow road. The car was sleek, a black matte finish and all muscle – it pulled in directly behind my car. The car's finish reminded me of the Nova from last night. I couldn't see the driver through the tinted windows, but I recognized the car: not the Nova from last night, but one of the show cars partially snow covered at Dave Brewer's garage. My heart began picking up speed in my chest as all the worst possible scenarios started playing at warp speed through my mind.

The car door opened and a shiny black motorcycle boot eased out onto the icy pavement. A second later I watched Dave pull himself out of the beasty car. I had gotten out of his shop before he could pounce, but he knew where I lived. My stomach sank to my toes. He had followed me here. He might have even told the creep in my house to wait for me to return, and Dave was going to finish me off. What had I ever done to him? I had been one of the few people who was nice to him back in school. If it weren't for me, he might not even have the auto repair place he has now. Why would he be involved, and why all the fuss over a few hundred dollars?

Mrs. Bavcock grabbed my arm, squeezing far harder than was necessary to pull me out of my daze, "Who is that? Do you know him?"

I didn't answer, but she must have read the fear on my face. She demanded, "Call the police. Now. Call them."

I watched Dave climb my front steps. He stood at my front door, using the glare from the storm door to check out his reflection and smooth his hair, then he pressed the doorbell. I wanted to shriek. I crouched down on the floor close to the ledge of Mrs. Bavcock's front window. This gave me a great vantage point, but the sheer floral curtains hanging in front of my face precluded any prying eyes from seeing me. I watched him press the doorbell a second time.

Dave shoved his hands deep into his pockets. He still didn't own any gloves? He eased himself a few feet to the left where an enormous picture window looked out onto the street. He tried to look in between the gap in the curtain, holding his hand over his brows in an attempt to cancel the glare. Walking back in front of the door, he rang the doorbell a third time, then proceeded to pound on the front door. I could see he was shouting something.

Mrs. Bavcock was crouched beside me on the floor, "What'd he say?"

I shook my head. "I don't know. I couldn't hear."

Dave bounded off the front porch, landing hard on the pristine snow surrounding the house. Dave walked around to each window on the first floor, desperate to see inside. What was he doing?

The third window he approached, he must have seen something that startled him, because he had been leaning in close to the glass then took three rapid steps away from it. Dave shouted at the window. It sounded like, "Hey!! What's going on?" But I couldn't be sure.

We were still peering like a couple of peeping Toms. Several things happened at once: Dave righted himself and stood tall, as if challenging whoever was inside. He cupped his ear as if to tell the person inside he couldn't hear him, then Dave nodded and strolled back around to the front porch again. Before his feet touched the first step, I felt the weight of the cell phone in my shaky hand. I pressed "send."

A nasally voice answered my call, "911 dispatch. What is your emergency?"

"This is Candy Kane. I live at 420 Elm Drive. There are two intruders in my house. Please send the police."

"Are you in the residence now?"

"No. I'm across the street with a neighbor. My roommate was attacked last night. Please send someone right away."

The dispatcher stayed on the line. Mrs. Bavcock and I didn't flinch, our eyes honed in on my childhood home. A gray and black tiger striped cat launched himself onto the window sill in front of us trying to get some attention. She reached up and pulled the curious cat to her for comfort. Several minutes passed with nothing to see, then a muffled bang sounded, as a man darted out the front door. He ran full-speed down the steps and up the street, passing directly in front of Mrs. Bavcock's window. My rapidly beating heart stopped completely as I saw the face that was already burned in my memory for all time. The man who had tried to shoot me last night was now fleeing up the street with Dave in hot pursuit. Dave looked like he was on fire, rage etched on his face.

The man who had tried to shoot me last night had a gun in his hand and was firing wildly behind him as he sprinted up the street, desperately trying to outpace Dave. His bullets were hitting everywhere but Dave, lodging into trees and cars lining the sleepy street. Dave seemed to pay no attention at all to the bullets whizzing around him. He was running full throttle, and as he passed Mrs. Bavcock's house, I heard his menacing warning, "If I catch you, I'll tear you apart with my bare hands."

Mrs. Bavcock said, "He's going to get shot. Is that boy a friend of yours?"

"Dave Brewer. I went to high school with him." The events made no sense. Was Dave mad because the guy hadn't killed me last night? Was I a loose end? A calico cat jumped onto the window sill to get a better view of what we were looking at. I reached up and moved her to the floor.

The dispatcher was still on the phone. I tried to keep her up to date with what was going on, so she could relay it to the police en route. "There must have been some sort of fight because one man has a gun and he's shooting at the other man. The one who just showed up is chasing the other one up the street."

The terrified man reached the end of our street, stopped, went down on one knee and pulled the trigger one last time. Dave grabbed his arm, hesitated for a half-second, then launched himself at the man running away again. It was tough to see what was going on because they were at the far end of the street, so I repositioned myself to try to get a better view. I caught just a glimpse of the man Dave was pursuing jumping over a privacy fence as Dave stopped short at the fence. He put one hand on his knee as if trying to catch his breath, while his other wrapped itself around his bicep.

Dave stood up, holding his hand over his arm, but started walking backward down the street toward my house, keeping his eyes fixed on the place where the fleeing shooter had gone. It was as if he didn't want to turn his back on where the man had fled. Halfway down the street, he must have decided it was safe because he turned around and began loping back toward my house. I expected Dave to slither back into his waiting car and hightail it out of there, but he didn't.

Before he even reached the bottom step in front of my house, I heard his cry, "Candy!! Candy!!" He stood waiting for some sort of a response, but when he didn't hear any, he ran back into my house, his hand still cradling his bicep.

None of this made any sense to me. What was he doing? His partner had just shot at him. The same guy who tried to kill me last night was waiting for me to get home. Dave knew him: the man had let him into the house. What was Dave doing?

Two police cruisers pulled up in front of my house, both blocking any potential traffic that wanted to pass on the street. The dispatcher knew which house I was hiding in, so the investigating police had to know I was safe, but both of them approached my house with guns drawn.

One officer had gone around to the back of my house while the other stood directly in front of it. They would catch him if he tried to sneak away. Even with this knowledge, my heart refused to slow down; blood pumped so vigorously I could hear my heartbeat in my ear. My face was flushed and my palms were sweating as I stayed riveted to the floor in front of Mrs. Bavcock's window.

Several minutes elapsed as other familiar faces began emerging from houses along the street. Curiosity was now getting the better of people. The commotion that had initially kept everyone safely tucked inside had quieted, and now interested bystanders were wanting to know what had happened to disrupt their previously muted morning. One neighbor was inspecting a bullet hole in his white Camry.

I watched as Dave walked through my front door, both his hands clasped on top of his head. When he was completely out of the house and standing on the porch, he knelt down as instructed. The policeman who had been around the back of the house put handcuffs on Dave while the first police officer kept his gun trained directly on him.

It was over. The man who had tried to kill me last night was long gone. Dave was in custody. Mrs. Bavcock was the first to respond: she grabbed an end table for stability and pulled herself back up to stand. I knew it was safe to get up, to walk outside again, but my body didn't want to move. I stayed crouched down, still processing everything that had happened.

More neighbors stood along the street, watching as Dave was caged in the back of one of the cruisers. The neighbors were probably speculating on what had happened. Had they all been woken up last night when the emergency vehicles took Libby away? Even those who had been able to sleep through it were surely being filled in now.

I overheard an old man from the corner lot say, "The block went to hell when the Kane's left town without taking that youngest daughter with them. It was bad enough she didn't mow the lawn. Now she has drug dealers shooting up the neighborhood."

Mrs. Bavcock gently squeezed my shoulder. Until she did it, I was too focused on the people outside to realize my whole body was shaking. She had heard him, too. "Don't mind him. You're in shock, Candy. You need to lie down. Come here."

The lady gently guided me toward her sofa. It was one of those old time sofas with the hideous chintz pattern, built to last fifty years. As offensive as it was to look at, I didn't argue as she instructed me to lie down. She tucked a throw pillow under my head, a second under my feet, and I grabbed a third one, hugging it tightly to my body.

I closed my eyes, my mind remembering the easy breezy days of high school. The most difficult part of my life had been trying to fit studying in around my social schedule. A few years later and I had almost gotten Libby and me both killed because I was hungry. I needed a change of scenery. There was no reason for me to stay here. My parents had left the cold winters and months of gray skies behind them for New Mexico. I could run away, make it to a warm beach before anyone even noticed I was gone.

Libby and I had always talked about taking off, but neither of us had a good reason to vanish – at least not until last night. I may never be anyone important, I won't change the world, but my life was worth more than a few hundred bucks.

A soft knock at the door sounded, and Mrs. Bavcock, who I hadn't noticed had been sitting beside me, whispered, "I'll be right back. Don't worry. You're safe."

How did this crazy old woman know the words that I needed to hear? *I'm safe*. Am I? Would I ever be again?

Heavy footsteps came back into the living room. A deep voice, tentative and kind asked, "Miss Kane, we have apprehended one of the two men who broke into your home."

I swung my legs onto the floor, embarrassed that the policeman had seen me not just hiding at a neighbor's house but probably looking like I was taking a nap. "Um, thanks. Do you have to dust for prints or anything, or can I go home now?"

"Actually, there was a mix-up at the station last night. A forensics team was to have been at your house first thing this morning to collect evidence from last night. That didn't happen. Now we have two crime scenes at the same place. Is there somewhere you can stay for a couple days while we try to sort this out?"

No, there wasn't. I had a few friends sprinkled around town, but none I knew well enough to intrude on their lives. When I didn't answer, the officer suggested, "Maybe a hotel?"

I nodded, knowing full well I couldn't afford more than Motel 6, and even that was only an option for a night or two. Mrs. Bavcock must have been partly psychic, "You can stay in my guest room, Candy. It's yours for as long as you need it."

Her eyes were full of compassion. All those times I'd begrudged her good nature and went out of my way to avoid her – she had never let it color her opinion of me. Now, my heart swelled at her offer, and I would never forget I owed her my life. Even if I had the money to afford a week's stay at the Hilton, I would never turn this lady down for anything again. I owed her and would owe her for the rest of my life. I gladly accepted, "If it's not too much trouble?"

Her sympathetic smile was all the answer I needed, but she affirmed, "No trouble at all. We would love to have you."

I knew her well enough to know that she wasn't speaking about her late husband and her; the "we" who would be glad to have me stay were the four-legged furry creatures who consumed so much of her life. I was grateful, and I would find a way to be extra nice to all of her roommates, too.

The officer seemed pleased with this arrangement, but added, "There is one more thing, Miss Kane. The man we took into custody says he's a friend of yours."

"I saw him through the window. It's Dave Brewer."

"He says you stopped by to see him this morning, and he was worried about you. He says he was only here to make sure you were okay."

"I don't believe it. The guy who was in my house when I got home is the same guy who tried to kill me last night at the gas station and beat my roommate into the ICU. He knew Dave. He let Dave into my house. We both saw it." Mrs. Bavcock nodded her head vigorously in agreement.

The policeman's eyebrows rose, "He must have left that part out. Sorry to bother you, Miss." He handed me a business card with his name and phone number on it. "Do you need to get anything out of the house before we seal it up?"

"Will Dave be able to see me?"

"We've got to take him to get his arm stitched up. I'll have my partner take him before I take you back through your house."

I shouldn't have cared, but the words were out before I could stifle them. "He was shot, wasn't he?"

Offering no concern at all, "The bullet grazed him. He'll be fine." He reached down and stroked the head of an orange tabby who was trying to leave her fur on his dark blue uniform. "It wasn't much worse than a cat's scratch."

The officer excused himself and left me with too many unanswered questions. Why would the man have shot at Dave? For that matter, why was Dave chasing him to begin with? Had my visit to Dave screwed up their plans? Had I thrown a wrench into everything by living last night? Dave had seemed genuinely happy to see me this morning: was he a great actor, or could that have been for real? Maybe he knew I was supposed to be killed last night, and after seeing me this morning, he had had second thoughts, and that was what the two had quarreled about.

CHAPTER 10

I watched the squad car pull away while I stood in the relative safety of Mrs. Bavcock's house. The police officer who had stopped by a few minutes before returned to walk me into my house to watch me collect the things I would need. He didn't try to make light of the situation, nor did he speak to me much at all. From the entryway, I went straight upstairs to my room, the second door on the left.

My room was exactly as I had left it last night. My covers were strewn in a large wad at the foot of my bed from my abrupt departure. A pile of clean clothes that Libby must have folded yesterday was perched on my dresser. I hadn't noticed them last night. I stared at the clothes, knowing the last person to have touched them was Libby. It didn't feel right to disturb them. Instead I reached into my drawers and pulled out four outfits. If I couldn't come back in the next few days, I'm sure Mrs. Bavcock would let me use her laundry.

The clothes I was wearing were the same ones I had thrown on in the dark. I had half a mind to ask the officer to excuse me so I could put on fresh, but I would wait to do that until I could grab a shower. When I had pulled up in front of the house, a hot shower was all I could think of. I had never considered more danger awaited me in my own safe haven. In addition to the danger waiting, more danger pursued me. I shivered at the thought of what might have happened if Mrs. Bavcock hadn't been watching out for me.

My hands shook as I looked around the room. My whole life was tied up in this house, but if anything happened to Libby, I knew I would never want to return. She had been attacked, right here, while I slept. When we were younger, how many times had she spent the night, and we stayed up giggling until the sun came up? How many times had I been stressed out about school or a guy, and it was Libby who picked up the pieces and told me everything would be fine. Too many to count.

An image of her hooked up to tubes, fighting for her life in a lonely hospital room, brought the reality of the situation in living color. I grabbed a backpack from my closet, stuffed it with clothes, and threw it over my shoulder.

The officer who had stood by the door cleared his throat, "Does anything look out of place?"

My eyes darted around the room. My desk looked just as I had left it: school papers strewn in an outrageously high pile, books from last semester piled up beside it on the floor with gnarled up notebooks piled underneath. The dresser, too, looked untouched, save for the neatly folded clothes that I hadn't noticed last night. I recognized them as Libby's handiwork – she folded t-shirts in this four-fold way that made them practically wrinkle-free.

Beside my bed was a small table where I charged my phone, with an alarm clock I never used other than to see what time it was. A picture of my two sisters and I set behind it – wait, the picture was missing. The frame was exactly where I had left it, but it stood empty. The freak wouldn't go after Carly and Kim, would he?

The words shot out of me like rapid-fire, "There on my nightstand, that frame had a picture of me with my two sisters." I went to reach for it, but the officer stopped my hand in mid-air.

"He might have left prints. I'll make sure it gets dusted." From his pocket he produced a large plastic bag, put a glove on his hand, and gingerly placed the frame in the bag. Looking around the room, he asked, "Anything else?"

I shrugged my shoulders, "I don't see anything else."

The bathroom was at the end of the hall. I grabbed my overnight make-up bag, toothbrush, toothpaste and took a quick look in the mirror. The events of the last day were wearing on me. I looked like I felt – like I'd been to hell and back. Absently running fingers through my hair rather than using a hairbrush did little to make me any more presentable.

The policeman stood in the doorway, "Anything here?"

Nothing looked out of place. I had cleaned the bathroom yesterday morning, and it still smelled faintly of bleach. "No. Nothing looks out of place in here."

I thought of something, "Hey, can I go into Libby's room to get something? I want to take it to her at the hospital."

He nodded and allowed me to lead the way. I hesitated before turning her door handle. When her door opened, the cologne she wore still hung in the air. The skimpy outfit she had worn to the bar was on the floor beside her bed. I tried to ignore it as I reached for the first thing I wanted her to see when she woke up – the stuffed turtle I had given her for graduation.

We walked slowly down the hall back toward the stairs. I gave no explanation of why I wanted the toy, and thankfully, the officer didn't ask me. When she woke up, if I wasn't there when her eyes opened, her turtle would be there for her – reminding her that she was tough, that no one could break her.

"Can I see where she was attacked?"

His expression told me he wanted to deny this request, but he reluctantly nodded. Both of us walked slowly down the steps. In the daylight, the kitchen looked much as I had remembered from yesterday. Dirty pans were still on the stove from the manicotti she had prepared when she got back from the grocery store while I was sound asleep upstairs.

Someone had turned off the television that was on last night. I took a step toward the living room, but the police officer stopped me. "Don't go in. The forensic team doesn't want anything touched."

Standing in the doorway, the evidence of the brutality was everywhere. Blood splatter was on the walls and pooled on the carpet. A lamp was on the floor, the glass smashed and the metal base bloody. The tan sofa was soaked in blood where she had been lying as I left for work. My stomach turned at the scene. I ran for the front door, grabbed hold of the railing and retched off the porch. The officer grabbed hold of me, holding me in place as a second wave of dizziness and nausea consumed me. After my body settled down and the frigid air cooled my burning face, he helped me back into the house and ushered me to a kitchen chair. The officer placed a cool glass of water in front of me. As I took a sip, his cell phone rang.

He pursed his lips as he looked at the display and answered, "Officer Bivens." His brows furrowed as he listened to who had called him. He looked back toward the front door, then answered, "Understood. I'll make sure she is aware."

He took a seat beside me at the kitchen table. "That was Dave Brewer's escort. He escaped custody. It'll only be a matter of time before we apprehend him, but I think it's time you get back to your neighbor's house. We'll post a patrolman outside until the two men are in custody."

Adrenalin pulsed through my body. Dave was loose? Without finishing my water, I stood up, gathered my backpack and my overnight bag, and hurried to the front door, worried I might lose it again. Officer Bivens walked me all the way to Mrs. Bavcock's house. He stayed at Mrs. Bavcock's house until another squad car pulled up. His eyes were kind as he said, "We'll keep an officer posted on the street. Stay inside. I promise I'll call you with developments."

I should have been dead on my feet, but I wasn't. Mrs. Bavcock had made chicken soup while I was gathering my things, but I wasn't hungry. I was restless. I lay down in Mrs. Bavcock's guest room, counting the faded yellow flowers on her wallpaper, but sleep refused to find me. Grizzly images of my living room haunted me. I glanced at the happy turtle on top of my backpack. I wanted to go see Libby, to be there if she woke up.

After over an hour my body was more frazzled than when I had arrived. I excused myself and promised I'd be back later this afternoon. Mrs. Bavcock didn't try to dissuade me when I told her I was going to the hospital. I took my backpack with me. She eyed it hung over my shoulder, but ignoring her eyes, I didn't offer any explanation. Somewhere deep down I knew I wouldn't skip town without Libby, but if the worst happened and she didn't wake up, I would never return to my house or this street.

Images of the blood in the living room were waiting for me each time my eyes closed. Libby had to be okay. She had to pull through. I delayed long enough to let the police officer parked outside know where I was going and to ask him to keep an eye on Mrs. Bavcock. He told me he had been assigned to keep watch on the neighborhood but would be watching her house closely. I tossed my backpack in the backseat of my car and ignored Dave's car still parked right behind mine.

When I arrived, a different nurse was at the station for ICU, but the doctor had put me on Libby's visitor list, so I had no problem getting inside. A second nurse gave me a set of scrubs and walked me through the procedures for visiting someone in ICU. I was told my visit would be limited to ten minutes.

A chair set beside her bed. I put the happy turtle on her nightstand and sat in the chair.

The only sound in her room was the sound of machines helping to keep her alive. The humming and periodic beeping were a little hypnotic. I sat for a full five minutes before I noticed the hum of the machines was making my eyes heavy. I didn't want to fall asleep, so words began falling out of me.

"I don't know if you can hear me. I brought you your turtle. I'm sure it's against the rules, but I put him where the curtain kind of hides him." My voice was unsteady, "Your doctor is a hottie. If I were you, I'd pretend to be in bad shape for as long as you can get away with it. But if you want to wake up early and get out of here, I got his card."

The babbling continued for several minutes until the words I needed to say rushed out of me. "I'm going to find this guy. I promise you, I'll find him." My hand took hers: it was cool and a little clammy. I rubbed her hand using both of mine to try to warm it up. "You need to keep fighting. I need for you to get better." Reaching across the bed, I took her other hand in mine and did the same thing. "I promise if you get better, I'll never give you a hard time about rent again. We can get another roommate, so you can live in the house for free, okay? You're never going to shark again because of rent or food. We'll figure out a different way to pay the bills, I promise."

The tears that rarely came even in the worst situations were now cascading down my cheeks. My voice was unintelligible, but I choked out the words anyway, "I can't go back home if you aren't there. It isn't home without you, Libby. So wake up." The sobs took over as I bent forward and rested my head against her mattress. "Just wake up. Don't leave me."

Unsure how long I stayed in this position, a nurse gently shook my shoulder. I had stayed well past the ten minute limit. I nodded to the nurse and gave Libby one more sorrowful look. I leaned down to her ear and whispered, "Keep fighting."

I returned the scrubs to the used laundry hamper and left the ICU. The waiting room which had been nearly empty last night was full of long faces and tears. I didn't want anyone's comfort, but it felt better to be around others in as much pain as I was.

I found an overstuffed chair away from the others, by a window looking out across the city. My stomach growled. No matter how hard I tried to stop the memory, the events from last night crashed in on me as I fell into a fitful sleep in the waiting room. I woke up abruptly, looking around the waiting room in a daze. The reality of where I was, and the events of the last twenty-four hours poured over me. I stood up and stretched. I felt awful. My watch told me I'd been asleep for nearly two hours.

The light from the window that I had fallen asleep beside was diminishing. It was going to be dark soon. I needed to get back to Mrs. Bavcock's house and get some real sleep.

CHAPTER II

The fine hairs at the nape of my neck prickled. Someone was watching me. There was a policeman posted on the ICU floor, positioned behind the same desk as the nurse who had welcomed me when I arrived. He hadn't been here earlier, so I wondered if he had been assigned here along with the patrolman on my street. I turned in a complete three-sixty, but no one seemed to be paying any attention to me in the waiting room. I felt eyes watching, but from where? I was still groggy from my nap and needed more sleep. I had caught a quick nap between 9 PM and midnight last night, and a couple hours just now, but I had been on a two-day stretch before that. In the last forty plus hours, I had had just shy of five hours of sleep.

That had to be what I felt. My body was overreacting to all the stimuli. I had once stayed awake for almost three whole days and nights. Remembering that it had taken days to recover afterwards, my body was telling me it needed some down time. I didn't want my body to melt down like that again, but I wasn't confident that I could calm myself enough to sleep anytime soon.

Larry was sitting in a chair on the other side of the waiting room, but he hadn't been paying much attention to me. As I made my way over to him, he looked up and seemed glad to see me. "I just woke up. Has anything changed?"

"No. No change."

"How long have you been here?"

"I left for a little while early this morning, but when I got to work, I couldn't stop thinking about her, so I came back. I must have been in the cafeteria when you came in." I had never thought much of him when the two were dating: he gave off clingy vibes or something, but in this moment I started to think he might be okay. I was glad he was here for her. If she gets better – scratch that, when she gets better, if Libby decides to let him hang around, I'll do my best not to get annoyed with him so easily.

Light from the window was nearly gone. The short days of winter were here; it was dark most days before 6 PM. I needed to make my way to Mrs. Bavcock's guest room. With any luck, when I woke up tomorrow morning, I would be able to stomach school again. I had already decided I would park two streets over on Maple and walk through the easements to get to Mrs. Bavcock's house. I didn't necessarily expect either Dave or the shooter to come back to my street, but as much as my car stuck out, I wouldn't tempt fate, either.

Even though Dave had known me in high school, he knew little about where I hung out now or who I spent my time with. From what little I had known of him, he didn't have any big ties to this area, so it wasn't out of the realm of possibilities for him to skip town – especially if he was on the run from the police. A shiver shimmied down my spine: how had he so easily gotten out of police custody?

Assuring Larry I would be back in the morning, I said my good-bye and made my way down the hall. I stood in front of the elevator door, watching the illuminated number above it. When it arrived on the eighth floor where I stood, the little metal car was already full. I let it go without trying to wedge myself in. After the doors closed and it began its descent, I reached to press the elevator call button again. To my right was a sign for the stairs. Going down the steps wouldn't be bad; it wasn't like I'd have to do any climbing. Maybe being off this floor would get rid of that nagging feeling that I was under surveillance.

Halfway to the seventh floor, the feeling of dread went from a dull annoying feeling to a sharp fear that I was being pursued. "This is silly," I told myself aloud. I could hear someone walking down the steps a few floors above me. My stomach cinched tight. Whatever these weird vibes were, I needed to be in a public place, not in a lonesome stairway. I pulled hard on the seventh floor door and emerged in front of the same elevator I had stood in front of one floor up.

I pushed into an overfilled elevator, not even apologizing for likely taking the car over its maximum capacity. My car was in the parking garage across the street, and I liked the idea of walking almost the whole way to my car in a brightly lit skywalk. My departure must have coincided with a shift change at the hospital because a steady flow of people were walking with me to the parking garage.

I got in my car and waited while several eager cars darted passed me before I could back out. Luckily, the nurse on Libby's floor had validated my ticket, so I wasn't scrambling for any loose coins in my purse to pay. I had considered going to Bank Shot to talk to Chris but decided I needed a clear head, and sleep was the only way that was going to happen. I began driving toward Maple Street. The radio played a favorite song; something about the familiar melody soothed me, and I was finally settling down from the weird feeling I had had in the hospital.

A light up ahead turned yellow; stepping on the clutch and easing my foot off the gas, I tried to be extra careful because I could see the shimmer of the icy pavement ahead of me. I came to a stop at the red light and began fiddling with the radio, trying to avoid the commercial that had cut off the song I liked. The last thing I needed playing in my head was a catchy jingle about new carpet.

Absently I looked in the rearview mirror – Dave's face was staring at me. I screamed so loud that the windows should have shattered. My foot slid off of the clutch, the car's engine and transmission jerking to a stop. Dave didn't flinch, his voice was smooth, "I'm sorry. I needed to talk to you. I need you to tell me what's going on."

I scrambled for the door handle, but it wouldn't budge. Dave's hand had reached around my shoulder from the backseat and was holding the manual lock on the car door down. I was trapped. "How did you get in here?"

He held up a bent metal coat hanger in answer to my question. I had gotten into the car the same way lots of times by sliding one through the closed window and pulling the manual lock up with the end, so it shouldn't have surprised me that he, too, had a master key. The street was clear, no pedestrians to hear my scream, and no cars behind me to see I needed help. His voice remained calm when he asked a second time, "Candy, what's going on?"

I put on a brave front that I wasn't feeling. "What's going on? You and your friends are trying to kill me."

Incredulously he stammered, "Kill you? Why would I want to kill you? And who was that guy at your house today?"

That's the same question my mind had had on constant replay all day. Why would Dave want to kill me? He had been so sweet to me at his garage this morning, yet right afterwards he'd come to my house after me. The light turned green, but I didn't move. I stole a glance at the passenger side door. I could slide across and run back to the hospital. If I timed it right, I could easily have a ten second head start. I ran three days a week and could outpace almost everyone I knew. "You tell me. He let you in," I spat.

Dave's brows came together as his forehead wrinkled in irritation. "He thought I was someone else." His eyes narrowed when he asked, "What happened in your house? It looked like someone butchered a deer in your living room."

My breath hitched as the memory of seeing my living room this morning returned. I saw a sincerity in his eyes I didn't expect. "That guy who let you in my house? He attacked Libby last night."

His eyes widened, "The cops who brought me here talked about a woman being in the ICU. They didn't say who. I was waiting for dark to leave when I saw your car pull into the garage. Is she. . .I mean. . .that was a lot of blood. Is she going to be okay?"

I wanted to scream, "Yes," but I didn't know if she was going to be okay. I didn't know if she would ever wake up, or if she did, what kind of brain damage she might have. "They induced. . ." I couldn't finish the sentence. What was he saying? He didn't know Libby had been attacked? What was he doing at my house if he wasn't meeting the psycho stalker? Instead of finishing my answer, I asked him, "He thought you were someone else? Who?"

"I don't know. When he figured out I wasn't the guy he thought I was, he started shooting at me. What have you and Libby gotten yourselves mixed up with?"

"He let you into my house. What were you doing there?"

Dave's left hand still held firmly to the door lock, precluding my exit, as his right hand eased onto my shoulder while he leaned up toward my seat. His eyes remained fixed on mine through the rearview mirror. "I'd never seen the guy before. I went to your house looking for you. I thought you were inside because your car was out front." The hand on my shoulder squeezed me gently when he added, "I didn't know what to think when you left my place this morning. I was worried."

Was he on the level? Was it possible he *wasn't* involved? I wanted to believe the earnest expression that held my gaze, but I couldn't be gullible, not after everything that had happened. I had seen Dave at Bank Shot last night. He obviously knew Teddy. The guy who shot at me and attacked Libby last night knew Teddy, too.

He must have read the doubt in my eyes, because his voice spoke softly, "I could never hurt you. Ever."

Turmoil erupted inside me. I wanted to believe him. I wanted to be able to trust someone. After everything that had happened, I couldn't pull off this strong façade much longer. I was close to losing it. Maybe my initial conclusion this morning was correct: he had a multiple personality disorder and truly believed he didn't know these people. That would explain a lot. From what little I knew about the disorder, I believed that as long as he stayed with this personality, I would be safe. But I had no clue what the trigger might be that would make him switch to the personality from the bar last night – the dangerous personality.

Dave's expression was solemn, as if I were hiding the truth from him, "Who was he, Candy?"

"I don't know," I flared. I took a deep breath, silently wishing I could know whether to believe him or not. "You're sure you don't know him?"

"Never seen him before. You left my garage so fast I didn't know what to think. I wanted to see if you were okay. You didn't answer the door, so I started looking in windows to see if you had collapsed on the floor or something. Your Chevelle was parked in front of the house, so I was sure you were inside. When I saw him through the window, he waved me toward the front door."

"So you came over to my house and some strange guy let you in? You didn't think that was odd?"

"I didn't know what to think. I hadn't seen you in a while. For all I knew he was your roommate or boyfriend or something."

Still skeptical I asked, "At what point did you figure out that something wasn't right?"

"It was weird. As soon as he let me in, he started talking to me like we were old friends. He said he hadn't expected to see me there and told me not to get pissed, he was doing Teddy a favor." Dave paused for a minute, as if he were still trying to make sense of what had happened. "You had asked me about a Teddy this morning, too. I meet a lot of people at the garage, and the way he was talking like he knew me, I didn't know what to think and was trying to place him. When I came up empty, I didn't want to be a jerk and ask who he was, so I asked him where you were."

Dave's eyes darted away from where they had held mine through the rearview mirror. "He said, 'Unfortunately, still alive. I'll take care of her as soon as she comes back from across the street. You better go before this goes down.'"

That awful sinking feeling grabbed my stomach when I asked, "What'd you say?"

"I don't remember. I saw red. Whoever the guy was, he wasn't a customer, and he had just told me he wanted to kill you. I attacked him, which is when I realized he had a gun tucked into the waistband of his jeans. We wrestled around for a minute, somehow he got loose, and he tried to shoot me as he ran for the front door."

"Then why did you chase him up the street?"

Dave must not have realized I had watched most of what had happened from Mrs. Bavcock's window. He shook his head as if he didn't know the answer to my question either. "I didn't know what to think. The only thing my mind processed was the part where he said he wanted you dead. I sort of snapped."

Dave was wearing a coat, so I couldn't see the bandage on his arm. It wasn't the same coat he wore earlier: this one was a brown and black ski parka. The police had said they were taking him to get stitches. To confirm what they had told me, I asked, "But you got shot?"

His smile was warm, "Yeah, talk about contender for worst day ever."

I startled from the sound of a car's horn behind me. I wasn't sure how many green lights we had sat through. No longer convinced I needed to escape, but still not certain I believed him, I restarted the car and eased it into a brightly lit convenience store parking lot. With what Dave had just said, I started to question my multiple personality theory. He was adamant that he wasn't there to hurt me. For some strange reason, I believed him. If Dave wanted me dead, he could have easily done it in the garage or here from my backseat. He had had every opportunity; instead he was trying to get his mind wrapped around what had happened. Everything he described seemed logical. What was I missing?

There was something in Dave's eyes, an honesty – a genuineness. He must have noticed that my fear was ebbing because his enormous legs and body crawled over the bench seat from the backseat into the front passenger side. When he was situated and looking into my face with the glow of the convenience store lights lighting his features, he asked, "Start from the beginning. Who was the guy in your house? What was he doing there?"

I shook my head, "I'm not sure. One of my neighbors had seen him looking out the windows before I got home. When I parked my car, she didn't let me go in."

"And you had never seen him before?"

I chewed my lip for a second, "He robbed me last night at the gas station. He tried to shoot me after I gave him the money, but I was behind bullet-proof glass."

Dave thundered, "He tried to kill you last night and then came looking for you?" Dave's eyes were full of alarm as his hand gripped my arm.

I eased away from him, trying to fade into the door. I stammered, "Not exactly, I mean, yes."

Dave saw his outburst had frightened me because he eased back toward the passenger side door, crossed his arms, and took a breath. "From the beginning."

"Libby and I were playing pool at Bank Shot last night. She bet this Teddy guy and won. He didn't want to pay up, but," my voice trailed off. This was the part that I didn't want to say, because if I were wrong and Dave did have multiple personalities, this might make the Mark guy come out.

Dave asked, "But what?"

"This guy who looked like you was there. He made fun of Teddy for Libby beating him, then said something about being respectful of ladies when Teddy threw her winnings on the floor. It didn't seem like a big deal at the time, but when I got to work a few hours later, the guy you met at my house showed up. He told me Teddy had been gambling with his money, and he wanted his money back. I gave him money out of the cash register, and that's when he told me he had already attacked Libby."

"Wait. The guy in your house this morning robbed you last night *and* attacked Libby?"

I nodded. "He said he did, but I don't know for sure. Libby's still unconscious. The doctor said her brain is bruised, so they induced a coma to help her heal."

"You're not going back to your place tonight."

"I know. I've already made other arrangements."

His eyes were fixed on mine. "Cancel them. You're staying with me." I wanted to argue, to tell him I could take care of myself. But when I looked at the lines etched in his face, the expression wasn't one for me to fear: it was an animalistic, protective look. Unexpectedly, he reached across the front seat and gently took my hands in his. We sat there motionless for several minutes with him stroking my hands with his fingertips before he leaned toward me, gathered me in his arms, and pulled my head to rest against his chest. Dave murmured, "We'll figure this out. I promise to keep you safe."

Thinking back to the Dave I had known in high school, he had always come across as sort of a hollow person, an exterior shell that could have completely caved in on itself in a strong wind. This man holding me in his arms wanted to protect me. He wanted to be a safe harbor, and my ship had seen enough turmoil for one day. I allowed my body to go limp in his arms, to feel the rigid strength encircling me.

After several minutes I eased away from his protective embrace to look into his eyes. "You're sure? This isn't your problem."

Dave pursed his lips together then answered, "It's mine if I make it mine. We'll stay at my garage tonight. Let's go."

I shook my head, "The cops are probably staking your garage out."

"We'll drive by. If we see any patrol cars, we won't stop. If no police are around, we can park your car inside the garage."

The one thing that kept bothering me as I pulled the car out of the convenience store parking lot was the image of Dave at Bank Shot last night. I had talked to him. Could I have been mistaken? This morning when I met with him, Dave was adamant that he hadn't been there, and that was before he knew any of the events that had happened last night. I wanted to believe him, but I couldn't afford to let my guard down.

As we turned on a main street headed toward his garage, I asked, "The part I don't get is, I am sure I saw you at Bank Shot last night. I even talked to the guy who looked like you."

I glanced at Dave. He didn't seem suspicious or at all on the defense about my revelation. He just shook his head and said, "Well, unless his name was Mark, you might have had too much to drink."

Without a second's hesitation, I slammed the brake pedal all the way to the pavement. My Chevelle gripped the asphalt hard as the lapbelt held me firm against the seat and I used my arms to cushion my face against the steering wheel; Dave's head crashed hard into the windshield. Without so much as a glance in his direction, I killed the car and bolted out the door, running down the street like a mad woman. I was a full fifty feet down the sidewalk before I heard his heavy footsteps giving chase.

I screamed for help as loud as my voice would allow, as frozen tree branches whipped past my head. We were in a residential neighborhood with cars parked in driveways indicating people were in their homes.

His voice boomed behind me, "Wait!! Candy, wait! Holy shit, you saw Mark?! Candy, stop!"

My chest was tight as the arctic air burned my throat. My eyes watered from the cold, and my heart thundered in my chest. He was only a car length behind me and gaining ground with every stride. He would catch me if I didn't do something quickly.

I was approaching a two-story brick home where I saw movement inside. Running at full speed, I propelled myself off the sidewalk to try to cut through the lawn to get to the front door. The foot that launched me off the sidewalk slipped on a spot of ice. Before I could even try to high-step through the deep snow on the lawn, I was on my back, looking up into the black sky above.

It took a millisecond to realize I was on my back only yards away from safety when Dave grabbed me and held me on the ground. His voice raw and his breathing labored, "You saw Mark? He's here? When did you see him? Candy, where's Mark?"

Confusion overwhelmed me. Dave didn't think he was Mark. His eyes stared down into mine while he grabbed my arms, holding me firmly in place in the snow. "Oh, my God, you saw Mark. You saw him and thought he was me. Holy shit, Candy, you saw my brother."

Dave's expression was full of joy. I wasn't able to form a coherent sentence as the front porch lights flicked to life on the house while I lay helplessly on their snow-covered lawn. A man in his mid-forties stood at the opened door and called out, "Are you okay out there?"

I opened my mouth to scream again, but when I did, Dave did the most unexpected thing: he leaned down and kissed me. Not a romantic, "I've been waiting for you my whole life" kind of kiss, but a kiss full of nervous energy. It completely disarmed me. I wasn't capable of thought, much less speech. When his lips released mine, his brown eyes were staring down into mine accompanied by a smile bright enough to light the night's sky.

In a daze, all I could choke out was, "Your brother? I didn't know you had a brother."

He must have decided his quick action had not only stopped me from screaming, it had bamboozled me enough to keep me from making an escape into the safety of the stranger's house. Dave rolled off of me and stood, holding out both of his hands to lift me to my feet. The homeowner still stood in his doorway, but no longer worried that I was being attacked. Instead he gave us a look that silently said, "Yeah, I remember being your age."

Dave held up a hand. "We're fine. She just slipped. It's a little icy out here."

Concern colored the man's face, "Is she all right? She's not hurt, is she?"

I shook my head, "No, I'm fine."

My breathing was erratic from the sprint. I wanted to put my head between my knees to catch my breath, but Dave wrapped his arm around me and started ushering me back toward my car. "Walk it out, we need to move your car before someone hits it." Not waiting for me to catch my breath, Dave asked, "You met Mark? What did he say?"

In my rush to escape, I had left my car in the middle of the street, keys in it, with the driver's door wide open. If someone hadn't yet called the police or stolen it, it would only be a matter of time. Dave's excitement was evident as he continued asking questions I could only nod or shake my head to because I was out of breath. "Was he looking for me? Does he live here? Do you know how I can reach him? What did he look like? Did you tell him I lived here?" I kept stealing glances at him. He looked outrageously happy, trying unsuccessfully to keep a goofy-looking grin off of his face in between all the questions. There was a cut on his forehead, and he used his coat sleeve to wipe the blood that was dripping down his cheek.

I tried to make sense of what he had said. Mark was his brother? How did he have a brother he'd never mentioned and I'd never met? Mark knew Teddy? Teddy called Mark "Boss." The man who was waiting in my house to finish me off this morning knew Mark? By the time we reached the car, I was still breathing like I had finished an Olympic sprint, so the questions sailing through my head were just stuck there. Dave let go of me about ten feet before we got to my car. No doubt he had just as many unanswered questions as I did.

He wiped his head a second time, this time smearing the blood that had already collected on his coat. He looked like a really bad Halloween decoration. As we approached my car, I noticed that in addition to the small hole with spider-web like cracks around it on the driver's side of the windshield, I now had a matching spider web on the passenger side of the windshield where Dave's head had bounced off.

Despite all the questions in my head, the only thing I asked was, "Do you want me to take you to the hospital. It looks like you need stitches."

"No. I'm a fugitive, remember. I can clean this up at my apartment. Let's go."

CHAPTER 12

Since his revelation that he had a brother, Dave hadn't said much of anything on the drive over. He was lost in his own thoughts and didn't seem to want to let me in. We pulled up in front of Dave's garage. I had planned to park on the street like I did at my house, but he motioned for me to pull into the driveway. "Hold on. Let me go in and open the door. You can park in the left bay tonight. I don't want anyone to see your car outside."

It took him little time to unlock the front door, go inside and open the large bay door on the left. A purple custom car was in pieces in the front of the bay. The flared fenders and boxy frame gave no indication as to what the car might be. Dave motioned for me to pull in behind it. He guided my car in, and when I got out to inspect his guidance, I saw that my car's bumper was less than a frog's hair away from the other car's back bumper.

"Are you sure I'm not too close?"

"What, you think it's going to roll back tonight?" Since the car pieces I had parked behind were just that – pieces, not even attached to a frame with wheels, I agreed that it was unlikely to scratch my bumper.

In the light of his garage, the wound on his head was clearly a gash; stitches weren't an option – they were a necessity. He pulled off his bloodied coat, grabbed a greasy rag off of a bench and held it to his head. The sight of blood had never bothered me before, but the torn flesh exposing his skull was another story completely. I motioned for him to take a seat near a bench, "Hey, we're going to need to call the paramedics."

He lifted the disgusting cloth away from his face as a second wave of blood flooded down over his eye. He quickly replaced the rag, "It'll be fine." His excitement was evident, "You're sure you saw Mark last night? He's in the city?"

Tentatively I answered, "Yeah, I thought it was you. He looks just like you."

"Everyone used to say that when we were little."

The cloth in his hand was soaked. Less interested in helping coordinate a family reunion, I told him, "Look, I'm going to call an ambulance. If you lose much more blood, I'll have to take over around here, and no one will want me fixing their cars."

His free hand grabbed my wrist. "I said I'm fine. What did Mark say? Does he live here?"

I shrugged my shoulders, "He didn't say."

"Well, what did he say?"

"I already told you: he made fun of that Teddy guy for losing to Libby."

"That's it?"

"I thought it was you, Dave. The fact that you were telling me to call you Mark was weird, so I didn't get wrapped up in a big conversation. He said something about being there again next Tuesday night. What's the big deal? You haven't seen him in a while?"

A solemn look gripped Dave. "You could say that."

"When was the last time you saw him?"

"I don't know. A long time ago." He pressed his lips together like he was trying to keep words from spilling out. He lifted the rag again, and although it was saturated, blood was no longer oozing from his head. "I've got to go upstairs and take care of this. I've got a first aid kit in the bathroom."

A first aid kit? He was in for a real shocker if he was planning on Neosporin and a Band-Aid. "C'mon up." Without so much as a backwards glance in my direction, Dave tucked behind a Coke machine that hid a staircase.

One of my jobs was as a housekeeper for a couple bachelors, so I assumed all single men lived like pigs. As I emerged at the top of the stairs, I was shocked to find an apartment that was spotless. A bright chandelier hung in the center of the room and lit the tiny room up like a carnival. Framed posters of cars were hung on the walls. A sofa and recliner faced a large screen television along one wall. A second wall was lined from floor to ceiling with cabinets – enough cabinet space for a commercial kitchen. A dinette with two chairs was tucked in close to a refrigerator and efficiency stove. On the far end of the room stood a massive king-sized bed, which also faced the over-sized television. Next to it was a Bo-flex machine wedged into the corner. There was no dresser and no obvious closet: it looked like a big open room pretending to be an apartment.

There was one door off to the side that must have been a bathroom because Dave disappeared into it as soon as he climbed the steps. Water ran inside, and I expected Dave to come marching out ready to take me up on my offer to go to the hospital at any second.

Minutes passed. The water that had sounded like a sink's faucet stopped, but was replaced by the sound of a shower. I looked around awkwardly, wondering where he kept his clothes. Without purposely trying to be nosey, I opened one of the kitchen cabinets along the wall. Perfectly folded t-shirts stood in a pile on one shelf, boxers on the shelf below, and socks in a plastic tub on the shelf even with the floor. I moved to the side and opened another cabinet: precisely folded jeans were piled up side by side on the shelf at eye level. Who used kitchen cabinets for a closet? I went down the line opening each cabinet: one held magazines, another blankets and sheets, a fourth one pillows. I had to admire his ingenuity. I counted the cabinets: there were eleven across, with two stacked on top of each other – a brilliant way to store things in an apartment which was probably never intended to be living quarters.

There was nothing out of place in the entire apartment. Remotes were perfectly lined up on the small table beside the recliner. No photographs of any kind were displayed, other than the framed posters of cars – but nothing personal. I didn't really even like my sisters, but I had several of their pictures framed in my bedroom and a couple scattered in the house. Where were Dave's pictures?

Looking into the tiny sink, not one dirty dish waited. Did he really live here? The water shut off in the bathroom. I came back to my senses and took a seat on the sofa before he could catch me snooping around his apartment. When the door opened, steam billowed out from the tiny room. My jaw tightened as he emerged. Dave wore a fluffy tan towel around his waist and a second one hanging over his shoulders which obscured his chest and partially covered his abdomen. Peeking out from under the towel over his shoulders, Dave's chest glistened from tiny droplets of water that clung to him. His chest was completely bare, not a single hair protruding from the towel hanging around his neck. I knew my mouth gaped, but I couldn't make my jaw close.

Opening the cabinet I had just inspected, he stood with his back to me, pulled the towel off of his shoulder and slid a burgundy t-shirt over his head. The t-shirt complained as his arms wedged themselves through the sleeves. If he knew I were transfixed on him, he gave no indication that my leering bothered him. Dave reached in and pulled a pair of nylon shorts off the top shelf, slid them under his towel and didn't let it drop to the floor until they were secured at his waist.

My pulse had steadily been climbing as I watched him. I hadn't noticed the hammering in my chest until he turned toward me and asked, "Care if I work out?"

"Not at. . . it's your. . .you can." I sounded like the village idiot. My mouth didn't work as all the blood rushed to my eyes capturing every contour of his body. His t-shirt was too tight on his chest while it hung loose at his waist. Dave returned to the bathroom to hang up a towel. His legs were as massive as his upper body, every muscle defined as he walked barefoot over to the awaiting Bo-flex.

I turned my back toward him, preferring to look at the dark television instead of the sex-on-a-stick that had just reduced me to a pile of goo. Humiliated at my school-girl reaction to him, I took a deep breath, and then a second, then a third. I could still hear blood hammering though my body as I willed my pulse to slow down.

The kiss on the front lawn couldn't have been more than a means to keep me from screaming like a banshee. It had worked, but afterwards I hadn't screamed or kissed him back. What kind of signal had I sent him by lying there in stunned silence? What sort of signal was he sending me coming out of the bathroom in a towel?

"Like what you see?" My back arched at his conceited question. My eyes were still reeling and wanted a good reason to turn my body around to get another look, but based on my reaction a second ago, I was frightened my legs might walk over and sit on his lap. "Hello, earth to Candy, the remote's right there on the table. Just hit the green power button on the top right."

The television, right. He was making fun of me for staring at a powered off television. I turned it on and absently scrolled through channels until I found TMZ. I was beginning to get my senses back under control before I made a complete ass out of myself when it hit me: his forehead wasn't bleeding.

My head whipped around and caught him doing presses. I couldn't even see the cut on his forehead. "What are you, a vampire?"

He had been flat on his back, using a bar attached to the pulleys as a bench press. He was breathing out when a throaty laugh escaped him and the bar flung up out of control, "Not that I know of, why?"

"Where's your cut?"

Dave reached back up and took the unruly bar in his hand again. "I glued it."

"You what?"

"Glue. It's the same stuff they use at hospitals. I get nicked on metal a couple times a week downstairs and got sick of paying doctors hundreds of dollars to glue my cuts shut. I told you I had a first aid kit."

I stood up from the couch and walked toward him. I saw the thin glossy line holding his skin together. "Are you sure you don't need stitches?"

He smiled through his measured breaths, "Not unless you prefer I look like Frankenstein. The glue'll hold; it heals faster this way, too."

After we had pulled my car into the garage, I was sure he needed an ambulance. I looked at his massive bicep and saw a similar glossy finish just below his shoulder. He had been shot earlier today and this was all there was?

Dave saw me staring and answered timidly, "It just grazed me. See, that glue," pointing to his arm, "cost me at least two hundred bucks. That glue," pointing to the closed gash on his forehead, "cost me less than ten."

"So you're cheap?"

He gently let the bar slide back up to the top as he grabbed a towel and dabbed perspiration from his brow then sat up. "I prefer 'thrifty.'"

I stood a few feet away, acutely aware of the body veiled in flimsy fabric in front of me. As stealthily as possible, I wiped my palms on my hips. He stood up and eased past me toward the kitchenette, grabbing a pitcher of water out of the refrigerator and pouring himself an enormous glass. As he slid the pitcher back onto the shelf, "I'm sorry. I'm not used to company. Do you want anything to drink?" He leaned down into the small refrigerator and began calling out options. "I've got Coke, beer, there might even be a wine cooler in here somewhere."

My eyes roved to where he was bent over, looking in the refrigerator for drinks. "Um, no. I'm fine," I stammered.

"Chips?"

"No, thanks." The apartment was so small that it barely qualified as a studio apartment. It looked like it had been a storage area at some point. It did not run the length of the garage below it. Or maybe the room/apartment wasn't too small, maybe Dave was just too massive for the tiny space. I was warm, really warm, and not because the apartment was balmy. This was a horrifically bad idea.

What the heck was I doing here? I tried to reason with myself: he was worried about my safety. Whoever had broken into my house had proved he could get in and out without any problems. After what happened this morning, my house was locked down from not one but two crime scenes. My best friend was in the hospital. The place where I worked had been robbed, and I had, by far, the scariest stalker in the world. What the hell was I thinking checking out Dave like he was an exotic dancer?

Ashamed of my hormones, I turned away from the kitchen. I should have insisted on going to Mrs. Bavcock's house. It was after seven. After everything that had happened, she was probably worried.

I reached into my backpack and pulled out my phone. "I need to make a phone call."

"Sure. You want me to give you some privacy?"

"Um, no. I mean, I just need to call my neighbor, to let her know I'm okay."

"No problem. I need to check messages downstairs. I closed up this morning and missed a couple appointments. I'm sure I have some ticked off customers to go suck up to." Dave took the towel he had used by the bench, wiped the bench down, hung the towel up, washed, dried and put away his empty water glass, and went downstairs. It was a little creepy, as if he were on autopilot and nothing could be out of place. Maybe he was just trying to make a good impression. After leering at him in his towel, he could have kept caged chickens in his apartment and I probably wouldn't have noticed.

I dialed Mrs. Bavcock, and she picked up on the third ring. Her voice seemed a little shriller than normal, "Hello?"

"Mrs. Bavcock, it's Candy. I'm going to stay at a friend's place tonight, and I didn't want you to worry."

There was a short pause. I began to think the call had dropped when her voice answered back shakily, "Where are you staying, in case the police come looking for you?"

"They have my number if they need me. Thanks so much for offering to let me stay in your guest room, but I'll be okay for tonight. Keep your doors locked."

She didn't answer right away. I sort of expected her to argue with me. I heard a cat hiss in the background then a low angry cat growl. Funning, I asked, "It sounds like Henrietta made it home. Did she bring a tom cat back with her?"

The shakiness was still there, "Roland is being difficult. You know how testy he gets when he's cooped up inside all day."

Something was wrong. Really wrong. Roland had been the only cat she owned that I liked. He used to come over to my front porch and bask in the sunshine. That cat had had a real affinity for Doritos and could smell a bag through two walls – it was still hard to eat a chip without thinking of him. Roland may have slept at her house, but he had been as much my cat as hers. When he was hit by a car two years ago, I had been heartbroken.

Something wasn't right. Playing along with her I added, "Roland must want to go hang out on my porch."

"He did. But I told him you were spending the night tonight and he would be able to see you. There would be no need for him to leave and go looking for you."

Someone was in her house. She was trying to tell me a man was in her house with her. "You know what? Tell Roland I'll be right there. With all the action going on in the neighborhood the last few days, he's probably a nervous wreck."

Her voice was less shaky. She knew her message had been delivered loud and clear. "Okay dear, I'll tell him."

She hung up the phone and I screamed, "Dave!! Dave!!" I sped toward his stairs, launching myself directly into him as he flew back up the steps to where I stood.

Dave's eyes were wide as he wrapped his enormous arms around me, "What happened? You're shaking. What's wrong?"

CHAPTER 13

"That guy – the shooter, he's in Mrs. Bavcock's house. He's there right now. We have to help her." I used every bit of inertia in my body to move toward the stairs, but Dave held me in place.

"Settle down." His voice was calm as his earnest eyes tried to make sense of my frenzied answer. Dave's arms pulled me back to him, refusing to let me push him away, "Tell me what happened."

Tears clouded my eyes. She had saved my life this morning. She wouldn't let me go inside, and now she was in danger because of it. Her warning was like she was saving me all over again. "Roland's dead. He couldn't have been the one hissing. But the shooter wouldn't know that. He wouldn't know that she told me he was there."

Dave eased me away from his chest as his eyes lay helplessly on mine. "Candy, slow down. What are you talking about? Who's Roland?"

Ignoring his question, I whimpered, "We have to go there. He doesn't know that she told me. If we go there now, he might not hurt her." I pushed hard against his weight still cementing me in place. His grip loosened, but he didn't let me go. Dave didn't move so much as an inch toward the door. I couldn't understand why he held me in place. I demanded, "Let me go!"

His answer was tender, calm as a lake at sunrise, "Listen to me. You aren't making any sense. Tell me what's going on."

I exhaled deeply, frustrated by his stubborn unwillingness to move. I collected my thoughts and explained, "I called Mrs. Bavcock to tell her I wouldn't be staying at her house tonight. While I was talking to her, a cat hissed then growled in the background, and she told me it was Roland. Roland's dead. None of her cats would hiss at her. There had to be someone else in the house with her that one of the cats was hissing at. By her telling me it was Roland, that was her way of letting me know that something else was going on. Please, can we go now?"

Dave was dialing before it even registered that a phone was in his hand. "I'd like to report a home invasion at…" He cupped his hand over the phone and whispered, "what's her address?"

"421 Elm."

"At 421 Elm Drive. It's an elderly woman, and I believe the man inside has a gun. I believe there may be a policeman stationed in the area because of an earlier disturbance." Dave hung up before the dispatcher could ask him for any additional information. His hands guided me to sit on the step halfway between his first and second floor. He knelt on the step in front of me so we were eye to eye, "We're not going there."

I jerked, "I have to go! She needs me!"

His head shook ever so slightly. "No, what she needs is the police. They don't need you in the way."

"You don't understand: she's an old lady. She's probably scared shitless right now."

Evenly, Dave's sweet voice refused to waver, "She's smart. She got the message to you. I called the police. She's going to be fine. You told me a patrolman was posted on your street. The dispatcher will radio him; she'll be fine." His hand reached to my wrist as his fingers gently caressed my forearm. He probably meant it to be a reassuring gesture, and if any other scenario were going on right now, it would have been, but his touch was so light it felt like a spider crawling on my skin and I swatted his hand away.

"Fine. You called the police. I'm going over there. I won't get in the way." I tried to get to my feet, but Dave held me in place on the step.

His voice was smooth, while his hands were firm as iron restraints, "You're forgetting: I can't go over there. The police are still looking for me. If I show up there with you, they'll take me to jail. I don't want you alone while things get sorted out. I'm not going to leave you to fend for yourself while I'm locked up. We stay put."

I had made a mess of things. Dave had already tried to come to my rescue once today, which was before he knew anything of the chaos that was going on. He'd gotten shot for his trouble, I'd probably given him a concussion on the drive here, and now I wanted him to go back to the lion's den with me. His hand cupped my face, forcing me to look into his dark brown eyes. His thumb nimbly caressed the sensitive skin under my jaw as his fingers spread out on my cheek. My eyes closed, allowing my senses to soak up his touch.

His simple gesture had captivated me. Dave's thumb continued to stroke down to the nape of my neck as I felt his breath close to my lips and could smell the wintergreen mint of his breath. As my eyes opened, the intensity of his stare held me still. I averted my eyes, embarrassed by the sensations rushing through me. When I spoke, my voice sounded feeble, even to me, "I owe her."

"She will understand. She wouldn't want you to put yourself in danger. She would want you to stay where you are – safe." My hand raised itself to his, which was still cradling my face, his eyelids slowly closed as he leaned his lips forward brushing mine. His kiss was apprehensive, as if he were silently asking me for permission.

My lips reacted to his, the suppleness of his lips lingered on mine as his other hand drew to my side and wrapped itself around me. I had kissed plenty of guys, but most were more interested in shoving their tongue down my throat. Dave's kiss was different, like a cool breeze on a warm day, a seductive caress. I leaned forward, pressing my lips more firmly to his as a dull moan escaped him. He stood from where he had been kneeling on the steps, bringing me to my feet and guiding me back to the top of the steps.

My hands wrapped around his elbows, as I registered defeat at the top step, wanting to give in to the building desire welling up within. As we both stood just inside his apartment, Dave's arms encircled me, holding me to him as his breath danced across my neck in a heavy exhale.

Before I could completely lose myself in him, the nagging voice that had been briefly locked away in a compartment inside my brain roared to life. Images of Mrs. Bavcock began playing in my head: her insistence that I not go in my house when I arrived this morning, her support as we crouched on the floor and peered through her front window, and her eager offer to provide me shelter no matter what kind of trouble I had gotten myself into. Each of these images sprung to the surface of my mind. I pulled away from Dave, trying to clear my head.

He eased forward as I stepped back. I put both of my hands against his chest to separate myself from him, acutely aware that he had briefly incapacitated any hope I had of rational thought while he kissed me. I took another step away from him. Dave's eyes snapped open while an apology poured out of him. "I'm sorry. Shit. I didn't mean to. . . Candy, I'm an idiot."

Dave believed I had rejected him. He distanced himself from me as he turned away. I had wedged space between us because I couldn't think with him that close to me, kissing me, caressing me. He made me want to shut the rest of the world out and get lost in him, but I didn't have that luxury right now. I couldn't let anything happen to Mrs. Bavcock, and I couldn't let Dave distract me from what I needed to do. Her life was in danger because of me – I would never forgive myself if something happened to her because I had done nothing.

His back faced me and his posture looked sullen: Dave had misconstrued my action. My head was still spinning from the impact his kiss had on me, but the fog he had created was clearing enough for me to say the words that had been muted in his embrace. "Look, I know why you can't go. It's okay. I just need to be sure she's okay." He remained with his back toward me, still on the other side of the room, fumbling with a remote for the television.

His voice was low, filled with remorse, "I'm sorry. I don't know what came over me. It won't happen again." His shoulders remained arched forward as if weary and defeated.

My backpack was in my hand. I didn't have much time, but I couldn't leave him like this. I bolted over to where he stood, wrapped my arms around him from behind and stood on my tippy toes as I breathed into his ear, "You'll do it again if you know what's good for you." His body went rigid under my touch, but he made no move to turn toward me. "I'll be back in twenty minutes. Promise."

I spun toward the steps, but Dave caught my forearm before I could go. He wore a confused expression, as if trying to detect a hint of deception. Before he could ask me anything lame, I planted a kiss just to the right of his lips. "Twenty minutes. Don't go anywhere. I'd like to continue what you started on the steps."

With no time for a sappy goodbye, I pulled my arm free from his grasp, and ran down the steps – only to see my battered car. The windshield looked far worse than I remembered it from when we had arrived. I looked for the lever to lift the bay door behind it when Dave's voice called from beside the pop machine. "Here." He tossed a set of keys. "Take my truck. I'm timing you." A brilliant smile flashed as he hit a lever behind him and the right bay door lifted.

It was a beautiful black truck, newer with leather seats and, surprisingly, an automatic transmission. It had been forever since I drove a vehicle I didn't have to shift. I would have expected him to have a restored truck, but this one had heated seats, so I wouldn't give him any grief later.

CHAPTER 14

I eased Dave's truck to a stop halfway up my street. The area in front of Mrs. Bavcock's house was completely blocked by police cruisers with flashing lights. At least a half-dozen uniformed policemen milled around the street and Mrs. Bavcock's yard. I breathed a sigh of relief when I didn't spy an ambulance, and none of the police had their guns drawn. Had I been wrong? Had I overreacted to what she had said on the phone?

A pit began to form in my stomach. If I had misunderstood her on the phone and called the police out on a false alarm, could I be charged with anything? I got out of the truck knowing Dave had been right: I had been stupid to come here. What did I hope to accomplish? I never should have left his apartment.

An energized voice echoed from Mrs. Bavcock's yard, "Oh my goodness, Candy! You're okay."

Mrs. Bavcock was running at me like a two-year-old leaving day care. I scrambled to get to the neighbor I would be forever indebted to. "I'm okay. Are you okay? What happened? Was he here?"

Tears streamed down her cheeks as she grabbed hold of me. "He was. He's gone. He was standing at the front window when the patrolman who had been parked up the street began walking toward my front door. He ran out the back door and through the alley before I realized what was happening."

I looked her up and down: not a mark on her or a hair out of place. All these grotesque images of the vile man hurting her had been on constant play in my head on the drive over – she was fine. "How did he get in?"

Mrs. Bavcock's head bowed as embarrassment clouded her face. "He knocked on my back door holding a cat, asking if it belonged to me."

It wouldn't take a criminal mastermind to know that cats were her weakness. It wouldn't matter who the stranger was; if it was someone who had a hurt cat, she would open her door to them. Where was the policeman who was supposed to be watching out for her? I grabbed hold of her, unwilling to chastise her for her lapse in judgment. I only wanted her to know how glad I was that she was okay. I gave her the strongest hug I thought her frail body would be able to absorb without hurting her. "I'm just glad you're okay."

Tears continued streaming down her face as she hugged me back and whispered, "I could sure use a guest in my guestroom tonight."

As I pulled away from her embrace, I saw the hopefulness in her eyes. She had every reason under the sun to be frightened and not want to be alone in a house full of cats tonight. I longed to go back to Dave to take whatever comfort he could offer me after the worst twenty-four hours of my life, but I couldn't tell this lady no. "Sure. Just let me make a call."

I pulled out my phone as she walked back to her yard. I didn't have Dave's cell, but given the fact that he lived over his garage, I called the number listed in information for his shop. Dave picked up on the second ring. His voice urgent with worry, "What happened? Is she okay?"

"He was here. She's a little shaken up, but it doesn't look like he hurt her."

He let out a grateful sigh, "Good. I'm glad she's okay." There was a pause on the line as I grappled for how to tell him I wouldn't be back tonight. His voice rolled back to the silky sound from before, "My watch says you've got eight more minutes before your promise is broken."

My heart lurched hearing his words as heat welled up within me, "Yeah, about that. She's okay, but she's pretty scared. She really wants me to stay with her tonight."

A disappointed breath echoed through the phone, but Dave remained silent without trying to tempt me with his seductive voice. I wanted to go back to his place. For a fraction of a second I had considered calling my sister to tell her what had happened so she would come stay with Mrs. Bavcock. If I did that, a family phone tree would be enacted, and I would spend the next two days reassuring every relative I had that I was fine, while they interrogated me about the events. I wouldn't call Kim or Carly.

I was striking out without even getting a chance to bat. "I know. Look, I'll return your truck before I go to school tomorrow morning."

Dave's voice was disappointed. "You don't have to. I don't need it. I've got a car I can drive."

The car he had brought to my house earlier today was still parked in front of my house. How many cars did he have? Trying to make sure he understood the only reason I wasn't returning to his place was that I couldn't leave Mrs. Bavcock alone, I said, "She needs me."

"I understand," although from his defeated tone, he didn't.

I cupped my hand over the phone so I wasn't sharing this with all of the people now standing within ear shot of me. "I want to see you. That conversation you started on the stairs, I had a few things I wanted to add."

Another sigh sounded in my ear. "The garage is open at eight."

Mischievously I answered, "So expect me at seven."

He gave me his cell phone number before I hung up, and I felt unforeseen butterflies taking flight in my stomach. His kiss had been unexpected, both of them, although the first one probably didn't count. Lying in the snow with his weight on top of me and his lips finding mine had been his way of keeping me from screaming for help. An enormous smile grew as I thought of how he had completely disarmed me. The second kiss was different, very different. It also disarmed me, but in a sensory overload sort of way. I thought of nothing beyond the sensations in the moment – as if the rest of the world would have to get along without us for a while.

A policeman approached while I was still reliving the moment with Dave in my mind. I probably looked like a dork standing with my phone in one hand, wearing a dazed look I was sure any passerby could see. The policeman was a little overweight, or maybe he had washed his uniform in hot water; regardless, it didn't seem to fit. He nodded in my direction, "Miss Kane?"

"Yes."

"Mrs. Bavcock indicated you called this in tonight."

Cautious with my answer, given the circumstances in the last twenty-four hours, "Yes."

"She also says you will be staying with her this evening?"

"Yes."

Narrowing his eyes at me, he asked, "What is your relationship to Mrs. Bavcock?"

I looked in the old woman's direction. "No relation, we're neighbors."

"The Sergeant's log says we responded to a disturbance at your place this morning." He motioned to my house directly across the street with wide bright yellow caution tape across the door.

A disturbance? Which one? "Right. The same guy who broke into Mrs. B's house tonight had been in my house this morning before I got home. A friend chased the guy out of my house and down the street."

The policeman looked down at his notes. When he did, a bald spot on the top of his head leered at me. "That friend of yours is a suspect. His name is David Brewer. Were you aware he escaped our custody earlier today?"

Now was my chance to get things cleared up for Dave. "Yes, Officer Bivens told me. But I don't want to press trespassing charges or anything against him. Dave was just worried about me."

The middle-aged police officer furrowed his brow, "You want to drop your charges against him? The report says he and the suspect who just did a home invasion on your neighbor are friends. Besides, trespassing is the least of his worries. He's looking at an assault charge."

"Assault? He didn't even talk to Mrs. Bavcock or me this morning."

"No, but the officer who escorted him to the hospital was assaulted when Mr. Brewer escaped custody."

I hadn't bothered to ask Dave how he got away. I figured someone turned their head and he ran. This was going to get ugly fast. Maybe if I could make the police officer understand that he shouldn't have been in custody to begin with, the other charge might go away, too. "They're not friends. Dave's brother might know the guy who broke into Mrs. Bavcock's house tonight and mine this morning."

"Who is his brother?"

"I've only met him once: his name's Mark. The guy who broke into my house mistook Dave for Mark, and I didn't know Dave had a brother until he told me."

The policeman shook his head as if my words were spoken in another language. "So you've spoken with Mr. Brewer since he escaped custody?"

Crap. Me and my big mouth. His expression was all business as he waited for my answer, "Yes. I saw him at the hospital this afternoon when I went to check on my roommate who had been attacked by the same guy you're looking for now."

He answered in a condescending way, "Mr. Brewer is a fugitive."

"That was my mistake earlier. How do I officially drop the charges?"

"You can fill out some paperwork at the station, but he's a person of interest in several crimes." The pen in his hand pointed at Dave's truck which I had left up the street, "I couldn't help but notice that vehicle is registered to Mr. Brewer. When did you borrow his truck? Is it safe to assume he is in the area, too?"

Double crap. "Um, he's not here. I just came here to check on Mrs. B." Several crimes? Could this be true? I couldn't get involved with a criminal, no matter how good a kisser he may be.

As I began to walk away from the astute police officer, he reached out and stopped me, "You, Miss Kane, are a person of interest, as well."

"What?!" My temper flared, "Are you nuts?" How could they think I had anything to do with shooting myself, attacking my roommate, or trespassing in my own house?

"You have to admit it looks a little suspicious. Your roommate is attacked in a house that is rented by you. Shortly after the attack, someone robs you, who you yourself told the police you owed money to. You paid that debt with your employer's money."

"I didn't owe the guy anything!"

"As I understand, you and your roommate were involved in illegal gambling activities, and the man wanted his money back. Who could blame him? He fired at you through bullet-proof glass, so you were in no danger. Why would you give him money from the register if he couldn't harm you?"

Fully on the defense now, I answered, "I was scared. I don't imagine he knew I was standing behind bullet-proof glass."

"Maybe not, but don't you think he would have figured it out after the first shot? Why would he keep shooting if it weren't for show?"

"Your theory sucks. Maybe he was trying to scare me. I pressed the silent alarm before he pulled out his gun. The police were already en route."

"Right again, you pressed the alarm because he was loitering by the bathroom. Are you sure this isn't some sort of scheme you had cooked up that has gone bad, and you don't know how to get out of it?"

"No! My roommate is in a drug-induced coma right now. Her doctor put her there because her brain is bruised. She's my best friend. I didn't have anything to do with any of this."

"Yet, you know the shooter."

"No, I don't know the shooter."

"My mistake, your boyfriend knows the shooter."

"I don't have a boyfriend! Dave Brewer is a *friend*, and it's his brother Mark who may know the shooter."

"Ah, yes, the mystery Mark. You just learned of his existence today? Convenient story. You return to your home and that same shooter, who you allege robbed you, was waiting in your house with one of your friends."

"Dave wasn't waiting in my house with him. Ask Mrs. B. He got here after I did this morning."

He scribbled illegible notes on his pad. I felt the watchful eyes of my neighbors gathered on the sidewalk now hanging on his every word. "You have an answer for everything, don't you, Miss Kane? So tell me: you are supposed to spend the night with a neighbor, but at the last minute you decide to stay elsewhere. Yet the man you have convinced the entire police force is pursuing you, is in your neighbor's house where you are supposed to be. Somehow, you know he's there, yet the patrolman stationed on your street is unaware. Have I missed anything?"

I was at a loss for words. I felt the heavy stares of my neighbors. Their whispers from the sidewalk were angry. They were angry and now all questioned my role in all the awful things that had happened. The policeman, too, noticed the mob of neighbors standing on the sidewalk. He asked, "So how did you know the shooter was threatening Mrs. Bavcock's safety this evening?"

My voice was meek, absent the earlier fury, "I called her and she told me."

He began scribbling again. "She told you the shooter was in her house?"

"No. I mean, yes. She didn't come right out and say he was there. I heard a cat hissing while I was on the phone with her."

The policeman actually smiled at me like we were playing some stupid game, and he was about to say "checkmate." "You're telling me her cat told you there was an intruder in the house?"

"Yes!" I shouted like a game show contestant. Feeling his contempt, I tried to explain, "I mean. Her cat didn't tell me. She told me it was her dead cat, so I knew it couldn't have been him."

I began shivering, and I wasn't sure if it was from the cold or from his ludicrous interrogation. "Miss Kane, how about you have a seat for a minute." He motioned for me to go to the closest police car. I shook my head, but he gripped my arm and led me toward the vehicle. When he held the back door open and tried to force me to take a seat, I did my impersonation of a cat being lowered into a bath, my fingers clinging to the body of the car as he tried to help me in.

"No!"

"You're refusing to cooperate?"

"No, I'm just not getting into the car. Look, Mrs. B wants me to spend the night with her. She's scared. Get out of my way."

His hand was on my shoulder as his other hand rested on a stun gun at his waist. "I suggest you get into the car, Miss Kane."

Something about his threat awakened the anger in me a second time, "I suggest you keep your hand off of me," I spat.

In a low voice, only loud enough for me to hear, he accused, "Here's what I think. It's a pretty peculiar situation. I don't think it's a good idea for you to be alone with Mrs. Bavcock. If I have to take you down to the station to keep you from entering her premises, I will. I may not be able to lock you up for good, but I can hold you for forty-eight hours."

I saw Mrs. Bavcock standing in her yard, desperately trying to see what was going on, worry etched on the lines of her face. Forty-eight hours. What could happen to her in that amount of time? Would he come back here? I'd already learned that a policeman staked out on our street was not enough of a deterrent to keep this creep away. Reluctantly, I agreed, "Fine, just let me tell her you don't want me to stay, and I can go somewhere else."

The overbearing, overweight, jackass of a cop followed me to where Mrs. B stood looking hopefully. I didn't want for her to know what this schmuck believed. She was frail, scared, and except for her furry roommates, she was alone. I couldn't have her thinking that I had any part in this. My lips pursed together in a thin smile when I delivered the news, "Mrs. Bavcock, I'm not going to be able to stay over tonight after all."

Her questioning glance shot between the policeman and me, "Well, why not?"

I looked at the arrogant moron beside me desperately wanting to spit out all the idiotic conclusions he had drawn, but decided that would for sure land me in jail. "Maybe another night, okay?"

"I don't understand, Candy." Her eyes began clouding with fright again, and I reached over her pristine white picket fence to try to reassure her that she would be safe, when the dork in blue held his hand up to stop me.

Nothing escaped Mrs. B. She saw his hand block me. I didn't offer an answer to her unspoken question, instead saying, "I'll call you tomorrow, Mrs. Bavcock. Have one of the officers check all your rooms before they leave, and then lock your door tight when they go. Don't open it for anyone."

She pressed her lips together, not understanding my change of heart. As I waved my goodbye, I made a straight line to Dave's truck. The same cop was just a few paces behind me. I'd watched enough television to know he was operating on theory only, which was fine because his conclusions were absurd, and unless he fabricated some sort of evidence, I would never be charged with anything.

He stuck out his chest as if trying to intimidate me. I wasn't biting. "I have a few more questions for you."

Ignoring his words and still fuming at him, "Great. Let me know when your boss wants to talk to me. I'm done talking to you." I climbed into the truck, and he grabbed hold of my door. Instead of quietly going away, I shouted, "One more thing. If anything happens to that little old lady because you stopped me from staying here to protect her, I'll talk to every reporter from here to New York City. I'll post interviews on Facebook,

YouTube and anywhere else I can find. I'll make it my mission to tell the whole world what a moron this city has working for it!"

Coolly, he responded, "That sounds suspiciously like a threat."

"No, a warning. She is your responsibility; you'd better make sure she's safe." I yanked the door free from his grasp, turned over the ignition and backed the wrong way up the street to leave because squad cars were still blocking traffic in both directions on the street.

Before I had rounded the second corner, I dialed Dave back. He picked up with a sweet tone, "Calling to wish me sweet dreams?"

I ignored his seductive words, "Not hardly. I'm not sure, but I think I just royally pissed off a cop. I'm on my way back to your place, but I'm not sure if we should stay there."

"What? Is the shooter following you?"

"No." I glanced in my rearview mirror on instinct and didn't see any headlights following me. "I don't think he's following me. Shit, I don't know anymore. Is there someplace we can go other than your apartment?"

"I'll think of somewhere. How quick can you get here?"

"Five minutes."

I hung up. When I pulled up to Dave's garage, the right side bay door opened, and he waved me in. Once I had pulled the truck inside, he closed the garage door behind me. Dave opened the driver's door to the truck for me to climb out. My hurt and anger must have still been pretty clear on my face because as I stood he gathered me in his arms. Dave's voice was full of concern when he said, "Tell me what happened."

I did, all the horrible details – everything the stupid cop had said. Dave shut off all the lights downstairs then guided me toward the steps. I shook my head, "We should go. We can't stay. If the jackass ran your tags, he knows this is your address. It won't be long until they bust in here."

"My registration and driver's license both have my address listed as Mr. Kravitz's house. I called Kravitz to fill him in on what was going on. He won't give them this address. If they pull my tax records, they could find this address, but if the cops think you had anything to do with what's gone on, I don't think we have to worry about their investigative skills. We'll be fine." He paused for a minute then gave my hand a gentle tug that sent shivers through my body, "Come upstairs."

A part of me started to argue, especially remembering what the jackass cop had said about the assault charge. Before I could say anything, Dave moved in close holding one solitary finger to my lips. "Shhh, come upstairs." Halfway up, on the step where he had sent my senses into a tailspin with his kiss, I remembered exactly why I ran back to him.

He turned the lights on in the apartment. Dave went to the kitchenette and opened the refrigerator. He uncapped a strawberry wine cooler and handed it to me. I gratefully took it. Underage drinking was nothing compared to what they were considering charging me with, and at this point, I seriously needed something to calm down. As I stood in his kitchenette, one of the policeman's questions was still bothering me: Dave was a person of interest in multiple crimes. "Dave, how'd you get away from the cops today?"

"It wasn't that hard. One of them left the room to get a coffee. The one who stayed with me after the doctor finished up was on the phone with his wife, engrossed in a conversation about a water leak in their basement. I walked out while he was on the phone."

"One of the cops at Mrs. Bavcock's house said you assaulted a police officer today."

"Assault? Not hardly."

"So how'd you get away?"

"Like I said: I walked out of the room when the one was on the phone. I saw the second one as I was going to the elevator. He tried to stop me, so I pushed a tray on wheels at him in the hallway, then took off up the stairs. By the time he got in the stairway, I could hear him going down. I went up to the fourth floor and hid in a supply closet. When no one found me, I got the idea to sneak out at the next shift change. I found a pair of scrubs, a coat jammed into a box on a shelf, and I walked out with a crowd of nurses from the hospital. When I was trying to figure out how to get out of the garage, I saw your car parked inside."

That didn't sound like much of an assault charge. He pushed a tray on wheels at the policeman? Maybe the cop had embellished the story so he wouldn't get in trouble for wandering off for a cup of coffee. I doubted the truthfulness about Dave being a person of interest in several crimes, too. There was nothing in his demeanor or actions that would make me believe he was any kind of a criminal.

"Any other crimes I should know about?"

"What? No. Why are you asking?"

"The cop said you were a person of interest in several crimes. Why would he say that if it weren't true?"

Dave looked baffled. "I have no idea. The last thing I did that involved the police was to report graffiti spray painted on my garage." He paused, then added, "Candy, I'm not a criminal."

CHAPTER 15

A question had bothered me; after the almost-interrogation on the street in my neighborhood by the stupid cop, I couldn't let it fester. I insensitively blurted out, "So why didn't you ever tell me you had a brother?"

Dave shrugged his shoulders, but held my gaze. "It never came up."

"Oh, come on. As much as I complained about my two sisters, you never once thought I would be interested that you had a brother?" I sensed there was more to the story. I took a big swig of the strawberry goodness and took a seat on the sofa, crossing my legs in front of me and pulling them to my chest. "Is he your twin brother? Because he looked just like you."

Dave smiled more to himself than to me, "No. Mark's two years older than I am." He stood in the little kitchen, making no move to sit with me.

"You said you haven't seen him in a while. When was the last time you talked to him?"

Dave placed his hands on the chair in front of him, as if he needed the support. "I think I was five, maybe six."

I felt my eyes grow wide, "You haven't seen your brother in fifteen years?"

Dave's gaze drifted off to the far wall, his voice distant, "Something like that."

Questions flooded me, but I didn't want to dig too deep and have him shut me out. Gingerly I prodded, "Where's he been?"

"I don't know."

I felt like I should ease up on my questions, this was obviously a sensitive subject, but I couldn't stop myself. "How can you not know where your brother is?"

Dave sighed. He slowly walked toward the couch, eyeing the empty space beside me. He took a seat just within arm's reach of me and answered, "It's complicated."

I scooted closer to him, reached out and took his hand in mine, "You don't have to talk about it if you don't want to, but if you do, I'll listen."

Dave's eyes stared at my fingers intertwined with his. I didn't think he was going to say anything. After several minutes his gaze shifted to the far wall of the little apartment where the picture of the '65 Mustang hung. His voice was low, barely above a whisper. "Our dad left. Mom didn't take it well. She stopped coming out of her bedroom for days at a time, sometimes longer. When she did come out, she wasn't really there. I don't remember Dad. When I try, I can picture Mom's face, but I doubt I could recognize her if I saw her on the street."

I already knew this much about his life. In high school I had been curious, and I had asked him how he got into foster care. He told me his mom didn't want him and had signed over her parental rights to the state before Dave went to kindergarten. When I asked him if his dad was dead,

Dave told me he didn't remember his father. He had never mentioned a brother – not even once.

"Mark and I got placed in a foster home together in the beginning. The couple was nice, but I don't think either of them were prepared for two little boys who basically had been taking care of themselves. I had never had any rules, so when a bunch were thrust on the two of us, I didn't adjust well."

I squeezed his hand lightly, but he didn't react or move his gaze in the slightest. I asked, "The two of you were moved?"

Dave shook his head, "No, just me."

Confused, I pressed, "Wait, the foster family kept your brother but sent you back to the state? I thought they always tried to keep siblings together."

"They try, but if it looks like one of the kids is going to be a problem, it's up to the foster family. Margaret and Dewey wanted to keep Mark. I was the reject. Our case worker said I had some sort of attachment disorder. She told Margaret and Dewy I might never adjust. She removed me so that Mark had a shot with them."

I stared at this beautiful man sitting next to me. He had always seemed so withdrawn and alone: I chalked it up to being abandoned by his mother. His words were methodical, as if he were a doctor describing a clinical procedure. It sounded as if he had distanced himself from this memory long ago. "You said you didn't adjust well? What's that mean?"

A forced grin showed on his face, but his eyes were still focused on the Mustang picture on the far wall. "I just didn't conform. After I left Dewey and Margaret's house, I was placed with a new foster family, a few months later, a third. Somewhere in the mix, my case worker changed. The new one wasn't assigned to Mark. Every time I saw her, which was next to never, she said Mark was fine, but I bet she didn't have a clue where my brother was or, for that matter, who he was."

"But you've always lived here?"

"No. I was in Missouri to start with, but one of my foster families wanted to adopt me. They did all the paperwork, got all the sign-offs, and then my foster father got a transfer out of state with his job. It looked like they were going to have to give me back to the state of Missouri until the adoption was approved. He must have had some friends somewhere because a couple days before my case worker was supposed to pick me up and place me in a group home, they got approval from Missouri for me to move with them to Nebraska."

I knew this wasn't the end of the story. When I met Dave, he was living with a vile woman two miles from my house. That couldn't have been the foster mother who wanted to adopt him. "So what happened?"

"A couple days before the adoption was supposed to go through, Troy and Shelia had some outrageous fight and ended up separating. Eventually they divorced. Shelia wanted to keep me, but she didn't work, so the state of Missouri wouldn't let her adopt me on her own."

Not fully comprehending, I asked, "So you were sent back to Missouri?"

"When the adoption didn't go through, a new case worker was assigned who, once again, didn't know me from a stray dog. The new case worker reviewed my file and decided I was adjusting better in Nebraska and somehow got me transferred – she decided to make me Nebraska's problem."

Dave didn't look at me the whole time. The strain in his voice told me this was something he didn't talk about. "How old were you when you moved here?"

He shook his head. "I must have been nine. I was in fourth grade. I can still remember Shelia telling me she was going to get a job and petition the state to be my foster mom again. I never heard from her after I left her house."

My heart ached. How could one person go through so much? "Your brother, you never saw him after you were five?"

Dave squeezed my hand, but said nothing. Instead, he stood up from where we had been sitting on the couch and went over to the bed. I couldn't tell if he needed privacy or what, but he didn't answer me. His nerves were raw. I took another sip of the wine cooler, wondering what could possibly be the right move.

A friend would poke and prod until she got out everything he had been holding in. If it were me, there's no way Libby would be sitting here on the sofa right now if I had just walked away. The pain in his eyes had been nearly unbearable to watch. Dave and I had just reconnected this morning, and I wondered if after everything we had gone through today, would added questions about his brother re-spark our friendship or drive a wedge between us.

The fiery kiss we had shared an hour or so ago was nowhere to be found. A coolness that had nothing to do with the temperature blanketed the air. If I were being honest with myself, the kiss had me re-evaluating our friendship. Friends didn't kiss. I hadn't kept in contact with him after high school, so how good of a friend had I been?

I wanted to comfort him. I wanted to share every minute detail of meeting his brother last night, and I wanted him to open up to me, but if I pushed too hard, would he push me away? It had been months since a man gave me goose bumps. Who was I kidding? No man had ever given me goose bumps before.

I downed what was left of the wine cooler. Glancing toward the refrigerator, I wondered if trying to find a little more liquid courage might not be in order. I wasn't much of a drinker, so weighing my options, a second drink would likely knock me out. I unlaced my boots and set them neatly beside the couch.

I stood and stretched my arms high into the air. From this vantage Dave was lying on the bed, with several pillows lining a wooden headboard which stood halfway up the wall. His back was facing the outside of the bed, with a pillow clutched tightly to his chest. His body may have been a few feet from me, but Dave was a million miles away. I resolved not to ask anything else – if he wanted to talk, I wanted to be there to listen, but I wouldn't pry.

Gingerly walking toward his bed, I felt the weight of each step I took. As I stood beside the bed, I didn't feel right forcing myself on him. "Mind if I sit with you?"

Dave looked at me with the saddest eyes I had ever seen. I wanted to gather him in my arms and tell him everything would be fine. His hand reached out to the empty space on the bed as he wordlessly patted the area in a silent invitation.

I sat upright, a little stiff. I was the least eloquent person I knew, and the fear of saying exactly the worst possible thing scared me into an uncomfortable silence. I scooted my body a little closer to his, away from the edge of the bed. When I did, he rested his head on my thigh. Instinctively, I began stroking his hair the same way Mom had done for me when I was a little girl scared of a thunderstorm.

Neither of us spoke for a long time. His straight dark hair felt like silk between my fingers. I resisted every urge for anything other than a comforting touch. I was here for him if he needed me. My eyes began to weigh heavily as the strokes of my fingers slowed.

Dave's voice was low when he finally spoke. "Mark warned me to behave. He told me if I didn't do what I was supposed to do, they would take me away."

Moisture clouded my eye. When I didn't ask anything, he continued, "I was a little Dennis the Menace back then. Margaret or Dewey would tell us to clean our rooms: ten minutes later Mark's was spotless and I was busy drawing on walls."

Dave paused as if the memory were tearing him up, but he kept going. "Or if we were told to go to bed, Mark would go without hesitating. I would need a drink, or a snack, or to go to the bathroom, or sometimes I would just go to my room and play with toys for hours. I found a lighter by the grill and melted the vinyl siding on the house. I figured out that curtains weren't supposed to be used to build forts, too, and if they were, painting the fort's name on the curtain was frowned on."

"Mark was the perfect son. It didn't matter how many times I was scolded, or how many times Mark tried to cover for me, I was the problem child. The day our case worker came to take me away, I swore I could change. I begged them to let me stay. I pleaded for one more chance. Mark even promised he would be double-extra good if I could stay."

Dave lay with his head still propped on my thigh. I couldn't see his face but felt the moisture from his tears on my leg. "But they wouldn't listen. I don't even remember what I had done, but it must have been pretty bad. Mark held my hand in the house's front entryway. The case worker had already put what few possessions I had in her car. The last words I ever heard him say was, 'But he needs me. Don't take Davey away.'"

"Instead of answering him, the case worker asked me if I wanted ice cream. I told her I did. I let go of Mark's hand and walked out the door." Dave paused, his voice full of remorse and suppressed pain. "I think I was too young to understand I wasn't coming back. I didn't know that was the last time I would ever see Mark."

"She placed me with a new couple that night. It didn't take long for me to learn that I wasn't going back to the house where Mark was. I begged my foster mom to take me back to him. The new foster parents who took me in told my case worker that I needed to see my brother. They even offered to take me to him. She would never set it up. I started acting out, way worse than I had done with Margaret and Dewey. I kept thinking that if my new foster parents gave me back, I would go back to Margaret and Dewey's house." Dave's voice trailed off.

The memory he shared was so raw and painful it left me emotionally vacant. I hadn't known him at all. I didn't have a clue how awful his childhood had been. I wanted to say the right thing, but there were no words. I just lay there holding him. I slid down beside him on the bed, draping my arm over his broad shoulder. Nothing I could say would offer even a sliver of comfort to this man who deserved so much more.

"When acting out didn't work and I had been placed in several new homes without Mark, I tried a new tactic. I became the model child, hoping I could go back to Margaret and Dewey. That didn't work either."

Dave reached over and shut off the lights. He let go of the pillow he had been clutching against his chest to make room for me next to him then covered us both with a blanket. Dave pulled me into him, grasping me instead of the pillow. His fingers glided over my back in a soothing way.

I lay in the dark listening to the rhythm of his breathing. After all the chaos of the day and heartbreak of Dave's memories, I soaked in the comfort he offered me. Dave gave me a kiss on the forehead, then closed his eyes. I didn't fight sleep. I welcomed the rest after one of the worst days of my life.

CHAPTER 16

Light streamed in from the miniature windows. They were so small they had probably been converted ventilation openings. Whoever had converted this second floor into an apartment had an architect's imagination.

Reaching over to the other side of the mattress, I felt the bare sheet where Dave had been. My eyes snapped open as I scanned the little apartment – Dave wasn't here. As grimy as I felt, a shower couldn't be put off for another second. Remembering my backpack with my change of clothes was still in my car, I crept down the stairs to find Dave working on the purple pieces of a car parked in front of my Chevelle.

"Morning!" His booming voice made me want to retreat into one of his cabinets upstairs.

I waved a hand and found a smile, but couldn't answer him. Pulling the heavy door of my car, I reached into the back seat and grabbed my backpack. He stood up from where he had been bent over the pieces of car strewn on the floor and offered, "Coffee's already brewed."

A twang of familiarity grabbed me – this was like being at home. Libby was obnoxiously chipper in the morning, too. I had class in two hours. That gave me more than enough time to get cleaned up, stop by the hospital to check on Libby and still be on time to class. "I'm going to grab a shower. I'll be down in a few." As I turned to go back upstairs, I noticed my car, asking incredulously, "You replaced my windshield? When did you have time to do that?"

He smiled, "Nice, right? I had one in the back for a restore I'll be doing soon. I didn't have a chance to put it in until this morning. The glue is still curing. It'll be roadworthy in twenty minutes."

Dave was beyond belief. Thrilled with the notion that no icicles would form on my nose from the hole in front of my face, "Thanks. What do I owe you?"

He tapped his head where the gash had been, "Well, since my head did the bulk of the damage to it, it'll be my treat."

Remembering how I had slammed on the brakes trying to throw him through my windshield made me cringe. He had to know I had purposely tried to knock him out, but he was going to pay for it? "Don't be silly. Tell me what I owe you."

Dave stepped toward me, his hands slid down my arms as he smiled and looked squarely into my eyes. "You're paid in full." He stood looking down on me for a second, his voice softer as he added, "Thanks for last night."

The memory of last night crawled back into my consciousness. My heart still ached for him, but the distant stare I had seen him wear last night was gone. He looked. . . hopeful. I leaned into him, absorbing his warmth, as I murmured, "Thanks." I motioned to my backpack over my shoulder, "Um, I'm going to grab that shower."

Dave let go of me as I headed for the stairs.

The bathroom was underwhelming. The room was hardly bigger than my closet. I was greeted by a metal freestanding shower with a vinyl shower curtain, and an avocado green sink and toilet. It was easy to forgive the bathroom's appearance when I turned on the water: the high pressure head shot scalding hot water into the shower stall. It felt so incredible I would have stayed until I had emptied the water heater if I weren't a guest – wanting to check on Libby was another reason not to camp out under the shower head.

A small cabinet hanging to the left of the mirror held towels, each stacked neatly. Drying off was difficult because it looked like I was in a steam room. I hadn't brought my hair dryer and opened the doors to the cabinet under the sink hopefully. I found a few toiletries, all standing label first, lined up perfectly, and spaced evenly from each other. I had never seen a more organized bathroom storage area. Everything in Dave's life was neat and orderly – everything except me. In contrast, I was a walking mess.

With my skin still partially damp, I dug through my backpack and found a sweater and jeans. I wondered what I was going to do about my hair. I couldn't go outside like this: my hair would freeze.

I tried to put the shampoo and conditioner back under the sink the way I had found it, hung the towel neatly beside the one already on the rack, and looked for anything that might be out of place. As I stepped out of the bathroom, Dave sat on his bed waiting for me. I sat on the couch to put my boots back on.

I still looked like a wet rat, but at least I didn't smell like one anymore. Dave's eyes locked on mine as he held out a steaming mug. It smelled wonderful. I was expecting coffee, but when I brought it to my lips, it tasted like a mocha latte. "Mmmm," my voice offered in thanks.

Dave smiled, "It's coffee with a kick. A packet of hot chocolate in a regular cup of coffee is a double shot of caffeine and a pretty sweet way to start the morning."

I drained it quickly, not sure if it was because of the taste or the fact that I had no idea what to say about everything he had shared with me last night. I had always been a restless sleeper, but after we drifted off to sleep, his strong arms held me all night. Regardless of the awful memories he had shared or my own circumstance, I had never felt safer.

At the forefront of my mind was the fact that he had a brother he hadn't seen in over fifteen years. Mark somehow knew the guy who had attacked Libby, scared Mrs. Bavcock and stalked me. It could have been an innocent relationship. For Dave's sake as much as mine, I hoped it was. I didn't want for Mark to be involved.

That kiss yesterday on Dave's stairs was unexpected. If I hadn't have gone to check on Mrs. Bavcock, I'm not sure where that kiss may have taken us. Dave had always been so guarded, not just around me, but with everyone. Last night when he opened up, it was as if once he started telling me about his past, he couldn't stop.

Through the night, memories of his electric kiss and the passion seeped into my dreams while stories of being ripped away from the only family he knew got all jumbled together. I wasn't sure where that left us. I wanted to be strong and supportive because I felt his pain last night, but I wanted to be more than a shoulder for him to unload on, too.

I should have had something profound to say: something to the effect that I would help him find his brother, or that I wanted to be tangled up in his bed again with him tonight, or maybe that I was here for him if he needed me. But the words didn't come. None of them. This new Dave was a stark contrast to the one I had purposely befriended in high school. Back then he was someone who looked like he needed someone to care, but for the life of me, I couldn't get close enough to learn why I felt that way.

Now, knowing the secrets he carried with him, he did need me. He was successful, strong, protective, and could send shivers through my body with just a light caress. Wet hair or not, I needed to get out of here before I made a complete fool of myself. I would say something either stupid or profoundly inappropriate. I liked where this relationship was going, but I didn't want to rush it.

Walking over to the opposite side of the little studio, I set the cup in the sink. "Well, I'm going to go check on Libby."

His eyebrows drew together, "You think that's a good idea?"

"It's early. Stalkers don't get up this early. Besides, if she's awake, I want to see her."

Dave stood up and moved to the sink, rinsing out the cup I had set there. "How would you know? How many stalkers have you had?" He asked good-naturedly. Before I could answer he offered, "I'll go to the hospital with you. Just give me a minute to put a sign on the front door."

He had already shut his business down yesterday because of me. I couldn't let him screw things up with his customers again. Based on my conversation with the policeman last night, having him out and about with an assault charge was a seriously bad idea, as well. "That's okay. It's Thursday, I've got a morning class, too. I haven't been able to get ahold of Libby's dad to tell him, either."

Dave squeezed my shoulder and looked down into my eyes, "I could try to help you find her dad, then we could go pick up your assignments. You could work on them here. If you tell your teachers what's going on, they'll let you slide."

"Speaking from experience?"

"Yeah, I was the king of 'I need more time' when I was in school."

"That was high school. I'm paying for this. If I wanted to learn from a book on my own, I wouldn't have written the tuition check. I'll be fine."

Dave put both his hands on my shoulders as his brown eyes warned mine, "I don't remember you being this stubborn. At least let me try to help to find her dad. What's his name?"

Defensively I flared, "Henry Merrick. And what do you mean stubborn?"

"Uh, yeah, you've got some killer stalking you, so I think you can skip a couple classes."

"And do what?"

"You can have the run of my apartment. I won't bother you. I'll be downstairs if you need me."

Run of his apartment? Like from one wall to another? "As enticing as that sounds," and spending more time with him today did seem decent, "I have a test to retake from yesterday."

Dave's hands squeezed my shoulders, as shivers erupted in my body. "I'd feel better if you were here – where I could be sure you were safe."

Leaning into him, I whispered a soft kiss on his lips, "I'm glad you'll miss me."

"I wouldn't miss you if you were here. I'd much rather not miss you."

Grinning, "I don't want to become a piece of furniture. I'll be back this afternoon." I started for the stairs, but paused at the top step long enough to see the disappointment shining back at me through his eyes.

"You could never be a piece of furniture." After a second he offered, "Hey, want to go to Bank Shot tonight and see if anyone knows Mark?"

Inwardly I sort of cringed. The only one I knew who would know Mark was one of the guys who was responsible for turning my life upside down – Teddy. After everything he had told me last night, there was no way I would deny him. "Sounds great. I'll be back late this afternoon."

Holding his position near the kitchen sink, he offered, "If you need me, for anything, call me."

A warmth spread through my body. I had no doubt he would drop everything if I needed him, not that I wanted to be someone who wasn't capable of operating independently. It made me feel good that Dave was only a phone call away. I blew him a playful kiss from the stairs and went to my car.

Dave followed me down the steps. I climbed into my car as he lifted the lever to let me out of the garage. Dave's expression was sad. . . maybe not sad – concerned. My hand rested at the top of the steering wheel as I gave him a quick wave and rolled out onto the street.

I spent less than fifteen minutes at the hospital, after conferring with Libby's doctor again and finding there had been no change. She was still sedated. Larry had spent the night in the waiting room. I offered to get him some coffee, but he held up an empty paper cup tucked under his chair.

Looking at my watch, I still had plenty of time. I drove toward the east side of town. It was too early for Bank Shot to be open, but I had an incessant need to drive by anyway. I slowed as I approached its empty parking lot. Thirty-six hours ago, this place had been nothing more than a means to an end, now it had a near sinister feel to it.

An image of Chris flashed in my mind. Regret clouded the image as I wondered if the psycho stalker had come looking for him, too. But why would he? For that matter, why would this guy be chasing *me*? Four hundred bucks was nothing, well, it was something, but it wasn't worth what he had done to both Libby and me.

School was a breeze. I expected to completely blow the test I had missed, but it was pretty easy. My lack of studying between Tuesday night and this morning had me nervous, but I was feeling much better after having finished it. As I emerged from the building where my last class had been, bright sunlight hit my face. It was still sub-zero outside, but something about feeling the sun was a real treat. Most of the winter was day after day of gray overcast skies. The sun's bright rays did something to me and put the events of the past two days in a better perspective.

Libby had been attacked, but her doctor was optimistic. However, he had reminded me several times they wouldn't know the extent of her injuries until after the swelling went down. Larry was spending night and day looking out for her – something I couldn't do if I had any hope of finding the lunatic who did this to her. Mr. Sanders had given me a week off with pay. When he had first offered, I was stunned. I sort of figured I'd take a couple days then let him know I'd be ready to come back, but I hadn't even driven past the place since I picked up my car yesterday morning. It was on one of the major streets, so I must have subconsciously avoided the gas station not to drive by it.

I turned the key to unlock my car door when a voice I hadn't expected came from a car parked right next to mine. "I've been waiting for you."

My body froze. Cycling through all the familiar voices, I didn't need to turn in its direction to know who it belonged to. I didn't turn toward him. If he had a gun trained on me, I didn't want to see it. Instead, I answered, "Hey, Tony. Does Teddy know you're here?"

CHAPTER 17

"Of course not. You know what he'd do to me, right?" I had backed my car into my usual space this morning. Tony's car was pulled into the parking spot beside mine so our driver's doors were side-by-side.

I whirled on him, "I've got a pretty decent idea. What the hell is going on?"

Sheepishly Tony answered, "I wish I knew. I overheard Teddy talking to Grey last night. Are you okay?"

"No, I'm not okay. Neither is Libby. Is Grey the guy who attacked us?"

Tony looked around the lot to see if there were any prying ears. Satisfied that there weren't, he started to answer, "Grey's bad. . ." He stopped abruptly. "Look, do you have somewhere you can go for a couple weeks? Grey and Teddy have short attention spans. If you can just disappear for a couple weeks, they'll lose interest."

"Disappear for a couple weeks? I can't just go into hiding."

Tony shook his head, "They aren't going to let it go right away. They're both on some insane adrenaline rush."

Disbelief colored my words, "Over four hundred bucks? Grey robbed my gas station for more than that."

"It doesn't make sense to me, either. Teddy just moved here from Kansas City. Grey came up to visit. I had met Grey a few times when I lived there. Just trust me. If you ever wanted to take a vacation, now is the time to take it."

I shook my head. I wasn't going to be bullied, not by these two losers or by the cops. If the two had known each other in Kansas City, maybe they had a record. Tony was already helping me. How much help would he give me if one of the crazies was his brother? One question, above everything else needed an answer. "How is Mark involved?"

Surprise registered on Tony's face at my question. "Mark? Mark Brewer? He wouldn't get his hands dirty with any of this."

Relief engulfed me. "How can I get a hold of him?"

"You don't get a hold of Mark. No one does. But that's someone you better never cross. You think my brother and Grey are bad news, they've got nothing on him."

My heart sank. Dave's brother was worse than Teddy and Grey? I felt the hair on my arms prickle under my sweater. Who could be worse than a hot-headed murderer and his sore-loser sidekick? I didn't doubt the sincerity in Tony's words, but what would have possessed him to try to warn me? "Why are you here?"

Tony looked nervous. "Your friend is the first one to get the better of Teddy, ever. I knew he was mad; I didn't know how mad at the time. Look, deep down he's not a bad guy. He had never been hustled before."

Did Tony know what the two of them had done? If he did, why wouldn't he have turned them in? "You know that Grey guy put Libby in the hospital, shot at me, shot a friend of mine, robbed the gas station where I work, and broke into one of my neighbor's houses?"

"I heard. That's why I'm here. They were both out looking for you last night, and when they couldn't find you, they decided you probably skipped town. You need to lie low so they keep thinking it, or better yet – leave town." Tony gave me a menacing scowl, "Coming to school today was a dumb move."

With a confidence woven into my answer that I didn't feel, I answered, "I'm not scared of either of them."

"Then you're an idiot, because both of them scare the shit outta me." Tony put his car in gear. "Pack up. Seriously, just leave for a couple weeks until this blows over. Right now they're both so hyped up neither is thinking straight."

I appreciated that Tony was trying to look out for me in his own way, but I needed more information about Dave's brother. Before he could drive away, I reached out and put my hand on Tony's driver's side door. "Tell me where I can find Mark."

"He doesn't live here. He comes through town every now and again to do business."

"What kind of business?"

"None I want to know about. Stay clear of all three of them. Don't go back to Bank Shot. Don't go to any places you would usually go."

Tony drove away. As I looked around the parking lot, I was suddenly acutely aware of the fact that I was alone. Mark blew through town to do business? He was worse than a killer? If I told Dave what Tony had just said, what would he do with this information? Dave told me he wanted to go to Bank Shot tonight, but from what Tony said, that would be one of the places Grey and Teddy would be looking.

I didn't know how accurate Tony's information was. Maybe he was wrong about Mark. As I watched Tony's car disappear around a corner, the reality of everything sank in. Grey knew where I worked, so even if I didn't want to take the full week off, going back to the gas station was a no go. Did he know I also worked at Cookie's Cuisine? I was due in again on Saturday. I had told Teddy that I was in college. There were several colleges in town, but my car stuck out – he could easily find it the same way Tony had, by just cruising parking lots. I couldn't go home even if I wanted to: it would be a crime scene for the foreseeable future.

My head was spinning, and I had the overwhelming urge to retch. I doubled over, waiting to see if my body was going to unload my lunch. My hands began shaking, and the cold from the air was doing little to cool the bile and heat rising inside of me. I took in several deep breaths, filling my lungs with the arctic air.

As I stood next to my car, grateful that my body hadn't betrayed me after all, I let Tony's words marinate for another minute. I hadn't seen Mom and Dad since summer, not even for Christmas. New Mexico was sounding better by the second, but even if I could swing a trip down to see them, I didn't want Libby to wake up without me. Then there was Dave. I liked where things had started to go with us yesterday. He was so much different than the guy I thought I knew. I wanted to get to know him better.

What little relationship advice my sister Kim had given me, she was adamant that starting any kind of a relationship under stressful circumstances was never a good idea. It was too tough to sort out what feelings were real and which ones were fed by insecurity. Maybe it would be best if I hit the road for a couple weeks as Tony had suggested. Dave wasn't going anywhere. If I left, he would be here when I got back. Maybe if I were gone, Libby would be safer.

The cold air began to permeate my jacket. My shaking fingers I had from fear had morphed into shivers from the cold. I took a seat in my car and turned the heater on full-blast. Eyeing my phone, my fingers dialed a self-preservation call. When the call connected, Mom's voice picked up, "Hello?"

Sounding as cheerful as possible, I said, "Hi, Mom. What're you and Dad doing?"

"Dad's at work, and I'm watching Rachel." My mom was a Rachel Ray fanatic. I didn't give her a hard time about it because dinner was rarely boring. I missed that since they had left. Dinner nowadays was Ramen noodles or whatever was on sale.

A little less enthusiastically I offered, "I was thinking of taking a road trip."

"Here? What about school?"

"Spring break is next week. You want some company?" That was a lie. Spring break was still four weeks away, but she wouldn't check. Once she and Dad left, they stopped paying attention to the little things in my schedule. Lots of students went south for spring break, so this shouldn't give her any cause for concern.

"Oh, I'd love that Candy, but it's such a long drive. Do you think Kim or Carly might want to drive down with you?"

Although I technically loved both of my sisters, I didn't want to be stuck in a car with either of them. Kim was seriously self-absorbed, and Carly seemed like she intended to be a career-student. She had been at Midland University in Freemont for four years with no tangible end in sight. "I haven't mentioned it to either of them yet. I wanted to make sure you had a guest room before I made any big plans."

"There is always room for you. But call your sisters to see if one of them will drive down with you. I don't like the idea of you driving that far alone."

"If they can't, I'll see if another friend wants to come along."

Mom answered, "It would be great to see Libby again. Will she be able to get off of work?" I couldn't tell Mom what had happened two nights ago: she'd be on the next flight back. That would completely defeat the purpose of the road trip. Sadly, even if there were no threat from Teddy or Grey, I didn't think I could even say what had happened to Libby out loud yet.

"I'll see."

Mom began telling me about her latest adventures. She was treating her new surroundings as if she were semi-retired and had several new interests. She had taken up knitting, scrapbooking, and extreme couponing. One afternoon she had called to brag that she was able to purchase $150 worth of groceries for less than $15.

At the time I had been envious, thinking this was a hobby Libby and I needed to take up. Then I learned she had forty boxes of cereal and at least that many boxes of cake mix – neither she nor Dad ate cereal for breakfast, and I couldn't imagine eating that much cake in a year.

She broke off in mid-sentence, as if sensing through the phone that I wasn't listening. "Candy, is there anything wrong?"

Taken a little by surprise, I answered, "No. Why would you ask?"

"I'm not sure. I just worry about you and Libby sometimes. I know I shouldn't. You've got a good head on your shoulders." She paused a few seconds, "Of the three, you were always the one I knew would be able to take care of herself."

Pride welled up in me. The shakes, whether they were from the cold or the fear, stopped in that moment. "I'm fine, Mom. I just miss you and Dad."

"Well, if that's all it is, get packed and come on down. But if there is something more going on. . ." She trailed off briefly, as if knowing I was keeping something from her, "But if you're having a problem, running away from it isn't the answer."

My breath hitched at her words. She was right. I had never run away from anything in my life. Despite how meager our existence was, Libby and I were making it on our own without any help from anyone. I cringed at the thought of her hospital bills. She would owe thousands by the time she was released. Or rather, we would owe thousands. It might not be my name on the bill, but I'd find a way to help her make good on them because that is exactly what Libby would do if our roles were reversed.

Mom's words were exactly what I needed to hear. Still sitting in my car in the parking lot – my decision was made. I wouldn't go to New Mexico, or anywhere else. Despite Tony's prodding, I had gotten us into this mess, I would get us out if it. The fear that had tried to attach itself to me diminished marginally. I wouldn't let it own me. I wouldn't let any of what had happened in the last couple days define me.

I hung up with Mom, a new determination boiling to the surface. Moving the stick shift to first, my mind was made up. I had some work to do, starting right now.

CHAPTER 18

My car eased into the visitor parking lot outside the police station. I had one advocate: at least I hoped his support hadn't been an act two nights ago. I needed his help. The sun was still shining brightly from the western sky, but the afternoon warmth was quickly diminishing. Turning off my car, I looked at myself in the rearview mirror: the eyes looking back were haggard. Too much had already happened, and more ugliness might be right around the corner. "*You can do this*," I told myself. As I swung the heavy door closed, I tucked my chin inside the neck of my coat and sprinted for the police station's front door.

Inside the heavy metal doors was a grand entryway. A large sign with an arrow pointing toward the steps, read, "All Visitors MUST report to the 2nd Floor Desk Sergeant." The police station had an intimidating feel to it, as if the designers purposely erected the most daunting entrance they could manage. Tall thin windows stood at attention along both sides of the entryway. The ripple in the lead-glass of the window panes gave away their age. A thin wooden overhang shielded the radiators on the floor running the length of the windows.

The floor and steps of the police station were a brilliant pattern of granite. The tan, brown, and black swirls were peppered with flakes of some shiny mineral, giving the appearance of gold dust embedded within. Thin black no-skid strips ran the length of each granite step. These strips seemed to be a minor precaution given the number of wet boots full of melting snow that likely climbed these steps.

As I emerged onto the second floor, an enormous wooden desk with two uniformed police officers greeted me. I unzipped my coat and draped it over my arm. No other visitors stood in front of the counter, and neither of the uniformed policemen looked up from their computer monitors to acknowledge I was there. I sized up the officer on the right as I stood in front of the intimidating desk. He was trim, having an athletic appearance which contrasted with the milky-pink complexion of his wrinkled skin. The policeman was bald on top, but a thin strip of light red hair, trimmed close, reached around the sides of his head. I'm not saying the guy was old, but if he were milk, I wouldn't put him back in the refrigerator. His tie was straight and his uniform shirt had enough starch to hold him in place for a month.

His words were kind, but the tone with which they were delivered was condescending. "How can I help you?" The officer barely glanced at me while he was doing something he obviously believed was important on his computer.

Standing up straight and in the most direct voice I could project, I said, "I need to see Officer Brown."

The officer rolled his eyes, "Which Officer Brown?"

"Um, Charlie Brown."

The officer looked at a large white board propped up against the wall and pulled off a single sheet of paper that had been stuck to it with a magnet. Still choosing not to make eye contact with me, he asked, "Do you have an appointment?"

"No. I didn't know I needed one. I just wanted to talk to him."

"He's out on patrol. You'll need to make an appointment with him." Finally turning toward me, he allowed his eyes to rove over me. They gazed at me from the boots I wore, pausing slightly at my hips, all the way up to my chest. He must have liked what he was leering at because a disgusting grin appeared on his face, which made the whole incident that much more gross.

"Fine." Taking a few steps away from the desk, I dug through my purse and found the business card Officer Brown had given me before I made my way back down to the first floor. I dialed the number and he picked it up on the first ring.

"Brown."

"Hi, Officer Brown." I scowled in the direction of the jerk who had basically dismissed me without even offering to call him. "It's Candy Kane from the other night. Are you busy?"

"Hey, I always have time for someone whose name is almost as ridiculous as mine. What's up?"

"I'm at the police station. I wanted to talk to you, but the desk sergeant said you were out on patrol, so I need to make an appointment to see you."

"He what? That must be Lewis. Short guy, no hair, a real affinity to starch?"

Officer Brown's description of the schmuck behind the desk tickled me, "That's the one."

"He's a putz. I'm on the fourth floor right now. Give me a minute and I'll come get you."

True to his word, Officer Brown walked down the steps and straight over to the uniform sitting behind the desk. "I need a visitor badge for Miss Kane." Officer Brown reached for a tattered white binder, setting on top of the desk with large block letters marked "VISITOR" and handed it to me. Neither of the two police officers looked happy to see each other. Once I had filled out my information in the binder, Officer Lewis gave me a red plastic badge with a clip on the back and an enormous "V" written in bright red on the front.

Officer Brown led me up to the fourth floor, then directed me into a small conference room halfway down the hallway. The walls were decorated with police academy graduation photos. His eyes looked around the tiny room holding a small table and four chairs. "My desk is in a bull pen, so this at least has a little privacy. What's on your mind?" Officer Brown took a seat and motioned for me to take one across the little table from him.

"First, I wanted to say thanks for the other night. I was pretty freaked out, and you were great to me."

He fished in his pocket and pulled out a business card. A genuine look of concern crept over his face as he offered the card to me, "I should have given you this Tuesday night. Here's a number you can call. The people who run this hotline help crime victims all the time."

He thought I wanted his help because I was scared? Well, I was sort of scared, but not from the robbery by itself. I started to give the hotline card back to him, but reconsidered and tucked it in my wallet. "Do you know what all has happened?"

"I can't discuss the specifics of an ongoing investigation, even with one of the victims, I'm sorry." He waited a second, as if to drive the point home, then added, "Those are the rules."

I didn't need a lesson on investigative protocol. I needed that jackass from last night read the riot act for being such a douche. "Last night there was a home invasion in one of my neighbor's houses. It was the same guy who beat up Libby, shot at me at the gas station, and broke into my house yesterday morning."

Given his reaction, it looked as though he was aware of all four incidents. "Look, Candy, it's all part of an investigation. I can't share any of the details with you. If you want police protection, I can arrange a detail." Reminding him that the protection on our street did Mrs. Bavcock no good would have been rude.

"I don't want protection. I need you to find this guy. I found out this afternoon that the guy's first name is Grey."

Officer Brown's expression changed, "And what is your source?"

"Teddy's little brother, Tony, paid me a visit at school today. He told me I needed to get out of town. He said Grey and Teddy were both looking for me." When Officer Brown didn't say anything, I concluded, "But you already knew his name because I used the security camera to zoom in on his license plate at the gas station and you checked his credit card receipt. Right?"

Officer Brown shook his head, "The license plate on the Nova had been stolen off of a late model GMC truck. The credit card was also stolen. Tell me everything Tony told you today."

"That was pretty much it. He said Grey and Teddy were both bad news, and he told me I needed to get out of town. I asked him about another guy who had been at the bar, but Tony said that other guy wasn't involved."

I wasn't sure where it had materialized from, but Officer Brown was taking notes on a small notebook in front of him, "Who was this other guy? You didn't mention him Tuesday night."

I teetered on whether I should tell him the truth or not. I knew his name, heck, I probably knew more about Mark than was in any police database, but I wasn't convinced he had anything to do with what had happened to Libby and me. From the way Tony had described Mark, implicating him could be bad on lots of levels if I were wrong. The last thing I wanted to do was to cause trouble for Mark, and possibly for Dave.

"It doesn't matter because Tony says everything that has happened is Teddy and Grey." I watched Officer Brown's expression. His face was relaxed; his green eyes watched me the way a cat observes a mouse: interested, paying attention to each minute detail.

Feigning ignorance, Officer Brown said, "I was under the impression the other man's name was Mark Brewer. Do you have any further information to share? Is there anything else you neglected to tell me Tuesday?"

Crap. These cops were comparing notes, and he no doubt knew about my run-in with the jerk cop from last night. He believed I was withholding information from him? Well, I was, but nothing important. Did he agree with what the stupid cop from last night accused me of? That I was involved? He must have noticed my reaction because Officer Brown restated his question, "I'm sorry – not neglected. You were in shock. Have you remembered anything else that might help us with the investigation?"

"No. But after that Grey guy broke into my neighbor's house last night, one of the cops basically accused me of being involved. I didn't cook this up. I wouldn't hurt Libby or scare Mrs. Bavcock." My emotions were gaining momentum, and I needed to get them under control.

Officer Brown nodded, "That was Fletcher." I raised my brow. Officer Brown clarified, "The officer on the scene who made those accusations – his name's Fletcher. He's very by-the-book, and his gut tells him there is no way something this elaborate was done over such a small amount of cash."

A sliver of hopelessness began gripping me, "What do you think?"

His hand reached across the table in a comforting way, "I saw you at the gas station, Candy. People can't fake that kind of fear. Your reaction is on the gas station's surveillance recordings." He paused, looking me directly in the eye. "No one can convince me you had anything to do with it."

A breath escaped that I had held involuntarily, "So, you believe me?"

"It doesn't matter what I believe. It only matters what I can prove." He must have realized he was touching me because he pulled his hand away from mine as if I had a snake attached to my arm. "Are you planning to leave town?"

Without hesitating, I answered, "No."

"If you change your mind, call and tell me before you go. It could look suspicious if you just up and disappeared." My eyes narrowed as I wondered if I were putting too much faith in Officer Brown. Reading my expression quickly, he added, "Hey, relax. Just make sure I know where you are."

"Why, so Fletcher knows where to pick me up after he fabricates enough evidence?"

Scowling at me, he answered, "No one is fabricating any evidence. If anyone needs to corroborate one of your statements, we have to be able to get in contact with you. Being scared and wanting to go somewhere safe is a perfectly reasonable action."

"I'm not scared." My words felt stronger coming out than they sounded.

Gently, his soft green eyes warned me, "Well, you should be. This Grey guy, whoever he is, seems pretty scary. I've watched those surveillance videos a dozen times – he's a predator. Mr. Sanders said you probably didn't know about it, but there was a hidden camera inside the store pointed in on the cash register – I saw the whole thing. You're lucky to be alive. Monsters like him, they keep hunting until they catch their prey or a better mark presents itself. Let me assign a security detail to you."

"No thanks." I didn't come here to have my hand held. I came here to get the investigation focused on where it was supposed to be – not on me. "So, the stolen license plate. Where was it taken from?"

Officer Brown's eyes narrowed marginally. "Why do you ask?"

"Because Tony lives around here. He wouldn't have made a special trip to my school today to warn me if he wasn't close. I assume you got surveillance video from Bank Shot, and you have Teddy's photograph from it. You have Grey's photo from the gas station, yet I haven't seen anything on the news asking people to contact the police with information. That must mean you have some idea of who these guys are, and you're trying not to scare them off."

Officer Brown didn't comment on a single word I had said. After several seconds of silence I asked, "So if the license plate was stolen from somewhere out of town, maybe that's where Grey lives. Tony says Grey and Teddy are from Kansas City."

As if reading from a script, Officer Brown responded robotically, "We are following numerous leads."

"But you're not going to tell the public that there is a psycho stalker running loose around town?"

He looked over his shoulder toward the door, as if judging what kind of super-sonic hearing would be required to listen in on our conversation. "Every criminal is different. Sometimes, giving them any kind of notoriety in the media only leads to escalated violence."

"So you're protecting the city's population by not warning them about a murderer on the loose?"

Through gritted teeth he answered, "Not every decision is made by me, Candy."

"It seems like you're waiting for something worse to happen." The pitch of my voice grew with my frustration. "Would my body on a slab at the morgue be enough for you to re-evaluate police protocol? That would for sure remove me from the list as a 'person of interest,' right?"

"There's nothing else I can tell you. Trust me that we're looking for both of these guys."

"You want me to trust you? Fine. Do something to earn it. Last night I tried to tell Officer Fletcher that Dave Brewer was just in the wrong place at the wrong time. He didn't have anything to do with any of this. I want to drop the trespassing charges against him for breaking into my house yesterday morning."

I was pleased when Officer Brown didn't feign ignorance of the circumstances, but the hair on the back of my neck stood up when he echoed Officer Fletcher's comments, "Mr. Brewer assaulted a police officer at the hospital yesterday. That trumps trespassing."

Goosebumps peppered my arms. Dave was in serious trouble, and it was my fault. "Dave didn't lay a hand on an officer! Get your facts straight. Are you forgetting, Grey shot Dave? Get the charges dropped, then I'll know if I can trust you."

Officer Brown stood up from the table and opened the door, signifying that our talk was over. "I'll see what I can do. No promises."

Feeling surly, I shot back, "Fine. I'll see what *I* can do. No promises."

He canted his head to the side, and asked, "What's that supposed to mean?"

"You won't go to the media to warn the public? I will. You don't think the local news would bury this story, do you? I bet it'd be the top story every night for a week. Think of it: they'll be calling the mayor, the chief of police, everyone. I bet they'd love to know a citizen who tried to stop a criminal you can't find got shot, got arrested for his efforts, then got charged with assault for rolling a hospital cart at an officer."

Officer Brown's teeth were clenched. "I already told you, giving this guy any kind of notoriety can only make things worse."

"Then get Dave's charges dropped, and I'll keep my mouth shut."

He shook his head at me. I didn't like the idea of two lunatics running rampant around the city targeting me, but the idea of Dave locked up when he was just trying to help made it far worse. Rather than wait for an answer, I looked at the open door and slid through it. Officer Brown called to me before I reached the steps, "I'll see what I can do. Stay away from reporters. Where are you staying?"

"I'd be staying at Mrs. Bavcock's if. . . never mind. You've got my cell. No one needs to know where I'm staying. No promises on the reporters until I know Dave's in the clear." I took the steps two at a time back down to the Desk Sergeant to drop off my visitor badge. I had accomplished what I had set out to do. Officer Brown knew as much about this creep as I did. He was probably ticked off right now, but I couldn't afford for Dave to get locked up over something dumb. I crossed my fingers that Dave hadn't been arrested while I was at school today.

My feet felt light as I rounded the last corner of the stairs. The same scowling Officer Lewis looked up from his desk as I pulled the visitor log and wrote in my time of departure. I put the visitor badge back on the desk without a word and turned my back on him.

It hadn't felt like I had been inside long, but when I emerged from the large double doors into the visitor parking lot, darkness had fallen. A feeling of dread washed over me. I had never been scared of the dark or of being alone, but the strength and threats I had used upstairs evaporated when the cool night air hit me in the barren parking lot. I stood at the door, eyeing my car – no others were parked near it.

I had heard stories of men in shopping malls hiding under victims' cars, ready to jump out and attack as an unsuspecting person walked up. Although unlikely in a police station parking lot, I couldn't shake the dreaded feeling. When I was about twenty feet away, I angled my head down while I was walking to get a clear view of the undercarriage of my Chevelle. It was clear.

Dave had gotten into my locked car yesterday. Old cars were easy to break into. I'd locked my keys in the car lots of times, and a metal coat hanger was all it took to get inside. Before I unlocked the door, I angled my head using the illumination from the streetlight to see that no one waited for me in the back seat.

Dave was probably worried. I told him I'd be back right after school today. I hadn't counted on making a detour here. Heat wrapped itself around me as thoughts from last night began assaulting me. That kiss on the steps had curled my toes. It was unexpected and intoxicating at the same time.

Who would have thought I would ever be attracted to Dave Brewer or that he would be such an incredible kisser? My attraction initially could be blamed on his post-high school physique: the physical change was remarkable. But the attraction only intensified when I learned what he had gone through: watching his eyes light up when he talked about Mark, and the sadness they hid when he shared how he had been taken from him. I thought it was great that he was helping one of Kravitz's students who shared a similar history with him. Given the circumstances, my first reaction was that Dave would be callous about the way he had grown up; the fact that he was helping a kid who didn't have a lot of options was admirable. I felt closer to Dave, or maybe realized that I wanted to be closer to Dave.

No one should lose the one person in the world who loves them back. Dave made a conscious decision to let me into his life last night. I'd bet that what he shared with me he had shared with very few others in his life. The feelings were too raw. I hated that he was so alone. I wanted to find his brother as much as he did.

CHAPTER 19

Driving toward the west side of town, I knew I should go to Dave's place, but I couldn't help driving past Bank Shot on the way there. It was after dusk, and the city was taking on that surreal silvery look in the moonlight. The enormous neon sign of a pool cue pointing at the place's entrance was like a beacon in the night. I had promised Dave we could both come here and ask around if anyone knew Mark, but I wanted to see for myself that Chris was fine. I turned into the parking lot, but I didn't look for a parking spot. Chris drove an old orange Dodge pick-up. If I saw it in the parking lot, I'd know he was okay.

I looked at each row slowly: the truck wasn't here. My stomach lurched. He could have caught a ride in with someone else, or maybe this wasn't his night to tend bar.

If I went in and either Grey or Teddy were inside, what would I do? Libby had friends at almost every bar we went to, but those were her friends, not necessarily mine. If the two were inside, would I be able to get help from others while we waited for the police to show? I pulled up beside a mountain of snow. Whoever had been clearing the parking lot must have been trying to make a pile that would stay until summer.

Coming to Bank Shot was a bad idea – bad on too many levels. I had nearly talked myself into leaving when I decided that if I went inside and Teddy and Grey weren't there, I could see when Chris would be working. If Chris were here, I could tell him what had happened, so he could keep an eye out for the two. The best defense was a strong offense, or maybe it was the other way around, but it seemed to fit.

If the police had come to Bank Shot and asked Chris if he had seen the two without giving him details, he would be less inclined to help, knowing that he had been complicit in one of them being hustled. He needed to know what had happened to Libby. No matter how angry he was with her, he wouldn't let something like this slide.

I looked at my outfit. I wasn't in Libby's uniform for hustling pool. The bar was really dark, so most people inside wouldn't even give me a second look. If I just took a quick peek to see if Chris were there, how dangerous could that be?

The inner turmoil was silenced when I lurched my car forward into a large parking spot near the back of the lot. The parking lot looked mostly bare. As I stood, the walls of my stomach tried squeezing themselves together. I pushed through the nervousness with one foot in front of the other as the front door of the bar beckoned me to it.

Less than ten feet from the front door, a voice called out to me. "Well, if it isn't my favorite eye Candy."

I had heard this particular "pet name" at least once a month since I hit puberty. I wheeled around ready to glare at whoever decided to give me grief, when relief flooded me. Dave stood under the glow of the neon light.

Butterflies took flight in my stomach, and my unease about going inside eased. "Geeze, you scared me. All done working for the day?"

Dave was all smiles, "I'm always working." He moved toward me in long strides. He stopped a few feet short of me, making no effort to move closer. Disappointment nibbled at me. It was silly. I had just seen him this morning, but it wasn't like I was his girlfriend: he had every right to keep a little distance in public. That's what I tried to tell myself, but memories of him holding me last night had flashed through my mind a good bit of the day today. Images of those few moments on his steps seemed to be on a near constant replay. Maybe he was just shy. I took a tentative step toward him, attempting to close the space between us.

Surprise registered silently in his expression. I didn't know what he was thinking. Maybe he hadn't meant to open up so completely to me last night. I forgot my filter and asked, "What? Having second thoughts?"

Dave took a step in my direction, effectively closing the little gap that remained between us. He didn't touch me, but I felt the warmth of his body a hair's breadth from mine. In a low sexy voice, he answered, "I have lots of thoughts. Just giving you space so as not to smother you. Glad you don't need time to warm up to me."

"After last night, I think we're past the bashful stage." I stood on my tip toes and pressed a light kiss to the right of his lips. His cheek was cool and smooth as summer cherries. Holding my position a second or two longer than necessary, Dave took my hint and turned his head, pressing his lips to mine. It wasn't tentative or restrained: it was an aggressive hungry kiss that promised passion with each press of his lips.

Car lights drove up behind us, effectively interrupting the kiss that felt like a long awaited sequel to the one on his stairs. Dave was breathless, as his eyes darted around the parking lot. "Where's your car?"

Smiling, I motioned toward the bar's entrance, "We've got time for that later. We're already here. I want to see if Chris has seen anything."

Dave's face looked confused. I took his hand and began walking toward the door. I made it exactly two steps before Dave's hand boomeranged me back into his arms. His feet were planted. "We've got time for it now," he answered seductively.

He stepped into me, pressing his body wholly against mine in the dim light of the parking lot. The hunger in him grew, even more aggressive than just minutes before. Smug that I had this effect on him, I tugged at his hand a second time and broke the kiss. "This'll take ten minutes, then we can go back to your place."

He shook his head in confusion, as if not comprehending what I was telling him. "Man, this is a switch. Usually that's my line."

Smirking at him, I asked, "You say that to a lot of girls?" He smirked but didn't answer. A quick feeling of insecurity washed over me, "You're not kicking me out, right? I don't want to overstay my welcome, but there isn't much I wouldn't do for another one of your special coffees."

Dave's eyes widened fractionally as I felt his muscles tense. Then he asked the strangest question, "Candy, when did I make you coffee?"

"Sorry, didn't mean to offend you. Hot chocolate with an extra shot of caffeine or whatever you call it."

All hint of flirtation disappeared in front of me when his voice turned serious and he asked, "Are you medicated or something?"

"Um, no. Call it whatever you want, but I've got to say that was better than slamming a Red Bull. Breezed through my test without any effort at all this morning."

Dave continued studying me as if I had just said something absurd. He took a step back from me, eyeing me suspiciously. I got the impression I might have been a disease-riddled leper. "Did I say something wrong? Hey, if you are sensitive about your secret recipe, I'll keep it on the down low."

Still confused, he answered, "I have no idea what you're talking about."

The look he gave me was strange, as if he really didn't have a clue what I was talking about. I studied his face: it was Dave. No, it wasn't! There was no shininess on his head from the glue holding the gash closed. I looked at his clothes: he wasn't dressed like Dave. I had been through most of Dave's cabinets and had only seen t-shirts and hoodies. The man before me wore a thick winter wool coat with a dress shirt peeking out from the collar. The word formed on my lips before I knew what I was asking, "Mark?"

He still eyed me suspiciously, but kept his distance. Words poured out of me, "OHMYGOD it's you. You're here. Holy crap! I didn't know that was you. I mean, I know your brother."

A foreboding look glared at me when he answered icily, "I don't have a brother."

Searching for something in his eyes, the playfulness from before was gone. He thought I was running some sort of scam on him or something. "Dave. Your brother is Dave Brewer."

Without warning, his hand was around my throat and lifting me angrily off the ground. "My brother's dead, you stupid bitch."

Air was cut off from my lungs and the constriction on my throat made speaking impossible. Rage showed through his eyes, and had I not been held inches off of the ground, I would have cowered away just from his glare. My legs kicked frantically while he continued holding me in the air, glaring at me. A voice yelled from across the parking lot, "You better put her down, friend."

I didn't recognize the voice, and for all I knew, an angel had descended from heaven to intervene on my behalf. Well, most angels wouldn't wear dirty blue jeans, Carhartt jackets and baseball caps, but I wasn't about to ridicule this stranger's wardrobe choices. Mark dropped me and pushed me away from him, landing me squarely on my butt on the frozen asphalt.

Coughing and gagging as my lungs desperately tried to fill with air, I held an arm up feebly as the stranger came to my side and helped me to my feet. The stranger watched Mark who walked off toward the far side of the parking lot, then asked, "Are you okay? Do you need an ambulance?"

My eyes darted around the parking lot. I had lost Mark for a second, but saw the lights flash on a sleek black Mercedes. Still trying to gather air, I launched myself away from the good Samaritan and jogged toward Mark's car. His expression was still full of fury when he glared in my direction.

I couldn't catch my breath, so I waved my arms like crazy trying to convince him not to go. It didn't work because he got in his car, revved the engine, and spun the tires on the ice-packed pavement. I did one of the stupidest things of my life and leaped in front of his on-coming car, despite seeing the rage on his face. The car skidded to a stop within inches of me.

The idea that I would be a new hood ornament for his car should have convinced me to jump out of the way, but after seeing the pain in Dave's eyes last night, I couldn't let Mark get away. Mark rolled his window down as his angry voice shouted, "Get out of my way. I'll flatten you."

"Dave's not dead." I coughed a few more times, my eyes locked hard on his. "Lives here." A loud wheeze, "He told me about you. I told him I saw you here Tuesday night."

My heart was still pounding like a jackhammer in my chest, but he had heard me. He didn't look convinced, but he put the Mercedes in park, opened the door, and stood up. "What do you mean he lives here?"

"He moved here when he was nine. He said you two got separated when he was five. I was supposed to come here with him tonight to try to find you."

The stranger who had come to my aid was watching the events unfold. He must have thought this better than daytime television because he didn't budge from the place where he had lifted me off of the asphalt. Mark walked over toward me, disbelief still coloring his expression. "Dave Brewer. My brother? You're telling me he's alive and he lives here?"

"Yes. He and I have been friends since high school. He restored my car," pointing absently at my Chevelle two rows over. "He told me about what happened with the two of you when you were little. How the foster family kept you and gave him back to the state."

Mark said nothing. As powerful as he had looked to me just minutes before, his whole demeanor had changed. I saw his mouth try to form words several times, but words weren't coming out. I offered, "I can take you to him. Or give you his phone number. You have no idea how badly he wants to see you."

Still not believing me, he asked, "He's alive?"

"Uh, yeah. At least he was when I left for school this morning." I gave him a smile that he didn't return. Instead he went back to his car and sat in the driver's seat. I looked toward the stranger who was still watching with morbid curiosity. I went around to the passenger side of Mark's car and tapped on the window for him to unlock the door. When he did, I took a seat beside him.

Much the same as last night, I had no idea what words could possibly comfort this brother any more than the words I couldn't find last night for Dave. When he finally spoke, his voice was absent any emotion, "I've got some things I need to take care of. You should go. Don't tell him you saw me tonight."

"What? Are you kidding me? Dave was beyond excited when I told him I met you. He would kill me if I lied to him about seeing you tonight."

"Give me some time. I need to tie up some loose ends before I see him again. You said he lives here?"

"Just let me get him on the phone. Five minutes. Please? Just talk to him for five minutes and let him know you're okay." I pulled my cell phone out, scrolling through contacts to find Dave when Mark's hand closed over mine.

His eyes were sad, which didn't make any sense. If I called Dave right this second he would be elated. Mark's reaction to learning that Dave was alive baffled me. Mark looked into my eyes, "So, when you kissed me, you thought. . .you thought I was him?"

"Well, yeah. I don't even know you." Embarrassed that I had confused the two, I thought of what Dave's reaction might be if I shared the parking lot encounter with him. He would probably think it was funny, except that I didn't know the difference. I was mortified.

He snapped his fingers and scowled. "My loss."

Strange response. Questions poured in on me. Why wasn't he pumping me for information on Dave? Why did he think Dave was dead? Why would he choke me like that? Mark had scared me, the same fear that up until now was reserved for Grey and maybe a little for Teddy. Not wanting to elicit an angry reaction, I asked the safest question I could think of, "Why did you think Dave was dead?"

"It doesn't matter. You're sure it's my brother? People steal dead people's identities all the time."

"He has the same eyes as you. The same cleft chin. Your hair is the same color, too, but yours is just a little longer. No, your appearances are too close not to be brothers." I studied him for a second longer. Dave had a much less intense personality, but a comment like that could only be offensive if I shared that disparity with Mark. Instead, I offered, "He only lives like ten minutes from here. We could go there now."

"No."

"I don't understand. You don't want to see him?" Without waiting for any kind of a response I said, "He's a great guy. He owns his own repair shop – all custom muscle. I know he wants to see you. He told me about you last night." My voice lowered, "It almost ripped his heart out to share it with me. Please go there with me."

Mark turned away from me and gazed out into the darkness in front of him. He shook his head as his voice turned to steel, "Not now. Soon. I'll find him."

He bobbed his head toward the passenger door, wordlessly dismissing me. I reached for the door handle when the reason I had come in the first place cascaded on me, "Hey, before you go, how well do you know Grey and Teddy?"

Mark's eyes narrowed. I might well be stepping onto thin ice, but I needed to know. "Teddy was one of the two guys that my roommate and I were playing pool with the other night."

His expression didn't change, but he clarified, "You two hustled Teddy, right?"

"Sort of. I mean, we needed groceries."

"Bad move."

"You know him? Because the police are looking for them now."

"You might as well be looking for a ghost. He has more identities than a shark has teeth."

"Can you tell me their last names?"

"Get out."

Get out? Did Mark know what Grey had done to Libby? What he tried to do to me? Grey had shot Dave, but given Mark's response to finding out Dave was alive, I wasn't sure that would make any difference. Mark didn't wait for my response as he reached across me and pulled the passenger side door handle. His voice commanded, "Now."

I slid off the seat not sure what to think. I closed the passenger side door as he pulled out of the lot without so much as a second glance in my direction. What had just happened? He thought Dave was dead, but when he found out he was alive, he wanted nothing to do with him? I asked if he had any info on the two scum bags who had turned my life upside down, and he kicked me out of his car? What was Mark involved in?

Tony's warning from earlier came in loud and clear – he said Mark was worse than Teddy or Grey. What was Mark? A mob boss or something? Teddy had called him "Boss" and had gotten nervous when Mark told him to be respectful to Libby. What had they discussed after we left? Mark knew Libby had hustled Teddy and his little brother.

The same voice from across the parking lot shouted, "Hey! He didn't hurt you, did he?"

The man still stood where he had helped me up. I shook my head and waved. Glancing toward the entrance, I saw a man walk out of the bar then stand in the shadow to the left of the entrance. As I held my position trying to make my eyes see into the dark corner, a shiver ran up my spine. I took a step toward him, then my whole body stiffened as his face emerged from the shadow: Teddy. Grey was nowhere to be seen, but I'd recognize Teddy anywhere. He blew me a kiss, stuffed a cigarette butt into an ashtray by the door, and disappeared back inside Bank Shot. I ran to my car at the far end of the lot. Reaching into my purse, my fingers latched on to my keys. I pulled them out, fumbling with them in the darkness while looking over my shoulder, trying to see if Teddy was coming after me.

In my hurry, I jammed my house key halfway into the lock on my car door. I jerked at it, but the key was stuck. I looked back toward the entrance, praying Teddy stayed inside. I wiggled the key which had no business being in the lock, peeked over my shoulder again while continuing to jiggle it. My breathing was labored, my heart pounding in my chest. A streetlight flickered to my left as a flashback of security cameras being knocked out at the gas station blew through my memory.

This was it. I'd done a great job hiding from everyone until now. These thugs would catch me here, where it all began. I looked for somewhere I could run to while still desperately trying to remove my house key from my car door. I reached into my purse, pulled out my cell, and hit redial on my phone. Officer Brown's voice answered in earnest, "Officer Brown, how can I help you?"

Although no one was anywhere near me, I crouched down beside my car and whisper-shouted, "It's Candy. He's here. Teddy's at Bank Shot right now. I just saw him."

"Has he seen you?"

"Yes. He's here. I'm in the parking lot. Please hurry!"

"Get somewhere safe and stay there. I'm five minutes away. I'll call it in."

Feeling the rubber of the tire up against my shoulder, my eyes remained fixed on Bank Shot's front door. I felt the iciness of the pavement coming up through the sole of my boots. Shivers began to take hold of me, whether induced by the cold or the fear, I'd never know. The stranger who had helped me when Mark had me dangling in mid-air was nowhere to be found.

A taxi pulled up to the front door; it was one of the new Green-taxis in a Toyota Prius. The front door opened. Teddy opened the back door of the taxi as his eyes scanned the parking lot over the roof of the car. I stayed crouched at the height of my wheel well, hidden in the shadow. I had an excellent vantage point to see him, but he would have had to know I was there for him to see me. A lady with a ruby-red dress and porcelain skin followed him out of Bank Shot as he held the door for her. When she disappeared inside the car, Teddy took one more concerted look around the lot, then tucked into the back seat with her.

The breath I had been holding released. The taxi cab had barely cleared the parking lot when I dialed Officer Brown a second time. "He just left. He's in a Green-taxi, headed north on Gordon. He's with a woman. I haven't seen Grey."

Officer Brown's voice answered back urgently, "You said he saw you?"

"Just for a second, then he went into the bar. He didn't see me when he left the bar."

"I'll call the cab company to get a location on the taxi. Don't go inside."

"I don't plan to." I gave one final jerk on my key, and it pulled free of the lock. I no longer wanted to go inside and talk to Chris. I didn't want to go back to my empty house, even if that had been an option. Libby could be awake by now, but I knew Larry would be there to take care of her. The only thing I wanted in this moment was one person, holding me against him, blocking out all the things I wanted to pretend weren't going on in my life. I unlocked my car, fired up the engine, and pointed it toward Dave's.

Just before I pulled onto Dave's street, Officer Brown called me. "The cab dropped him in a parking lot. I've got men canvassing the area. We'll find him." I thanked him for the update. Fear ebbed as Dave's garage came into view. Mark wanted me to pretend we hadn't seen each other tonight. I couldn't do that to Dave. I'd have to find a way to tell him that I had seen him, but gloss over the fact that Mark refused to meet him.

CHAPTER 20

I pulled in front of Dave's garage. He must have been watching for my car from the upstairs window because the moment my lights touched the door, it lifted open. My heart danced as I saw Dave in the corner pressing the lever to let me safely back into his world. His hair was wet; either he had just worked out or he was freshly showered. Either possibility was inviting. I got out of my car, my eyes locked on his. As we stood across the garage from each other, neither of us spoke to the other, but the torrent of desire between us was palpable. Dave reached for the lever to close the garage door behind my car and wordlessly began climbing the steps to his apartment.

I followed him. When I cleared the top step, all the lights were out, and candles danced lightly in the darkness on nearly every flat surface of his apartment, giving just enough light for me to see his silhouette standing in the center of the room. He was perfection in the flesh. I succumbed to stunned silence as my body drew closer to his.

When Dave brushed against me, the familiar heat he generated in me returned. I grabbed hold of him like there would be no tomorrow. Remembering how delicious his chest looked under the towel last night, I wanted to see it all, to feel his flesh against mine.

The t-shirt he wore was just as tight as the one he wore last night. I wrapped my fingers around the hem of his shirt and gave it a tug up. Surprisingly, his hands pulled it out of my grip, anchoring it in place. He hadn't been a lady's man in high school; maybe he was insecure around women. I couldn't be sure, but it felt like some sort of game he wanted to play; I was as competitive as they come and loved a challenge.

I slipped my hands under the back of his shirt, allowing my hands to glide over the smooth skin beneath. Dave's breath hitched in response to my touch, and before he could disarm me with one of his kisses, I grabbed hold of the material a second time and pulled hard to lift it over him.

Dave stopped me a second time, securing the shirt, then he distanced himself from me. A curtain of rejection billowed over me. What kind of signal was he sending me? The candles gave the apartment a romantic feel. The look in his eyes and the warmth of his touch were a welcomed invitation. His insistence that his shirt stay on made no sense. What was the turmoil going on inside him? I believed his longing burned just under the surface with mine. Had I imagined it?

Dave had stopped several paces away from me. My eyes drank in his silhouette: his sculpted body was a true work of art. Men with bodies in the same league as Dave's normally walked around in as few clothes as possible. He had had a tough life growing up, so maybe he was shy about his body. What little I knew of his past had been difficult. Maybe he hadn't told me every grim detail. Maybe there were physical scars he didn't want me to see.

Maybe I needed to give him some space. There weren't many places to go off to in the apartment for any kind of privacy. Actually, other than the bathroom, there weren't any places for privacy. I began to wonder if I had crossed a line. Glancing toward the stairs, I considered going down to the lobby of his garage, or maybe to my car. I didn't want to force myself on him.

Dave walked over to his enormous bed and lay down, much the same as he had done last night. Conflicting emotions ran rampant within me. Part of me wanted to escape to the seclusion of my car and forget his rejection, while the more convincing part of me longed to go stretch out on top of him where he lay.

I asked, "Did I do something wrong?"

His flirtatious smile beamed at me with humor in his voice, "No." He patted the space beside him on the bed, as his voice returned to the silky sound from earlier, "Come lie down with me."

The sound of his baritone request launched a fresh wave of butterflies in my stomach. Even from twenty feet away, Dave's eyes were locked on mine. His seductive look drew me to him as my body responded of its own accord. Before I could talk myself out of it, I was seated beside him on the bed.

Neither of us spoke. I watched him intently, looking for any sign that he had lost interest. His gaze held me locked in place. Dave leaned toward me, barely brushing against me. I felt the heat from his skin as I longed to feel the softness of his lips against mine. I wanted to reach out to him, but I didn't want him to push me away. After the silence between us became nearly unbearable and neither of us made a move for the other, I asked, "So that kiss yesterday. . . any regrets?"

The black pupils of his eyes were so dilated in the diminished light that they had nearly swallowed the walnut color whole. His eyes narrowed when he answered, "No. You?"

His hand tentatively found mine, while his eyes refused to look away. He began gently stroking the top of my hand: his feather light touch made circular motions on my skin causing goose bumps to erupt along my flesh. "Only that you haven't kissed me like that since."

In one fluid motion, Dave rolled toward me, pressing his weight against me, as his lips sought mine like a precision missile. I welcomed his lips as his hand continued doing its dance along my side, under my sweater. I deepened our kiss as a sensual groan escaped him. My arms guided him as he pressed himself against me.

I wanted my skin against his, to feel the friction of our bodies colliding in the dimly lit room. Whatever had given him pause as we stood just minutes ago seemed to have evaporated: he wanted this as much as I did. I tugged at his shirt again, but he took my offending hands in his and held them where they couldn't pull his clothes off. Uncertain what to make of his action, I asked, "Are you okay?"

Dave shook his head, "I'm fine. I just don't like my shirt off."

His words stung. So I was taking this further than he wanted it to go. I concluded he wanted to slow things down, just rekindling our friendship rather than starting anything more. My hands went limp in his as I eased my body away. His eyes snapped open wide as regret colored his face. "Shit. Candy, don't."

I turned toward the opposite wall, I murmured, "Don't what?"

His voice begged, "Don't move away from me."

I didn't flinch. I couldn't understand what was going through his head, and on top of everything else going on, I didn't think my ego could take a crushing blow. The "I just want to be your friend" line would be more than I could take. I didn't move.

Dave's voice sounded defeated. "Oh, hell. I might as well tell you. You're going to find out anyway."

"Tell me what? Let me guess – you have a girlfriend. You aren't over a recent breakup? You aren't at a place in your life where you have room for me. Go ahead. Whatever you're going to tell me, I'm fine with it." My voice was peppered with resentment, ready for whatever stupid rejection he was going to throw my way.

He turned my body toward him as a shy look took over his features. "Uh, no. Nothing like that. You'll probably think it's funny. And just so you know, I prefer funny to creepy." He paused as if trying to get up enough courage to go on. "So I was out on a date with a girl just after graduation. We had both landed a couple fake ID's and were wearing them out. I was lit, so was she. We thought it would be fun to go out and get tattoos." Dave paused, as if assessing my ability to keep up with the conversation.

I let his words marinate for a second. He had been on a date, he was drunk, and he thought it would be fun to get a tattoo. The pieces fell into place – he had a woman's name tattooed on him and didn't want me to see it. From his desire to keep it hidden from me, it was probably an "Eternal Love" or sappy "Love of my Life" design. Jealousy flared for no good reason as I felt my eyes narrow on him. My reaction was absurd. Who cared if another woman's name was permanently written on his chest?

Dave studied me for a minute before deciding, "I can tell from your reaction you're going to see it and think it's creepy. So I'll just do us both a favor and keep my shirt on."

My posture stiffened. What kind of idiot gets the name of a girl he hardly knows tattooed on his chest? The words were out in a flash, "So what was her name?"

Dave leaned in questioningly, "Who?"

"The girl you went and got a tattoo with?"

Confused, he answered, "Jill. I still see her every now and again. The guy she's dating owns that purple custom downstairs."

Now it was my words that were confused. He had tattooed her name on his chest, and now her boyfriend was one of his customers? "That's got to be awkward."

He shook his head, "No, not really. She and I only went out the one time."

"Wait, you just said you see her every now and again. What's that mean?"

He smiled as if he had to explain a horrifically complicated concept to a moron, "I mean when her boyfriend comes into the shop – I see her then. I don't hook up with her or anything."

"Oh." I wanted to be okay with it. I've made some tragically stupid decisions – not stupid enough that any of them were permanently etched on my body – but some things I wasn't too happy about after I had done them. We both lay there awkwardly on the bed. His hand reached for mine. I didn't push it away, but I wasn't overly eager to pick up where we had left off just to be shut down again. Curiosity got the better of me when I rolled over on my side and said, "Show me."

Dave grinned. "I'm a betting man. And I'm betting that if I show you my ink there are only a few possible outcomes. Most of them are bad," he paused. A charming grin that reached all the way to his eyes studied me until he continued, "I'm not willing to risk it. My shirt stays on."

His summation of the possible outcomes made me giggle. "What if I promise not to react one way or the other after you show me?"

Dave's head cocked to the side in consideration, but answered, "Not good enough."

"What if I promise no matter what it looks like, I know that it was done when you weren't in your right mind?"

He smiled, not the sweet grin from before, but the perfect wide smile of a Cheshire cat. "I didn't say I wasn't in my right mind. I said I was drunk."

"Whatever. Show me."

Dave's hand began gliding up my arm. Sternly I accused, "You're purposely delaying. Either show me now, or I'll think of all the worst possible tattoos you could have. If it's really bad, I promise to wake up before you every morning and color it in with a black Sharpie."

"Every morning?" I worried that I had said something wrong and began thinking of something clever to say to cover up the fact that I would like the idea of a sleepover at his place for more than just a couple nights. His lips began nuzzling my neck, whispering kisses just under my jaw. Heat spread over my skin as my body made me more acutely aware of his touch. His breath was labored and with each new sensation, I fell a little deeper under his spell. Dave turned toward me, hiking his leg up over my hip and pressing his body firmly to mine. "Just promise me you won't think I'm creepy."

Creepy? Images of skulls, zombies, even a swastika came to mind, but I needed to know. "I promise."

Dave eased off of me, boosting himself into a seated position on the other side of the bed. He shook his head as if having an internal argument with himself. I faked disinterest, taking my boots off and setting them beside the bed. He turned away from me, his muscular back facing me, and then in one quick motion removed his shirt and proceeded to fold it into a six by six square laid neatly beside him. Nearly a minute passed before I heard an audible sigh and he turned toward me.

As my eyes took in the tattoo on his chest, my mouth gaped. Even after he had prepared me, I wasn't prepared. My breathing sped up and tingles spread from my head to my toes. It wasn't creepy. It wasn't even remotely offensive. It was the most unexpected cartoon tattoo I had ever seen. On top of his beautifully sculpted chest, directly above his heart was a tattoo of a bright red heart. The heart had big brown cherub eyes, white gloves and sneakers, with oversized cartoon lips. It looked a lot like one of the M&M guys from the commercials. The heart's two little gloved hands were holding a red and white striped candy cane.

I was speechless. His eyes desperately searched mine. He made no excuse and didn't try to play it off like it was a joke or anything; instead he quietly offered, "I told you I've had a crush on you forever."

I sat motionless, my eyes darting between his chest and his eyes. "You have a tattoo of a candy cane on your chest?"

"Yeah. Still want to wake up early and cover it up with a Sharpie in the morning?"

My hand was drawn to the happy cartoon figure smiling back at me from his muscular chest. My finger traced the outline as the implication of the happy message crashed on me.

"You were on a date with a girl and got this? What did she say?"

"I think she assumed I had a strange fascination with Christmas or something. She didn't try to talk me out of it. She sort of egged me on when I said I wanted a candy cane over my heart. She's the one who told me to get a cartoon heart holding the candy cane. People get dumb tattoos all the time." His eyes bore straight into mine, "This one means something to me. I was letting the world know that my heart wanted to hold you."

Frozen in place, my memory raced to yesterday morning after finding him in his garage. He had confessed he had always had a crush on me – I had dismissed it. The proof of his feelings were staring at me. I wanted to gather him in my arms and get lost in his embrace. I wanted all the fear and craziness in my life to evaporate so I could truly enjoy this moment. I stammered, "I don't know what to say."

Dave's lips were at my ear when he answered, "You don't have to say anything." His hands slid under my shirt and glided across my skin. The goose bumps returned at his touch. He whispered, "Just promise me you'll be here when I wake up tomorrow."

"I promise."

Dave kissed my neck, gently nuzzled the sensitive skin by my ear lobe then slid under the covers. He held the comforter up for me to slide in beside him. Before accepting his invitation, I walked over to each of the candles still dancing in the darkness and blew each one out. When I returned to the bed, I slid my sweater off and climbed in beside him. Dave's massive body spooned against me.

My head rested on his bicep, as his other arm draped over me, gently motioning circles on my front. His whisper so low, I barely heard his words, "I love that you are here."

Gripping his arm draped over me, I answered, "Me, too."

CHAPTER 21

Friday morning I again awoke to an empty bed. . . a little disappointed. I had hoped to see his happy heart tattoo first thing this morning. Dave continued to surprise me. How could I have ever believed I knew him? I hadn't known him at all.

Dave was confident, attractive, he finally had conversational skills, and judging from this place, he must be a savvy businessman. What had happened? The Dave I thought I knew didn't make eye contact, wouldn't speak unless he was answering someone's question, and had never been the poster child for Tide.

Had he watched one of those, "You can do it" infomercials on television? Taken a Dale Carnegie seminar? People change. Everyone matures, but nothing like the change I had witnessed in Dave. It was almost as if he had gone through a finishing school or was abducted by aliens. I liked him before, but I liked him because he had done me a favor by restoring my car. The more I learned about him while I was in high school, the more I felt sorry for him. The truth was, the feelings I had for Dave right now were nothing like how I felt before. I no longer thought of him as a wounded puppy I could try to save.

Dave was a catch – a real catch. Lots of guys I had met in college had been okay, but the few I had dated were so consumed with their own lives, I felt as if I had been intruding. Time with me had been squeezed in between football games or road trips with their friends. I had gotten semi-serious with a couple of them, well, maybe not serious, but exclusive. None ever broke my heart because I didn't care about any of them enough for their departure from my life to be more than a blip on a screen. There was one other major difference between Dave and everybody else, too – my eyes couldn't get enough of him.

I snuggled back into the sheets that still retained his scent. My eyes closed as I escaped into a fantasy where it wasn't just his bare chest I was snuggled up against. The candles had been a nice touch last night. The way the flickering light danced across his skin and accentuated the crevice of each ridge on his muscular arms and chest, it was beyond a turn-on – nothing short of erotic.

Breaking myself out of my own little world, I sat up in bed and stretched my arms, letting an enormous yawn free. It was just after 7 AM on a Friday. Regardless of Tony's warning yesterday, I didn't have any classes today, so there was no need to rush across town or to worry about dodging any stalker who could be lurking outside one of my classes.

Gazing around the apartment, everything still looked as it had the first time I laid eyes on it: nothing out of place. I thought people only lived like this on television shows. My house as a whole, and my room specifically, always had that "lived in" feel. I thought of the last guy I had dated, Calvin. He was nice enough, but every time we went to his place, it smelled like a locker room. I could go for obsessively organized and clean as opposed to grimy and gross any day. Dave was a huge step up from Calvin.

I plodded to the bathroom, checked myself in the mirror, grabbed some clothes, and decided I was presentable enough to score a cup of coffee downstairs. It was still early, so I thought Dave must be getting in some work before he opened the place. I wouldn't pass for a supermodel, but sweatpants and a t-shirt had to be acceptable this early in the morning.

Halfway down the steps, I saw a figure wearing a pair of blue coveralls bent over the engine of a green Chrysler. A quick glance told me it wasn't Dave: the body was too thin. I froze in place and considered returning back to the apartment when Mr. Kravitz looked over his shoulder and caught me watching him from the stairs. Instant relief flooded me. Although never one of my teachers, he was always great to me, with his easy smile and welcoming demeanor. His skin was weathered, and although it had only been a couple years, gray hairs had begun to take over the hair on his head and face. Mr. Kravitz wore the same scraggly beard and mustache he had the last time I had seen him; his hair was cut short and from what I could see, he was still sporting the same grease under his fingernails as he had in high school.

He called a happy greeting, "I wondered when you were going to come down. Dave told me to keep a lookout for you."

My eyes darted around the garage. Dave's truck had been parked inside last night, and it was nowhere inside now. How hard was I sleeping? I should have heard him leave. Where would he have gone? "Hi, Mr. Kravitz. What are you doing here?"

"What? You think only kids cut school?" He grinned mischievously, then added, "Around here, I'm just Ryan."

Something felt insanely wrong calling him by his first name. Still not sure what to think about Dave's absence, I asked, "Where's Dave?"

Flashing me a smile, he answered, "He's sort of an early riser. Dave needed to find a part at a salvage yard. He left a little earlier than normal to catch some gym time first. He didn't want to leave you here alone, so he asked if I'd come try to work a miracle on this car until he gets back."

"Oh." I looked at the coffee pot in the lobby, "I was just going to grab a cup of coffee, and I'll get out of your way."

Mr. Kravitz put down the wrench he was holding onto the Chrysler's radiator. "I'll join you."

I went to the little cup tree and took two cups, filling them both and passing one to him. I wondered what he thought about me spending the night. Did he know why I wasn't at my house? My teeth sunk into my lower lip, the way they did every time I got nervous about something. How much had Dave told him?

He interrupted my errant thoughts when he asked, "Dave tells me you met Mark?"

"Yeah, well, at the time I didn't know it was Mark. The two of them look a lot alike." After the tattoo revelation last night, I had completely ignored the fact that I had seen Mark a second time. It didn't feel like I was keeping it from Dave last night because my thoughts were occupied elsewhere, but in the light of day, I regretted not telling him about the encounter as soon as I got here, candles or not.

"You know, Dave has been searching for his brother nonstop for years. Funny how fate works."

His statement took me off guard just as I was bringing the steamy cup to my lips. "He never mentioned to me that he even had a brother until two days ago."

"Dave's a pretty complicated kid." That was the understatement of the year. Mr. Kravitz paused for a minute before he added, "He's come a long way in the last couple years. I hope he's not disappointed when he finally meets Mark."

Did Kravitz know Mark? I swallowed the steamy coffee slowly, worried that I wasn't the only one keeping a secret from Dave. "Disappointed?"

His smile was warm, "No one is able to live up to a memory. Dave's been holding on to the memory of his big brother for fifteen years. It would be great if people were as perfect as we remember them to be, but no one is without flaws."

That was sort of profound. I felt a little more comfortable; he didn't seem to be hiding anything about Mark from Dave. Rather than speculating on Mark, or worse yet, letting it slip that he'd choked me last night, I was much more interested in learning what had happened to Dave in the last couple years. "Dave's a lot different than I remember him being in high school."

A thoughtful smile crept across his face. "Different? You mean he's taller?"

"No!" I answered with a laugh. "I mean, he was sort of a loner before. He seems, I don't know, energized or something."

"I wish I could take the credit for the changes I've seen, but most of the big improvements were Emily's doing."

My heart sank. Dave hadn't even hinted that he had a girlfriend, or an ex-girlfriend. I was naïve to think just because he had a heart hugging a candy cane on his chest that he had been pining away for me for the last couple years.

"Oh." I felt my face blush. What would Kravitz think of me staying here if Dave had someone else in his life? Especially someone who had done for him what I hadn't been able to do. My eyes rested on the floor as I confessed, "He didn't mention her."

His voice was rich as he warned, "You'd better keep that tidbit of information to yourself. She is pretty possessive of him, and I doubt she'd forgive him anytime soon if she found out he was having sleep-overs and wasn't telling you about the other woman in his life."

Did he think this was a joke? The light pink on my cheeks morphed into a deep red as I felt the blush stretched all the way to my ears. My teeth gnawed on my lower lip again, and I wanted to escape, not hide, but melt into the wall.

"Now, don't get like that. Here. . ." Kravitz whipped a cell phone out of his pocket and flashed his screen at me. A child with light blonde curls, pouty lips, and bright blue eyes scowled at me from his phone. She looked like a cherub, with chubby cheeks and a look that said, "I will have my way whether you like it or not."

Aside from her demanding look, she was an angel. "Ah, if that's my competition, I forfeit."

"You're a smart girl." He tucked his phone back into the side pocket of his coveralls. "When he came to stay with us, he tried to stay locked up inside himself. She wasn't having it."

"When he came to stay with you?"

"You met the hideous beast the state placed him with while he was in school? He turned eighteen and aged out of the foster care system. His guardian didn't want anything to do with him when the checks stopped coming in."

A wave of sorrow spread over me, "He never told me."

Kravitz nodded. "That was my doing. I told him he was welcome to stay with me and my family as long as he wanted. But there are lots of sad stories out there: I couldn't take in any other students. I didn't want any of the faculty or students to find out he stayed with me because I didn't have room for anyone else in my home."

"That's pretty awesome of you." I looked around the place and remembered Dave had told me Mr. Kravitz was his silent partner. "You helped him open this place, too?"

"Only out of necessity. He was fixing cars so fast that my classroom was starting to feel like Jiffy Lube. I had people calling from Nebraska, Iowa, and Missouri trying to schedule Dave for a restore. A couple here and there would have been fine, but even the principal noticed we had a significant turnover."

"Really? While he was still in school?"

"Yep. There aren't many people who have the kind of attention to detail he has. Word gets out fast in the custom world. He needed a place of his own."

"You rented this place for him?"

"I negotiated the lease, and introduced him to an accountant." His voice morphed into a proud parental brag when he said, "You know that kid pocketed every penny he earned on every job he worked? Students aren't supposed to make money on the school's shop, but several of his restores netted him some healthy tips from appreciative car owners. He never spent a dime on anything that wasn't an absolute necessity. He had the money for the lease on his own; he just needed the encouragement to do it."

"But he told me you were his partner?"

Shaking his head. "Yeah, he tells everybody that. Every month his accountant sends me a check, too. Initially I tried to give them back, but it always turned into a full-blown argument."

"Really?"

"Yeah. Rather than bicker with him, I started a separate account. Every penny he's ever given me is in there." He looked around the little garage and commented, "He's outgrown this place. When he decides he wants something bigger, that cash will be ready for him."

"You're not much of a partner then."

"I help whenever he needs it. I'm more of a skilled cheerleader." His gaze focused squarely on mine. "I've seen students come and go. There have been the over-privileged, the undernourished, the troublemakers and everything in between, but there has only been one Dave Brewer."

"You sound like a proud father."

"Dave's a part of my family. He doesn't see it that way, but I do."

"I know he appreciates everything you've done."

"Yeah, I know. You asked me what happened to him? The answer is a little bit of my wife and a whole lot of Emily."

"Your wife? I've never met her."

Kravitz nodded, "You should see his eyes light up when she pays him a compliment. It's something to see. Like the sun rises and sets on her shoulders." Conspiratorially, he added, "It's the same way he's looked at you for years."

My cheeks heated up again, "There was never anything between us back in high school. We were just friends."

"You two were just friends because he didn't know how to tell you how he felt about you. He was too intimidated to let you into his world back then."

I didn't agree with his conclusion, and it felt strange talking about it to Mr. Kravitz. Instead of carrying on a seriously embarrassing subject, I pried him for information on the changes that had happened with Dave. "Is Mrs. Kravitz like a clean freak or something?"

A sad look shone on his face. "Don't let that scare you away from him. He doesn't do it on purpose." He must have read my confusion because he explained, "He said when he was little he tried like hell to get back to the home where Mark was at. He became compulsive – everything having to be in its place to prove he was a good boy. I'm sure the foster family who kept Mark were good people, but they really did a number on Dave by asking the state to take him back."

Dave's emotions were so raw, I didn't feel right prying the other night. Kravitz seemed to know everything about Dave, and one question had been eating at me since he told me what had happened. "I thought they didn't do that? I thought the state kept siblings together?"

"I don't know, Candy. Two states in the mix, several different case workers assigned, an adoption that fell through – none of it makes sense to me, either. That kid may be built like a Mack Truck, but he's got a model airplane for a heart. It's been snapped together, glued, and painted so that it's a thing of beauty, but it's fragile." He pressed his lips together, as if arguing with himself before he added, "If you aren't sure you can love him back, you need to cut bait soon."

His word choice sent shivers through me. Loving him back was absurd: we hardly knew each other. "Mr. Kravitz, we've just spent a couple days together."

"You've just spent a couple days with *him*. I can guarantee you, a day hasn't gone by in the last four years where *you* weren't the last thought he had before his eyes closed for the night."

Disbelief colored my words, "He didn't even like me when he first met me."

He waved a hand in front of my face. "Are you blind? You remember the day you came into my classroom trying to sweet talk me into letting you into the class? Who do you suppose was rubber-necking and trying to get a better look at you when he thought I couldn't see?"

"That doesn't mean anything."

"You're right. Back it up a little. When you had detention with me your freshman year?"

I rolled my eyes, "Yes."

"Dave showed up for detention, without a detention slip."

"So?"

"When I asked him for it, he didn't have one. He said he just wanted to get some extra studying done."

I didn't remember Dave even being in the room anytime during the two weeks. Defensively, I shot back, "That didn't have anything to do with me."

Kravitz furrowed his brow at me, "How many times do you think Dave studied the whole four years he was in school? Still not convinced? You had a small part in the school play your senior year, right?"

I nodded. "Small" was a kind description. I got to say two sentences. Kravitz's voice dropped lower, "He didn't miss one performance."

Dave's simple admission, "I've had a crush on you," took on a whole new meaning when put in Mr. Kravitz's context. Dave wasn't being kind or flattering: he really had thought of me that way for much longer than I knew. I still felt the embarrassment showing brightly on my cheeks.

Not wanting to continue this trip down my oblivious memory lane, I asked, "You said Emily and your wife helped him come out of his shell? What was their secret? How'd they do it?"

He rubbed his chin, considering my question. "It wasn't one single thing either of them did. Emily used to play I-Spy with him for hours, which made him ask questions. She told him about her day, and wanted to hear about his. I guess it was a lot of little things." He let out a hearty laugh, "You should have seen my wife's face the first time he put groceries away in our kitchen pantry. When he was finished, all the cans were stacked neatly and grouped according to the contents. All the labels were facing front. I swear she went in and would purposely move cans around only to find them back the way he had arranged them hours later. It used to drive her nuts. She tried to teach him that life is supposed to be messy."

"But he's that way about everything. Have you seen his cabinets upstairs?"

"Oh, yeah. Lots of times." Kravitz pointed over his shoulder toward the garage, "His tool box, too. It's his way of coping. For most of his life it was the only part of his life he could control. When he was younger, he thought it was the key to getting back to Mark."

"And now?"

"I think it just makes him feel good to live an orderly life."

I had always liked Mr. Kravitz, but I never knew how insightful he could be. "So someone with a chaotic life is probably a big turn off for someone like Dave?"

"Dave's had a thing for you for as long as I've known you. A little chaos might do him some good."

Sheepishly I countered, "Do you know everything that's been going on with me?"

"I know some of what's going on. Dave's worried about you, enough that he's let you interrupt his routine."

"What do you mean?"

"His routine. He's established this schedule he never varies from. What time the garage opens, when he works out, when he eats, everything is planned meticulously. Two days ago when you came here – he closed his shop down for the day. That kid works through blizzards, power outages, floods; he is here when no other place in town is open." He waited to let it sink in then added, "He closed the place down when he went looking for you."

I wasn't all that impressed: he lives upstairs – it's not like he has to drive through snow. Likely sensing that I wasn't getting the gravity of his statement, Kravitz continued, "He works out every day of the week from 5 AM to 6 AM. He didn't want to bother you while you were sleeping, so he drove across town to hit a gym this morning, rather than using the one he's got upstairs after you woke up. He called me last night to ask if I'd come over here to make sure you were okay while he ran errands."

Defensively, I said, "I never asked him to do either of those things."

"Don't you see? You are the first person he has let into his life that he has allowed to vary his routine. It's a huge step."

"Or a colossal inconvenience."

"You asked about the changes in Dave. You want to know how that happened?"

"Yes."

"It happened because he wanted something more. He wanted to fit in. It was my daughter who first showed him how to use a washing machine. She was six."

"I don't understand."

"Dave wants to be like everyone else, but when he was growing up, no one took the time to show him how to be like everyone else."

"He's changed a lot from the guy I remember. He seems a lot more confident when he talks."

Kravitz was excited, "I know. That was all Emily. He had only been at our house a couple days when the two of them were at the table in the kitchen, and she was telling him about a project she had for school. A couple minutes into the conversation she reached over and pinched his arm, then told him, 'It's rude and disrespectful not to look at someone when they're talking to you. Are you disrespecting me?' My mouth about hit the table when I heard her say it, but Dave looked her square in the eye and told her, 'I'm sorry, I didn't know.'"

I didn't know what to say. Mr. Kravitz relayed several stories of how Emily corrected Dave on things that most people do naturally. "Call her Little Miss Manners when you meet her."

I drained what was left of my coffee. After setting the mug in the sink, I turned back to Mr. Kravitz. "I like him." He didn't respond. Everything he told me made me want to be around Dave more. Dave was complicated, but I felt like I knew him a little better. I wanted him to know I wasn't planning to cut bait. "I care about him. I don't want him to get hurt any more than you do."

He nodded. He returned to the Chrysler without another word, when I asked, "Hey, when's he coming back?"

Kravitz grinned, "Within the hour. You better get showered. He's taking today off to spend with you." A smile formed on my lips. After everything Mr. Kravitz had said about routines and the fact that Dave had never not worked, I didn't know what to say. He must have picked up on my surprise because he answered anyway when I hadn't posed a question, "So you'll want to use positive reinforcement with him. If you want him to be more spontaneous, you've got to be ready to react when he tries. Go!"

I took the steps two at a time, leaving Mr. Kravitz to his own devices in the garage. I had learned far more than I expected to this morning. I was glad Dave and I had the history we did, but that was only a small element of who he was now. He may be compulsive about some things, but he wanted to spend the day with me. I wondered what we might do. If he left it to me, I'd vote for a quick trip to Mt Crescent Ski area. It was in Honey Creek, Iowa, but that was close and would be fun. If Dave didn't know how to ski, they had a great tube run that would be great for laughs, too. All of my ski gear was in my garage. I was sure I would be able to get into that even if my house was still off limits.

I thought of other activities as I bounded into the shower in case Dave didn't want to spend the day in the snow. When the steamy water washed over me, I thought of finding Mark last night and the fact that I had kept it from Dave. Not intentionally, but I made up my mind to tell him about it as soon as he got back today.

CHAPTER 22

Dave stood in the kitchenette as I emerged from the bathroom. He wore a mischievous grin. Unable not to smile back at the silly look on his face, I asked, "What's so funny?"

"I picked something up for you while I was out."

"A mocha latte?" I asked hopefully.

"I can make you one if you want, but no." He handed me a black sharpie marker. "In case you wanted to cover up my ink."

I shook my head, still loving that my name might as well have been written in block letters over his heart. "No, thanks." Tossing the marker onto the little kitchen table, "It sucks that it's not summertime. I'd make you go all over town with your shirt off today."

Dave closed the distance between us as his lips leaned down close to my ear, "I'd do it right now if you wanted me to."

He pulled my wet hair off of my shoulder, then kissed the tender skin below my ear as his teeth grazed my ear lobe and shivers rocketed through my body. His hands slid under my t-shirt caressing the small of my back as tingles erupted under his touch. My hands did the same thing to him, sliding over his smooth skin as his lips found mine. My body began pressing against his as heat rocked me to my core.

A satisfied moan escaped him as I deepened our kiss. I gripped his shirt, much the same as I had last night, but he didn't try to stop me as I lifted the material over his head and tossed his shirt to the floor. My hands greedily took in his exposed flesh as his breath grew shallow.

Electricity erupted between us as I pulled my shirt off and tossed it next to his on the floor. Dave's eyes took me in as he murmured reverently, "You are beautiful." His lips slowly skimmed the arch of my neck, down my shoulder, and continued moving lower.

A tool clanged against metal downstairs and onto the floor as the sound reverberated around the quiet building. My breath hitched as I remembered we weren't alone, "Kravitz is downstairs."

Dave's lips returned to my ear, "Shhh, it's just you and me." My heart pumped wildly in my chest trying to convince my mind it hadn't heard anything. He whispered, "I want you." His groin pressed into me, as his hands slid under my thighs and lifted them up so my legs were wrapped around him.

My pulse pounded hard, its drumming was all I could hear, beating a loud rhythm drowning out everything else. Dave took choppy steps toward the bed, easily carrying me as I clung to him. We needed to slow down, but my body refused to listen to my mind. A hunger grew inside me that would be satisfied with nothing short of the friction of his body against mine.

Dave eased me onto the bed, the weight of his enormous frame pressing against me. Our chests were bare as his skin coerced me into an unfamiliar bliss. A sigh of pleasure escaped me which made Dave's eyes light up, "I love that sound. I want to make that sound come from you over and over again."

Light tingles had morphed into an outrageous desire. I pressed my lips to his ear as my teeth grazed his ear lobe, much as he had done to me only minutes before. A pained whisper answered my wordless invitation, "Don't do that, Candy, unless you're ready to shed some more clothes."

My fingers slid just under the waistband of his jeans as I watched his eyelids grow heavy while a lustful expression shone on his face. He held my hands in place before I could make a move to make good on his warning. His eyes snapped open as they looked directly into mine, "You want to do this?"

Without hesitating, "Yes."

He rolled over pulling me on top of him. Sliding my hair to the side, I nuzzled into the crook of his neck feeling every inch of his bare chest against mine. His voice was low, as if he were arguing with himself, "This is too fast."

I chuckled at him, "Too fast? It took you four years to make your move."

"Six," he confessed with a grin. Both his hands cradled either side of my face. His callouses were rough against my jaw, while his dark brown eyes stared directly into mine. I wasn't sure what he was looking for until he warned, "I'm not up for a fling."

Had I heard him say the same words last night, I would have been wounded, but after speaking to Kravitz, I knew Dave wasn't rejecting me. He was proposing much more. I turned my head, kissing one of the hands that had been holding my face, "I wasn't offering one."

Confusion shone on his beautiful face. I could get lost in his eyes if I weren't careful. He cleared his throat and asked, "What are you offering?"

"Popcorn, backrubs and the remote."

My answer did nothing to remove the confused expression he wore, so I elaborated. "I love going to the movies and eating buttery popcorn. After a full day of leaning over cars, your back must kill you – so a backrub might be something to look forward to. As long as you don't choose sports every time we sit in front of the television, I'll let you pick what you want to watch at least half the time."

Dave still wasn't making the connection, so I drew it out for him, "You are who I want to sit next to while I'm eating my popcorn. I'm volunteering a backrub every evening if you want it because I seriously like the way your muscles feel under my touch. I promise not to make you watch chick-flicks every time we hang out in front of the television. That's the best offer I can make right now."

"You don't have to be my girlfriend because you're in fear for your life. You can stay here as long as you want. No strings."

"I'm not here because I don't have anywhere else to go." That was debatable. "I'm here because I want to be with you. You've changed a lot since we were friends in school. I liked you back then, but I. . . really like who you have become."

Another tool clanged against metal downstairs, as if Kravitz were reminding us that he was still here. The bell on the front door of the lobby sounded. I asked, "Do you need to see who that is?"

Dave shook his head, "Kravitz can take care of it." He pressed his lips hard against mine. When he pulled away, he looked thrilled. "So, you want to go find a latte?"

"You just said the magic words."

I began to ease off of him to retrieve our shirts when I remembered what I had been agonizing about before he distracted me. "Wait. I need to tell you something." Dave's eyes searched mine, still sexy in a playful way. "Last night, before I came back to your apartment, I drove by Bank Shot."

He grinned, "We can find a pool table today if you want. I'm not bad." He made a motion with his hands like he was taking a shot with an invisible pool cue.

I rolled my eyes at his offer. Pool hadn't been a game for me in a long time: it was more of a part-time job with Libby. "No. I mean, maybe another time. When I was there. . ." my voice trailed off. I didn't know how he would take it, but he needed to know I'd seen his brother. "Mark was in the parking lot."

"What?!" he roared. He stood up quickly from the bed. "Why didn't you tell me? Did you talk to him? Where is he?"

Hurt registered on his face, and I knew anything I shared with him could only make that look intensify. "I talked to him. I told him I knew you."

"You did?" The hurt change to hopefulness as his eyes held mine. "What did he say?"

"He thought you were dead. I had trouble getting him to believe me at first. He wants to see you, but said he had to take care of some things first."

Dave looked at me with a wild gaze. "Why didn't you tell me any of this last night?" He walked over to where our shirts were lying on the floor and grabbed his angrily, pulling it hard over his head and shoving his arms through the holes.

"He made me promise not to tell you I'd seen him. I was going to tell you anyway, I swear I was. When I got here, we started talking, the candles were lit, I got lost in the mood, and I just didn't think about it."

"You saw my brother. I told you I've been looking for him forever. You didn't think I'd want to know that you saw him?"

Biting my lower lip, I waffled about how much to tell him. I didn't know how accurate Tony's information had been, but Mark had done nothing to dispel anything Tony had said when he choked me and shoved me to the ground, then threatened to run me down with his car. Tentatively I answered, "I think he might be involved in some bad stuff."

My accusation hung in the air. Dave watched me, waiting for me to clarify. When I didn't respond right away, he asked, "Bad stuff?"

I picked up my shirt off the floor, put it back on and took a seat on the sofa. I told Dave everything Tony had said, about my trip to talk to Officer Brown, and how I'd threatened to go to the media if the charges against him weren't dropped, then everything that had happened in the Bank Shot parking lot.

When I was done speaking, Dave sat beside me with a blank look. I offered, "Tony says he didn't know what Mark was involved in, and it's not like I trust Tony. He could have been wrong."

Dave's voice was hollow. "He didn't want to see me?"

"He did. I'm sure he did. But whatever he's involved in, maybe he didn't want to drag you into it. He said he'll find you after he takes care of a few things."

Dave stood, his face emotionless, "I need to go."

I grabbed my purse and stood up, "Okay."

He shook his head at me. His voice sounded distant, "Sorry. I need to go somewhere by myself for a while. I don't know when I'll be back." Without so much as a glance in my direction, he disappeared down the steps. Whoever had walked into the lobby was talking to Kravitz.

I heard Mr. Kravitz say, "Dave, you got time to look at a Camaro?"

Dave didn't answer him, but I heard the bell on the door clang from Dave's departure. A few seconds later his truck started up outside. Peering through the window, I watched Dave drive away. Muffled voices spoke in the lobby for a minute or so, then the bell on the door sounded again as the customer departed.

Kravitz yelled from the bottom of the steps, "What happened? What's wrong with Dave?"

I felt awful. Why hadn't I told Dave last night? I knew how badly he wanted to see Mark. It should have been the first thing I said when I arrived last night. The hurt on Dave's face wasn't just because of what Mark had said, the hurt was there because I hadn't told him right away. I scanned the little apartment. My backpack lay up against the wall outside the bathroom door. I threw it over my shoulder, went downstairs and grabbed my coat off the hook at the bottom of the steps. How had I screwed this up so royally?

CHAPTER 23

Friday night I returned to Dave's garage. It didn't look like there was a light on anywhere in the place. I couldn't see the flicker of a television from any of the second floor windows. His garage doors didn't have any windows to peep through, so there was no way to see if his truck was inside.

He hadn't called or texted me all day. A little neurotically, I had checked my phone every five minutes all day long until I had almost killed my battery. Libby was still unconscious, but her doctor said the swelling had gone down. They planned to wake her up tomorrow if her condition continued to improve. Larry and I sat in the waiting room together for hours this afternoon. It was difficult trying to make conversation. The only thing we had in common was Libby, and as much as I didn't want to, I started to remember why he had never been one of my favorite people.

Before I could get seriously annoyed with him and say something I'd regret, I stood up to go visit Libby.

Donning the visitor scrubs again, I stood by Libby's body. Her face was pale. The stuffed turtle still peeked out from behind the curtain on her table. I was pleased no one from the staff had stashed it away. "So this is your last night, Sleeping Beauty. Doc says tomorrow's the day." I reached down and squeezed her hand – it felt cool. I slid her hand under the covers, then did the same thing with her other hand. Her hair on the side of her head that hadn't been shaved laid against her cheek. Reaching into my purse I pulled out a clip and pulled her hair out of her face for her. "I haven't found him yet – the guy who did this to you. I saw that freaky Teddy last night. The cops almost got him."

I stared at her, hoping to see some indication that she had heard me. "Dave Brewer has a brother. Remember when we were at Bank Shot and thought we saw Dave? It wasn't. That was his brother Mark. They're hard to tell apart." Still nothing. "I kissed him. Well, technically I kissed both of them. I don't think kissing Mark counts, because I thought it was Dave at the time. I know what you're thinking, but Dave is different. He's not shy or awkward anymore – he's sexy." Conspiratorially I added, "I spent the night with him the last two nights." My cheeks flushed, "It was G-rated both nights, well, maybe PG, but I don't think it'll be that way for long."

I pulled a chair over and sat down next to her bed. Even though I had placed her hand under the blanket, I put mine over the lump where I knew her hand was. "He has a tattoo. He tried to hide it from me because he worried I would think it was creepy. It's a tattoo of a heart holding a candy cane." I checked again to see any reaction – nothing. "Can you believe it? It sort of made me want to melt. He told me he's had a crush on me since high school." I couldn't make the goofy grin on my face subside even if I tried. "I can't wait for you to see it."

The weight of my last sentence settled heavy on my heart as my grin disappeared. What if the doctors tried to wake her up tomorrow and she wouldn't wake up? What if she woke up and didn't know who I was? What if her brain were damaged and when she woke up she was no longer Libby?

"You have to wake up tomorrow." Sorrow choked me, "Don't. . .you can't. . .just wake up, okay? No matter what else happens, wake up tomorrow. I promise I'll do whatever you need me to do." I slid my hand under the blanket and locked my pinky finger with hers. "Pinky swear. If you need someone to take care of you, I'll do it. Just wake up. I need you."

We sat there with our pinkies linked together. I didn't want to let her go. I wished it were already Saturday. The not knowing was killing me. I could take any curve ball her condition dictated, but the uncertainty of what tomorrow would bring was excruciating. I leaned down close to her ear, "I'll be here tomorrow afternoon as soon as I get off work. It's okay if you wake up before I get here. Just wake up."

There was no response at all. "Larry has been in the waiting room since they brought you here. I still think he's a loser, but if you wondered, I'm pretty sure he loves you. He has only left the hospital a few times to change clothes and shower. If you. . ." I corrected myself, "when you wake up: I won't give you a hard time if you want to see him again." I squeezed her hand through the blanket draped over her. "I'll never give you a hard time about anything again – just open your eyes. You're more of a sister to me than Kim or Carly. I love you, Libby."

She didn't react to anything I said, and I could no longer take it. I hurried out of her room, deposited the scrubs in the used bin and hurried into the waiting room. Larry looked hopeful as I rushed through the doors, but I shook my head, a silent answer that she was still in her coma. My one-sided conversation with Libby had taken everything I had not to break down into a blubbering mess. As much as I wanted to leave without trying to speak, Larry stood up and walked toward me. I held up a hand, and choked out, "I'll be back after work tomorrow." I squeezed his forearm and reassured him, "She's going to wake up. I know it." Ducking my head, I walked away. I didn't want to consider the possibility that I was wrong, or any of the other possibilities.

I drove back to Dave's. The place was still dark from the curb. I got out of my car to look and see if there was any hint of movement inside. As I attempted to see through the blind on the front door of Dave's garage, it looked like he wasn't here, or if he were inside, he wanted to be alone. How had things gone wrong so quickly?

He was different from all the other guys I knew. He let his guard down with me, letting me see the real Dave, right up until the second he believed I had betrayed him. I knew why he was so hurt. If I were him, I would be furious with me, too. Just because I understood his reaction, I still hoped he might forgive my lapse in judgment.

I knocked on the front door of Dave's garage, but again, there was no answer. I tried calling his cell, but it went straight to voicemail. I had called several times today, but I hadn't left any messages. When I heard his voice asking me to leave a message, words began spilling out of me. "Hey, it's Candy. I know you don't want to see me. I don't blame you. If I could do it over, I swear I would have told you about Mark right away. I just got swept away by you last night. I know it was selfish. I'm sorry. I didn't expect the candles, or your tattoo, or to feel the way I do about you. You have my number. You once told me you live your life by expecting the worst and hoping for the best. So, I guess I'll hope one day you can forgive me. Bye." I almost hung up, but added, "If I don't talk to you again, thanks. I'm glad I finally got to meet the real Dave. I'll never forget you."

From Dave's garage I decided to hit the college library and do some searching. I tried everything I could find to try to locate Mark Brewer on the internet. Phone records, public utilities, property searches: each Mark Brewer I located was either too old or too young or in the wrong state. By eleven PM I was exhausted, and the library was getting ready to close.

I couldn't go back to my house. I hadn't heard from the police all day, but it was too late to knock on Mrs. Bavcock's door even if they had concluded I was no longer a person of interest. I considered driving back to Dave's place, but decided against it. I had friends who stayed at the dorms on campus, but it was Friday night and none would be home yet. It was too cold to sleep in my car. I was quickly running out of options, and Motel 6 looked like it might end up a reality.

A thought occurred to me that there was one person who might let me stay. I did an internet search and found the number. I hated to do it, but short of getting a motel room that I didn't have money for, I was coming up empty. A surprisingly friendly voice answered the phone for such a late hour. I took a deep breath and answered, "Hi, this is Candy Kane. I'm sorry to call so late. Is Mr. Kravitz home?"

Mr. Kravitz was quick to agree to let me camp in his guest room for the night. When I arrived it was close to midnight. It must have been eating at him all day, because I had barely crossed the threshold when he asked, "What happened with you and Dave this morning?"

There was no reason to hide anything from him. "I saw Mark last night."

He tried to correct me. "You mean Tuesday night?"

"Then, too. I ran into him at the parking lot of Bank Shot before I went to Dave's last night. Mark thought Dave was dead. When I told him he lived here, he wouldn't meet him."

"You told Dave the brother he has been looking for most of his life doesn't want to see him?"

"No! I told him what Mark told me to tell him: he was tying up some loose ends and he would find him soon." Mr. Kravitz gave me a disapproving stare. I explained, "I tried to get Mark to call him. I told him I'd get Dave on the phone if he wouldn't meet him, but he said no. He told me he would find him when he was ready."

"What loose ends?"

"I don't know. He didn't say." I paused, remembering what Tony had said. "I think Mark might be a big time criminal. Someone told me he's really dangerous and to keep away from him."

"Did you tell Dave?"

I shook my head. "Not in those words." I felt awful about the whole situation, especially about not telling Dave right away. "I don't know anything about Mark. If I'm wrong, I don't want Dave to think badly of him, but if I'm right, I don't want Dave hurt, either." I wanted to add that I knew first hand that Mark has a propensity for violence when he's angry, but chose to keep that tidbit of information to myself.

Mr. Kravitz shook his head in frustration, "Dave hasn't returned any of my calls all day. I locked up the garage at five o'clock, but he didn't come back."

I confessed, "I drove by the shop: there weren't any lights on. Where do you think he went?"

"I don't know. It's not like him. I've got keys, we can go over tomorrow and check on him." He looked at my backpack still slung over my shoulder. "C'mon, let's get you settled in, and we can come up with a plan in the morning." Mr. Kravitz led me to a guest room with ivory walls. The bed was soft; it was draped with a comforter depicting green ivy in an ornate pattern all over it. Matching curtains hung from the single rectangular window. The carpet was a thick pile under my toes. For such a welcoming room, I couldn't wait to close my eyes and forget everything that had happened today.

Nightmares consumed my night: Grey's face smiling at me through the glass at the gas station, Teddy standing over Libby's body at the hospital, but worst of all was the agony on Dave's face when I told him over and over his brother didn't want to see him. I woke up to sun pouring in through the curtains while I was utterly exhausted.

When I awoke Saturday morning, I was grateful for the place to stay, but it was time to get my life back. It had been three full days since my house was declared a crime scene. That should have been more than enough time to gather whatever evidence may have been there. It was early, so I made the bed, put on a clean set of clothes from my backpack, and tiptoed down the hallway.

I could hear a television in a room adjacent to the kitchen. I chose not to follow the noise, instead I found a note pad and scribbled a quick thank-you on it for letting me use their guest room. As I started for the door, a high-pitched voice startled me, "It's not nice to leave without saying good-bye."

I turned toward the voice and was struck by the angelic face scowling at me. The photograph on Mr. Kravitz's phone hadn't done the little girl justice. Her face was round with enormous blue eyes and pouty lips. The blond ringlets hung at her shoulders as she stood in the doorway with her hands on her hips.

"I'm sorry. I didn't want to wake your parents. You must be Emily. It's great to meet you. I'm Candy."

Her little blue eyes narrowed suspiciously, "You weren't here when I went to bed."

"No. Your parents let me stay in the guest room last night."

She considered this for a second, then told me, "You haven't eaten breakfast. When I stay at Beth's house, I always stay for breakfast."

"Um, I usually just have coffee for breakfast, and I don't want to wake your parents."

Emily went to a cupboard to the left of the refrigerator and grabbed a canister of coffee and a coffee filter. "Here you go. I don't know how much to put in."

She stood beside me as I put in enough for a fresh pot and pressed the start button. Within seconds the aroma filled the air of the kitchen. She continued watching me as I stood by the coffee brewer. Finally she asked, "You stayed in Dave's room. Do you know Dave?"

"I do. He's a friend of mine."

A sad look shown on her face, "You don't have a momma, either?"

Taken aback at her logic, I answered, "I have one. She lives in New Mexico with Dad."

After considering my answer for a minute, she volunteered, "Momma says not everyone has a mom. All my friends at school have moms. None of them live in New Mexico, but one lives in California."

"Then your friends are really lucky."

I poured myself a cup of the fresh coffee in a mug. I kept glancing toward the doorway every few seconds to see if our exchange had awakened Mr. or Mrs. Kravitz. When my mug was drained, I smiled back at Emily, "Thank you for breakfast and for letting me borrow Dave's room last night. I need to get to the hardware store before I go to work. Tell your parents I said thanks, okay?"

"Okay." Having completed her hostess duties, she smiled and walked me to the front door. She offered, "Bundle up, it's cold out today."

"I will. I hope to see you again soon."

"Dave doesn't use his room anymore. You can come back tonight if you want. But Aunt Jean needs the room when she comes to town, so you can't put any posters on the wall."

I smiled at her. There was something about this girl. I could see how she could have easily broken through Dave's defenses when I had failed. "Okay. If I come back, I won't bring any posters."

While I sat in my car waiting for it to warm up, I called Officer Brown. He confirmed that the police were done collecting evidence, so I could indeed return to my house today. He also told me that all charges against Dave had been dropped. Officer Brown told me there was some pending disciplinary action for the police officer who had accused Dave of assault during his escape from the hospital. I thanked him and hung up.

The thought of sleeping in the big house by myself was not all that appealing, but I didn't want to take advantage of Mr. Kravitz. I doubted Dave would welcome seeing me any time soon. Before I pulled away from the curb in front of Mr. Kravitz's house, I tried calling Dave. It went right to voicemail. I didn't want to come off like a stalker, especially after the long message I had left for him last night. "It's me. Um, the doctors are supposed to wake up Libby this afternoon. I'll be at the restaurant today, then the hospital after. I just wanted you to know where I was if you were looking for me. Bye."

Tossing the phone in my purse, I drove to a hardware store. If I was staying at my house, I was going to need a little better lock than the ones I had now.

A half-hour later I was at my house. When I opened the front door, an envelope had been jammed under the door. Libby's name was on the envelope with a big smiley face drawn next to her name. If it were a get well card, I'd take it with me, but since it hadn't been mailed, I wanted to make sure it wasn't a message from a friend who hadn't heard what had happened. I took it to the kitchen and opened it up. It was a thank-you card from Jayson, a guy she worked with, accompanied by three hundred dollars. I knew I shouldn't read it, but I couldn't stop myself. It said: "Thanks for the loan on Monday. If you hadn't have helped me, I would have lost my car. I owe you big time. Thanks for not telling anyone. Jayson"

My vision clouded as tears threatened to escape. When I accused her of blowing her whole paycheck, she had let me believe she had been irresponsible rather than telling me she had loaned her money to a friend. That was just like Libby: twelve dollars in her coffee can, and she had loaned everything else she had to someone she believed needed the money more than she did. I sat at the kitchen table re-reading the thank-you note several times. Each time only made me feel worse.

When I rose from the chair to put the money in her coffee can, I saw there was over two hundred dollars in it already. She had given Chris money at Bank Shot and bought groceries Tuesday night – the rest of Teddy's money was safely tucked away. Why wouldn't she have given the money she had to Grey when he showed up? Had she denied she had it? Why wouldn't she have handed the whole thing over? Had she told Grey I had the money?

I had seen the living room and the aftermath of what had happened to Libby when I stopped by with the police officer Wednesday morning. I wanted to avoid the room. I didn't want to see the blood-soaked sofa again. I filled up the sink with food encrusted dishes that had set on the stove all week. I washed, dried, and put them away, glancing over my shoulder several times at the ominous living room. My hands grabbed the dishrag to wipe down the counters while the dishwater drained.

Reluctantly, I walked out of the kitchen and stood in the doorway to the living room where Grey had attacked her. The tan sofa had several pieces cut out of it, no doubt gathered for evidence. Two very bloody patches had been cut out of the carpet, as well.

I slid down the doorway, my back braced against it, unable to move as my eyes took in the horrific sight. I don't know how long I sat there staring at the place where Libby had nearly been killed. Unable to stand, I crawled over on my hands and knees to where the attack had happened. My hand smoothed over the carpet caked with dried blood. It was thick and hard, feeling like dried paint under my fingers.

There was so much blood. It was dry and the carpet and couch that had been soft before were both hard to touch and gruesome to see. I remembered glancing into the room as I ran out of the house Tuesday night; Libby looked like she had fallen asleep in front of the television. Why hadn't I gone in and told her to go to bed? Why hadn't I gotten out of my own bed when she called for my help? If she died, it would be because I hadn't prevented it. I hadn't helped her when she needed me.

I couldn't leave the sofa in the house. I needed to get it out. I couldn't bear to look at any of it. I pushed the sofa out of the living room, through the kitchen, the entryway, and on to the front porch. Trash day was Monday, but it was too large for pickup. I started to walk back inside, but I couldn't leave the couch out for the world to see. She deserved better. I went back inside and grabbed my coat, hat and gloves, then dragged it through the snow to the backyard.

When it was in the center of the backyard, away from everything else, I doused it with gasoline from a can in the garage and set it on fire. I was sure one of my neighbors would probably call the fire department, but I didn't care. I stood there watching it burn as the flames enveloped every inch of it. When one of my neighbors stepped into her back yard, I waved my hand but offered no explanation of the bonfire I had started. In this moment I wished for Grey's face to appear around the corner of my house. The rage inside me grew with every bit of flame that flew into the air. He wouldn't get away with this.

As the flames died down and the springs were visible, I turned away from it, then returned to the house. I opened a drawer in the kitchen, took out a knife, then cut every bit of the carpeting and padding that had blood stains on it. I ripped the carpet free of the floor, took it outside and threw it on the still smoldering sofa. I poured more accelerant on the fire and watched the flames dance high again.

I spoke into the fire, willing my words to find my nemesis, "Stop by for a visit now, Grey. You'll pay for this."

After the flames died down and I was satisfied that no part of anything Grey had touched still remained, I went inside again. Hopefully Mom wouldn't try to surprise me for a visit until after I had replaced her sofa and carpet.

Two hours later I was sitting on the floor by my front door frustrated beyond belief. My phone rang in the kitchen as I scrambled up off of the floor to retrieve it from my purse. I caught it on the third ring, hoping to hear Dave's voice on the other end. I tried to hide my disappointment when I heard Kravitz. "Why'd you leave so early this morning?"

I sighed into the phone, "The police said I could have my house back today. I thought I'd install some floor deadbolts, but I can't get the stupid hole I drilled to line up with the lock in the door, and I have to be at work in an hour." I didn't bother to mention my bonfire in the back yard.

"I've got some time. I can help you with them."

"Seriously?"

"What, you think I'm only handy with cars? I'll be over in ten minutes. You still live on Elm?"

How did Kraviz know where I lived? He'd never been here. "Uh, yeah. Car's out front."

True to his word, ten minutes after we hung up, he was standing at my front door inspecting my work. "Yikes, Candy. You suck at this."

"Thanks, Mr. Kravitz. Like I hadn't figured that out for myself."

He shook his head at me, "Go get ready for work. I'll finish up here."

Tentatively I said, "There are two more exterior doors if you're feeling ambitious."

Chuckling at my ineptness with hand tools, he directed, "Go. I've got this."

I bounded up a few of the stairs when the wave of discomfort hit me again. My eyes narrowed as I saw him cutting a new hole in the floor. I didn't get an ax murderer vibe from him, but after everything that had happened the last few days, I didn't want to be naïve, either. "Hey, how did you know where I lived anyway?"

"How else? Dave."

"Dave told you where I lived?"

"I wouldn't say he told me." He leaned back against the wall. "Remember that schmuck Dillon Ford you went with to prom?"

Schmuck was an understatement. He turned out to be a grade-A loser. I had cut him out of every picture the two of us were together in and tried to block out the whole experience. "I'd rather not."

"Dave was trying to get up the nerve to ask you to prom. He and I sat in my car on your street for almost an hour one Saturday. Eventually he talked himself out of asking you at your house, thinking he wanted to ask you at school instead, so we drove away."

"Dave never asked me. I only went with Dillon because prom was like two weeks away."

Mr. Kravitz smiled, "I know. Dave tried lots of times, but could never close the deal."

I tried to think back. I couldn't remember ever talking about prom with Dave. The subject had never come up. After finally getting to know the real Dave, I wish he'd have found a way to ask. Prom was one of the worst dating experiences of my life. It was supposed to be a special night, but ended up being little more than an evening of Dillan trying to grope me while he attempted to shove his slimy tongue down my throat.

I showered and dressed in record time. I had fifteen minutes to get to Cookies' Cuisine, which was only five minutes from my house. After being pulled off of the lunch shift during the week, I couldn't afford to lose my weekend hours, too. Mr. Kravitz wasn't at the front door when I came downstairs. No tools lay anywhere around it. As I looked, the shiny new deadbolt was secured into the floor and all the wood shavings that had been lying on the carpet were gone.

The sound of the drill echoed from the back of the house. He'd finished this and started on the second in less than a half hour. I didn't know how he was working so fast, but I was grateful. I found him kneeling beside the door for the entrance to the basement. He looked up after he felt my eyes watching him. "One down, two to go."

"The front door looks great. Thanks so much for doing this for me."

"No problem. It was a smart idea to install these. They won't keep out someone who wants in, but they'll force them to make enough racket to wake the dead, so no one can sneak up on you. Here," he tossed me a single key. "That's for the front door. I'll lock the front door on my way out, you'll be able to get back in with that one. I'll leave the other keys on the table for the two back doors."

"Thanks," I stumbled for a second, "Ryan." He smiled when I had finally been able to call him by his first name. It felt strange and wasn't something I'd easily be able to make a habit out of. "I'm going to work. If you see Dave. . ." my voice trailed off.

"If I see him, I'll let him know you're worried. Don't think just because I'm putting these locks in that you aren't welcome at my house. The guest room is yours if you need it."

"At least until Aunt Jean's next trip."

Mr. Kravitz laughed, "Right."

CHAPTER 24

I checked in with the manager as soon as I arrived at the restaurant. I wasn't sure what was going on today, but the place was packed while people were huddled in the front waiting for tables. Saturdays were busy, but not typically saturated with hungry people.

I grabbed an apron from the back. Kelly saw me, and directed, "Tables two and four." Kelly was one of my favorite people to work with.

"Got it," I called. The next three hours were non-stop. Although I was deemed unreliable because my morning classes routinely ran long during the week, I was one of the better waitresses on staff. My tips showed it. Just as the lunch crowd was beginning to clear, I did a quick calculation and had pocketed almost fifty dollars. That was almost a full tank of gas.

Kelly called over her shoulder. "Some guy in a black truck stopped by a while ago to see you. He was delicious! I told him you were off at four. He said he'd be back then."

My heart lurched, "Did he say his name was Dave?"

"He didn't say. You been holding out on me?"

What could I tell her? The last time I had worked, Dave hadn't been in the picture; it was hard to believe that was less than a week ago. "It's sort of recent. Dark hair, dark eyes, big arms?"

"I didn't see past his chest. He had to turn sideways to make it through the doorway. My God I want his babies."

"So, should I plan on seeing him a little closer to four-thirty?"

We both giggled as Kelly straightened her uniform and said, "That should be adequate enough time for me to convince him you aren't as good of baby momma material as I am."

The manager eyed us from the kitchen. Gossip was frowned on, and I was already under his scrutiny for breathing. Having the sudden urge to look productive, I announced, "I'm going to go wipe down tables."

"Hey, Amazon, can you grab some napkins from the supply cabinet first?" Kelly was five foot three in heels, so anything past the third shelf required climbing on her part.

I laughed at her, taking a detour to the back, "No problem, my little Pygmy friend."

Dave had stopped by to see me. I felt giddy. I looked at my watch; he would be here in less than two hours. If he were still angry with me, he would have left a message or just continued to ignore me. Driving all the way here meant he wanted to talk. If I could get him to listen, he'd know I didn't purposely hide the fact from him that I had seen Mark.

Thoughts of Dave stretched out beside me assailed my memory. I stopped by a mirror hanging in the back hallway and checked my hair in case he came back early. I couldn't wipe the stupid grin off my face. A heaviness that had been on my chest since yesterday morning eased.

Shaking my head at myself in the mirror, I stepped into the supply closet, quickly eyeing each of the shelves, and finding the box of napkins all the way in the back of the fifth shelf. I could reach it without a step stool, but had to do it on my toes holding a lower shelf for balance. The door opened behind me and slammed shut hard. "Geeze, impatient much?" I called to Kelly.

My fingers grasped the packet of napkins as I turned toward the door to toss the packet at her. My heart stopped as my eyes took in the man who I last saw sprinting down my street with Dave giving chase. A knife glinted in his hand.

I screamed, a high-pitch I wasn't even aware I was capable of producing. He jumped forward shoving his hand over my mouth. He glared menacingly, then whispered, "Not a sound or your little waitress friend doesn't make it home tonight. Clear?"

A second later Kelly swung the door open to the supply room. Grey stood behind the door glaring at me out of her view.

"Are you okay?"

"I saw. . . a rat, I think."

"A rat?" Her voice hitched up two full octaves as she bounded back into the hallway holding the door open, "Oh my God, where?"

"I'm not sure. Something moved behind the door and scared me." Kelly leaned back in and moved the door slightly to get a better look behind the door when I reached out and held it in place. "It's fine. I'm sure I imagined it. Here." I tossed the package of napkins to her. "I'll be right out. I just need to calm down a little."

"You look a little pale. Do you want to take your break? I can cover for you."

Glancing back toward the killer behind the storage room door, he mouthed the word, "Yes."

"Uh, thanks. Yeah. I'm going to go get some air."

"Okay. I'll tell Cookie. She's going to freak when she hears there's a rat in the store room."

Kelly left the door cracked when she walked back toward the front. Grey's voice was sinister and made my skin crawl. "Nice. At least you're smarter than you look. Let's go."

He grabbed hold of my shoulder, hard. He was leaving a bruise, but I was too scared to ask him to loosen his grip. As we walked out of the storage room, we had to go past the entrance to the vacant bar. I peeked inside and saw Cookie tallying up lunch receipts. I tried to catch her eye, but she was consumed with the slips of paper in front of her. Just before we reached the back door, there was an opening into the kitchen where the dishwasher worked.

The dishwashers were on a constant rotation. None of them stayed on the job longer than a couple of months. Working for minimum wage in a steamy room whose temperature routinely topped 100 degrees did little to inspire long term employment. The dishwasher today looked Asian, and was wearing headphones, so calling out for his help would have been wasted breath. He didn't even notice Grey and me walk past the area where he worked.

Grey shoved me through the back door as the blast of cold air assaulted me. Our uniform was a thin short sleeved t-shirt and black trousers. Within seconds I was shivering. Grey wore a thick leather jacket and seemed to enjoy the goose bumps holding the hairs on my arms at attention. "Oh, so sorry, it's a little chilly out today, isn't it?"

He zipped up his coat while the smug expression on his face grew. I told him, "My coat is just inside on the hook. Let me reach in and grab it."

He shook his head as a smile grew in front of me, "I don't think so. You're as slick as a greased pig. Avoiding me the way you have has been quite an accomplishment. You must be very proud of yourself."

"You tried to kill me!"

"*Tried* being the operative word. You've proven yourself a worthy opponent."

"Opponent? I don't even know you! You attacked my roommate – she's still in the hospital. You scared the crap out of the old lady across the street. What is your problem?"

"My problem is you are still breathing. Teddy didn't appreciate the scam you played on him and Tony."

My face was numb and my arms freezing. The high today was supposed to be five degrees. Shivers rocked me as I stuttered from the cold, "There wa-wa-wa-was no sc-sc-scam."

"No sc-sc-scam," he mocked. "No one plays Teddy and gets away with it, no one. Your roommate is lucky she's still alive." He reached into his pocket and pulled out the photo of my two sisters and me which he had stolen from my bedroom. "Give me a reason to hunt these two down, too."

Pure fear rocked me. I had to stop this guy. Two men were walking toward us in the alley, neither paying much attention to us, so I screamed to catch their attention, "H-H-Help me!"

A fist crashed hard into my jaw as my body landed face-first in the snow. The snow was even more cold against my uninsulated skin than the subzero temperature of the air. I lay there a second as the pain registered from my jaw. I had never been punched before – ever. The sharp throbbing brought tears to my eyes. I heard Grey warn the two men, "Keep walking. Nothing to see here. Just teaching my girl some manners."

Their footsteps crunched faster in the snow as they ignored him and drew closer. Grey reached down and pulled me up from the ground by my hair, holding my body in between him and the approaching men. His voice was raw, "I said back off. It'll be worse for her if either of you take another step."

I saw one pull out a cell phone, then Grey punched me hard in the kidney from behind as I went to my knees. I prayed the guy had called the police. I lost focus of the two men through the searing pain, but heard one of the voices shout, "Easy man. Take it easy. Just let her go."

Grey dragged me by my hair and shoved me toward an awaiting car. It wasn't his Nova. It was blue with four doors. He pushed me through the driver's side door while he held a fistful of my hair in his hand. My jaw ached, but the throbbing in my back from his punch was indescribable. My neck was wrenched at an odd angle from him using my hair as a handle.

Grey let go of my hair long enough to turn the key in the ignition. Away from his grasp, I fumbled for the door handle in the few seconds I wasn't under his control and was rewarded with a punch to the throat. I saw spots and couldn't make a sound if I had wanted to. I gasped for air.

The car fishtailed out of the alley as he sped down the narrow road. Welcomed heat blasted on me from the dashboard. I was too frightened to move, even to flinch. I tried to watch where he was going but had difficulty paying attention to my surroundings. A jacket lay bundled on the floorboard. If he stopped at a red light, I would grab it and run. Grey's brutality in the last few minutes told me I wasn't going to be breathing if I didn't escape.

He slowed as I recognized the entrance to Pioneers' Park. I ran the trails here during the summer months and was familiar with this place. This park offered the advantage of me knowing my surroundings, but the distinct disadvantage that it was a nature preserve, so hardly anyone came here during the winter months.

A few lonely tire tracks stretched out in the snow in front of us. The car wasn't built for off-roading, so he would need to keep it on the pavement if he hoped to get back out. The sky was overcast: it was still light out, but the day's sunshine was completely blocked by the blanket of winter clouds. A heavy hit against my temple landed so hard my teeth clanged together, then everything went black.

CHAPTER 25

I came to in a small wooden structure, possibly a toolshed or an equipment shelter. There was enough light to make out shapes, but not bright enough to make me wince as my faculties slowly returned. I was covered by a jacket. It smelled of cheap cologne and sweat. The stench made me want to gag, but I breathed through my mouth to keep from alerting Grey that I was no longer unconscious.

I wiggled my toes: they were numb, but functioning. My fingers were the same. I was suspended a few feet off the ground, lying on what appeared to be an old Army cot. The canvas was stretched tight on metal poles. Knowing my slightest movement would make the canvas complain, I held very still. From what I could tell, I wasn't tied up or bound, just dumped on the canvas. My temple throbbed, my neck ached, and I could feel the tightness of a fresh bruise that had formed on my back.

It was cool in the structure, but not cold. Something was giving off heat, but the throbbing in my head and my desire to stay motionless persuaded me not to turn to see what that source might be. The scent of kerosene was heavy in the air as I overheard Grey's angry voice, "I'm freezing. You want in on this, you've got thirty minutes." He paused briefly, then answered, "She's still out." Another short pause, "I don't give a shit what's on television. You want a piece, you got thirty minutes, then I'm gutting her."

My body reacted to his words: the fine hairs on my arms stood at attention, every muscle in my body tensed while I sucked in a silent breath. I tried not to let my body betray me by outwardly reacting to his words, preferring instead to stay stiff as a board so as to remain silent. If he believed I was still unconscious, that was preferable to being gutted. Without moving a muscle, I scanned as much of the structure as my eyes could take in without giving away my current state.

A door stood along the same wall where my cot lay. The building had a cement floor. Light shown from the other side of the room as the cot I was lying on cast a shadow against the wall. Grey was pacing the floor on my right – his footsteps echoing a sinister march in the little shack. I believed the heat source behind me was a fire because the shadow from my cot danced along the wall. If he had built a fire, there was a good chance his back was to me. People normally faced a fire when they were cold. With his back turned, I'd have a two second advantage if I could make it through the door, maybe more.

I discreetly made a fist with my right hand, then my left, proving to myself that my hands worked and neither were bound. Both fists relaxed again in the position I had awoken to. I wiggled my toes in both of my shoes a second time to be sure. My head throbbed, but my vision wasn't blurry and I didn't see double, so I didn't think he had given me a concussion. I slowly filled my lungs with as much air as they could hold, then released it just as slowly.

His pacing continued as if he were a caged animal. I didn't know where we were – I hoped we were still in the park he had pulled into before knocking me senseless. The park was on more than 500 wooded acres. Once I got outside I'd have to look for landmarks to tell me where we were. If I were lucky, I'd be able to find one of the trails that I routinely ran after work in the summertime. Many of the trails in the park overlapped, and I knew nearly every route back to Cookie's.

I took my third lungful of air, then instead of releasing it slowly, I jumped off the cot, grabbed the jacket that had been draped over me, and bolted to the door. It wasn't locked, and it flew open easily under my grip. My legs took enormous strides: I was running for my life – my body knew it.

I had been running full speed for at least thirty seconds before I saw a landmark I recognized – a large oak tree with trail signs tacked on it. Choosing a trail I was familiar with, I continued to run full speed, peeking over my shoulder every few strides to see if I was being pursued. I couldn't hide my tracks in the snow, but it had been an overcast day today and the clouds hadn't lifted. The moon's illumination was poor from the clouds, and if Grey were trying to run as fast as I was, he would have a tough time seeing my tracks.

After a full ten minutes at a dead sprint, I could hardly breathe. Each breath I took felt like knives piercing my lungs, so I slowed my pace and tried to push through the ache. I couldn't feel my fingers, and my toes were growing more numb with each stride. The park was empty. I hadn't passed a single person my whole trek through. The paths were hardly visible this time of year on the clearest of days, so trying to stay on the snow-covered path proved daunting in the dark. Every few strides my feet would land on a patch of ice, threatening to send me sailing into the air if I continued running.

Just to the right of my path I spied a thick grove of evergreens. Jogging the last few feet to them, I crouched down in the shadow of the largest evergreen bush to try to catch my breath. The sounds of traffic in the distance were all I could hear over my own labored breathing. I don't know how long I stayed cowering next to the bush, but it was long enough that the breaths I took were no longer burning my lungs.

I had escaped. Grey hadn't caught me. I tried to get my bearings, looking for another landmark I recognized in the deserted park. I had veered off the trail I started on; this was an area I wasn't familiar with, too far out from the trails I frequented in the summer months. Gauging the tree line off to my left, if I could find a path that breached it, I should end up on Windom Street. From there it was less than a mile back to where my car was parked near the restaurant. As I stood up, I heard heavy boots running on the frozen snow in the direction where I had come from.

I quickly crouched back down, hoping he hadn't seen me, when his voice echoed around the deserted area. "It's my lucky day. I thought I'd lost you. Nice of you to wait for me to catch up."

Terror gripped me, as the fine hairs at the nape of my neck shouted for me to run. I didn't think, I just reacted. I spun around and sprinted away from the voice. There was no path in front of me, but I didn't let that dissuade me. My feet high-stepped through the thick crunchy snow. I had outrun him once: I could do it again. The ground was sloping down, adding to the momentum of my pace. I allowed the pull from the slope to let me nearly fly over the ground, dodging whatever vegetation peeked out from the frozen ground beneath my feet.

A snow covered obstacle, possibly a trash can on its side, lay directly in front of me. I leaped over the obstacle more gracefully than an all-state hurdler. His heavy steps crunched in the snow behind me, but I was gaining ground as his footsteps seemed to be further and further away. I chanced a glance over my shoulder to see if I could see him. I couldn't. In the silence of the night, I could hear he was still pursuing, but he was further behind me with every step I took.

Satisfied that I was going to make my escape a second time, I turned my attention back to where I was running just in time to see a gleaming sheet of ice stretched out in front of me. I was four full strides onto the ice before I realized I was running on a frozen pond.

The ice under my feet was smooth and spongy. It was strong enough to hold me upright, but with each step, the ice grew thinner. I slid to a stop, scanning in all directions. I couldn't go back the way I had come because I didn't have enough of a head start to find the safety of the bank and distance myself from Grey again. Instead I would try to run at an angle toward the outside of the lake, to find an adjacent bank where I could get off of the ice.

As I had committed to my plan, the ice under me complained, then spider web cracks formed under my feet. I took a tentative step as more cracks formed under me. Paralyzed by the fear that I would fall through if I continued or die if I went back: I stood still, searching for a better option. A single large crack opened up between my feet. The ice supporting my weight wasn't nearly as thick as it needed to be. I stood where I was, my mind racing: I was at least thirty feet from the closest bank. Grey had caught sight of my dilemma and was closing in fast.

Fear that the pond would swallow me whole took hold. Grey reached the bank where I had run onto the ice, as he mocked, "For a college girl, you don't read very well." He pointed to a sign facing away from where I stood. "Says right here: keep off thin ice."

I couldn't go back the way I had come: Grey was waiting. I couldn't stay where I was because the crack underneath me would give way any second. I couldn't go toward the center of the lake for the same reason. Going left would get me back to my car if I could just outpace him one more time. The muscles in my legs were already shaking, and my lungs felt like they were on fire. I had no other options. I jumped as far as I could to my left. As soon as the ball of my lead foot hit the ice, I was running full-speed toward the lake's bank.

Grey anticipated my move, and his feet were in motion in the same instant mine were. I reached the short bank and pulled myself up the berm using the naked winter saplings for grips. I climbed with every ounce of strength I possessed. As I reached the top of the berm, Grey's hand grabbed the back of my jacket and pulled me back down to the bottom of the berm. I scrambled to my feet ready to spring forward up the berm a second time when he lunged and was directly in front of me.

Grey grabbed both my arms and attempted to shove me back out onto the ice. I hooked my foot under an exposed root of a tree to anchor myself in place. When I didn't topple backwards, Grey lost his balance, and I shoved him hard out onto the ice. I didn't look where he had landed and could only hope the patch he had slid onto would be thin. I ran forward up the berm and refused to let my eyes look back. I did not listen for footsteps or breathing behind me, nor did I tear my eyes away from where I was going. If I didn't make it to safety this time, I wouldn't make it at all. I had run for too long, and my body couldn't take the abuse for much longer.

I dodged trees, low hanging branches, roots protruding from the ground, tall grass and thin shrubs, making my own trail through the trees. The vegetation pelted my numb face and cut my hands as I clawed my way through. Lights ahead of me from cars on Windham Street were my beacon of hope in the night.

As my body cleared the tree line, I was right: Windham Street lay directly in front of me. The fear and adrenalin in my body heightened. Without looking, I darted directly in front of the traffic, ignoring oncoming vehicles from both directions. It felt like playing that old video game Frogger as I dodged cars driving in both directions. Surprised motorists lay on their horns as I dashed in front of several unsuspecting drivers.

I was nearly exhausted after my escape through the park. My Chevelle was less than a mile from here, but I didn't have the strength to make it that far. I looked for a police car or an emergency vehicle of some kind. Traffic was heavy, but all the motorists seemed to pay little attention to me once I was on the far side of the busy street. My eyes scanned for a dark entryway or crevice where I could hide and catch my breath.

Despite the heavy traffic on the street, most of the businesses that lined it were closed for the day. To my left, a half block down the street stood an Irish pub. A brown overhang above the entrance with gold lettering proudly displayed: Finnegan's. The pub's name was flanked by shamrocks on either side. A public place was far safer than trying to hide on the street. I ran to the pub's front door as a sharp cramp stretched along my side.

Peering into the darkened front window, I could see there were at least thirty people inside. I could get lucky and Grey could run past this place, but even if he found me inside, he wouldn't attack me in front of that many witnesses. I grappled for the oversized brass door handle as my hand shook violently. A voice touched with humor called out from just a few feet away. "Are you training for a marathon? There are better activities to be had on a Saturday night."

The voice stopped me short. I let go of the door handle and turned to see a sleek black Mercedes sedan parked on the street. Adjoining the pub was a neighborhood grocery store, and directly in front of the store's front door was Mark. Too much was happening at once; I ignored Mark and grabbed the pub's handle in favor of the relative safety it offered.

A car horn blared behind me. I turned and saw Grey nearly get mowed down by a green Hyundai. A second shout from Mark, "Ah, an interesting way to train for a marathon. Someone chasing you is excellent motivation to push yourself. Don't let me interfere."

Mark confidently strolled toward his car, ignoring the fact that a lunatic had just chased me out of the woods. My eyes snapped back to Grey. Silently I wondered how Mark could be so callous. In that moment I wasn't convinced he could possibly be a distant relative to Dave, let alone a brother.

Grey stood in the median of the street. He saw exactly where I was. Re-evaluating my condition, the pub was still my best option. No way could my body outrun him again. Grey warned, "You'll regret it if you take one more step."

Did he think I was stupid? Maybe he should have said, "Wait for me so I can hurt you." I reasoned that I could find a sympathetic bartender or a backdoor – maybe both. Pulling the front door open to make my escape, a surprised couple darted through the door I held open. Neither commented on my wild appearance, choosing instead to put their heads down and walk in Mark's direction. The momentary delay was all Grey needed. He ran through the three lanes of traffic, leaped onto the curb and stared at me with angry eyes.

My fear and exhaustion morphed into anger when I turned toward him and shouted, "Back off. I'm calling the cops. You lose."

He stopped short. The threat of police may have slowed him, or possibly the fact that he knew chasing me into a public place could only end badly for him. I gave him a triumphant grin.

Grey placed both his hands on his knees, his eyes never leaving mine. I didn't back down, or rush into the pub: I stood answering him with the same angry glare he had just offered me. Wearing a forced smile, his winded answer was difficult to understand, "No one cheats Teddy and gets away with it. Remember that."

I let go of the door handle like an idiot, instead taking a step forward to face the brutal man who had pursued me for nearly four days. "I never cheated Teddy. Neither did Libby. It was a fair game. Ask his little brother."

"Teddy says you cheated."

"How did we cheat? And even if we had, Libby's in the hospital right now and you already got your money back. You nearly gave my neighbor a heart attack. All this over a few hundred dollars is insane." He didn't respond so I shouted, "Kidnapping just got added to your attempted murder charges. When the cops find you, you're done!"

He stood up straight, an evil smirk wide on his face, "I'm going to make an example out of you. No one messes with Teddy in this town. Others need to know there are repercussions when they cheat him."

A confidence resonated loud in my voice which I did not feel. "I got news for you: Teddy lost fair and square. Word gets out that all of this happened over a few hundred dollars, and he won't be able to show his face anywhere around here. This is my town. This is Libby's town. Teddy's new here. Libby has lots of friends who aren't going to be happy about what the two of you have done."

His smirk returned to a glare. "Are you threatening me?"

I was tired of running and furious that these two losers had turned my life upside down and had come a fraction of an inch from killing my best friend over nothing. The image of our sofa on fire in my back yard resonated in my head – my fury from earlier returned. I wanted him to know that there would be backlash for both of them.

Before I could answer, Mark's smooth voice came from the other side of me, "She's right. I asked around. She's not lying. Teddy's always been a hot head. He may have led you down a path you didn't need to go. He wasn't cheated – he lost."

All my energy had been focused on Grey in front of me; I had nearly forgotten Mark was behind me. Grey's over-confident voice instantly turned submissive when he realized Mark had just interjected himself into our conversation. "Oh, hey, I didn't know you were still in town." Grey's posture straightened and his glare dissolved when he answered, "This is a favor for Teddy, you understand."

Grey's comment didn't make any sense. It was almost as if Grey were asking permission from Mark, but permission for what? To kill me? To give me an adjoining room with Libby? Then it hit me: I had a weapon in my arsenal I hadn't even considered yet. Turning toward Mark, I asked Grey the question, "So, Grey, why don't you tell Mark how you tried to kill his little brother Wednesday morning." Instead of waiting to see Mark's reaction, I turned back toward Grey. "You shot him on my street. You knew that was Mark's brother, right?" Grey's eyes grew to the size of quarters as his shoulders slumped and his body shrank. Grey had been so focused on teaching Libby and me a lesson, he hadn't realized he had just grabbed a Bengal's tail in the process.

Mark glowered through me. If looks could kill, a grave digger would be thawing dirt right now. "What's she talking about, Grey?"

The table had turned as I watched the fear I had been feeling for four solid days materialize on Grey's face. He stammered, "I don't know. I never shot your brother, Boss."

Proof that I had selected the right weapon was standing in front of me. Enjoying the way Grey was squirming, I added tartly, "You shot him all right. Then the cops arrested him for your break-in. Nice. I'm sure Mark doesn't mind in the least that you almost killed his little brother and left him to answer for your breaking and entering charge."

I turned toward Mark, "You thought your brother was dead all those years? This lunatic almost made that a reality this week." I may have exaggerated a little, but Grey had shot Dave, and I definitely had Mark's attention.

Mark's hands balled into fists. His knuckles turned white. Angry lines formed on his forehead as he remained silent, eyes focused squarely on Grey.

Grey held up both his hands, "Hey, I didn't kill anybody. I shot at some guy who was chasing me. It was self-defense. He never told me he was your brother. I would have never pulled a gun on your family, never!"

Remembering how Dave had described it to me, I used every bit of leverage I had. "That's funny? Dave told me that you let him in my house because you thought he was Mark. Maybe you were trying to kill Mark?"

Pure horror showed on Grey's face. His complexion that had been flushed just seconds before from running drained of all of its color as he turned sheet white. "That is not what happened!"

Mark's voice was calm, turning his attention to me, "C'mon, Candy." Mark held out his hand to me in a friendly gesture. "I believe your altercation with Grey is over. I'll give you a ride to your car." Without looking at Grey, Mark warned, "You, Teddy and I may need to have a chat later, Grey."

My eyes darted between the two men. Neither seemed like a safe option: a flash of Mark holding me off the ground by my neck and tossing me like a rag doll Thursday night made me take an unintentional step away from his outstretched hand. Mark scared me almost as much as the buffoon I had outrun. I looked again at the Irish pub's door handle. I had screwed up royally by not telling Dave right away after I had seen Mark on Thursday. Fear or not, I wouldn't screw up again by letting Mark drive away tonight.

Grey still sounded as if he were scared of Mark when his smooth voice leaked the fear that was written on his face. "Hey, this situation is something Teddy initiated. You and me," he wagged his finger wildly between Mark and himself, "we're good, right?"

Unamused, Mark answered, "Funny. This situation," Mark made a circle in the air pointing at the three of us, "as of right now, no longer includes Candy. The new players are you, Teddy and me."

Grey's eyes went wide as both his hands shot further up into the air. "Oh hell, Mark, I'm sorry. Miss Kane never mentioned the two of you were friends." Grey made eye contact with me briefly, then averted his eyes to the ground and added, "Our misunderstanding is over. I hope your roommate has a speedy recovery."

Miss Kane? A speedy recovery? The hairs on my arms prickled. Who was Mark? Why was Grey all of the sudden willing to let his vendetta drop? Grey began walking backwards away from us.

Mark's voice still smooth as silk inquired, "Medical bills?"

"Way ahead of you, Boss. I'll take care of Miss Merrick," his eyes glanced back at me, "and any Miss Kane has as a result of my misunderstanding this evening."

I didn't have to look far for the salt pellets to pour into Grey's wound. As a final reminder, I asked, "What about Mark's brother? He was shot as part of the same 'misunderstanding.'"

Mark had kept a completely cool exterior throughout the exchange, but at the mention of his brother, his nostrils flared and his eyes widened. Grey saw the rage ready to break free when he answered in a rush, "Of course. Yeah. I'll take care of any your brother has, too." He looked humbly at Mark, stumbling, trying to find the words to calm the fury, "I'll apologize in person. I'll make it right. I swear I will, Mark."

He was easily ten feet away when Mark warned, "I don't want to hear of either of you around Candy or my little brother again. Leave town. You've got two days. If I hear you're still here on Monday, we will have a different kind of chat."

Grey froze in place at Mark's words. As if not believing what had just been said, he pleaded, "Monday? C'mon, Mark."

Mark gave a winning smile while pointing at his own wrist, "Tick tock, Grey. Make sure Teddy gets my message, as well. I would hate to have to deliver it in person on Monday." He turned his attention back to me. "Now, how about that ride to your car?"

CHAPTER 26

I was at a loss for words. Grey nodded his head respectfully and darted back across the street and into the park. My mind spun. I didn't know what to think. Mark's index and middle finger rested under my jaw as he used them to close my gaping mouth. Unable to wrap my mind around what had just happened, I clarified in a whisper, "They're not going to be coming after me or Libby any more, are they?"

Mark smiled. "Grey is about as sharp as a marble, but I left little room for misunderstanding. If you see either of them, even at a checkout stand at Target, make sure to glare at them and drop my name."

Sure that I did not want to know the answer, I asked anyway, "So, are you a mob boss or something?"

"Hmmm, I'm in the 'or something' category."

Mark took my elbow, guiding me toward his car. He opened the passenger door for me then walked around to the driver's side. He started his warm car, reached over and pushed a button to turn on my heated seat, then turned the vents on me full blast. It felt like heaven.

My eyes settled on Mark's face. He looked so much like Dave. The two could have been twins. Before he could pull away from the curb, I confessed, "I told Dave I saw you Thursday night – in Bank Shot's parking lot."

Mark's tone, which had been almost playful outside on the street, hardened. "I thought I asked you to keep that between you and me?"

"You did. I'm sorry, especially after what you just did for me out there. But, you have to understand, Dave is really important to me. He's been looking for you forever. Please, can you just talk to him for a few minutes?"

The hardness in his voice did not soften, "I told you I had some loose ends to tie up. I'm not accustomed to anyone ignoring my instructions."

"Ignoring your instructions? Hey, I don't know what you're mixed up in, and, frankly, I don't care. Neither does Dave. I know Dave's been through hell, and he is the most amazing guy. When he told me how he was taken away from the foster family you stayed with, it tore him up. Fifteen years later he's still torn up. He doesn't care what's going on in your life, he just wants you in his."

Mark pursed his lips together, "Compelling. But, not now."

The hurt on Dave's face yesterday morning when he left his apartment haunted me. Looking in Mark's eyes, they were the same color, but Mark's held no emotion at all. I needed him to understand whether he wanted to listen or not. "He folds his shirts in six by six squares. His apartment doesn't have a single speck of dust anywhere. His cabinets are full of items that are perfectly organized. There isn't one dirty dish in his whole apartment."

Mark's only answer was a confused look. Words were spilling out of me whether they made sense or not. "From the day he was taken away from you, he tried to do everything perfectly so he would be sent back. He loves you. I can't tell him I saw you a third time and couldn't convince you to see him. The rejection would crush him."

Something I said had finally struck a chord. I could see a flicker of emotion in his eyes. "Candy, as much as I would like to see him again, now is not the right time."

"Fifteen years ago would have been the right time. Hell, eleven years ago when he was almost adopted wouldn't have been bad, either. Or ten years ago when the adoption fell through. Or five years ago when I met him and he didn't have one single friend in the whole school. All of those times were the right time, but now, today, I'm telling you, you don't have a choice. You're going to say hi to your brother if I have to put a knife to your throat and drag you there."

I wondered if I had suddenly grown horns, because Mark looked at me as if I were a space alien. When he didn't respond to my threat with any threat of his own, I pointed at the corner. "His apartment is on West Eighth Street, so take a right at the end of this block." I buckled my seat belt and looked out the windshield, waiting to give him the next set of directions.

He sat in place, both hands on the wheel, staring out at the street in front of us. "Look, I'm a man of my word. As soon as I finish a couple projects, I will find Dave. I'm glad he has a friend who cares about him as much as you do, but now is not the right time for a reunion."

Turning toward him, I dug my heels in further. "Five minutes. Give him five minutes. That's a hello, a cell phone number and a hug." I reached over and put my hand on Mark's bicep, giving it a gentle squeeze, "He needs those five minutes more than he needs air." When his expression didn't change, I clarified, "I'm not kidding about holding a knife to your throat."

Mark's reaction surprised me. He smiled: not a smirk, or a grin, but a full-blown toothy approving smile. He didn't protest. He nodded, put the car in drive and took a right at the end of the block as I had instructed.

We drove in the quiet for several minutes. As we approached Dave's street, Mark inquired, "So, are you his girlfriend?"

"I don't think so. Maybe. I'm not sure."

"For someone who isn't sure, you seem to know a great deal about him."

"I've learned a lot in the last week. Tuesday night, at the bar? I thought you were Dave."

Surprised, he asked, "We look that much alike?"

"Yeah. Even Libby thought you were Dave."

"You said something about he folds his shirts in squares – I don't do that."

"I don't know the full story, but you'll see what I mean when we get there. Dave is meticulous about everything. Mr. Kravitz, that's a teacher from high school, said people come from all over the Midwest to have him restore their cars."

"Really? It's good to hear he's doing well for himself." Mark eyed me suspiciously. "So, for curiosity's sake, where were you planning to find a knife? I have to assume if you had one, you would have used it on Grey."

His question took me off guard. We were talking about Dave. I had threatened him: given Grey's reaction to Mark, that was probably a bad thing. "The way Grey high-tailed it away from you, I'm guessing there's one somewhere in your car," I offered lightly.

Smirking, "Sadly, no. I try not to keep weapons in my car. I admire your tenacity, but you need to be more careful about who you threaten and what you threaten them with. Grey isn't the worst man in the city, and you can't count on me to run interference for you."

"I would have been fine without your help," I spat confidently. As if to convince him I added, "I had outrun him twice. He wouldn't have attacked me in the pub."

"Your spunk is to be commended, but spunk is only worthwhile when backed up with brawn. Don't pick fights you can't win, and never threaten anything when you are unwilling or unable to follow through."

"Noted. But Dave needs you. There isn't much I wouldn't do for him. I gooned things up with him the other night, and I need to make them right."

Mark's eyebrows furrowed together when he asked, "How does one 'goon up' something?"

"I got back from Bank Shot and didn't tell him I'd seen you. The next morning when I did, he was upset with me for lying."

Mark countered, "An omission isn't a lie."

"Any form of deception is a lie. You didn't see the hurt in his eyes. He had given me a glimpse of the emptiness in his heart when it comes to you. That's a void I can't fill – only you can."

Mark took his eyes off the road as if searching mine for something. He answered back quietly, "I'm damaged. What happens when he meets me and he finds out I can't fill that void, either?"

"I don't pretend to know what you two went through. But you are the only one who can fill it. You just proved to me that you care. Geeze, you ran the guy who shot him out of town."

Mark smiled warmly, "Let's keep that bit of information between us, shall we?"

"I thought that would be my opening line, 'Hey, Dave, Mark scared the snot out of my stalker. Can we keep him?'"

"You're funny. I can see why you're his friend. Davey was always the funny one."

"So, what were you? The tough one?"

"I was older. I took care of Davey. At least until the day that the state of Missouri took him away from me."

His hand sat on the arm rest. I put my hand over his and gave him a squeeze. "I can't wait for him to see you." Still confused by everything that had happened, I wondered if Mark could tell me why Grey came after us. "So, thanks, by the way, for running Grey and Teddy out of town. I still don't understand how this escalated. It was only four hundred dollars."

Mark shook his head. "It isn't the money. It could have been four dollars or four thousand dollars. It's more about position. In their business, neither one of them can afford for others to think they are suckers."

"What business is that?"

"Never mind. They will steer clear of you. Neither will cross me." Mark drove exactly where I told him to. When we arrived in front of Dave's garage, the place was once again dark. My heart sank. If he wasn't inside, the hissy fit I had just thrown to get Mark here had been for nothing.

I didn't get out of the car for fear that Mark might change his mind and I'd never see him again. "Can I use your cell? Mine's in the pocket of my coat at work."

Mark rolled his eyes. "It doesn't look like he's here. I've got somewhere I am supposed to be. How about I take you back to your car and I'll promise to find him soon."

I shook my head. "Not good enough. He has to be here. Let me use your phone."

Mark reluctantly handed it over. I dialed Dave's number; it went directly to voicemail. I called the number to the garage; it also went to a recording. I called Kravitz. "Do you know where Dave is? He's not answering his phones."

"He's not answering my calls, either. I haven't talked to him since yesterday morning. Where are you?"

"I'm outside his place. It's dark."

"I don't know where he would be. If you find him, tell him to call me and let me know he's okay."

I could hear the defeat in my own voice, "Okay, thanks. If you hear from him, tell him I need to see him, okay?"

I hung up with Kravitz. Dave had stopped by the restaurant looking for me today, so he wasn't avoiding me anymore. What little time I had spent with Dave, I learned he was a creature of habit. If he were anywhere in the city, he was in his apartment. "I'm pretty sure he's inside."

Mark sighed, "It doesn't look like he's here."

Not expecting a favorable response, I asked, "I don't suppose you know how to pick a lock, do you?"

Mark shook his head, "Not my specialty."

I opened the passenger door, turned to Mark and said, "Don't leave." I ran up to the front door. It was a heavy steel door, and I pounded and kicked it mercilessly. The sound of my plea to get in was muffled by the cinder block structure. If Dave were inside, I wasn't convinced he would have heard me from the lobby, let alone from the second floor apartment.

I grabbed a handful of snow and launched the snowball at one of the second floor windows. The snowball bounced off with a heavy thump. I sent a second one and then a third. Nothing. A pile of white rock was setting under a holly bush: I grabbed one and threw it hard against the window. If he were in the apartment, it would be impossible for him to ignore my onslaught.

Mark grabbed my hand as I was about to send a second rock up to his window. "He's not here. Stop before you break something."

"He's here. I know it. He's upstairs in the dark, all by himself. You didn't see him yesterday. He was angry with me. But that wasn't the worst of it: his heart froze when he learned that the one person he could love with his whole heart didn't want to see him."

Mark's eyes narrowed, "I never said I didn't want to see him. I said the timing was bad."

"I told him, but that's not what he heard."

Mark shook his head and scowled at me. He walked back toward the steel door examining the side. "If he isn't inside, you're ready to face a breaking and entering charge?"

"He's in there. I know it."

Rolling his eyes, Mark murmured, "This is ludicrous." He stomped back toward his car. Part of me wanted to run in front of him and hold him in place because I thought he intended to drive away. Just as he approached his car, the trunk popped open. Mark dug through a compartment where his spare tire was kept, removed a tire iron and a can of lubricant.

"We're fortunate that a dimwit installed his front door backwards. The hinges are on the outside rather than where they're supposed to be on the inside." He shook his head at me as he walked back up to the garage's front door. "This won't be elegant, but it's better than a broken window." Mark sprayed the hinges for several seconds each. After each one was saturated, he placed the tire iron under the lip of the hinge and took each pin out with no more effort than inserting a key in a door.

He placed the third pin on the ground and turned to me. "If we go in and he's not there, I'm leaving you to explain to the alarm company why it was so imperative you get inside."

"Deal." My smile stretched wide. A giddiness travelled through me as I had a sudden urge to hug him. Mark shook his head then planted his foot hard against the wall and pulled. His arms took the door completely off of its resting place as a gaping hole now stood before us. He gestured for me to go in first. No alarm sounded, and I wondered if that meant we had triggered a silent one, or if one wasn't installed.

I had just made it through the lobby and around the corner into the garage when Dave was flying off the stairs with a baseball bat in his hand. I held up my hands and shouted, "It's me! Dave, it's me!" I cowered as the bat was already over his shoulder before he realized who "me" was. He let the bat fall to the floor when he stopped at the bottom of the steps. From the light of the Coke machine, I saw relief showing in his eyes.

"Candy? What are you doing here?" He looked at the doorway to the dark lobby, then asked, "How did you get in?"

Ignoring his question, I was unable to contain my excitement, "He's here. I found him. Well, he found me, but he's just outside."

Mark's voice called from the lobby, "I'm not paying for a new door. This was her idea."

Dave's eyes grew wide. He walked slowly from around the pop machine. He looked from me to the lobby door, back to me, then his eyes rested on the lobby's doorway. A single word escaped him, "Mark?"

Mark was somewhere in the pitch black lobby. He answered jovially, "In the flesh. Why don't you have an alarm system? Did you forget to pay your utility bill or something?" The light flickered on in the lobby when Mark located the switch, and a second later he stepped from the lobby into the garage. The two brothers stood motionless for a second staring at each other. Dave glanced back at me for a fraction of a second then launched himself at Mark, taking him in a bear hug.

Neither spoke. They both clung to the other. Their embrace was the most beautiful thing I had ever seen. It was a full minute before they let go of each other. Mark was the first to speak. "Sorry about your door. She was pretty adamant that we were getting inside."

Dave laughed, brushing moisture from his cheeks with the back of his hand. "Her persistence is only rivaled by a pit bull's."

Mark shared a warm smile with me, "You have no idea."

Dave motioned to his apartment upstairs, "You want to come in?"

Mark said, "Just for a minute. I'm in town on business, and as I tried to explain to Candy, I need to meet with a client tonight."

Before the two brothers could go up the steps, I called their attention to the gaping hole in the front of the building. "Um, should one of you put the door back on first?"

Mark smiled, "Right. Need to keep the riffraff out. So, do you always answer the door with a bat at night?"

Still all smiles, Dave answered, "When I heard the snowballs on the window, I thought it was just neighborhood kids. I heard someone monkeying with the door and thought it might be vandals, so I was coming to investigate."

"With a bat?"

"Better than a gun."

Mark raised a brow, "I'll let Candy fill you in on her day. I bumped into her on Windham Street and offered to give her a ride to her car. Your pit bull analogy? Yes, she was pretty adamant that I bring her here instead of to her car."

Dave smiled sweetly to me, "Thanks."

My eyes darted between the two brothers. "Put the door back on already. It's freezing out." The two of them went to the door and had it back on its hinges in less than a minute. Dave turned on the lights in the garage and hit a switch to illuminate the apartment, too. I didn't want to intrude on their reunion, so when they went upstairs, I took a seat in the lobby and grabbed a magazine from a rack on the wall.

Motor Trend had never been a favorite; in fact, I'd put it in the same category as *Better Homes and Gardens*. I had always liked cars, but was far more interested in old school muscle instead of a showdown between the latest BMW, Viper and Mercedes.

The five minutes I had begged Mark to give came and went, so did fifteen, and after I had been in the lobby for a full hour, curiosity began to get the better of me. I tentatively walked toward the stairs. Hovering beside the steps listening to the humming of the Coke machine, I strained to hear the conversation upstairs.

Dave asked Mark, "Are you hungry? I've got a roast and potatoes I can warm up."

Mark's voice was a little lower than Dave's when he commented, "Very domestic. I'm impressed. No, don't go to any trouble." The rustling of a chip bag sounded. "I haven't had Wavy Lays in years. Remember how we used to make little ice cream forts in our bowls and use the chips for fences?"

"You're stuck with just the chips. I don't have ice cream."

"No ice cream? You have a roast and potatoes but you don't keep ice cream in the freezer? You aren't as domestic as I had believed."

Dave's answer was strained. "I don't eat ice cream."

"You don't eat ice cream? You used to love ice cream. I used to bribe you with it to get you to make your bed."

"Yeah, I remember." Dave paused for a few seconds before he added, "I haven't eaten ice cream since. . . well, you know."

"Since when?"

"Since our case worker asked me if I wanted to get ice cream and I followed her out to her car."

Mark didn't answer, but I heard his footsteps overhead. A muffled response echoed half a minute later, "It's not your fault. You were just a kid. Let it go."

"So, were you looking for me, too?"

"No." A long pause hung in the air before Mark added solemnly, "I told you, I thought you were dead. I never considered my caseworker got it wrong." Another long pause before Mark said, "I'm glad she was wrong. Hey, listen, I've got somewhere I need to be, but I promise I'll be back soon."

I heard both men coming down the steps and quickly made my way back to the lobby. Both were all smiles. I marveled at their similarities: they were the same height, similar builds, nearly identical features on their faces – in a glance it would be next to impossible to tell them apart. Lucky the two did not dress alike. The only discernable difference was the cut above Dave's brow that was still shiny from the glue he had used on it.

Mark was the first one down the stairs, his face all smiles when he grabbed me in a hug. Mark whispered directly into my ear. "Thank you. I needed this meeting as much as he did."

Mark let go of me and took Dave in a bone-crushing hug, "I'll call you in a couple days, little brother."

Dave held onto Mark, but looking over Mark's shoulder, his eyes rested on me. When the two of them let go, Mark turned to me, "You want that ride to your car now?"

My eyes darted to Dave, not sure where things were between us. He answered for me, "I'll take her to it. I'm pretty sure I made you late for whatever you had planned." I didn't want to go to my car. I wanted for him to hold me the way he had the last time I was here. I wanted him to tell me how important I was to him, and most of all, I wanted him to tell me he wasn't angry with me anymore.

Mark tipped his head in a wordless good-bye, then let himself out.

It was just Dave and I standing in his garage. He walked up to me and leaned down as his lips softly whispered against mine. As he eased away from me, his eyes widened, he took a step away and reached for a hanging pedestal light above a work bench and angled it in my direction. Perplexed, he asked, "What happened to your neck?"

My hands slid to my throat as the sting on my neck registered under my fingertips. Grey had hit me hard in the throat behind the restaurant, and I had been able to ignore the pain until Dave's eyes stared at it. Before I could answer, he instructed, "Wait here."

He ran up the steps to his apartment and returned holding a plastic bag of ice cubes. As Dave gently pressed the cold bag to my neck, his eyes darted to my hands covered in cuts and scrapes. His deep brown eyes looked sadly into mine. "What happened to you?"

"That Grey guy kidnapped me from the restaurant today. I woke up in a shack in Pioneers' Park with him talking on the phone telling someone that he was going to gut me. I bolted."

Dave's nostrils flared. "I'll kill him."

I shook my head, "He's gone. Mark told him he had until Monday to get out of town."

Dave answered menacingly, "That gives me two days to find him."

Dave carefully repositioned the ice on my neck. I didn't want Dave to go looking for Grey. I didn't want him to leave for any reason. The last two days had been unbearable – I needed him to stay with me. "No. Don't. Mark scared him. He's going to pay Libby's medical bills, yours, too. Just let him go."

Dave eased his hand to the small of my back to pull me toward him. I winced. Instead of asking me, he took a step to my side, removed the too large jacket I was wearing and lifted the back of my t-shirt. "What the. . .?" His fingers ever-so-slightly pressed the spot where Grey had kidney punched me. "Grey did this?"

I felt tears welling up in my eyes. I pressed my lips together and nodded my response. Dave took the ice bag which he had been holding against my neck and pressed it to the bruise on my back. In a calm voice, absent any emotion, Dave asked, "What else did he do?"

If I tried to speak, I knew I'd break down before I could get a full sentence out. I pulled my hair back with one hand and touched my temple with my other. It, too, felt sore. Dave's eyes narrowed, but he didn't move the bag of ice from my back.

Dave confessed, "This is my fault. I'm sorry, Candy. I wasn't there to take care of you." His expression was earnest and his voice sorrowful.

"This didn't have anything to do with you. He's a psycho. I was working when he kidnapped me. There were at least twenty people around. He didn't care who saw him."

Dave's gaze held mine. "I knew I should have stayed. I came by when you were busy. I told a waitress I'd be back after your shift." He paused as his voice lowered, "When I came back, she told me you saw a rat in the storage room and left early. I thought I'd blown it and you didn't want to see me. I should have grabbed a table to begin with. None of this would have happened if I'd stayed."

"You don't know that. He shot at you before; if you'd have been there, he might have killed you."

He shook his head as if dismissing the possibility. "Have you reported this to the police?"

"No. Mark took care of it. Both of them are leaving town. But a police report isn't a bad idea – it might keep the manager from firing me."

He raised an eyebrow. "Fired? You can't go back there."

"I have to go back there. Tips from the restaurant are how I keep gas in my car."

Dave kissed my temple softly, "We'll talk about it later. For now, call the police. Hopefully I don't still have a warrant for my arrest."

I smiled. "You don't. I talked to Officer Brown this morning."

When the police arrived, I told them everything that happened from the moment I tossed a package of napkins to Grey in the storage room until I saw Mark on Windham Street. Dave's anger wasn't masked as he listened to everything that Grey had done to me. I left out the part about Mark telling Grey to get out of town, but ended with a truthful statement about Mark intervening and giving me a ride to Dave's house. After my statement was complete, the policeman who took it departed. Dave had called to check in with Mr. Kravitz then offered to take me to the hospital. I wanted to go see Libby, but I felt awful and looked worse – I didn't want her to see me before I got cleaned up.

Dave was remarkably quiet as we slowly climbed the steps to his apartment. Dave was massive and there wasn't room for both of us on the same step, but he gently guided me up the steps from behind, at the ready to catch me if I lost my footing.

As I started for the sofa, Dave walked past me to a beautifully carved wooden box on his coffee table. He opened it, then removed a handgun, sliding it into the waistband of his jeans. He saw me staring in disbelief, as he walked up to me and kissed my forehead, "I'll be back soon."

"Where are you going? And why are you taking a gun?"

"I'll find him. Get some rest. I'll be back in a couple hours."

My scratched up hands gripped his shirt before he could walk past me. "No. Dave. Don't go." I wanted to shout at him and tell him he was being reckless. I wanted to tell him I didn't want a murderer for a boyfriend. But neither of these things would stop the rage I saw in his eyes. Instead, I was unable to pretend to be brave for one more second. I confessed, "I'm scared to be alone."

His eyes softened. Dave made a loose fist and caressed my cheek with his knuckles. "I can't let him get away with this."

"Please. Don't leave me." Tears streaked my cheeks. "I need you."

Dave gathered me in his arms gently. I turned my head, resting it against his chest as his arms completely encircled me. My voice pleaded again, "Mark already took care of both of them. Stay with me."

Barely above a whisper, Dave answered, "I'm here." He kissed my forehead a second time, "I'm here. I won't leave." Dave gestured for me to take a seat on the couch. He removed the handgun from the waistband of his jeans, returning it to the carved wooden box. Dave alternated pressing the ice to each of my injuries. When I didn't think I could take another second with the ice, he took the bag to the sink and returned with a pan of warm water. Dave cleaned each of the scrapes and cuts on my skin, put Neosporin and Band-Aids on several of the bigger scratches, then glued two gashes shut.

Neither of us spoke as he took care of my injuries. His touch was feather light. When he was done, I wrapped a hand around the back of his neck and whispered into his ear. "Thanks."

He spoke against the back of my neck, "You're welcome. Are you okay?"

"As long as I'm with you, yes. Promise you won't leave?"

"I promise."

"When I wake up tomorrow, will you still be in bed?"

Dave grinned. "I'll be wherever you need me to be."

"I want to see you when I wake up."

His breath was minty and warm; I felt his kiss resonate through my entire body. Not in a tingly sexual way, but the warm glow like stepping into the sunshine from a dark cave. Dave's lips travelled down my neck and back to my ear. His invitation, "Come to bed."

I tried to stand, but when I did, my legs were wobbly. Dave leaned down and gathered me in his arms. I wrapped my arms around his neck as he carried me across the little room and gently lowered me on to his bed.

CHAPTER 27

The next morning I woke up with Dave's enormous arms holding me against him as his fingers lightly caressed my arm. He was warm, his touch inviting. We had survived, to hell and back for sure. My body ached after the adrenalin from last night had worn off completely. Without looking in a mirror, I knew the horrific bruise around my neck would be there for a while, and my temple was sore from Grey's fist. The tiny cuts on my hand from my escape weren't that noticeable since Dave had taken care of them last night.

None of those injuries concerned me when Dave's arms held me. The warmth of his body was intoxicating. I looked at the tiny apartment: it was still so orderly. Dave's voice whispered, "What do you want to do today?"

I stretched against him, allowing my whole body to press against his. "Libby should be awake by now. Will you go with me?"

"Yeah." He pressed his lips to the back of my head while he pulled me tighter to him. "Shower?"

Neither of us moved. It could have been an offer to let me go first, or it could have been an invitation for me to join him. I decided I wanted for it to be the latter. My hand slid up his arm to his shoulder, then all the way back down to his fingertips. An audible sigh sounded behind me as I asked, "You know I'm a conservationist?"

"Mmmm," his response.

"It would be a waste of water for us to take separate showers."

He kissed the back of my neck as he chuckled. "You're right. Let's make a pact to stop wasting water."

I rolled over so I faced him. His eyes were heavy and he had never looked sexier. I kissed the sensitive skin under his chin as he sighed into me and murmured, "I could get used to this."

My eyes roved to his chest where the happy heart smiled back at me, holding the red and white striped candy cane. My index finger traced the lines as I considered what all had happened in the last five days. I had nearly lost my best friend, several years were likely shaved off an elderly neighbor's life, but I had found Dave.

It wasn't a reconnection, because the Dave I thought I knew was nothing like the man who I now knew. It was difficult to reconcile in my mind that had all the awful things that had happened to me this week not happened, I would likely never have known the real Dave. I wouldn't have known he had feelings for me or how deep they ran. I wouldn't have understood why he was so unwilling to let people into his life.

Had that creepy Teddy not have set everything in motion, not only would I not be wrapped up with Dave, he would still not have seen a brother he had been looking for for over a decade, and that brother would still think Dave had died. Some amazingly cool things had happened as a result of actions which made no sense.

Is this how life was supposed to be? Good things could come from bad things if you looked for the good hard enough? I thought of Libby's body in the hospital, clinging to life this week. She wouldn't have wished for one moment of the brutality and neither would Larry, but the result of the action brought two people together who had sort of given up on each other.

I tried to think of something positive that had come from Grey's home invasion on Mrs. Bavcock. She was old and set in her ways, but thank goodness for her concern. I'd always been friendly to her, but I now owed her my life – a debt I would never fully repay. If I had to find something good that had happened as a result, I would have to say that I would never again think of her as just a crazy old cat lady; she was brave. I hoped to live as long as she has, and I hoped to be just as strong as she was when I got there.

I hadn't asked Dave much about his reunion with Mark. One thing still didn't make sense to me, "Did Mark tell you why he thought you were dead?"

Dave stiffened. I didn't think he intended to answer at first, but just as I was about to sit up in bed and cover my awkward comment with something funny, he answered, "When my foster parents petitioned Missouri for me to move with them to Nebraska, a notification was made to my next-of-kin that I was no longer under the care of the State of Missouri. When he got the notification, he called his case worker to ask her what was going on. She must have gotten her signals crossed because she told him I had been in an accident."

"An accident? What kind of an accident?"

"He could never get a straight answer. She showed up with a grief counselor and told him I was in a better place."

"His case worker told him you were dead?"

Dave shook his head, "She never came out and said the words, but Mark said he sort of shut down after that. He had been in a group home at the time and stayed there until he was fifteen."

"A group home? So he didn't stay with Margaret and Dewey after you left?"

"No, that's the jacked-up part. When I was placed with another foster family, I did everything I could to be good and be placed back with him. He did the opposite. He turned into a hellion trying to get moved to wherever the state had put me."

"Why wouldn't your case worker have seen that and put the two of you together again?"

"I don't know. It wasn't long after I moved from Margaret and Dewey's house that a new case worker was assigned to me. I'd like to think that she just didn't know, rather than she purposely tried to keep us apart."

I hugged Dave again, "I really am sorry for everything the two of you went through."

"We both made it through. If it weren't for you, I'd still be looking for him, and he would still think I was dead." I guess I wasn't the only one trying to find the bright side. Dave eased off the bed and held out both of his hands for me to get up, too. As he helped pull me to my feet, his eyes looked toward the little bathroom door off in the corner.

I took his hand leading him toward the door. The room was barely large enough for one person. I qualified as one person, and Dave was easily the size of two. He reached behind the vinyl shower curtain and turned on the water. Not looking the least bit tense about sharing a shower with me, he slid off the short nylon shorts he had been wearing and stepped behind the curtain.

My eye muscles flexed at the brief glimpse they had seen. My heart raced so fast it could have kept time with Jeff Gordon's Chevrolet. I looked at myself in the mirror, the ugly purple just under my chin, the scrapes that peppered my hands, and my hair all but knotted. I didn't feel very attractive, and I wasn't sure this was the image I wanted burned into his memory of our first time together.

Just as I was beginning to lose my nerve, the shower curtain gapped and Dave warned, "I'm giving you to the count of three, then I'm reporting you to the Water Company." His enormous arm jetted through the opening between the wall and the curtain, as his finger beckoned me to join him.

"*Be brave,*" I thought to myself. Dave had opened himself up to me: it was time for me to do the same. My exterior wasn't as formidable as Dave's, but before him, there had never been another man I let into my heart. For the first time, I would let a man see my darkest secrets, the insecurities I hid from everyone, and the flaws I hoped nobody noticed. Beyond sharing my body, Dave was the first guy I had ever wanted to share my heart.

I slid the shower curtain to the side and stepped into the welcoming arms of the man who not only displayed his heart for the world to see, but as of this moment, owned mine.

We left his place and decided to stop at a little diner on our way to the hospital. I was conflicted, my emotions were on overload and running in different directions. One minute I was excited and full of joy over Dave, the next I was nervous and scared to find out what Libby's condition was. Dave must have sensed the conflict because he was driving and he chose a detour. When I tried to argue that I needed to get to the hospital, his response was, "An hour's delay won't make a difference to Libby, but you need to eat."

I hadn't told Dave that my fit over food was what had set all of these events in motion. As much as I wanted to argue with him, I remembered I had eaten almost nothing Saturday and it was now approaching lunch time on Sunday.

He pulled into the parking lot of a diner close to his garage. I had never been there before, but the waitress who took our order was friendly. As I looked across the table at Dave, he was still all smiles. He reached over and took both my hands in his, "You are beautiful."

I wanted to laugh, knowing full well that the gnarly bruise on my neck was less than attractive, but the sincerity in his voice touched me tenderly. Blushing, I answered, "You're pretty sexy yourself."

"Is the chair okay on your back? We could switch to a booth if that would be better."

I hadn't even thought about the bruise back there; it didn't bother me much at all. "No, this is okay. So, tell me about Mark. What's he do? Where's he live?"

"He's still in Missouri. He moved to Kansas City when he was fifteen. He was a little vague about what he does."

"Fifteen? That's pretty late to be moved to a foster family, isn't it?"

"He wasn't with a foster family. He just left."

"At fifteen? How did he survive? He wasn't even old enough to get a job."

"He didn't say, but I'm guessing he wasn't bagging groceries." Dave's hands began playing with the salt shaker on the table. As terrible as the woman had been that the state placed Dave with in high school, he hadn't lived on the streets.

"What happened to your mom? Does he know?"

Dave pressed his lips together as I saw the sadness turn to anger before my eyes. "She's alive, at least she was seven years ago."

"Has Mark talked to her?"

He shook his head. He had still been holding the salt shaker when I asked the question, but he squeezed it and it skidded across the table. Dave groped for the little shaker, glanced at me and answered in a clinical tone, "He said that's why he left for Kansas City. Mark said he was standing on a street corner and saw her driving a minivan stopped at a red light. He had been excited to see her. She saw him standing there, then drove away."

My stomach knotted. Who could do that to their child? "Oh. Poor Mark. Maybe she didn't recognize him."

Absently he answered, "Maybe. But Mark told me that's why he took off. He believed I was dead. There had been no sign of Dad since a few years after I was born. Our mother had given us up. When she saw him on that street corner and drove away, Mark said he couldn't take it. He said he wanted a new life."

I brushed my knee against his, trying to offer whatever comfort I could. "One day, maybe the two of you will get a chance to talk to her – to make peace."

Dave shook his head. "I don't need to make peace. There is hate and love. To feel either of those things about someone you have to have feelings for them – I don't feel either. I don't feel anything for her and I don't ever need to see her." He must have been surprised by my expression because he clarified, "Mark may need to make peace. I don't."

"You said you don't remember her?"

"No. Not really. I think I remember what she looked like, but I was four when she gave us to the state." His eyes focused on the wall behind me, "I'll never do that. If I have a kid, he'll know I want him."

I reached under the little table and put my hand on his knee, giving it a reassuring squeeze. His hand gripped mine, as his eyes left the wall and focused on me. Barely more than a whisper, Dave asked, "How could she do that?"

"I don't know."

"She threw us both away. She didn't even give us a chance."

"It was her loss. Look at what you have become."

"Yeah, look at me. I'm such a catch."

Squeezing his hand under the table, I agreed, "Yes. You are." A look of disbelief stared back at me. I wished he could see himself through my eyes. "You're honest. You're kind. You're successful. You have done it all on your own: you've beaten the odds."

Dave's eyes stared at the table. "I hate being alone."

I squeezed his knee again. "You're not alone. You've got me."

"Until I start to drive you crazy. I'm obsessive compulsive, not just about my things, but about everything. I'm that way about my schedule, my garage, even my laundry."

I stood up from the table, walked around to his chair, sat on his lap and draped my arms over his neck. He looked embarrassed by my PDA, but his arms encircled me. A few curious stares from the other customers shot my way, but I didn't care. "I think you're perfect. I'm not going anywhere." His arms cinched tight around me as he buried his face on the still sore bruise on my neck. It hurt, but I didn't pull away.

I noticed our waitress standing a few feet back holding our plates. I kissed his forehead and stood up returning to my seat. I had ordered an omelet. It was easily big enough for three people, but I didn't care. I didn't stop until my plate was completely empty. Dave must have been as hungry as I was, because the waitress collected two empty plates when she brought our check.

He asked, "Ready to go see Libby?"

I was. I thought of her still body that I had visited Friday night, remembering the worry I had shared with her while she was unconscious. I wanted my friend back. I would take whatever I could get, even if it was just a piece of the Libby I loved. A sliver of the person she had been was better than nothing at all.

CHAPTER 28

We arrived at the hospital and for the first time all week, Larry wasn't in the waiting room. Compared to other visits, there were remarkably few people in the ICU's waiting room. An initial feeling of dread washed over me. The doctor was supposed to wake her up yesterday; what if he tried, and she didn't wake up? Why else would Larry not be here?

The large windows along the west wall allowed a great deal of natural light through. I looked around the room desperately trying to locate Larry; there wasn't a dark corner anywhere for him to be tucked away in. The room's decor was just as inviting as it had been the other times I was here, but I stood frozen in place. Tears welled up in my eyes as my feet planted themselves. Dave took two steps past me before he realized I was stuck. He turned and must have seen the panic on my face because he pivoted and was directly in front of me. "What's wrong? Are you okay?"

I shook my head indicating that I wasn't okay. Just two nights ago, I had been in her room, begging her to wake up – there had been no response. What if, when she woke up, there was so much damage she wouldn't know me anymore? Dave's hand took mine, his voice strained, "Not knowing is worse than even the worst case scenario. C'mon, let's ask the nurse how she is."

My feet reluctantly followed as Dave led the way to the nurse's station. A young friendly nurse looked up from her desk, "Can I help you?"

My voice wouldn't work. Dave saw me struggling, so he asked for me, "We'd like to see Libby Merrick."

The nurse's fingers hammered hard on the keyboard in front of her. When her screen produced the info he had asked for, she looked up at the two of us as a wide smile spread on her face. "Sorry, you're on the wrong floor."

Wrong floor? Libby *had* been moved. Had she been moved to a regular patient room? Was she okay? The knot in my stomach refused to unfurl, as images of Libby in a long-term care facility or even a hospice wing flashed through my thoughts. Dave must have sensed I was still unable to form questions, because he asked her, "Oh, okay. Where can we find her?"

"Room 230."

Dave tugged my arm in the direction of the elevator, but I needed to know. I let go of his hand and lay both of my palms on her desk. I swallowed the lump in my throat then whispered, "Is she okay?"

The nurse answered warmly, "She's awake."

The pressure on my stomach eased at her answer. I could feel an enormous smile form on my face. "Thanks!" I spun around and was pulling Dave toward the elevator. My steps were as light as Libby's the night she told the school superintendent that she was the gingerbread girl while she skipped over his front lawn at two in the morning. Libby was okay! Wait, the nurse hadn't said she was okay. She said she was awake and had been moved out of intensive care.

When the elevator doors opened on the second floor, Larry was sitting in a waiting room watching a NASCAR race. He looked thrilled to see me, "You made it! I was beginning to worry about you! She's been asking for you."

His words brought me up short. "Libby? She's been asking for me? So, she's okay?"

He shook his head as if in disbelief, "She's been getting better the last two days. Where have you been?"

"Two days? I thought the doctor was going to wake her up yesterday afternoon?"

Larry chuckled. "That was the plan, but you know Libby. She does everything on her terms. It was the strangest thing – she woke up right after you left Friday night."

"What?!"

"Yeah. You should have seen the hospital staff scrambling. Her doctor told me they had enough meds in her to keep a Clydesdale sedated. She woke up within a half hour of you leaving on Friday."

"Why didn't you call me?"

"When she woke up the doctors were running tests for hours. By the time I saw her it was after midnight. She asked for you right away – I told her you had left but were going to be back after your shift at the restaurant on Saturday. She told me not to call you because she wanted to surprise you. When you didn't come last night before visiting hours were over, I called your cell and left a bunch of voice mails. Didn't you get them?"

My phone was still in my coat pocket hanging on a hook at the restaurant. We hadn't gone back to retrieve my coat or my car after my run-in with Grey. "No, I got. . . sidetracked yesterday. I left my jacket at the restaurant with my cell in the pocket. The restaurant is closed today."

Larry motioned toward her door, "Well, she's anxious to see you." I was going to introduce Dave to Larry, but when I turned to make the introduction, Larry was staring at him. It was strange, Larry's look was uneasy.

"Larry, this is Dave. He went to high school with Libby and me."

Larry held out his hand awkwardly. "Dave. . .Brewer?"

Strange. I didn't remember ever talking about Dave when Larry and Libby were dating. Dave took Larry's hand, "Yeah, nice to meet you. Have we met?"

"Um, no, thanks for finding Henry. He's in with Libby now. How did you find him anyway?" The strange look on Larry's face didn't change. His words were shaky and his height seemed to shrink in front of us.

Dave shrugged his shoulders. "There aren't that many Henry Merrick's in the area. I just asked around. A guy I had rebuilt an F100 for last spring knew him. He gave me some places to look for Henry."

Staring at Dave in disbelief, I asked, "You found Libby's dad?"

He smiled. "After I went back to the restaurant and they said you left because of the rat, I drove back to my place. I was hoping you would call or stop by. I got to thinking about you telling me that you didn't know how to get a hold of Libby's dad to tell him what had happened. I called a couple customers who seemed to know everyone in Lincoln – one of them knew him. He gave me a couple bars to try. I called around while I was waiting for you."

Why hadn't I thought to do that? I leaned in and kissed him just to the side of his lips. "That was really sweet of you."

Before he could tell me it was no big deal, Larry pointed me toward Libby's room. The room was bright from sunshine pouring in through the window. Her head was propped up on pillows. Her skin was pale, there was a large bandage on the side of her head just behind her temple, where the huge tube had been the last time I saw her. No machines were hooked up to her, and her smile beamed back at me. "Candy! You're here!" The turtle I had smuggled into her ICU room from her bedroom was setting beside her on her hospital bed.

Aside from the color of her skin and the area where her head had been shaved, she looked good. She looked like Libby. She sounded groggy but like the Libby I had known forever. I hadn't even noticed her dad sitting in a chair against the wall in her room until he offered, "There you are. I've been keeping her company waiting for you to get here."

I glanced in his direction. "Hi, Mr. Merrick. I haven't seen you in a while."

"I intend to fix that. You two girls will be seeing a lot more of me."

Libby was all smiles. All those times we had carefully avoided him around town, something must have changed, because she seemed pleased with the prospect of seeing him more frequently. "Sounds good to me. You know where we live. Come by anytime."

Libby's dad held out his hand to Dave, "You're Dave?" I nodded enthusiastically as Henry added gratefully, "Thanks for letting me know about my little girl."

"You're welcome."

Larry joined us and, between Libby, her dad, Larry, Dave and me, our happy voices carried up and down the hall. No one, not even a grumpy nurse popped in to tell us to keep it down. Whispers weren't an option when someone had so narrowly beaten death. I used Dave's phone to post on Facebook to let everyone know Libby had been in an "accident" but was able to have visitors. A steady stream of friends and her co-workers began arriving within a half hour and didn't diminish until visiting hours were over. Dave and I stayed the entire day and well into the night.

One of the nurses commented that Libby must have been some sort of a local celebrity because they'd never seen so many people all looking for one patient. It was selfish of me to believe that only I loved Libby. People we had gone to high school with, played pool with, gone to bonfires with, and even her coworkers all popped in to check on her. When one of the nurses gently reminded us that visiting hours were over fifteen minutes ago, Dave took my hand and led me toward the door.

Libby hadn't asked me anything about what had happened to her. I assumed Larry had filled her in. Libby motioned me back toward her bed, took my hand, and asked, "Are you okay?"

I wasn't sure if she had seen the scratches on my hands, the bruise on my neck or what, but I answered without a moment's hesitation. "I have a lot to tell you. Thanks for waking up."

She leaned in conspiratorially toward my ear, "Have you seen my doctor?"

Worry crept into my voice when I answered, "No, do you need me to go get him?"

"I'm pretty sure Larry would never forgive me if I asked for his number, but holy crap, he was an eyeful when I woke up." Libby was back. Only she could come through an ordeal like this and notice the hotness wearing a stethoscope and a lab coat. I gave her a gentle squeeze and whispered into her ear, "Don't worry, if things don't work out with Larry, I got his phone number."

CHAPTER 29

Two months later

Libby stood in the doorway of the kitchen, resting up against the thick wooden frame. "I got paid. You want me to pick up anything at the store?"

Shaking my head, I didn't look up from the pot on the stove. I had made jambalaya, and it was ten minutes from perfection. Cooking had never been my thing, but lately I'd been hitting Rachel Ray's website for recipes. "We just went yesterday; I think we're good on everything."

"Well, here," she handed me a wad of twenties, "at least let me chip in on the rent."

I waved her money off, "We're already paid up through next month. Keep it."

She wore a sorrowful look when she pleaded, "Candy, I can help."

I shook my head as my eyes went to where her hair was finally growing back. In the hospital, the staff had shaved the side of her head so they could put the tube in to drain fluids from her brain. Libby had had long blonde hair for as long as I had known her – naturally blonde, nothing she had to touch up every couple months. She ended up getting a short cut to try to camouflage the fact that it had been bare skin from her ear to her temple. The style looked cute on her, but each time I saw the thin patch of hair on one side of her head, guilt washed over me all over again.

It wasn't until after she had been out of the hospital and home for over a week that I could ask her if she remembered what had happened the night she was attacked. Her memory was blotchy. She remembered answering a knock at the door, Grey forcing his way into the house, but she didn't remember the attack. Neither one of us knew how Grey learned where I worked, but we concluded he must have still been in the house when I left in a rush for work, and he followed me there.

Libby concluded that my abrupt departure probably saved her life that night. Her doctor told her one more hit to the head would have been a death blow. I shared that had I not been sleeping like the dead, I should have heard the attack going on in our living room.

Her hand still held the folded twenties she had offered. Instead of accepting them I reminded her, "That was the deal, Libby. You fought back and didn't die: I told you I'd get another roommate to help cover the bills."

"I never agreed to it. I was unconscious, remember? Let me help."

"A deal's a deal." I meant every word of my promise to her that night. I didn't want her to shark anymore, or if she did, I didn't want her ability to con some guy to be the means for us to eat. I had kept up my end of the deal. She still went to the bars and played, but nowadays she had a new partner. She never told him to wear skirts, either. "When's Larry going to be here?"

She shrugged her shoulders, "Soon. He got off at five. He was going to stop off at his place and change." She leaned up against the table watching me for a second before she asked, "So what's your deal? Larry doesn't make your skin crawl anymore?"

Her question caught me off guard. Before the assault I had been very vocal about how little I liked him. I had even done a happy dance in the kitchen the day she told me they had broken up. "Nope. He's okay."

"Did you two bond or something?"

Larry never left her side. He slept in the waiting room of the ICU for almost a week, then camped out in her hospital room for three days after her condition had stabilized. He went so far as to try to set up payments with the hospital before she had been discharged, though not needed: the bill had been paid in full by an anonymous benefactor. He loved her and nothing short of a crowbar would have removed him from her life after she recovered. "Yeah, I guess so. I still think you could do better, but if you're happy with him, then I'm happy for you."

"Wow, Candy, that was almost an endorsement. Why the change of heart?"

Libby had talked to her doctors, so she knew how lucky she was to be alive. What she didn't get was how much her attack had affected all of us. Larry took a leave of absence from his job because he couldn't stand to be away from her for any length of time, not just while she was in the hospital but throughout her recovery.

Henry popped in at least once a week since she'd left the hospital. This was strange, because I'd now seen him more since her accident than I had the whole time we were in high school. She had carefully avoided him before, but seemed excited about each of his visits.

Mrs. Bavcock stopped by at least three mornings a week for coffee and had recently begun dropping off cookies, too. Her family was in the area, but after everything we had been through together, she decided to take on the role of Honorary Mom to both Libby and me.

I called Mom and Dad after Libby was out of the hospital and told them what had happened. Mom was on a plane the same night – she wasn't the least bit upset about the carpet or sofa. Mom spent the weekend with us and was pleased to see the floor deadbolts Mr. Kravitz had installed. She was pretty happy to see Larry and Dave keeping an eye on Libby and me, too.

When I finally found Chris, I learned that neither Grey nor Teddy had ever bothered him. Chris couldn't believe what had happened to Libby. He brought a vase of flowers and a plate of chicken wings to her hospital room when he found out. Ever since she had been discharged, Chris called every Tuesday night to see how we were doing. At first I thought it was a little eerie, but it was his way of letting Libby and me know he was thinking about us. When he called last Tuesday, he told me that Bank Shot had a new policy in place to walk female customers to their cars in the evening. It didn't sound like a big deal since Libby hadn't been attacked in the parking lot, but Chris said he had recommended it at an employee meeting, and it was now a new policy at the bar.

All of these people seemed like bystanders, yet one dreadful evening proved that they were much more than decorations in our lives.

Libby was staring at me, waiting for an answer. "I dunno. He was there for you when you needed him. Up until your nap at the hospital," *nap* was the word I used instead of *coma* whenever we talked about her stay at the hospital, "he always seemed a little too happy to be breathing."

"He's still pretty upbeat."

"I know. It's not as annoying now."

The front door sailed open as a strong spring gust nearly pulled it out of Dave's hand. His smile was so brilliant it could have morphed the sun. With his long strides, he came directly to me, lifted me off the floor, and swung me in a circle. "It's official. Finished the papers. Should be able to open it in thirty days."

I beamed back at him, "Was Kravitz with you?"

"Yeah, he tried to bail out at the last minute, but Emily helped me convince him to go."

Kravitz had told me that Dave had outgrown the shop he was renting. A place just a few blocks from my house came up for sale while Libby was still in the hospital. It had six large rollup doors and was ten thousand square feet with a fenced-in area for jobs waiting to be started. Kravitz and I both prodded Dave to take a look, but it was Mark who told Dave he needed to think bigger. Mark had stopped by Dave's shop a week or so after they reconnected and saw several of Dave's restorations.

Mark still lived in Kansas City. He blew through town a couple of times per month on business. He didn't share with either of us what his business was. It bothered me because I was sure whatever he did was illegal, but Dave didn't care. He had his brother back.

I had always had an active imagination, so I envisioned everything from him being a drug mule to working directly for a drug cartel, possibly even as a hired hit man. It still nagged at me inside, but after a few visits and angry glares from him, I stopped asking. He had saved my life, he probably saved Libby's life, and he assembled Dave's missing pieces. Whatever he was to the rest of the world, to me he was Dave's only family. Maybe we'd find out the truth someday, or maybe we wouldn't – regardless, Mark was a regular visitor and I had never seen Dave happier.

Dave and Mr. Kravitz came to an agreement on the expanded Bodies by Brewer, where students with promise would have part time jobs on the weekends learning from both of them. The two were even talking about establishing a co-op program with the school. Dave had given up his studio apartment and moved in with Libby and me over a month ago. It wasn't as convenient for him to walk down the steps for work in the morning, but there is something to be said for closets.

To Mark's credit, Teddy and Grey left town. Occasionally I would see Tony, but he never said a word to me about where either had gone. The few times I had seen him had nothing to do with bars: once at the grocery store, once at McDonald's, and once while Dave and I were on a walk on Windham Street. Dave didn't know who Tony was and seemed oblivious to the fear Tony wore when he saw the two of us strolling toward him. I didn't bother to do introductions, so I was sure Tony believed I was walking with Mark, the same guy who had tossed Tony's brother out of town.

"So, thirty days from today?" I clarified.

Dave, still holding me in a tight hug, nuzzled my neck with his lips. "Looks that way." He reached over to the stove and stirred the pot in front of me, then looked at Libby, "Hey, can you watch this for a few minutes? I need to talk to Candy upstairs."

Libby took the spoon from him, "Sure."

As he led me by the hand, I noticed his palms were sweating. He must have still been freaking out about the big real estate purchase. Dave internalized everything. Over the past two months he had opened up a great deal, but anytime someone got on his last nerve, or he was frustrated, he would keep it inside and stew about whatever was bothering him. I had finally gotten him to the point that he might vent to me, but that was a pretty tall order for someone who had spent most of his life hiding himself from the rest of the world.

He led me into our room and closed the door. Dave looked nervous, and I was prepared to give him the same pep talk Kravitz and I had offered multiple times for the last month. For a man with so much talent, he was reluctant to expand.

Dave backed me up against the closed door. He took me by surprise when he stepped closer to me, placed both his hands on either side of my face and gently kissed my lips – not one of the impassioned kisses I always hungered for, but a sweet one that lingered.

Dave could melt me into a puddle of goo with no effort whatsoever. I slid my arms on either side of him, reaching up underneath the back of his shirt, allowing my fingers to lightly caress the smooth skin underneath his t-shirt until I elicited his "happy moan." He let go of my face, sliding his hands down to my hips and rested his head on my shoulder. I could spend hours like this with Dave.

The more I learned about Dave, the luckier I felt to be a part of his life. The first week when we reconnected, Dave had told me about the foster kid he was helping. The kid's name was Byron, and he wanted to sign up for Kravitz's class, but didn't have money for a car or the parts to fix it. I thought it was great that Dave bought the stuff for him so he could be in the class. Dave was going through classes to become a foster parent. Once he had completed the training, he would be one of the youngest foster parents the state had ever had.

His voice came out raspy, full of emotion. "You know I love you, right?"

I did know. Initially, it was hard for him to say the words. It wasn't that he didn't feel them, he just had difficulty saying them. "Yeah, I love you, too."

His head still rested on my shoulder when he confessed, "But I don't want to be your roommate or your boyfriend anymore." My heart stopped. My fingers froze where they were. My whole body tensed. When he saw my reaction, he quickly added, "Shit. I don't want to break-up with you, either."

Defensively, I let my hands that had been pulling him toward me go limp. I didn't respond. I couldn't. What was he saying? I knew we had fast-tracked our relationship. Was it too much, too soon? I had opened my heart so completely that the thought of him pulling away now would shred me. He took my limp hands in his, looked directly into my eyes and confessed, "I want this to be permanent."

Permanent what? "What are you saying?"

"I'm saying I didn't know how lonely I was until you came into my life. Before you I had a frozen heart, and you were like a nitro charge. I never wanted a big life. I never hoped for anything more than surviving. You've changed everything. You've owned me since before I had this heart drawn on my chest. I'm saying I want to own you the same way."

Confused, I still didn't know what he was saying, but at least I was sure he wasn't breaking up with me. "You want me to get your name tattooed on *my* chest?"

Dave's serious expression transformed to a smile as he eased down in front of me onto one knee, "I'm saying I want you to be my wife." He produced a diamond solitaire in a platinum setting. The design was simply elegant, the diamond dazzling, and his proposal took my breath away.

It had only been two months, was this too soon? I loved him. I craved quiet moments alone and relished waking up in his arms each morning. My sister's warning played in my head about relationships fizzling out when they were based on intense circumstances. What did Kim know? She'd never known Dave. She had never thawed a man's heart. Holding out my hand to him, I said, "Yes."

He slid the ring on my finger.

NOTE FROM NANCY:

I hope you enjoyed *His Frozen Heart*! This is the first book in my *Brewer Brothers Series*. The second book is *Fractured Karma* and it is Mark's story.

I am an independent author, which means I do not have an agent, a publicist, or a publishing company backing me up. I DEPEND on word-of-mouth advertising. If you enjoyed *His Frozen Heart,* it would mean the world to me for you to recommend it to a friend (or ten friends!). If you recommend it to someone who does not have time to read, let them know it is also available as an audiobook! (The narrator did a superb job!)

Independent Authors live and die by reviews from readers. Before I became an author, I believed reviews were only written by professionals. I did not know that my opinion mattered. If you are in this category, please KNOW that your opinion does matter!! If you could take a few minutes and write a review of *His Frozen Heart* and post it to the store where you bought it, I would be very grateful. It doesn't have to be long, just a few words to tell others what you thought of it.

If you enjoyed my writing, I would love for you to check out my other books. If you enjoy Greek Mythology, my *Touched Series* is a modern take on the old fables. This series consists of four books, and the first book, *Blood Debt,* is free. If you ever believed that certain people are supposed to be in your life and you have lived several lifetimes with them, my *Destiny Series* may be for you. *Meeting Destiny* is the first book in a three book series and is also free. All of my books are available in print and audio.

Finally, if you would like to chat with me, here are the best places to find me:

My Author Page on Facebook:

https://facebook.com/NancyStraight.Author

My blog: http://www.NancyStraight.com

Twitter: https://twitter.com/NancyStraight

Goodreads: https://goodreads.com/NancyStraight

Email: NancyStraight@gmail.com

I read and respond to every message I receive. (Sometimes a day or two late, but I do respond to everyone who reaches out to me).

I hope to hear from you!

Happy Reading,

Nancy

www.ingramcontent.com/pod-product-compliance
Lightning Source LLC
Chambersburg PA
CBHW070639310726
48982CB00001B/331